PRAISE FO[...]
THOMA[...]

"The most inventive novel you'll buy this year . . . by turns funny, unsettling, and heartbreaking."

—*New York Times* bestselling author Christopher Golden

"Tightly focused and deftly handled . . . a smart and playful story."

—*Publishers Weekly*

"Engagingly believable characters in a series noted for flashes of humor despite its overall serious tone. . . . Followers of Jim Butcher's Dresden Files will enjoy." —*Library Journal*

"Engaging [and] tightly written. . . . You won't find a dull moment."

—*Sacramento Book Review*

"At turns frightening, tender, heartrending, and full of twists and turns." —*News and Sentinel* (Parkersburg, WV)

"A fun book . . . a thought-provoking book." —Innsmouth Free Press

"A very powerful, very personal tale that is equal parts gut-wrenching, heartwarming, and awe-inspiring." —The Ranting Dragon

continued . . .

Also by Thomas E. Sniegoski

The Remy Chandler Novels

A KISS BEFORE THE APOCALYPSE

DANCING ON THE HEAD OF A PIN

WHERE ANGELS FEAR TO TREAD

A HUNDRED WORDS FOR HATE

IN THE HOUSE OF THE WICKED

WALKING IN THE MIDST OF FIRE

A DEAFENING SILENCE IN HEAVEN

THE
DEMONISTS

Thomas E. Sniegoski

A ROC BOOK

ROC
Published by New American Library,
an imprint of Penguin Random House LLC
375 Hudson Street, New York, New York 10014

This book is an original publication of New American Library.

First Printing, April 2016

For more information about Penguin Random House, visit penguin.com.

LIBRARY OF CONGRESS CATALOGING-IN-PUBLICATION DATA:

Names: Sniegoski, Tom, author.
Title: The demonists/Thomas E. Sniegoski.
Description: New York City: Roc, [2016]
Identifiers: LCCN 2015044949 (print) | LCCN 2015049268 (ebook) |
ISBN 9780451473523 (softcover) | ISBN 9780698185517 (ebook)
Subjects: LCSH: Demoniac possession—Fiction. | Spiritual warfare—Fiction. |
Demonology—Fiction. | Exorcism—Fiction. | BISAC: FICTION/Fantasy/Urban Life.
| FICTION/Horror. | GSAFD: Fantasy fiction. | Horror fiction. | Occult fiction.
Classification: LCC PS3619.N537 D46 2016 (print) | LCC PS3619.N537 (ebook) |
DDC 813/.6—dc23
LC record available at http://lccn.loc.gov/2015044949

Printed in the United States of America
10 9 8 7 6 5 4 3 2 1

Penguin
Random
House

ACKNOWLEDGMENTS

Love and gratitude to my lovely wife, LeeAnne, whose help on this book was invaluable. Love and thanks also to Kirby for keeping it real, and making my office smell so sweet.

Special thanks to my brother from another mother, Christopher Golden, the amazing Jessica Wade, Ginjer Buchanan, Jim Moore, Howard Morhaim, Kate Schafer Testerman, Nicole Scopa, Frank Cho, Thomas Fitzgerald, Dale Queenan, Larry Johnson, Pam Daley, Mom Sniegoski, Dave Kraus (gone, but never far from my heart), Kathy Kraus, and the demonically infested down at Cole's Comics in beautiful Lynn, Massachusetts.

It's a lovely day for an exorcism!

THE
DEMONISTS

PROLOGUE

Nine years ago

John Fogg preferred the company of ghosts.

Although he appeared perfectly relaxed at the podium in front
of the standing-room-only crowd, he would much rather have been
prowling the shadows of an abandoned insane asylum in search of
vengeful spirits, or listening for the sound of a ghostly child's laughter
near a Tennessee lake notorious for the lives it had claimed through
the centuries.

He had spent the last ten years of his life traveling the world and
studying the weird, the unusual, the paranormal, his eyes opened to
a secret reality of wonders, and the potential for great danger. Some
of the *things* he had discovered did not care to be looked upon, and
sought to close his eyes—permanently. But John Fogg had also learned
to fight back. From the myriad faiths of the world and their most holy,
he was taught the sacred rituals of banishment, of exorcism, and the
demonic entities that roamed the planet unseen, un-believed in, learned
to fear him.

He was promoting his latest book, *Spirits Around Us*, regaling the audience with a tale of poltergeist activity in the Philippines that had sent his jeep plunging into the jungle and nearly cost him his life. With a smile, he informed the group that both he and his driver had survived the crash with only minor bumps and bruises, and that their mysterious accident had more to do with poor automobile mainte-nance than with the angry machinations of spirit creatures.

The crowd laughed, and some applauded as Fogg's eyes darted down to the Cartier watch on his wrist. Thankfully, it was time to wrap up and deliver his trusty catchphrase.

"I'd like to thank you all for coming tonight," he said, smiling ap-preciatively, briefly making eye contact with as many as he could of those crowded into the main floor of the large bookstore. "And ask you to remember . . . that the world is a far stranger place than you realize."

He paused, feeling their anticipation. He could see some of their mouths begin to move, reciting what had become his signature sign-off. It would have made his nana beam.

"From ghoulies and ghosties, and long-leggedy beasties, and things that go bump in the night, Good Lord, deliver us. Thank you, and good night."

The room erupted in applause, and he offered a wave and a smile as the store manager approached to escort him to the autograph area set up in the back of the store. She was an older blond woman wearing an oversize sweatshirt with a cat on the front, but it wasn't she who caught his attention as he was about to turn away from the lectern.

From the corner of his eye, he saw another woman, and was com-pelled to look back.

She was sitting in the center of the room, and he was surprised that he hadn't noticed her earlier. She was stunning, with skin like porcelain, and hair as dark a black as he had ever seen. She wore black jeans and a gray T-shirt with the yellow-and-black Batman symbol emblazoned upon her chest. It was her eyes that captured him, holding his gaze—even at this distance he could see that they were the most striking shade of icy blue.

She realized that he was staring at her, and raised her hand. "Mr. Fogg," she called out.

John gently pulled his arm from his escort's grasp, and lifted his eyebrows to acknowledge the young woman. "Is there something I can do for you?" Her eyes reminded him of Arctic ice, but they had a warmth that drew him in.

She gave him a smile, and it was something John wouldn't have minded seeing again, and again.

"I'd like to thank you for dragging the science of parapsychology out of the darkness and into the mainstream." She held up a copy of his first book, *Haunting Season*, as a smattering of applause broke out from those who had stopped to listen to their exchange.

He acknowledged her thanks with another smile and a nod.

"However, you did write something to which I take great offense." She flipped through the book, a piece of paper she'd used to mark her page fluttering to the floor as she began to read aloud. "'I have never encountered a medium who was able to convince me that his/her talents were genuine. Sure, there were the occasional few who offered interesting information that proved semiuseful to an investigation, but I remain unconvinced that most so-called mediums have a direct line to the spirit realm, as so many claim.'" She closed the book and placed it beneath her arm. "I realize it's been some years since you wrote those words, but do you still feel that's true?"

Fogg chuckled nervously. "Why do I get the feeling that I'm being set up?"

The young woman smiled again. "Not setting you up, Mr. Fogg. Just looking for an answer."

"Okay," he said slowly, buying himself some time by stepping forward to the first row of chairs. "How shall I word this?" He considered what he was about to say, then took a deep breath. "Since that book was written, I must say that I've had many more relatively successful encounters with mediums." He paused again. "But I'm still not convinced," he finished.

"Not convinced, even though you admit you've had successful encounters since—"

"*Relatively* successful," John interrupted. "Mediums have accompanied me on cases and shared that ghostly entities were sad, or that their name was Frank, or that they wanted us to leave a particular location."

"But that's not enough for you."

Fogg shook his head. "No, not really."

"Do you believe that those messages, no matter how inconsequential you feel they are, came from spirits inhabiting those areas?"

"I believe that some people are more adept at picking up random signals—like tuning in a weak radio station. They are able to catch words, phrases, names here and there, but are they actually communicating with the spirit world? No, I don't think so."

"So you wouldn't call those people mediums?"

"Not in the true sense, no," Fogg said. "They are more than entitled to call themselves what they like, but I'm looking for the precise definition of the word—someone who has the ability to converse with spirits just as *we* are talking right now."

"So those who pick up these . . . sporadic signals," the woman continued to press. "In your mind, they haven't really earned the title of medium."

"No," John admitted, then placed a hand on his chest. "But that's just me."

The woman nodded, ever so slightly, then turned to leave. "Thank you," she said.

"Excuse me," Fogg called out as she stepped into the center aisle. "I didn't catch your name."

She stopped. "You didn't ask me."

"What is your name?"

"Theodora, Theodora Knight."

The name was familiar, and then it dawned on him. "Your mother wouldn't happen to be Agatha Knight?"

"As a matter of fact, she is," Theodora replied.

"Ah, now I see." He slipped his hands into his pockets.

"Do you, Mr. Fogg?"

"John," he corrected.

"All right, John," she said. "What is it you see?"

"I see the daughter of one of the world's preeminent mediums, come to defend her mother's honor."

"My mother's honor is perfectly fine," Theodora retorted.

A few years before, Agatha Knight had appeared with John on a network news segment that focused on the paranormal. She had refused to show off her supposed psychic ability, then stormed off the set when pressed. The incident had done little to change his opinion of mediums, and their oft unreliable talents.

"Remember, it was she who refused . . ."

"My mother didn't feel that it was polite to relay information that wasn't meant for public knowledge," Theodora told him. "So she said nothing."

"In other words, the spirits didn't want to talk to her?"

"I'm sure your grandmother would have conversed with her just fine, only what she had to say wasn't for common consumption."

"My grandmother?" John asked, startled, an uneasy smile on his face.

"Your grandmother," Theodora confirmed. "She wanted to speak with someone that night, but it wasn't my mother, and it wasn't a television audience."

John chuckled. "Okay, so who was she there to speak with, if not a medium of your mother's reputation?"

"Before your segment, my mother was supposed to participate in a separate story involving the passing down of psychic gifts. I was to be with her that night, but I was feeling a bit under the weather—a stomach thing, not very pleasant."

"So it was you my grandmother wanted to talk with?"

"That's right." Theodora's icy blue gaze bored into him as she cocked her beautiful head slightly to one side.

John suddenly felt a familiar chill, and his spine straightened. "Is my grandmother here now?"

"She is."

"And is she speaking with you?"

"She is."

"And is that something you might share with me?"

Theodora turned and headed up the aisle toward the front of the bookstore. "She said you should take that stick out of your ass," she tossed over her shoulder with a laugh.

Fogg couldn't help laughing as well. "Is that it?"

The young woman stopped but didn't turn to face him. "And that you should offer me a job on your television show."

"That hasn't even been announced yet," he said, taken aback.

"Well, after it is, your grandmother thinks you should offer me a job."

"And what exactly would you be doing on my show?"

Theodora turned and stared at him with a dumbfounded expression. "You know, I was hesitant to agree with her, but now I see that she's right."

John began to walk toward Theodora.

"You really aren't the sharpest crayon in the box." She shook her head and pushed through the doors, out of the store and into the night.

Fogg chuckled. That box-of-crayons metaphor was something his grandmother had often used to describe members of their family.

But she'd never used it to describe him.

He stood for a moment, staring at his reflection in the bookstore's glass doors. Maybe this time she was right.

His musings were interrupted as the manager in the cat sweatshirt eagerly grasped his arm and directed him to the back of the store where a line had formed in front of a long table piled high with his latest work. Apologizing profusely, he allowed her to lead him behind the table to greet his fans, making a mental note to call his producer at the Spirit Network in the morning.

How about we add a medium to the show?

1

Now

At first glance, the house at 145 Westview Lane, Pittsburgh, Pennsylvania, was nothing special. It was a typical ranch-style home built in the early seventies on a plot of land where an old farmhouse had once stood, before it burned down in 1961.

"Got anything?" John asked his wife.

Theodora stood silently beside him in the near darkness of the living room, using her special gift—her enhanced senses—to find and touch any residual spirit energies left by the home's previous occupants. "Nope, same as the last time you asked me—nada. The place is strangely—pardon the expression—dead."

"Nice," Fogg said dryly. "I'm surprised you didn't save that one for our viewers."

"Only the best for you, shnookums," she gushed, and although it was too dark to see it, John imagined that special twinkle in her icy blue eyes, accompanied by a smile that could melt even the stoutest of hearts.

"Hey, Jackson, how are we doing for time?" John asked the cameraman behind them. They were in the midst of a commercial break.

Jackson touched his earpiece and listened for a moment. "Two minutes, twenty," he replied, hefting the night-vision camera back onto his shoulder.

"Think we'll take a look at the stain next," John said. He clicked his flashlight on and moved the beam over the hardwood floor. They'd seen it earlier when they were doing their prebroadcast walk-through. Supposedly it was blood, but John had his doubts.

"That stain is gross," Theodora complained.

"Gross is good for Halloween," John answered.

"We're back in ten," Jackson warned. "Nine . . . eight . . . seven . . ."

John and Theodora positioned themselves near the stain and waited for the signal that they were live.

"Showtime," the cameraman whispered, and John immediately began.

"Welcome back to the special, live Halloween broadcast of *Spirit Chasers*," he said, staring at the tiny red light on the night-vision camera that Jackson was pointing directly at him. "For those of you just tuning in, I'm John Fogg, and I'm here with my wife, Theodora Knight, and my *Spirit Chasers* team investigating a home in rural Pennsylvania. We've dubbed it the House of Tribulation because throughout its history, its many residents have almost all been victims of troubled, almost cursed lives."

John moved through the inky black, flicking his penlight across the floor as he walked. "Right now Theo and I are examining a strange stain that, according to the house's current owner, Fritz, grows more pronounced when paranormal activity begins to escalate in the home."

He shone the beam of the flashlight on the living room floor, illuminating a dark stain, shaped like the state of Florida. "Jackson, can you show this to the folks at home, please?"

John continued as he watched the red light on the infrared camera turn away from him and down toward the floor. "Fritz believes that this is a bloodstain left when the previous owner murdered his wife, supposedly in this very spot."

"Just one of the many disturbing events that have transpired in this seemingly cursed home, and part of the reason why Fritz refuses to live here anymore," added Theodora as she knelt beside her husband for a closer look at the darkened spot.

"Right," John agreed. "Once he began renovations on the old property, he started to notice odd sounds and smells. He even reports seeing shadow figures from the corner of his eyes."

"John, why don't you get some EMF readings while I get out the blood test kit?"

John heard the sounds of Theo rummaging through her things as the red light on the camera again faced him. He removed the cellphone-sized device from his pocket and held it over the spot on the floor, slowly moving it over the area. As he did so, he reminded his viewers that he was looking for the high electromagnetic fields emitted by ghostly beings, then expressed disappointment that the device remained perfectly silent, as it had throughout the evening's investigation.

John felt his wife poke his arm in the darkness. "Here's the kit, hon."

He reached for the offered items. "In this bottle is a hydrogen peroxide mixture that reacts with the chemical found in blood called catalase. If this really is blood," John explained as he removed the cover on the plastic bottle and squirted some solution onto a cotton swab, "the liquid will start to bubble."

He knew it wouldn't, but he had to go through the motions for the live show. Again the camera panned down to the stain. He could imagine the viewers at home, sitting on the edges of their seats, eyes glued to the screen, hoping that John would confirm a bloodstain. He waited a moment, letting the excitement build, then slowly rubbed the saturated swab across the stain.

"No bubbles," he announced. "This stain is definitely not blood."

"I'm guessing some sort of petroleum product maybe," Theo offered from where she squatted next to her husband. She placed the tip of a well-manicured finger in the center of the dark spot and gently rubbed at it. "Whatever it is, it's saturated the wood. It could be that it reacts to temperature fluctuations within the house during changes in the seasons, and that's what led the homeowner to believe it's a hint of paranormal activity."

John's walkie-talkie squawked and he removed it from his belt, hoping for something, anything that would save the show—maybe some disembodied footsteps, or better yet, a creepy voice recording from the EVP session Phil Carnagin and Becky Toomes were conducting in the basement.

"Go for John," he said.

"John, it's Phil. We've found something I think you should see."

"We'll be right down," John said, forcing himself not to sigh with relief. "How are we doing for time?" he asked Jackson.

"Commercial coming up," the cameraman replied.

"Excellent," John said. "We'll break here, and when we return—"

"The basement, with Phil and Becky," Theodora finished.

"And we're into commercial," Jackson announced, lowering the camera.

"To the basement, then," John said, clicking on his flashlight.

"Where our ratings are going to be if something doesn't happen soon," Theodora added, turning on her own flashlight.

"You've done it now," John warned, already heading toward the kitchen where the door to the basement awaited them. "Now all hell is going to break loose."

"We can only hope," Theodora said wryly.

John chuckled. He had to agree with her. They'd researched this place pretty thoroughly, even sent in a preinvestigation team that had garnered good results—EMF spikes, interesting electronic voice phenomena (EVP), shadow entities. The place had seemed perfect for their Halloween broadcast. Hell, it had won out over a Scottish castle!

So why is it now so silent? John wondered as they headed down the stairs. "Let's hope for something good," he said aloud. "Or next Halloween, we'll be at home handing out candy."

"Full-size?" Theo asked.

"Excuse me?"

"Will we be the house that gives out full-size candy bars, or the mini bites?"

"If we lose the Halloween show, we'll have no choice but to go cheap—bite-size all the way."

Theodora carefully descended into the basement, following the beam from her husband's flashlight. Again, she reached out to the house, trying to rouse dormant energies of those who had once resided there.

And still there was silence.

That wasn't unusual in newer homes, where the structures hadn't had enough time to collect the residual energies of life and death. But this place, a genuinely old house that had seen a lot of living and dying throughout a lot of years, offered her nothing.

It just wasn't right.

"We're back in one and a half," Jackson announced, clumping heavily on the wooden steps behind them.

John had reached the bottom of the stairs, where his flashlight played over the cobwebbed surface of some old apple crates that had been stacked there.

"Phil!" he called as he stepped around the crates. "Becky!"

"Back here!" Phil yelled.

The cellar was larger than Theodora had expected, probably extending beyond the house and under the backyard. She allowed her defenses to remain down as she and Jackson followed her husband through the darkness, skirting rusted old bike frames and farm tools.

And still there was nothing.

They finally came upon Phil and Becky in a tiny, shelved room where the products of fall canning had probably been stored for the winter. Now the shelves were empty of everything but a thick coating of dust, as was the rest of the room. Except for a single sealed jar on the floor in the center of the room.

"What is it?" Theo asked from the doorway, feeling Jackson trying to maneuver around her for a better shot.

"Less than a minute," he said as he pushed past her.

"We'll pick up with a discussion of this," John said, his flashlight beam illuminating the jar.

Theodora couldn't take her eyes from the object. There was something about it that didn't seem right.

She saw Jackson give John the signal, and he launched into the next segment of their live show.

"Welcome back to the *Spirit Chasers* Halloween show, and thanks again for joining us. Just before the break, Phil and Becky called, asking Theo and me to join them in the basement, where they found this." He squatted and moved the beam of his flashlight across the bronzy surface of the jar on the floor.

He continued to talk, but Theodora was only vaguely aware of the words leaving his mouth. Her eyes were transfixed by the surface of the container as her husband's light played across it.

The sound was faint, like that of ice cracking as it was warmed by the afternoon sun, and then she saw it—a crack in the smooth surface of the rounded jar.

Her breath caught in her throat as her senses were suddenly bombarded, her head filled with staccato images—images of heinous acts committed in this house, in this basement.

"Where did you find it?" she gasped, interrupting her husband's monologue. She felt the eyes of the team fall upon her, but she couldn't take her own from the jar on the floor as more spiderweb cracks appeared on its surface. "Where did you find it?" she repeated, nearly screaming. "Tell me!"

Jackson had turned the camera directly on her. After all, it was a live show and this kind of thing was great for ratings, but ratings were the furthest thing from Theodora's mind.

"Theo, are you—" John began, but was interrupted by Phil.

"In here," he said, a hint of fear and uncertainty in his voice. "It was over in that corner, on its side."

"So you touched it?" Theodora asked. "You touched it and moved it here?"

She saw the raw image of a little girl falling down a staircase, and felt her pain as her baby teeth smacked the edge of a step, gouging the wood as they were knocked from her mouth. Theo's stomach roiled as she struggled to raise her psychic defenses against whatever was seeping from the container.

"Something's happening," she heard Becky say from across the room. Theo had always suspected that Becky was a bit of a psychic as well.

"Would someone care to fill me in?" John asked cheerily, although his wife could hear the edge to his voice.

She ignored it and asked a question of her own. "Did you drop it?"

"No," Phil replied, sounding a bit defensive. "We just moved it to the center of the room so we could see it better. What—?" He abruptly stopped as another, louder crack sounded, followed by the frantic beeping from one of their EMF detectors.

Another wave of images poured over Theodora, and made her witness to more pain. She tried desperately to block it out, but the events were coming so fast and furious that she could barely discern what she was seeing. All she knew was that it was horrible, and that death was always the outcome.

"You shouldn't have touched it," she said breathlessly. "You shouldn't have—"

More, louder cracks came from the jar, and she pushed back the surge of panic that threatened to overtake her. "We have to leave," she managed, her eyes still glued to the object. "We have to get out of here before—"

"Theo, what's going on?" John demanded, reaching out to grasp her arms.

The container shuddered then with a whiplike snap, and a dense mist began to seep from the growing fissures.

"I know why the house was so quiet," Theo cried. She gazed at the vapor filling the small room, and at the glowing white sigils that were beginning to manifest on the walls. "How could I have been so stupid?" She tried to pull away from John. "It wasn't that they weren't here . . . they were silenced."

The beeping of the EMF detectors suddenly stopped, their batteries drained.

Images were pounding at Theo's skull, demanding that she look at them.

To see what was about to be released into the world.

"Oh God," she whispered, a new image worming its way onto the screen of her mind's eye. She saw Fritz . . . as well as others, dressed in bloodred robes, painting the symbols upon the walls.

Symbols that would silence the voices of the home.

Silence the spirits so they could not warn the investigators.

Theo fell against her husband.

"That's enough," John said, wrapping his arms around her and holding her tightly. "Go to commercial," he ordered Jackson, but the man kept right on shooting.

Theodora managed to lift her head to look at Jackson, and what she saw filled her with absolute dread. Jackson did not do what was asked of him because he was no longer in control. She could see the spirits around him, manipulating him, bending him to their will.

While at first the small room had been empty, it was now filled—filled with the dead, and something more.

"It's too late," Theo said as the atmosphere became even more oppressive.

"That's it for me," Phil announced. "I'm getting the fuck out of here while—" He exploded before he could finish his sentence or take a step. Blood and shreds of clothing and skin covered the ceiling and walls of the tiny room.

And Theo could see what it was that had done this to their friend.

Within the mist that had leaked from the container were terrible things, demonic things.

Harbingers of something larger, and far more terrible.

Jackson's camera ceased to function midway through the slaughter, but until that moment—

He'd had no desire to continue filming, sending scenes of the bloodletting into the living rooms of millions of viewers, but he'd had no choice.

He'd wanted to drop his camera to the cellar floor and flee for his life.

But something held him fast and made him continue to perform what had been his chosen profession for the last eleven years—something that chortled happily, its amusement echoing painfully in the hollows of his skull.

Watch! it commanded him. *Watch and see the fate that will soon befall the world.*

Becky was closest to the container as it began to vibrate to the point that its image through the camera's viewfinder was blurred. Then it exploded in a flash of black so intense that it was darker than the darkness of the environment surrounding it. Pieces of the jar spun through the air, hissing shrapnel that sought out the warmth and fragility of Becky's flesh. The pieces were drawn to her, to her life, and each and every jagged fragment found its way into her body.

The presences inside Jackson's skull laughed hysterically as Becky's body danced and twitched, before it finally collapsed in upon itself, bones shattered, muscles shredded, tendons cut.

John was picked up by something that glinted wetly in the dark of the storage room. It lifted him as if he weighed nothing and slammed him against the nearby wall of stone, again and again, until the white rock was stained black.

Theodora's screams allowed Jackson a brief moment of focus. The beautiful medium hung above the dirt floor, her head tossed back, the tendons in her neck straining as she screamed, and screamed, and screamed. Ghostly things—demonic things—swam about her: serpents of shadow, eels of darkness, entering her body, dissolving into her flesh. The spirits inside Jackson's head cheered excitedly as the entities flowed into Theo's helpless body.

John's pathetic moans filled the basement space as he crawled into the camera's view, a bloody hand reaching up toward his wife.

She is the vessel now, the voices chimed, and Jackson did not understand, nor would he ever, for the evil spirits were done with him then. He began to cry, crying for his friends, but mostly for himself, because he knew he would not be spared this day.

But then he felt himself released from the evil's loathsome clutches, and he almost fooled himself into thinking that he might live. He dropped the camera, ending the horrific transmission as it smashed on the dirt floor, and he spun away from the blood-drenched storage room, running through the near pitch-blackness toward where he remembered the stairs to be.

They let him find them, one of his sneakered feet falling upon the creaking wood of the first step as he prepared to propel himself upward.

He thought of the happiness he would feel as he ascended to the kitchen and raced through the mudroom door into the yard, where he would hungrily gulp the cool autumn air. And he knew that he would cry tears of sadness for his friends, but also of sheer joy that he had not shared their terrible fate.

That he had survived.

He would have experienced all of that, if only he had been allowed to live.

If only.

2

In this place, John Fogg was a child again. In puddles that spread across the vast city street, he could see the reflection of himself clad in his favorite pajamas.

He was remembering a time, so very long ago now, when he had gone to New York with his folks to see a holiday show. He hadn't been paying attention, caught up in the excitement of the city and the season, and had stepped away from his parents, eager to see the next of Macy's wonderfully magical display windows. And suddenly he could no longer find them in the always moving crowd of people that flowed around him.

No matter where he looked, he saw only unfamiliar faces, and he had cried out for his mother and father for what seemed like an eternity, until finally they were before him. The looks of relief on their faces slowly dissolved to anger, and then the scolding began.

But he would take the scolding and the nearly painful squeezing pressure of his mother's grip upon his hand.

They had found him, and that was all that mattered.

John was back on those cold winter streets, only now it was nighttime, and it was raining. He was alone, clad only in his pajamas.

Why had he gone out onto the city streets wearing only his pajamas?

He had no answer, just an ever-increasing sense of dread that expanded in his belly like a balloon.

"Hello?" he called out, but the only response was the patter of freezing rain on the hard, puddle-dappled streets.

Why am I here? Why am I alone?

It was the first time that you let the fear in, answered a voice from someplace nearby.

John spun, looking about Herald Square, finding only parked cars and gray, rain-drenched buildings—not a soul to be found, except for him.

"Who's there?" he demanded. "Ma? Dad?"

Someone laughed. At least he thought it was a someone—hoped that it was a someone.

Your fear was like a door, John Fogg, the mysterious voice said. *So intense that it swung wide, opening you up to all sorts of possibilities.*

"Why can't I see you?" John asked, his eyes darting to every corner, every shadow. "Why don't you show yourself?"

Do you want to see me, John Fogg? the voice asked with all sincerity. *Do you really want to see me?*

John didn't know how he should answer at first, but he managed to push past the expanding bubble of fear in his gut. At least he would have one answer; and for him, it was always about answers.

"Yes." He braced himself. "Yes, I really do want to see you."

Again he heard that laugh, only this time it was joined by others—many others.

Well, who am I to deny a child's wishes?

A patch of shadow across from where John stood in front of one of Macy's blackened windows shimmered and waved like a stretch of ocean caressed by the wind. A shape pulled free, standing motionless, watching the boy.

John felt the nearly uncontrollable urge to run but held his ground, watching the man.

Maybe . . . maybe he would help him.

Slowly he began to cross toward the figure. A vague swath of light from a nearby traffic light suddenly illuminated its face, and what John saw stopped him dead in the middle of the deathly quiet Manhattan street.

The face was as white as the moon in the sky, with eyes as round as the planetoid but void of anything other than deep, sucking darkness. Its mouth was pulled back in a smile that—*John supposed*—was to be considered friendly and comforting, but couldn't have been further from that. It reminded him of an old animal trap he had once seen in his uncle's shed while on a summer visit to West Virginia—wide and jaggedly sharp, stained black with old blood.

Somehow John knew this face. An older part of him, buried within the dream child, had hoped never to see its terrible visage again.

Do you remember me, John Fogg? it asked, its pointed teeth clicking and clacking as it spoke.

John remained silent, carefully backing away, back toward the dark department store windows.

Your silence speaks volumes, the monster said with a chilling laugh as it began to casually stroll toward him, joined by more shadows that detached themselves from the shimmering black mass. *And I'm not alone, John.*

John wanted to run—but where? He looked about, desperate to find a safer place, but saw only darkness, darkness that pulsed and moved as if alive. Darkness that throbbed and stretched like the skin on the belly of some great beast, ready to disgorge its babies into the nightmare world.

There's nowhere for you now, John, the nightmare man said. *You are trapped here, with us.*

The creature stopped and stood in the middle of Herald Square, waiting for the other monsters that continued to crawl from the shadows.

John found them familiar as well, and felt his terror grow even more. Painful flashes of memory thrummed within the core of his being like the plucked string of a badly tuned instrument. He saw himself as an adult, as he dealt with each of the demonic things that were gathering in the street before him.

They were minor supernatural pests, the demonic equivalent of fruit flies, but they were still annoying, and potentially dangerous. And he had disposed of them, performing rites of exorcism that had removed them from the earthly realm, depositing them—*he now realized*—in this nightmarish place.

We always said we would pay you back in kind, the monstrous leader spoke. *If we ever had the chance.*

The darkness around John continued to birth more things that shambled, crawled, flew, and hopped. He had nowhere to go. Everywhere he looked, there was danger.

And now we do. With that, the leader's jaw snapped loudly and the creature started toward him, a wave of jabbering nightmare following in his wake.

John could do nothing but stare, imagining the horror that was about to overwhelm him. He didn't turn around, but he could hear other things converging on him from behind. And then accepting his fate, he took a deep breath and closed his eyes, tensed, but ready for the nightmare that was certain to never end.

A sudden sound made him cringe. At first, he thought it might have been some sort of prehistoric beast baying its joy as it was about to consume him in a single bite, but then he recognized it as the blare of a truck horn.

John opened his eyes to find the leader, and the flow of shadowy entities, mere inches from him. He turned in the direction of the nearly deafening horn, and saw an eighteen-wheeler barreling down the street, right into the beasts, scattering some like road waste, while crushing others beneath its large wheels.

Falling backward onto the wet street, John looked up in awe as the truck ground to a halt, brakes screeching as it skidded upon the crushed bodies of the demonic entities that had been crossing the street to claim him. The door of the truck's cab swung open to reveal the driver, and John could not help smiling.

"Quickly now," the old woman ordered, holding out her hand. John immediately reached for her and Nana Fogg grasped his wrist, hoisting him up into the cab with ease. "Close the door. My interference won't keep them at bay for long," she said. Then she gunned the engine, and with a roar the truck was moving again, crushing more of the monstrosities as they threw themselves at it.

John could only stare at the silver-haired old woman, who worked the clutch as if she'd been doing it her entire life. "You saved me," was all he could manage. Where once his chest had expanded with fear, now it was filled with a nearly overwhelming love for his nana, who had saved him—

Again.

Margarite Alice Fogg—*Nana*—had always looked out for him.

As a small child, he had found the arms of the tall, statuesque woman who wore her silver hair in a tight bun at the back of her head far more comforting than those of his parents. Nana Fogg always knew how to make things right. She'd chased away bad dreams and wiped away his tears. She'd even stood up to his overbearing father, who had never seemed to have enough patience with his overly sensitive son.

And she had continued to watch over him, even after her death, as when she'd warned him from beyond the grave of a vengeful spirit's plan to set fire to his college dormitory. Now here she was, saving him from demons in the realm between life and death.

"You're driving a truck." John suddenly realized the strangeness of the situation.

"One uses what one has on hand," the old woman said, checking the side-view mirror for stragglers. "Would have used a jet plane if it had been handy." Nana looked at him then, her gray eyes swimming with emotion. "We need to get you out of this place."

"But we're safe now," John said. He watched through the expanse of windshield as the city changed, the buildings of New York growing less and less defined. "Right, Nana? We're safe?"

His grandmother's boney hands clutched the large steering wheel as she drove them farther into a world of blackness. "For now," she reassured him. "But we have to get you home before she—"

John was confused. "Who?" he asked aloud. And then with a sudden rush of emotion, he remembered. "Theodora," he whispered.

They were immersed in a universe of shadow now.

"Is she all right?" John asked, frightened by the look of worry he saw on his grandmother's pale face. "Nana?"

"I don't know, John," Nana said finally, her eyes on the darkness ahead as if she was concentrating on something that he could not see. "Since you escaped them . . ." She stopped talking and stepped on the gas, sending the great truck leaping through the shadows.

"What, Nana? Tell me—what will they do?"

"Since they've lost you, they'll look for the next best thing," the old woman said. "They want to hurt you, John—in any way they can."

The fear was back inside him, ready to consume him with the horrific realization.

"They'll go after your wife."

John Fogg's eyes snapped open, the blare of a truck's horn fading in the distance. He tried to move, but there was only pain and a terrible numbness that told him things were not right.

That things were terribly wrong.

Eyes that felt as though they'd been rolled in sand before being placed inside his skull darted about, trying to adjust to his surroundings.

Where?

A woman whom he did not recognize moved about a room that he did not know as he lay in a bed that felt unfamiliar to his body. John tried to speak, but the only sound he could make was like the rustling of dry fall leaves.

The woman moved too quickly for his eyes to capture, but then they found her at the side of the bed, pushing buttons on machines that chimed and beeped with her touch. Tubes trailed from the machines, and his eyes followed them down to where they disappeared into the flesh of his exposed arm.

RV, his soggy mind defined. *Got an RV in my arm.*

He knew that was wrong when an image of his nana waving from the driver's seat of a monstrous recreational vehicle spattered with the blood of the demonic exploded inside his head, making him gasp aloud.

The woman was suddenly hovering over him.

"IV," he croaked. "IV—not RV."

"That's right, Mr. Fogg," the woman said, placing a gentle hand upon his chest and pushing him back down to the bed. He wasn't even aware that he had been trying to sit up.

"What . . . ," he began, but lost his train of thought as his eyes again scanned the unfamiliar room.

A hospital room. He was in a hospital.

"There was an accident," the woman was saying, her hand still firmly on his chest. "Do you remember anything about that?"

At first he didn't, but then the images rushed in: a flood of staccato moments that made his body thrash and the machines beside his bed protest with furious beeps and alarms.

His team . . . his wife . . . He didn't want to see this—he didn't want to remember. Someone was screaming, a raw, ragged sound. It took him a while to realize it was him.

There were more people in the room now, rushing around his bed, trying to keep him down. They were doing something to his RV—IV, and he felt himself begin to slip away again, the slide show of utter carnage growing less distinct, the corners of the nightmarish images growing darker, obscuring what he no longer wanted to see.

He tried to remain conscious, fighting with everything he had so that his question might be answered.

"My wife," he managed. A thin man in a white lab coat turned his shaggy head to look him in the eye. "My . . . wife," John croaked again, just as the world fell out from beneath him and a yawning oblivion drew him down.

But not before he'd seen the look in the man's eyes, and he took it with him on his journey to nothing.

It was a look of sympathy.

John Fogg sat in a chair by the window in his hospital room, refusing to look at the bed that had been his prison for the last six weeks.

He was afraid that if he did look at it, the bed would draw him back into its embrace, whispering that it was not yet time for him to go, that there was still much more healing to be done.

As if in solidarity, his broken ankle encased in a walking cast throbbed painfully.

The doctors had told him that it was still too early for him to be mobile, but they had cut him some slack, considering his situation.

His situation.

John looked at his watch. *Where is Stephan?*

"Ready?" Stephan asked from the doorway as if he'd heard John's unspoken question.

"I've been ready for quite some time," John grumbled, pushing off from the chair. He winced in pain from multiple places all over his body.

"Use the cane," Stephan reminded him. "Remember what the doctor told you."

"I know what the doctor told me," John snapped, grabbing for the cane that leaned against the windowsill. Instead his hand brushed it, sending the cane crashing to the floor. On reflex, he reached for it, and nearly lost his balance, managing to steady himself by grasping the windowsill with an agonized hiss as pain stabbed through his ankle.

"Did you hurt yourself?" Stephan asked as he retrieved the cane.

John attempted to snatch it from Stephan's grasp, perhaps a bit too roughly, but Stephan held on. "I'm fine," he said curtly.

"No, you're not," Stephan replied, releasing the cane, causing John to stumble slightly. "And as soon as you recognize that, you'll be in a much better place."

They glowered at each other for a moment, before John begrudgingly accepted that the man was right, but he was in no mood to admit it aloud.

"Could you get my bag?" he asked instead, forcing calmness into his tone. "It's over by the bed."

Stephan did what was asked of him, as he always had done. Barely thirty years old, Stephan Vasjak nearly single-handedly managed all the business affairs of Rising Fogg Productions, as well as the rather hectic schedules of John and Theodora's personal lives. John wasn't sure what he would have done without Stephan there to guide him, and he knew that Theodora would . . .

The realness of the moment hit him like a sledgehammer and again, he nearly lost his balance.

"John?" Stephan was in front of him, suitcase in hand. "Are you all right—do you need a minute?"

John shook his head vehemently. "No, no more minutes. I have to do this now or . . ."

Stephan gently took his arm and guided him toward the door. "We," he corrected. "It's *we* who have to do this. C'mon, I'm parked out back, not far from a maintenance exit."

"Are they still camped out there?" John asked wearily.

"Oh yes," Stephan answered. "The paparazzi and the institutions they serve continue their voracious pursuit of pain and misery."

"Thought they might've lost interest by now."

"Not a chance," Stephan said as they entered the service elevator. "The fact that they haven't been able to talk to you or . . ." He stopped speaking and stared pointedly at the LED display as it counted down the floors.

John's lower leg was throbbing again as he leaned on his cane. The longer he was up, the louder his ankle objected. "Where did you say you were parked again?" he asked, breaking the uneasy silence.

"Just out back," Stephan said as the doors slid open. "Hopefully Dr. Snider wasn't planning on using his space or we might be walking farther than we thought," he continued as they headed out an unwatched side door.

Stephan's Audi was right where he'd left it. "Must be a golf day," the man said, unlocking the car with the push of a button on his key.

John lowered himself into the soft leather of the front seat as Stephan put his suitcase in the trunk.

"Need some help?" Stephan asked.

"I'm good." John carefully lifted his casted leg and pulled it into the car.

"Set?"

"Yeah."

Their eyes met as Stephan leaned in to close the passenger door.

"Thank you," John said suddenly. "For everything."

"No sweat." John's personal assistant shrugged as he slammed the door closed and hurried around to the driver's side.

Stephan started the car, then sat for a moment as the engine thrummed and Freddie Mercury sang about a Killer Queen over the satellite radio.

"Are we ready for this?" he asked quietly, not looking at John.

John's eyes were locked on the brick wall of the hospital that had been his home for the last several weeks. A small part of him would have liked to go back to his room and accept the painkillers that would send him to that wonderful womblike place that only narcotics could create.

But then, what would happen to his wife?

"I think we have to be ready," John finally answered his friend with a deep breath, and Stephan backed from the parking space, beginning a journey that both were anticipating and dreading with equal measure.

The look that John had read as one of sympathy that day so long ago when he first awakened had been exactly that. Something had indeed happened to his wife that Halloween evening, but it wasn't until he was stronger that anyone had shared the details with him.

He remembered the doctors prefacing the discussion by saying that her primary injuries were not life-threatening, that he had sustained much worse. And then they had paused, which had made him all the more anxious and angry.

He'd demanded to know her condition, and they'd finally told him.

There had been an official investigation into what had happened in the House of Tribulation that Halloween night, and the conclusion had been that a gas leak had caused an explosion that had taken the lives of most of the *Spirit Chasers* crew. John had said nothing to refute those reports, nor did he correct the doctors when they kept describing his wife's injuries as caused by the explosion. However, their reports of her actual condition continued to confuse him. They kept telling him that she was stable, yet she remained unconscious. And when the countless tests had been run, and still there was no apparent reason why Theodora Knight was not awake, they had stopped looking and transferred her to another hospital.

"Did you call this morning?" Stephan asked, interrupting John's thoughts.

"Yeah, no change."

Theodora had been sent to the Cho Institute, at the urging of Dr. Franklin Cho, a friend of the family who thought he might be able to help her, so John had agreed to the move. He'd called Dr. Cho at least five times a day since then, each time hearing the same rhetoric in Dr. Cho's oh so patient style. "Still no change, but we're preparing a new round of tests that we hope will . . ."

Elvis Costello was singing about something to do with angels wanting to wear red shoes as John tried to prepare himself for this visit to his wife. It would be the first time he had seen her since the incident that had nearly killed them, and he needed to be strong.

For the umpteenth time he thought of his nana's words.

They'll go after your wife.

Is that why she won't wake up? he wondered as they drove. Were his past battles with the forces of darkness somehow responsible?

"We're here," Stephan announced.

They drove up a heavily wooded road and around a corner, where they came upon a tall wrought-iron gate, the sprawling Cho Institute on the other side. A security guard approached the car with a friendly smile as Stephan brought his window down. The guard's name tag said he was Max, and he checked a clipboard in his hand to confirm that they were indeed welcome there, before opening the gates to allow them through.

"Have a good visit," Max said with a wave as Stephan drove past.

John sincerely doubted that would be the case.

Stephan parked not too far from the institute's entrance and helped John climb out of the car with a minimal amount of pain.

"You good?" he asked, handing John his cane.

"Yeah," John said, looking past the man to the imposing structure before him. He was already anticipating the heavy, antiseptic smells familiar to places like this, and the oppressive atmosphere, as if a powerful storm was brewing, only this time, in this place, it would rain misery.

It took him a few tries to get going, his body stiff and protesting, but he managed, slowly loosening up as he walked beside Stephan toward a ramp that snaked around the side of the building.

Just as they reached the front doors, John's cell phone began to ring. He fished it from his jacket pocket and felt his heart rate quicken as he saw who was calling.

"Yes, Doctor," he answered as Stephan watched him with a cautious eye.

He listened a moment, then started for the doors. "I'm here right now," he said before breaking the connection and entering the building.

"What's up?" Stephan asked.

"Don't know exactly," John said, scanning the lobby for the doctor. "He said to wait for him here."

Dr. Franklin Cho appeared from around a marble pillar, followed by three associates in white lab coats and two security guards.

"Doctor," John said, moving toward him, hand outstretched.

Cho shook his hand, and John at once noticed that the grip was cold—damp.

"Is everything all—"

"John, I need you to come with me." Cho let go of his hand immediately and turned away.

"Is it my wife?" Fogg asked, attempting to keep up with the doctor as his ankle painfully throbbed.

"It is," Cho said, without turning.

They were heading for a heavy security door, with a placard attached that read No Admittance Without Proper Authorization.

"Your wife regained consciousness a little over two hours ago," Cho said as they slowed down long enough for one of the security guards to open the door using a card key. "As a matter of fact, it was right after we spoke this morning."

"She's awake?" John repeated, following Dr. Cho through the door as the guard held it open. He knew he should be happy but instead felt an odd sense of trepidation that he couldn't understand.

"I'm sorry, you'll need to wait here." Cho stopped and pointed at Stephan.

"No, he should come," John said as Stephan opened his mouth to protest.

Cho looked at him. "John, I really think—"

"It's okay, John. I'll be fine here," Stephan interrupted.

John fixed him in a powerful stare. "You're coming." Then he turned to the doctor and added, "He's family."

Cho wasn't pleased but didn't argue. Without a word, he continued on down the white corridor to another security door.

"Where are we going?" John asked as they went through the door into another long white corridor. "I thought Theo's room was on the third floor?"

"It was, until she woke up," Cho said. "Your wife began to exhibit symptoms that we really don't understand," he explained, appearing uneasy.

"What kind of symptoms?" John asked.

Cho stopped in front of a closed door. "See for yourself," he said, unlocking the door and opening it wide.

John went into the room expecting the worst, but finding the most amazing of sights.

His wife, although looking tired and sickly, was sitting up and smiling weakly as several doctors and nurses attended to various tasks around her. John paused for a moment, hearing Cho behind him begin to question his staff about Theo's condition. John made his way toward the woman who had made his life complete, catching snippets of the team's responses as he drew closer to her bedside.

"I've never seen anything quite like it. . . ."

"Vitals were all over the place and suddenly they were normal. . . ."

"It's like she became another person. . . ."

John was standing at her bedside, gazing into those bleary, yet still beautiful icy blue eyes. "Hey, you," he said, reaching to take her hand in his. It was then that he noticed the restraints binding her wrists to the side of the bed.

"I guess I was pretty wild," she said, pulling on the bonds.

John didn't even hesitate, freeing one hand, then reaching across her to undo the other, ignoring Dr. Cho's urgent warnings.

"John, wait! Not yet! Be careful!"

And then John heard the laughter. At first he thought it was a happy sound, his wife joyfully chuckling at the idea that he would need to be careful of the woman he loved with all his heart and soul.

But then he realized that it was not his wife who was laughing.

The blow was savage and unnaturally powerful, sending him hurtling backward into some medical equipment before crashing to the floor. The room was suddenly alive with activity, but no one had a chance to touch Theodora before a pulsing, preternatural energy burst from her body, scattering doctors and nurses like leaves in the wind.

John had lost his cane, but he hauled himself up from the floor, using the radiator for support. It was as he'd feared.

Actually it was worse.

His wife floated above the hospital bed, her face twisted with an expression that looked like a grimace of pain. But John knew otherwise.

It wasn't pain at all.

"What's wrong with her, John?" Stephan cried from the corner of the room where he recoiled in terror. "What's wrong with Theodora?"

It was absolute joy.

John lurched toward the bed under the woman's watchful eyes.

"It's not her," he said.

A smile split her face wide, showing off razor-sharp teeth. "Hello, John," she said with a voice comprised of a multitude of demonic voices. "We've been waiting for you."

3

The alarm clock rattled.

It didn't really ring anymore, the mechanism inside the windup travel clock muffled by something mucking up the works.

But it still did the job.

Barrett Winfield turned over in his bed and fumbled with the back of the clock, silencing the alarm. He lay there on his side for a moment, gathering his thoughts—booting up, so to speak—and stared at the face of the clock. He'd never noticed the bodies of dead insects that had been trapped inside the clockface, crumbled at the bottom, just beneath the six. On closer inspection he saw that they were the remains of cockroaches and thought how odd it was that they'd found their way inside the plastic.

Now he knew why the alarm was probably muffled. Barrett smiled with his newfound knowledge and sat up in his bed. Once again he found the old adage to be true—one truly did learn something new every day.

He picked up the clock and gave it a little shake, watching the buggy remains crumble even more inside.

"It's the damnedest thing," he muttered as he climbed from the worn and sagging mattress and made his way across the cluttered bedroom to the bathroom, where he voided his bladder in the waterless toilet.

Relieved, he returned to his bedroom and assessed his domain.

The room was filthy, the floor littered with the remains of fast food meals, old newspapers, and clothes, both dirty and clean. He made a mental note to clean the place up soon, but right now just wasn't the time.

It seemed so long since Barrett had had the time to actually do things for himself. He'd been so damn busy with this new job.

But at least he enjoyed this job, after he'd been let go from Rothmore Elementary. . . .

He felt the emotions well up inside him as they often had done since that dark Halloween day. The costume parade for grades one through five had just ended when he was called to the principal's office. Mrs. Gornett had never been one of his favorite people, but he'd believed that they had shared a mutual respect. After all, Barrett had considered himself one of the best third grade teachers and was sure the other teachers at Rothmore knew that to be so.

Or at least he'd thought that to be true.

Barrett pushed the thoughts of his past away and rummaged through the clothes on the floor. The shirt and pants he'd worn for the last few days still seemed to be fine, and he figured he could get another day at least out of them. But when he slipped the yellow dress shirt on, he noticed the red stains.

"Damn it," he hissed. He'd thought for sure that he hadn't gotten any on him.

Shaking his head in annoyance, he pulled off the yellow shirt and tossed it aside. He riffled through a pile of clothing on an old folding chair and pulled a white shirt with vertical red stripes from the heap. He gave it a sniff—a bit musty, but it would air out as the morning went on.

As he slipped the shirt on and began to button it, his mind drifted back to the day he was fired.

No, he corrected himself. He was not fired—he was let go.

But was there really a difference? What they had done to him—to his self-esteem—that Halloween day was more than he could stand.

They'd said that he wasn't performing up to Rothmore standards, whatever the hell that meant. They even had the nerve to comment about his personal hygiene, as if that had anything to do with a child receiving the best possible education.

But in their pathetic little minds, he guessed, it did.

Barrett found his sprits sinking, and forced himself to remember the good that had come from such a horrible incident. For if he hadn't been fi—let go, then he would never have found his dream job.

That put a smile on his face and he went to a mirror leaning against the wall in the corner to look at himself. The mirror was cracked, and it distorted his reflection, but it was good enough to show that he still looked the part. That no matter what some near-sighted individuals with no true vision couldn't see in him, he still saw it in himself.

He was still a teacher, and he still had so much to give.

Satisfied with his appearance, he left his bedroom in the house he'd shared with his mother for his entire life.

She sat in a chair in the center of the living room, directly in front of the television.

"Good morning," he said as he passed through the archway, going into the kitchen.

He felt pangs of hunger but wasn't sure if his stomach was up to handling anything of substance this early. He still got the butterflies before heading into work.

He decided on some toast, going to the bread box and removing the plastic bag. The bread was covered in green and white mold, but that didn't bother him in the least as he selected two slices and placed them in the toaster. Four cockroaches ran for cover beneath filthy cups and dishes as he pushed the lever down.

"The place could do with a little bit of tidying up," he called over his shoulder to his mother, still in the living room.

She remained silent. But he knew how she hated it when he criticized her housekeeping skills.

The toast popped up, the odd smell of burned bread and cooking mold wafting into the air. Barrett took a dirty plate from the stack near the sink and dropped the hot toast on it. Looking in the fridge, he found a plastic container of margarine, but the contents of the tub were black. Barrett looked at it and sniffed it before deciding to eat the toast dry.

Besides, he had to get moving. Today was a special day.

"You might want to do some grocery-shopping, too," Barrett said as he carried his toast from the kitchen into the living room.

His mother continued to sit stiffly in her chair in front of the silent television. Usually she would say that he was picking on her.

Picking on her, he thought as he munched on his toast while he stood beside her chair. He was picking on her when he suggested that she might want to do a little bit of cleaning, or maybe a little bit of shopping. He stared at her, wondering what she thought she was doing to him when she complained that he worked too much, and that he needed to find a nice girl to marry and give her some grandchildren.

His mother just couldn't understand that his students were his children, and really, his job was his wife; that he was totally dedicated to both.

He took another bite of the toast, finding his thoughts drifting back to that day again, and how the horribleness of it all had seemed to flow into the night as well. He and his mother had been watching television, in between running to the door to dole out candy to trick-or-treaters. He hadn't told her that he had been let go, hadn't been able to find the right words. Besides, she'd been transfixed on one of her foolish paranormal reality shows—*Spirit Chasers*—convinced that it was all the God's honest truth. They'd had many an argument about those TV shows, and she'd usually ended them by shushing him quiet and saying it wouldn't be on television if it wasn't true. Sure, as if television couldn't lie.

He'd planned to wait until her show was over before finally telling her that he'd been let go, but he just couldn't wait any longer.

Barrett ate the last of his moldy toast, watching his mother, remembering how she'd reacted. He wondered if it would have been different had he waited until a commercial break, or until the show ended as he'd originally planned.

Instead he'd blurted it out, standing in front of the television. She'd screamed for him to get out of the way as he'd bared his soul and sadness to her, not sure he'd ever get over the devastation of it.

But he had gotten over it, that very evening actually. It was right after she had shown him her true face. His mother had always been cruel, but that night she took her cruelty to another level entirely. She'd called him a failure, telling him that if she'd known when she spent twelve hours in labor with him what a disappointment he would be, she would have visited the abortionist and saved them both a lot of misery.

A part of him still wanted to believe that his mother hadn't meant what she'd said, that she was just annoyed because he was interrupting her television program. But he knew her, and he knew that she very likely had meant every hurtful word.

Trick-or-treaters had been knocking at the door, and people screamed on the television behind him, when Barrett had gathered his courage and strode toward his mother, demanding an apology. Instead she'd just leaned sideways in her chair, telling him to get his failure of an ass out of the way, as her clawlike hands tried to push him to the side.

She'd demanded to see.

And he had shown her.

He had shown her the depths of his despair, the sadness, and the rage.

He'd grabbed a handful of candy corns from a bowl beside her chair. He'd always hated those things, and she used to tease him about making him eat all the candy corns in the house if he wasn't good.

If *he* wasn't good.

But what about *her*?

He remembered grabbing her by the front of her housecoat and pulling her toward him. He remembered her expression, how the anger had turned to fear. Fear of what he was going to do with a fistful of candy corns.

Barrett looked down on the hand that had held the candy corns, and at the scars on his knuckles, left as her dentures raked across the back of his hand while he'd forced handful after handful of the colorful confections into her mouth and down her throat.

The bowl beside his mother's chair was still as empty now as it had eventually been that night. When he had finished, she appeared to have had enough of the candy.

And hadn't asked for any since.

Barrett stood in front of his mother, between her and the dormant television set, as he had on that Halloween night so many nights before. Her skin had turned an ugly black, reminding him of the peel of a rotten banana. Her mouth hung open, her jaw obviously broken. Candy still filled her gaping mouth, and some had spilled out onto her lap. There were living things moving on her blackened skin, more than the last time he had looked at her. He smiled at the thought that these were her new children, and wondered if they would disappoint her as much as he had.

"I'm leaving for school," he told her, not expecting an answer. He just wanted to say it aloud. Her failure of a son was going to work. Her failure of a son had a very important job now.

He wondered, as he had many times before, if the new opportunity he had embraced would have come about that Halloween night if he hadn't struck back at his mother.

If she hadn't been watching that television show.

Barrett remembered the sounds of that night: the pounding on his door, his mother's foul venom spewing from her mouth, and the screams from the television. When it was all over, he'd simply stood there, looking at what he had done, and feeling the sheer terror begin to envelop him. He had been considering calling the police and confessing when a voice spoke to him.

He'd realized then that the screaming on the television had stopped, but now a voice whispered to him from its speaker. He'd thought it strange, and turned to see that the screen had gone to static, but the longer he'd looked at it, the more he had started to see something in the gray-and-white snow.

There was a face in the haze, and it was speaking to him.

Speaking directly to him.

At first, he was sure he'd lost his mind, that losing his job that day had pushed him over the edge, but then the voice commanded him to listen, and he'd had no choice but to do just that.

The voice had told him that it had need of someone with his talents.

It had need of a teacher.

All Barrett had to do was swear his fealty.

He could think of no other answer than yes. And then the voice had whispered to him from behind the static, telling him what he was to do and all that he had to know.

When it was done, Barrett was ready to teach them all.

"Well, how do I look?" he asked his mother as he straightened his tie.

She remained silent, but he already knew the answer. He looked fine . . . better than fine, which was exactly how he needed to be to satisfy the needs of his new employer . . . his new master who'd lifted him up from the depths of despair and given him new purpose.

Today Barrett would prove to himself, to his mother, to his new lord and master, that he was every bit the teacher he knew he was.

Today was the day he would begin to gather his students, and he would teach them about things long forgotten, and as they learned, that which had been lost to the ages would know life again.

And the world would never be the same.

"What's the matter, Johnny boy?" a legion of voices asked, using his wife's mouth. "Surprised to see us?"

John crawled across the floor under his wife's dark, watchful eyes—*No*, he corrected himself—it wasn't his wife at all. He used a nearby chair to haul himself up from the floor, purposefully displaying his weakness.

"A bit under the weather, Johnny?" asked the terrible voices.

Holding on to the chair for balance, he turned his gaze to the woman, locking his eyes to the windows of her soul.

"Are you there, Theodora?" he asked, his words calm, even though he was filled with fear and rage. He could not show it—would not show it.

Her face twisted unnaturally, the hint of a struggle within.

"Oh, she's here, Johnny," one voice answered, a voice as ragged and as old as the grave. "But she's a little busy at the moment." And then it began to laugh, the other horrible voices joining in.

"John, what's wrong with her?" asked Stephan, who cowered in the corner by the door. He'd forgotten that Stephan was there, and brought a finger to his lips to quiet him.

But his wife had already noticed.

She drifted back down on the bed and dropped to all fours, crawled to the end.

"There's nothing wrong with her—yet," the voice told Stephan. "But it's only a matter of time before—"

John made his move, pushing off from the chair and lunging toward the bed. He reached out and grabbed his wife's body by the shoulders.

"Theo, if you can hear me," he began.

The woman recoiled, trying to pull away, but he held her tight. "Come forward, Theodora," he said firmly, his eyes locked to hers. "Push past the filth of these intruders and—"

The stream of vomit was scalding hot, and alive with writhing maggots. John quickly turned his face away as the stinking stream covered him, but still he held on.

"Take your fucking hands off her! She's ours now!" the voices screamed.

"Theo, it's me," John said, ignoring the voices as he turned his gaze back to his wife's eyes. "Listen to the sound of my voice . . . take strength from me and come forward."

"Are you fucking deaf, Johnny boy?" the dominant voice demanded to know. "She isn't going anywhere but down. Do you understand, John Fogg? Your wife is gone now."

But John wasn't giving up. He willed his strength through his hands and into her body, hoping to give his love the help she needed to come forward.

Her body squirmed in his grasp, and he readied himself for whatever new and grotesque defense might be hurled at him.

"Let me go," the dominant voice ordered, the smell of its breath like the stink of a thousand corpses.

The maggots in the foul puddles at his feet began to change, shucking their sickly white skin to reveal fat-bodied flies beneath. The insects swarmed about John's face, nearly choking him, and still he held fast to Theo's shoulders, his eyes on her eyes, filling her with his strength, with his love.

"Take your hands from us!" the voices screamed.

There was a pounding on the room's door, and from the corner of his eye John watched as Stephan, stepping over the unconscious staff, grabbed for the doorknob, yanking on it fitfully . . . futilely.

"Theo, come to me," John ordered. He knew she was in there somewhere; she just had to be shown the way.

The flesh beneath his hands began to writhe, as if something alive crawled beneath. He was disgusted by the feeling, but he would not let her go.

"Theo, I'm here. Follow the sound of my voice."

"Oh Johnny boy, we are going to hurt your ladylove so bad," the voice said. Large, bleeding gashes began to appear upon her face, as if the skin was being sliced with an invisible knife.

"No," John said, with a desperate shake of his head. "I won't let you . . . she won't let you."

She was screaming now, fighting to be free of his grasp, but he held on tightly. She was close; he could feel it. *Just have to hold on for a bit longer,* he told himself, fighting through the pain that racked his body.

The curtains covering the windows suddenly burst into flames, blackening the walls before the sprinkler system activated, filling the room with a cleansing artificial rain.

The power that set the curtains on fire was directed at John. He felt it first at the base of his neck, a tingling sensation as if thousands of fire ants were biting at him. The pain quickly intensified as the flesh on his neck and back began to blister.

But still he held on to her, still he gave her his strength and love.

"You're gonna burn, Johnny," the demon said with a smile that was supposed to steal away his hope.

His wife's eyes began to leak tears of blood.

"Theo," John urged, the smell of his own hair burning filling his nostrils.

The demonic expression on his wife's face suddenly changed from perverse pleasure to something different.

Surprise.

"You're actually going to try this, bitch?" the demon asked. It glanced quickly to the side, then back at John. "I guess we're done for now, Johnny boy," the voice growled. It leaned in and planted a kiss on John's cheek with his wife's lips, lips that were as hot as lava, branding his skin with their impression.

But he didn't cry out; he would not give the loathsome entities that satisfaction.

"But we'll be seeing you again real soon," the demon added with a chuckle that quickly multiplied into the mocking laughter of hundreds of demonic entities.

It was then that John almost lost it . . . the hope that he had desperately held on to.

How many are inside? How many demons now call my wife home?

But he was saved by her expression, Theo's twisted face softening.

"John?" she said, the sound of her voice so weak . . . so frightened.

"I'm here," he said, taking her into his arms as her body went limp, succumbing to the degradation and exhaustion. "I'll never let you go."

The alarms continued their clamor as they both slumped to the floor. The door at last surrendered to Stephan, and security and medical personnel flooded into the room.

"Please," John begged as they tore her from his arms and returned her to the bed, where they began to work on her.

He sat there, the pain in his body attempting to capture his attention, but nothing could distract him from the moment. The realization was worse than anything he could ever have imagined, and it pummeled him again and again as the words of the demonic entity echoed inside his brain.

"I guess we're done for now."

The realization that he might not be able to do it.

"But we'll be seeing you again sometime real soon."

The realization that he might not be able to save her.

Brenna Isabel returned to the child's room one last time.

Maybe there was something she had missed, a piece of evidence staring her right in the eye, daring her to find it—to expose it to the light—providing her with what she needed to find this missing child.

As well as the others.

Her eyes moved over the bedroom again, trying to look at each thing as if it was new, trying to keep it all from being so familiar.

This case was the same as the other two—a young child missing from his home. The first was a seven-year-old boy, the second, a girl of six, and now this young boy, six as well.

Brenna slowly turned in the center of the room, her eyes absorbing every detail, wanting to see it all, hoping there might be something . . .

The children had nothing in common other than being school-age children from middle-class families who went to sleep in their beds and disappeared without a trace during the night—

And a strange symbol that resembled a badly rendered number 8 drawn on a discarded piece of cardboard . . . on the back of a closet door . . . and now on the roof of the missing child's favorite racing car. Marks hidden, but all in plain sight—visible if you looked for them. Her team was already working on the possible meaning. Was it a number 8? And if so what did that mean? Were there five more children who would go missing? Or maybe it wasn't an 8 at all. It was something, she was sure of it—but what?

There were no signs of struggle, no signs of forced entry. Nothing was seen, nothing was heard.

The children were just gone.

Forensics had gone through the room with a fine-tooth comb, gathering what they hoped would be evidence in tiny plastic bags. But Brenna knew it was useless. Whoever had done this was far too careful.

For now.

The only consolation she had was knowing they always got sloppy. Their confidence never failed to get the best of them, and they invariably let something drop. And that was when she would be there, to snatch it up, use it to bring whoever was responsible to justice.

But how many more children would be taken before that happened?

She couldn't think of that. Instead she forced herself to scan the toys and stacks of video games and books.

"Agent Isabel?" someone called from the doorway to the child's room. She turned to see Agent Niles standing there.

"I think we're done here," he said.

She nodded but turned back to the room.

One more time, she told herself. *One more time just to be sure.*

4

Stephan Vasjak leaned back in his chair, telephone clasped to his ear.

"He's not available, Ken," Stephan said for what seemed like the hundredth time. "I'm not going to tell you if he's physically here or not. It just doesn't matter. John is not available."

Stephan felt his frustration growing with each new phone call, e-mail, and text. They all wanted—needed—to speak with John Fogg.

But John Fogg wasn't—*here*.

"I know he told you to find him a new home, and he'll be ecstatic to learn that you think you've found the perfect property, but right now he is not available."

Stephan stood and began to pace, feeling as though the phone were grafted to his ear. "Well, if it's gone, it's gone and I'm sure your amazing talents will find him something else in no time." He could hear the annoyance creeping into his tone. Ken could be quite insistent.

"Fine," Stephan finally agreed. "E-mail the listing and I'll make sure he sees it." He breathed a sigh of relief as he finally ended the call—only to hear his cell begin to ring.

He set the office phone back in its cradle and reached for the cell attached to his belt. It was playing Queen's "Flash Gordon," and Stephan immediately knew he was in trouble.

"Hey, hon," he answered, trying to sound casual.

But Raphael wasn't buying it.

"Yes, I know what time it is . . . it's just been supercrazy around here. . . ."

Raphael promptly reminded Stephan that he hadn't been home at a decent hour in weeks.

"I know, Raph, and I'm working on it."

And Raphael wasn't buying that, either.

"Look, I don't want to do this over the phone." Stephan was trying to keep his cool, but Raphael's answer was quick, and cutting, asking him where else would they do it, seeing that he was never home.

Ouch!

"I know, and I'm really sorry. Truly I am." Stephan tried but knew his husband wouldn't believe him. When Raphael got like this, there was no reasoning with him. And, after all, he did have a point, but since that Halloween broadcast, John and Theo needed Stephan more than ever.

"We'll talk about this when I get home. I'm leaving right now, I promise."

Of course, Raphael had to remind him that he'd promised other things of late—promises that had been broken.

"I'll see you shortly. And I do love you."

Raphael hung up without responding.

Stephan stood there for a moment, staring at his phone before striding to his desk. Pulling the drawer open, he retrieved his satchel and slipped his phone into the side pocket. He threw the bag over his shoulder as he took one more look about the office, then quickly made his escape.

His office was on the first floor of the three-story town house that served as the main offices of Rising Fogg Productions, as well as home to John and Theodora. He stopped at the staircase across from the front foyer and propped his bag on the first step as he retrieved his car keys from another of its side pockets. He glanced up the stairs as he turned back toward the front door and stopped.

Keep going, and head right out that door, a voice inside his head ordered, and he almost listened.

Almost.

"John?" he called out instead. "I'm leaving." He waited a moment, but there was no response. "John?" he tried again.

He knew he should have taken that as a sign and just gotten the hell out of there before he ended up divorced, but he couldn't help himself. John was going through a lot—they all were—and he couldn't stand the thought of his employer, his friend, suffering alone.

He had to be sure he was all right, and as he headed up the stairs, he tried to convince himself that he would only check in and then be on his way.

"Hey, John? You all right?" he called as he entered the open-concept kitchen and living area.

He was met with silence, and no sign of John. Although Stephan was sure he knew where he would find him.

Where he always was now.

His office.

Stephan crossed the living area and proceeded down a short corridor, stopping outside a set of double doors. He hesitated only a moment before knocking.

And still there was no response, other than faint sounds of movement from inside the room.

"Hey, John?" He knocked again. Ordinarily he would have just left at this point, but since the business with Theo, John had become quite distant, preoccupied, and a little lost. Stephan wanted to respect John's grief, but he also needed to know that he was all right.

He grabbed the doorknob and cautiously opened the door. "John, are you okay?"

John was at his desk in the far corner, and slowly lifted his gaze. They stared at each other across a bridge of silence.

Stephan couldn't help himself, the annoyance of the day, mixed with the moment, powering his tongue. "Well, are you?" he demanded, walking into the office. It was an absolute mess.

"Am I what?" John asked.

"All right," Stephan said. "Are you all right . . . ? And looking around, I'm not sure you are."

"I'm fine," John said, going back to whatever it was he was working on. "Why are you fucking bothering me?"

Stephan felt as though he'd been slapped, and suddenly he couldn't help himself. John's attitude combined with the pressures of the day overwhelmed him. "Wow, you have some fucking nerve!"

John looked up again, anger in his gaze this time.

"You heard me," Stephan said. "I'm downstairs morning, noon, and night trying to hold this place together so that you can . . ." He stopped, turning his attention to John's desk, and the catastrophe that his office had become. "So you can do whatever the fuck it is you're doing up here."

"I think it's time that you went home."

"Is that it? You're dismissing me? I should have been home hours ago, but I was here, trying to keep things going so you don't have to worry about anything other than Theo."

"That's enough," John shouted.

"I'm worried about her, too." Stephan ignored John's outburst and stepped closer to the desk, seeing the open bottle of scotch and half-empty glass before John. "You're not alone, John. A lot of people care about you and Theo. *I* care. If you need anything, all you have to do is ask."

"I need you to leave me alone, and stop worrying about things that you're not being paid for," John said. He nearly jumped up from his chair and for the first time, Stephan saw how disheveled he appeared.

He stared at him in disbelief, not sure whether he should respond or not.

"Have I made myself clear?" John asked.

"Perfectly," Stephan replied, then turned and headed for the still-open door. "I hope you and your misery have a nice night," he tossed over his shoulder as he shut the door forcefully behind him.

How dare that little shit? John fumed, slamming his hand down on the desk.

Maybe it was the sudden burst of pain that finally made him realize what an amazing ass he had just been.

"Hey, Stephan!" he called out as he rushed around his desk and to the door. "Stephan, wait up!" He headed for the stairs, hoping he wasn't too late.

But as he descended to the silence of the floor below, he realized that Stephan was already gone.

"Shit," he muttered, and sat down heavily on the last step. *How could I have been such a jerk?* he thought as he wrapped himself in the solitude of the first floor.

He wasn't sure how long he had been sitting there, brooding, when he caught sight of movement in the mirror hanging in the foyer, reflecting from the office.

"Stephan?" John called out, standing up and heading for his friend's office. "Listen, I'm sorry . . ." He stopped.

The office was empty.

He was just wrapping his brain around the fact that he was alone when music began playing from the iPod station in the corner of the room—the beginning chords of Lynyrd Skynyrd's "Sweet Home Alabama" blaring throughout the office.

"Jesus," John hissed, feeling his heart begin to race. He walked over and turned the music off, the silence nearly deafening as he headed back out of the office.

The music began again, this time in the middle of "Homeward Bound," by Simon & Garfunkel.

He turned to the player again, studying it with a questioning eye. After a moment, he strode over and turned it off, watching it, as if daring it to play again.

He waited several minutes before turning away—and "Take me Home, Country Roads" by John Denver began to play.

"Country roads, take me home," the seventies superstar warbled, and being the genius that he was, John suddenly saw the common theme.

Home.

Since the incident at the hospital, he had been consumed with finding a place where he could take Theo when . . . *if* . . . she was released. Someplace where she would be safe, while he searched for a way to take care of her . . . affliction.

Evidently, something or, better yet, someone was aware of his plans.

"Is that you, Nana?" he asked aloud. This type of visit was unlike her; she usually preferred dream visitation to physical manifestation or mechanical manipulation. "Home," he said as he walked about the room, looking for signs of her presence. "You want me to bring her home."

John Denver continued to play.

"It would be nice," he agreed. "But it's impossible." His ankle began to ache, so he stopped and sat down at Stephan's desk.

"It wouldn't be safe here," he explained aloud, sadness nearly overwhelming him. The last time he had visited her, she was heavily sedated, but he knew the demons continued to plague her. And there was nothing he could do.

"In her current condition . . ." He paused, the words feeling like pieces of glass wedged in his throat. "She's dangerous, Nana. Dr. Cho says that he isn't sure how much longer she'll be able to stay at the institute before . . ."

That was what he'd been looking for when Stephan interrupted, a place where she would be safe until he found a way to help her.

"Not here, Nana," John said with a sad shake of his head. "With all my heart I wish it could be, but . . ."

He stood, his movement sending the chair rolling backward into the desk, where the bump seemed to bring Stephan's computer monitor to life. The image of a fabulous stately home appeared there.

Finding it curious that Stephan had left a file open, John leaned across the desk to grip the mouse beside the keyboard, and closed the file. The music—Michael Bublé crooning, of course, a song called "Home"—suddenly cut off, plunging the office into silence.

John had paused a moment, finger ready to click and close the file, when the phone began to ring.

"Hello?"

There was a long pause, and he was about to hang up when he heard . . .

"Hello?"

"Hello," John repeated.

"John?" asked a vaguely familiar voice.

"Yes. Who . . . ?"

"Ken . . . Ken Matheson, at Matheson Realty," his real estate agent answered. "I'm so glad you called. Stephan showed you the house, then?"

John let go of the mouse. "He did," he lied, playing it by ear as he stared at the stately old mansion on the screen.

"When I saw it come up on the listing, I thought of you immediately, and after I checked it out . . ."

"Where is it?" John asked.

"Marblehead, Mass," Ken said. "The North Shore. It used to be a sanitarium for the very wealthy. It closed in the mid-sixties and the current owner . . ."

There was something about the place, something that spoke to him. Something that told him yes, this was the place.

Home.

"I'll take it," John said.

"Excuse me?"

"I said I'll take it. I want to buy it."

"Wouldn't you like to tour the property first?"

"I've seen enough," John said. "Do up the paperwork, and I'll have a payment to you right away."

"Seriously?" Ken asked, obviously flustered. "Are you sure?"

Leonard Cohen's "Hallelujah" began to play, filling the office with its glorious sound. John's nana loved that song, and he did as well.

"I've never been more sure."

The man was talking on his cell phone as he walked up the driveway to the Cho Institute.

"Yes, I'm here now."

He could see movement in the guardhouse as he approached the gate, and a security guard exited.

"Let's see if your mojo is working," the stranger said into the cell phone as he approached the guard. "Evening."

The guard said nothing, simply clicking on his flashlight.

This had better work, the stranger thought as the beam of light illuminated him.

"Would you mind not shining that in my face?" he asked as he held his hand up to shield his eyes.

Without a word, the guard lowered the light.

"Thank you," the man said. "I want you to know that I am nobody, and as nobody I am here for nothing."

The guard stared blankly at him.

"Does that make sense to you?" the stranger asked.

The guard nodded.

"Good. Would you mind opening the gate for me?"

Silently, and without hesitation, the guard turned and disappeared into the guardhouse. A moment later, the metal gate swung open.

"It worked like a charm," the stranger said, talking into his cell again as he walked through the gate and headed up the curving drive to the main entrance. "I'm in."

"How long exactly will this magickal wonder be potent?" he asked, approaching the stairs leading up into the building. "That long? That's some serious stuff." He climbed the stairs. "Listen, I'm about to go inside. I'll call you back."

He broke the connection and slipped the cell phone into the side pocket of his leather jacket. It was relatively late, so the building would be fairly deserted. If he played his cards right, he'd be able to avoid almost everyone.

Pulling open the door, he stepped into a small foyer and climbed three marble stairs to the front desk. A security guard at once looked up and started to stand.

"No need to get up," the man said, and the guard immediately sat back down, returning his attention to the open book in front of him.

The stranger smiled and continued on to a back stairwell that would take him into the hospital's security wing. He passed an orderly whose expression went from surprise to nothing in mere seconds, as the stranger acknowledged him with "Evening." The hospital employee continued on his way as if he hadn't encountered a soul.

He reached the bottom level and opened the door into the coolness of the special floor. Looking left, and then right, he got his bearings and walked to the end of the corridor, where two nurses—a man and a woman—worked at a medication cart. They both looked up as he approached.

"Don't bother with me," the stranger said. They seemed to consider his words before returning to their medication pass.

The stranger continued on down the hallway and stopped before a room at its end. He paused for a moment before letting himself in.

The room was cold, unusually so, and his mind flashed back to the long and painful hospital stay he himself had endured while recuperating from the burns. At times, he was thankful for that experience, for it had prepared him for the life that would follow, and the work he had to do to make the world a safer place for his daughter.

Which was what had brought him here, to Theodora Knight.

Slowly he approached the bed, staring at the woman lying there. She was surrounded by machines that beeped and hummed. Her wrists were bound to the sides of the bed.

He reached down to pull the sheets aside, and jumped as he realized that her eyes were open. She was staring right at—through—him, the gaze so intense it was practically something physical.

He said nothing, imagining that the spell that had been placed upon him would continue to do its job, but . . .

The language that left her mouth was unlike anything he had ever heard before, and he removed his phone from his jacket pocket to record the strange flow of speech.

"I'm guessing you can see me," he said as he put away his cell phone.

Theodora smiled, and he felt the burn-mottled flesh on his neck and back prickle with sudden unease. Her teeth were razor sharp, like those of some primordial predator from the ocean's deepest depths. A tongue purple and forked emerged from between the jagged rows, seductively stroking the awful teeth as she chuckled.

From another pocket in his jacket, the stranger removed a hard case and opened it to reveal a needle and syringe. He carefully removed them, attached the needle to the syringe, and slipped its tip into the soft flesh at the bend of the woman's arm.

She said something to him then, her dark eyes going to the new wound in her arm and the bead of blood that formed there. The bead broke free of the needle's point of entry and began to move about the skin like an odd insect larva, leaving a slight scarlet trail on the pale flesh of her arm.

The woman began to laugh insanely.

Quickly the stranger finished collecting the blood sample and returned the needle and syringe to their case. He turned and left the room, the woman's raucous laughter seeming to follow him down the corridor and out of the building.

The man walked down the drive toward the exit, moving faster than when he'd first arrived. He wanted to be away from this place as quickly as he could. Away from the hospital and the twisted thing it housed.

As he stood before the gates that seemed to take an interminable time to open, he took his phone out and made the call.

It was answered on the first ring.

"It's Royce," he said, passing through the gates and hurrying down the lonely road into darkness to where he'd left his ride. "It's true.

"And it appears to be even worse than what we were led to believe."

5

One month later

The renovations were coming along quite splendidly.

John Fogg stood in the grand entrance to his new home—*their* new home—taking in the changes made since last he'd visited. He was satisfied, but couldn't help wondering if the work could be completed even faster.

"Mr. Fogg!" someone called, and he saw Burt Lansing, his contractor, come out from the side hallway that led to the kitchen.

"Burt, hi," John said, reaching out to take the man's hand in a hearty handshake.

"What do you think?"

"It's great," John said with a smile, imagining what it would be like once it was finished.

"Everything is moving along according to schedule," the contractor said. "Plumbing and electrical are coming along nicely, with drywall waiting in the wings, ready to go as soon as they're finished."

John nodded his pleasure with the enterprise, but still the question danced at the edge of his thoughts, trickling down to his mouth and . . .

"Don't you dare," said Stephan Vasjak, entering through the open front door, satchel slung over his shoulder, wagging a finger at him.

"What?" John asked.

"Just don't," Stephan said, taking off his sunglasses and looking around. "I know that look."

"What look?"

"The look that says thanks a wicked lot, but here's twenty-nine other things that I'd like done in the next half hour."

"I wasn't going to ask for anything," John lied.

Stephan stared at him as Burt Lansing laughed.

"I don't believe you," Stephan said, putting his sunglasses in his bag.

"Well, if you need anything don't be afraid to ask," Burt said, patting John on the shoulder and heading back from where he'd come.

"Thanks, Burt," John said, waving before he turned to Stephan. "I can't believe you embarrassed me like that."

"You were going to ask him for something. Admit it. I know," Stephan said.

"I was going to ask him if it was possible to speed things up."

"John," Stephan said, heading for the library that had been made into a makeshift office to the left of the main staircase. "They're already working seven days a week at a price that I find totally obscene." He tossed his bag down on top of a desk made from two-by-fours laid across three horses. "They can't work any faster than they already are."

John followed him into the library. "It's just that . . ."

Stephan pulled his laptop out of his bag, flipped open the lid, and powered it up. "I know, you want Theo to come home."

"I'm afraid the longer she's in the hospital, the harder it's going to be to make her well."

Stephan pulled an old folding chair over to his makeshift desk and sat down, refusing to look at him. John knew that he was keeping something to himself.

"What is it?" John asked.

Stephan shook his head. "It's nothing."

"No, just like you knew I was going to pester Burt, I know that something's up. What? Spill it."

"I know you're doing all this for her," he said. "But . . ."

"But?"

"Are you sure that this is the right thing to do? I saw what I did back at the Cho Institute and it scared the living shit out of me, and I've been with you and Theo for how long? Believe you me, I've seen some scary business. I'm just not sure how safe it'll be for her here . . . for us."

"The process to cure Theo will be a long and complex one," John explained. "And I'm sad to say that there are no guarantees that she will even survive the process."

It was the first time he'd said these words out loud and they were like a physical blow to him.

Stephan got up from his chair and came to him. "John, I don't want you to think that . . ."

"I completely understand your concern," John said. "I'm pretty damn afraid myself." He chuckled. "I'd completely understand if you wanted to step back from this, maybe take a leave of absence until—"

"Like hell I will," Stephan said. "I can only imagine what the business would be like when I came back. If you think this is right, then there's no reason for me to doubt you. I'll be right there by your side for as long as it takes."

"Thank you, Stephan," John said.

"You're welcome," Stephan answered, returning to his laptop. "Now that all that's out of the way, I thought you were supposed to be traveling today?"

"I am," John said. "I called the car service. They're picking me up here."

"And you did that all by yourself?"

John laughed. "Remember, there was a time before personal assistant business managers when I had to handle these sorts of things all by my lonesome."

"Who are you kidding?" Stephan said. "I'm sure Theodora took care of most of it."

John laughed again. "Yeah, she probably did."

They were quiet for a moment.

Stephan's fingers fluttered over the laptop keyboard, the faint clicking sound interrupting the pregnant silence.

"Romania?" Stephan questioned. "And what do we hope to find there?"

"I've been invited to an archaeological dig," John explained. "It appears that a vast and unexplored library has been located beneath the ruins of a monastery in Wallachia. I don't want to get my hopes up, but this library could contain information that just might help me make Theodora well again."

"We can only hope," Stephan said.

The sound of multiple car horn beeps made them look toward the window.

"Car service?" Stephan reminded. "Airport?"

John looked at his watch. "Shit," he muttered, already on the move. "Gotta go."

John left the library office, heading out into the foyer to the corner where he'd left his luggage.

"Make sure to text me when you get there," Stephan said.

"Yes, Mother," John answered, slinging his travel bag over his shoulder. "Hold down the fort. I'll be back as soon as I can."

"I hope you find what you're looking for."

"Me, too," John said as he slipped out the door, hurrying down the front walk toward a waiting black sedan.

A woman was coming toward him wearing a dark suit, white blouse, and large sunglasses.

"Good morning," he said, dropping his bags on the ground in back of the car. "Can you pop the trunk? How's the traffic? We should have plenty of time to get to Logan, but if it backs up into the Ted Williams Tunnel we'll be screwed for sure and—"

"John Fogg?" the woman said abruptly, removing her sunglasses.

"That's right," John said impatiently. She still hadn't opened the trunk.

"Mr. Fogg, I'm Special Agent Brenna Isabel from the FBI." She held out her hand.

John was startled, but took her hand. "I'm sorry, Agent Isabel. I mistook you for my driver." He shook her hand as he looked around and spotted another sedan on the other side of the driveway. A man with a face he recognized waved him over.

"That's quite all right," the agent was saying. "I've phoned you a few times, but we haven't been able to connect. I chanced a drive over this morning, but it looks as though I've caught you at a bad time."

"Actually yes," he said, releasing her hand and bending slightly to retrieve his bags. "I've got a flight in less than two hours, and with morning traffic and all . . ."

"I completely understand." She smiled, but there was no warmth in the look.

John felt her official coldness, and was certain that Agent Isabel was a no-nonsense type. He glanced back to the waiting car and the driver impatiently tapping his watch, although he had to admit that the agent's visit did pique his curiosity.

"Look, would you give me a call when you return?" She reached into her jacket pocket and produced a card, handing it to him.

He dropped his bags again and took the card from her. He quickly looked at it, then pulled his wallet from his back pocket and slid the card inside. "Certainly," he said, picking up his luggage and starting to his ride on the other side of the driveway.

"When will that be?"

He stopped and looked at her.

"Your trip? When will you be returning from your trip?"

"I really don't have a return time planned yet," he said. "I'm going to be doing some pretty heavy research, but I'd like to be back as quickly as I'm able. I promise I will call you."

"I'd really appreciate that," she said, and he caught wind of something very serious in her tone, something that almost made him stop and ask what was so important that an FBI agent had come looking for him.

But time was wasting, and he didn't want to miss his flight.

He lugged his bags to the waiting sedan and tossed them into the open trunk, slamming it closed. The driver held the back passenger door open for him as he quickly climbed in, catching sight of Agent Isabel still standing beside her own car, watching him. He gave her a brief wave as his driver pulled away.

She did not wave back as she slipped on her sunglasses and walked to her car.

Theodora Knight lay curled on a bed of shadow within a dwindling circle of light.

Her circle.

She knew that the light was coming from her, from within her own body. And she knew that it would not be long until it was gone, until the darkness rushed in to fill the space.

To swallow her whole.

But until that time she would fight, she would stoke her inner light, letting it radiate from her body to keep the encroaching shadows, and the things that lived inside them, at bay.

Yes, she knew they were there, those foul, horrible things, just outside her glowing sphere, just beyond the touch of light.

Waiting.

For they, too, knew that the illumination would not last forever, and eventually they would be able to claim her.

Until then she would do all that she could to keep the glow alive and hold the darkness back, and pray that there was still hope for her.

That the darkness would not win.

With those thoughts she felt the pressure of the shadows all around bear down upon her, squeezing the sphere of light, testing its strength.

And something just beyond the searing influence of her soul's illumination, something hissed with confidence—

Soon.

Barrett Winfield knew that he was dreaming, but it seemed so very real.

He stood upon the rooftop of his old school, looking out over a vast and once thriving city, now reduced to rubble. Teachers with whom he had worked knelt on the rooftop around him. They were filthy, covered in the dirt and dust of destruction, their tears leaving winding trails through the grime on their faces.

And they all looked to him, begging for his knowledge.

"Teach us," they pleaded. "Show us how to live in this changing world."

He wanted to tell them to fend for themselves, but he could not bring himself to do so, even though they had treated him so unfairly. The spirit of what he truly was wouldn't allow him, no matter how badly they had mistreated him. He was a teacher, after all, and now it was his turn to teach *them*.

"Look," he commanded, pointing at the ruins of the city.

In the distance, alarms wailed mournfully, mixing with the cries of the injured and terrified. What still remained standing of the many ruined buildings began to vibrate and crumble, falling apart as the ground beneath the city's center began to crack and swell.

As something forced its way up from beneath.

His fellow teachers were all sobbing, their eyes fixed to the falling structures and the heaving Earth below them.

"Listen," he told them, turning his head ever so slightly as a terrible howling filled the air. The sound was everything, deafening in its intensity, so loud that it caused the flesh to tingle, the bones to ache.

Glorious.

The teachers had covered their faces, ducking their heads.

"Watch!" he ordered, for this was how they would learn. And even though they were frightened, they did as he commanded.

As their *Teacher* ordered.

And the world's new, dark lord pushed up through the deep rock, dirt, and concrete, born to this new time and place. It—he—was a thing to behold. To describe his awesomeness would have been impossible.

And the Teacher reveled in the sight, while the others were stricken silent, thick tears raining from eyes wide with wonder and terror.

"Do you see?" the Teacher asked them. "This is the beginning of the new," he explained. "The world that you know now will soon be nothing more than a fading memory. This will become real."

The demon-god surged upward, its many mouths open and belching thick clouds of black, oily smoke that stuck to the sky and swallowed the sun. Darkness fell upon them, and the Teacher knew that it was only a matter of time before the entire planet was wrapped in a cloak of shadow.

The immenseness that was his god continued to spread out over the ruins of the great city, flowing out and beyond, some of its many,

many mouths singing the most beautiful of songs, while others vomited the clinging darkness.

The Teacher listened to that special song, and heard in its beautiful tune a message only for him. A message that sacrifices would have to be made for this wonder to be true.

To actually become reality.

And then Barrett realized that this fantastic moment, this transcendent experience had yet to occur.

That this was all a dream.

And his sadness and rage were like a thing alive. He looked at those who had spurned him, cast him out from their tribe, and he hated them more than ever before. One by one he took them, tossing them from the rooftop of the school, down into the enormity of his master, to be swallowed up by his awesomeness.

To be one with the god.

There was nothing he wanted more for himself, but he knew that his work was not yet done.

To see this dream—this beautiful fantasy—come true, he had to do his job. He had to teach. He had to plant the seed.

And in order for that seed to grow, the soil had to be rich, and moist with the blood of the innocent.

Barrett Winfield opened his eyes to the new day.

He lay atop the stained mattress, wrapped in sweat-soaked sheets, and realized that something had happened—that he was no longer the same—that he had been transformed.

His old self was gone. Only the teacher now remained.

The Teacher.

He smiled. Barrett had been weak, without purpose, but now . . .

The Teacher rose from the bed, filled with the drive to continue his holy mission and fulfill his purpose. He stood in the center of the room, surrounded by the filth of his old life, anxious to wash away the last remains of Barrett Winfield, to slough off that skin and reveal the Teacher beneath.

Walking atop the detritus of years, he made his way to the bathroom. It was as filthy as the rest of the house. He had to pull out dozens of trash bags filled with old clothes before he could climb into the dirt-caked tub. Then he cast off his undergarments, adding them to the piles of dirty clothes that already littered the floor.

Standing naked and exposed, the Teacher reached for the knobs, turning them, hearing the moans and groans of ancient pipes asleep from lack of use. The center knob turned with a whining shriek, and a blast of icy, rust-colored water vomited forth from the showerhead, gradually turning to warm as he shivered beneath the liquid spray. He stuck his face beneath the gout, to rinse away the last vestiges of Barrett's appearance, his hands now moving across his dirty body, scrubbing at what remained of Barrett's skin. He closed his eyes, imagining layers of skin sloughing off from his body, dissolving away and washing thickly down the drain.

His hands moved over his stomach and chest, but stopped when he felt something that he hadn't felt before.

Something that shouldn't have been there.

For a moment he felt that sudden, typically human fear.

Cancer.

But he was beyond human thought now. He stroked the odd, fleshy growth just beneath, and in the center of his chest, feeling it move beneath his fingers. Strangely it did not concern him.

In fact, it excited him, filling him with a sense that it was supposed to be there, that this was a message.

The Teacher smiled and continued to scrub at the filth that was Barrett Winfield, until only the pristine form of the Teacher remained.

Then he dried himself with some towels he'd found wedged beneath boxes of crusted cleaning products and returned to his bedroom to stand before the broken mirror.

The Teacher admired his naked body, surprised at how different he appeared, and yet so familiar. Moving closer to the mirror, he brought a tentative hand to the discolored growth just beneath his chest and stroked it gently.

Lovingly.

And practically burst into tears as he watched it move with life and begin to grow.

6

John Fogg had been too excited to sleep.

The flights had been inconsequential, giving him the opportunity to catch up on some reading, but he found himself horribly distracted. His mind was crackling with the potential of his journey, and what it could mean to the health of his wife. He could hardly focus on reports of increased paranormal activity across the world, or the latest offers from television and streaming networks.

The more he tried to concentrate, the more they transformed into gibberish, and he eventually gave up, closing his eyes and attempting to sleep.

But sleep had been as elusive there, as it had been in his hotel room.

He leaned his head back against the cool wooden paneling as the elevator descended to the lobby, feeling the tug of exhaustion. If the journey down had been just a little bit longer, he very well might have fallen asleep. But the elevator lurched to a stop, and with a cheery ding, the doors slid open on the richly decorated lobby. Pushing off the wall, he exited, his every sense attuned to one thing for this particular moment, and one thing only: the location of coffee.

He smelled the rich scent of the morning necessity, and then viewed the large copper urns placed against the wall in an open area with seats. It was still early enough that there weren't many people up yet, so he didn't have to wait for his first cup.

Thank God.

He scanned the area, looking for a sign that someone might be watching for him. The sponsor of the monastery dig had promised to send somebody to collect him and drive him out to the site. Fogg grabbed a cup and selected a coffee from one of the four urns. It didn't matter what kind it was, as long as it was hot and strong.

The first sip was like Heaven, and he felt that little kick, probably more psychological than anything else, lift his energy level, prompting him to take the next.

"Do you notice the difference?" a voice asked him.

John turned around to see an older, well-dressed gentleman behind him. He was immaculately dressed, but John's eyes were drawn to his face, the left side of which was badly scarred. Looking at the old wounds, he could only think of the vestiges of some sort of wild animal attack.

"Good morning," John said, stepping aside so the man could serve himself a cup.

"I was talking about the coffee," the old man said, moving to the center urn. He took a cup, placed it beneath the spigot, and filled it with the dark liquid. "This here is the elixir vitae, while what you drink in the United States . . ."

The old man smiled then, making the left side of his face appear even more horrible.

"Maybe it has something to do with the urns," John said, pointing out the copper containers, before taking another, larger sip from his own cup.

The old man stared at him, slowly bringing his cup up to his mouth, where he carefully drank. A handkerchief then appeared from out of his suit coat pocket and he dabbed at the damaged side of his mouth so as not to dribble. "The container is just that—a container." He paused, his stare suddenly intense. "It is what is inside that is the key."

And suddenly John's thoughts weren't of coffee and copper urns, but of another container and the evils that it contained, evils that had been unleashed that horrible Halloween night.

Evils that had taken, and changed, his wife.

John stared at the man who continued to sip his coffee and delicately dab at the left-hand side of his face.

"Why do I suddenly think you know more about me than I know about you?" John said, moving toward the urn to refill his cup.

The older gentlemen stepped aside so John could pass.

"I apologize, Mr. Fogg," the old man said. "Your celebrity precedes you, especially since the tragic events of Halloween last. Oh yes, even in Europe we are aware of the incident that claimed the lives of your *Spirit Chasers* investigators and severely injured both you and your wife."

John stared at the man, attempting to figure him out. There was something odd about him.

"Your wife, how is she recovering?" The old man turned his good eye to John.

"She's doing well, thank you," John said. Looking around, he found a cart that held clean cups, mugs, and saucers and set his cup down. "I don't believe I got your name, Mr. . . . ?" He held out his hand for the man to shake, but he was left hanging.

"That evening, Mr. Fogg," the scarred old man said. "It has affected us here as well."

"I'm not quite sure I understand," John said, feeling his ire on the rise.

"Just a simple utterance to make you aware that you, and your wife, are not alone," he said.

John was just about to barrage the man with questions when he heard his name called from the lobby behind him. He turned only for a moment to signal the driver that he was there, but it was long enough for the scarred old gentleman to disappear.

The only sign that he had even been there, the second dirty coffee cup sitting on the cart beside John's own.

The scarred old man walked around the corner of the hotel and approached a waiting silver sedan. He opened the back passenger door, slid inside, and pulled the door closed again behind him.

The driver's eyes found his in the rearview mirror.

"Well?" the driver asked.

The old man thought for a moment, a tentative finger stroking the damaged flesh around the corner of his mouth. "I don't know," he said slowly.

"But you did make contact?" the driver asked.

"Yes."

"Word from the States is that Fogg has bought and is renovating a new home. He's planning on bringing his wife there, when and if she's able."

"I'm not quite sure how I feel about that," the old man said, gazing out the tinted passenger window.

"You'd know if you had seen her," the driver said, reminding him of his journey to, and observations at, the Cho Institute. "There was nothing good going on in that hospital room, let me tell you."

"Let's head back," the old man said as the sedan pulled into the flow of traffic. He could feel the driver's eyes returning to him, and looked to meet the man's gaze in the rearview mirror.

"What are we going to do, Elijah?" the driver asked.

Elijah turned back to the window, watching as the ancient city of Bucharest passed quickly by. "We'll wait. Watch—see if he can be trusted."

"And if he can't?" the driver asked.

"Then we'll be forced to do something about our Mr. Fogg," Elijah said. He had started to gently stroke the damaged part of his face again.

"Him and his wife."

The Land Rover rocked up and down, driving over the rugged terrain up into the foothills of the Southern Carpathians, heading for the ruins of the Wallachian Monastery.

"How exactly was it discovered?" John asked as he bounced from side to side.

"That's actually a pretty interesting story," the driver, whose name was Scottie, said as he carefully drove the SUV up the pitted dirt road. "My employer bought the property to build a luxury resort. The demolition team discovered the storage chambers beneath the monastery."

"Your employer was tearing down the remains of a seven-hundred-year-old monastery to build a resort?" John asked in disbelief.

Scottie glanced at him and then back at the road. "That's right," he said with a smile. "It would have been another jewel in the crown of my lord and master, Cyril Anastos."

"Nice," John said sarcastically, holding on to the strap above the passenger-side door as the car continued to buck and dip. Anastos was considered one of the world's richest men, his vast fortune accrued through real estate and the Anastos family's shipping empire.

"Hey, at least he didn't continue the demolition," Scottie said. "As soon as the subchamber was unearthed, Mr. Anastos stopped the build and brought in a special research team to figure out what it was they'd found."

"A secret library," John said, the knot of anticipation that he'd been feeling since being contacted by Johan Booth, the head of the research team, intensifying.

"Indeed," Scottie said with a happy nod. "I do have to say, Mr. Anastos was quite pleased when he heard that you would be coming to help. He's quite the fan of your television programs."

The Land Rover rolled up over a small hill and that was when John saw it, an ancient stone structure, the front looking as though it had been erected yesterday, while the back portion had partially crumbled to ruin.

"Here we are," Scottie announced, parking alongside a row of trailers that appeared to be serving as a base of operations.

John could wait no longer. He quickly unsnapped his seat belt and climbed from the car, and that was when he noticed them—men armed with automatic rifles pacing around the back ruins of the monastery, keeping a watchful eye on all activity.

He must have looked startled, because as Scottie joined him, he said, "Not to worry—just our security team. Mr. Anastos is very protective of what he believes is his and he doesn't want to risk anything being taken."

John counted at least ten heavily armed guards. It seemed a little like overkill, but over the years he'd seen countless excavations looted of priceless antiquities, so he guessed that he couldn't blame Anastos. This just made him even more anxious to see what had been uncovered.

"Hello there," someone called from behind them, and John turned to see a large, heavily bearded man emerging from inside one of the trailers.

"Ah," Scottie said. "That's Professor Johan Booth. He's in charge of the dig."

"Professor Booth," John said, watching as the large man descended the four steps to the ground. He grabbed John's hand, shaking it vigorously.

"Very nice to meet you, Mr. Fogg," the man said. "When Scottie told me they were bringing you in, I was first a little surprised and then a bit concerned."

"And why is that, Professor?" John asked pleasantly.

"Let's just say I was only familiar with the more sensational aspects of your career." He released his powerful grip on John's hand. "But now . . ."

"But now I've been deemed worthy," John said with a smile. "Or at least I hope I have."

"After a brief Google search, I stand corrected and welcome your opinion on what we've found here," the professor reassured him.

"I can't wait," John said as Professor Booth started to usher him toward the ruins. "Will you be joining us, Scottie?"

"Oh no," the driver said with a slight shake of his head. "I'll leave this to the experts." Then he excused himself, walking toward the Land Rover, taking his phone from his pocket and starting to make a call.

"Right this way, Mr. Fogg," the professor said.

"John—please."

"Of course, and please call me Johan."

They walked toward the back area of the monastery where the damage was the most pronounced.

"The monastery is believed to have been the home of an anchoritic order of monks known as the Brothers of Heaven. They were a small and secretive brotherhood that lived lives of total isolation as they attempted to make their monastery the most blessed place on the planet in preparation for God's return to Earth."

"They were also known as the Order of the Golden City, if I'm not mistaken," John added as they made their way toward two heavily armed figures who gripped their automatic rifles tightly as they approached.

"Very good," Professor Booth said, glancing at John with a raised eyebrow and a nod, before acknowledging the guards in front of them.

"Good afternoon, gentlemen. This is the esteemed John Fogg. He will be accompanying me down into the library today."

The guards did not say a word as they coldly eyed John. Then they stepped aside, allowing him and the professor to pass.

Though badly damaged, the interior of the once holy place still held a certain presence and majesty. John took it all in, attempting to file away every detail of the impressive structure.

"An earthquake a little over a year ago caused the back end to crumble," Booth explained.

"Was this before or after it was decided to knock it down to make way for a luxury resort?" John asked.

"Actually before," the professor said with a chuckle. "Nobody wants a broken monastery, especially after the amount of money Mr. Anastos tossed around to the local politicians to acquire it. The earthquake helped to speed up the process a bit, which resulted in . . ." He waved toward a section of stone corridor that still retained part of a ceiling. "The demolition crew found the sepulcher, mummified remains and all, behind a section of wall that had crumbled with the force of the quake."

The corridor seemed to head underground; lights had been strung along the ceiling to illuminate the way. Finally John saw where the corridor wall had been breached, a burial chamber beyond it. Inside the chamber, the walls were honeycombed with tombs carved into the stone where the Brothers of Heaven made their final resting places.

"The workers were pretty freaked out by this, and a team from the local university was called out to take a look."

John stepped into the chamber and stopped, surrounded by the remains of the dead. But his eyes ignored all that as he searched for something else.

Something that had brought him to this place filled with the potential for hope.

"Have you found it yet?" the professor asked. "The entrance to the secret chambers below?"

John looked to the man whose bearded face was grinning from ear to ear, his eyes twinkling in the harsh lights strung across the ceiling.

"You're killing me here," John said as the burly man laughed.

He looked about the chamber, his eyes slowly taking in every inch of it. Looking to the stone floor, he saw that it was cracked, partially raised in some areas.

"A result of the quake?" John asked, pointing to a particular section of floor.

The professor nodded.

John moved farther into the chamber, making his way toward a raised stone base upon which the tightly wrapped remains of one of the monks lay.

"The abbot?" John said, pointing to the body.

"The most holy of the brotherhood," the professor confirmed.

John loomed above the enshrouded corpse, studying every detail of it. "What secrets do you keep?" he whispered to the withered remains.

The floor beneath the stone seemed strangely crumbled, the accumulation of dust and dirt pushed away. John looked down and slid his foot over the broken floor. He then looked up to see that the professor was staring at him intently.

Believing he was on the right path, John placed his hands upon the corners of the stone altar and gave it a push. Nothing happened at first, but then he planted his feet and applied a bit more force and—

The stone platform slid to the left, exposing an opening in the floor and high stone steps that led down into the darkness of the earth.

"That is awesome," John said, his eyes attempting to penetrate the darkness.

"We actually found another less dramatic way down that was caused by the quake, but I figured you'd appreciate this."

"You are so right," John said, taking the phone from his pocket and turning on the flashlight feature. "May I?" he asked.

"Please," the professor said, motioning for him to enter.

Carefully John descended, feeling the temperature dropping considerably the deeper he got. The last step ended in a large circular chamber with multiple doorways, and over each of the doorways was a symbol.

A symbol that caused the hair on the back of his neck to prickle with anticipation.

"Do you know what this means?" John asked as he slowly walked toward one of the passages, his eyes riveted to the symbol above it. He held up his phone to better illuminate it. "What these mean?"

The sudden roar of a motor practically made him leap from his skin as bulbs strung around the room came to life, flooding the chamber with light. John turned to see the professor setting down the plastic container of gas for the generator.

"I believe I do, but I was hoping that you would be able to shed some more light on the topic." Professor Booth walked over to stand beside him. "What do you know about the Demonists?"

John studied the drawings about the doorways. They depicted a monstrous version of some demonic entity—who many believed was a version of the Devil himself—trapped inside the confines of a cagelike structure, clawed hands closed tightly around the bars of its prison.

"Probably not much more than you," he began. "A mysterious brotherhood of holy men who combated the spread of evil in the world with their vast knowledge of the supernatural. Many in fact don't believe that they actually existed, seeing as evidence like this is nearly impossible to come by."

"And if you think this is impressive," the professor said, ushering John through the center doorway into an even larger space.

The room was enormous, and John couldn't even begin to think of how it had been created. It was as if the large space had been gouged from solid rock. Everywhere his eyes looked there was something that took his breath away. He recognized objects haphazardly scattered about the room: objects he had read about in his extensive research of the arcane, items of power that had likely been collected by the brotherhood as they traversed the globe.

"What do you think?" Professor Booth asked.

"I think this is one of the most historic discoveries ever made," John said, unable to hide the awe in his tone.

"Do you think this actually belonged to them . . . to the Demonists?"

John couldn't stop looking around. "I do."

"But why here?" the professor asked. "Why hidden away beneath this monastery?"

"Perhaps they believed that the items they gathered would be safe here," John suggested. "Unnoticed."

"But what makes this place more special than any other?"

"Didn't you say it was the sole purpose of the monks who lived here to make their residence the holiest place on the planet for God's return?" John asked.

The professor nodded.

"This is the heart of it, then . . . the heart of Heaven," John said, still looking around. "Where better to store items that could potentially be used for evil?"

"You do have a point," Booth agreed thoughtfully.

John stood in the center of the chamber, imagining the great brotherhood of holy men as they traversed the globe finding these objects of potential evil, and returning with them here, to be cleansed of their evil.

Cleansed of their evil. The words echoed in his skull, each reverberation driving its meaning home to him.

John looked about the room as if for the first time.

"A library," he said aloud, still searching. "Is there a library?"

The professor laughed as he walked over to a concave section of wall where an ancient shelf stood, still holding some lesser forms of danger. "I was wondering when you were going to get around to asking," he said. He then placed both hands upon the ancient stone to the right of the dilapidated shelf and pushed.

The shelf swung outward with barely a sound, revealing another darkened passage.

The professor looked to him and beckoned with two fingers as he went through first. John could barely contain himself, rushing toward the darkness.

But wasn't that what he had done most of his life? Drawn toward the black of the world, attempting to drive it back to make room for the light? He liked to think so.

Another generator rumbled to life, filling the room with a weak artificial light that temporarily caused the blackness to recede.

John stood in the entryway, breathless. This room—this chamber—was even larger than the storeroom they had just left. But where the other room had held items of potential evil—baubles, bones, accursed blades, and the accoutrements of black worship—this room held items of even greater power.

This room held the answers to questions long hidden from the world.

The library of the Demonists was where their true power existed.

"This is incredible," John said breathlessly. As far back as he could see, there were shelves, and on those shelves were heavy, leather-bound books. Stacks of rolled scrolls and parchment littered the tops of long tables between the shelves.

All of them, every book, scroll, and piece of paper, demanding to be read, the knowledge contained there brought into the light.

The tiny flame of hope that he'd nurtured at the beginning of his journey began to grow. To burn. He could feel its heat, starving to be more, desperate to be fed, the potential knowledge here quite possibly enabling him to help those afflicted with the most horrific of curses.

He thought of his wife, lying in a bed, swollen with evil, and realized that the answers he sought could be somewhere in this vast library—mere feet, or even inches, from his fingertips.

"Have they been cataloged?" he asked, his eyes tracing the leather bindings as he passed the shelves.

"It's been started," Booth said as he followed.

"Do you have a list that I might see?" John asked, moving down the makeshift aisles, searching.

He reached an area at the back of the library chamber where the thick wooden shelves had been arranged in a circle. John walked to the center and saw that they were all empty. It was strange to see open space where everywhere else he looked there were volumes of every conceivable thickness.

"Where?" he asked, saying no more as he imagined what wasn't there.

Booth chuckled, coming to join him in the center. "Mr. Anastos knows you better than I would have imagined," the professor said.

John looked at him, confused.

"He said that this would be the area you'd be drawn to."

"What was here?" John asked, imagining the ghostly apparitions of books on the shelves. Books that were now denied to him. "What books were they?"

"Books of exorcism," Professor Booth said. "Volume after volume, chronicling the Demonist Brotherhood's battle with the diabolical across the world, as well as their methods."

The flames of hope inside John surged. "I have to see them," he said, attempting to keep his heartbeat steady, trying to stay calm.

"Mr. Anastos thought as much. He had all the volumes taken to his home."

John waited, unsure of what was to follow. He had to see those books; he had to study and learn their ancient words of power.

Booth abruptly turned and started from the area.

"Wait," John called out. "I need to . . ."

The professor stopped and removed a cell phone from his pocket. "He wants you to call him," the professor said, waving the phone. "We'll have better reception above."

John hated to leave, but the answers that he sought in the dusty, ancient chambers below the holy place were no longer there.

He stood just outside the ruins, watching Booth speak softly into his phone. After what seemed like an interminable amount of time, the professor turned and offered the phone to John without a word.

John took it and brought it to his ear. "Hello?"

There was a pause and then a voice.

"John Fogg?"

"Yes."

"Cyril Anastos."

"Yes, Mr. Anastos. What can I do for you?"

"I believe it's what I can do for you, John. I have some old books I think you'd like to see."

"I think you do."

John imagined the wealthy man smiling on the other side of the call, wielding his power over him.

"Would eight o'clock be good?" the man asked.

"For what?" John questioned, suddenly not sure about where this was going. He knew where he would like it to go, but . . .

"For dinner, of course. You will come to my home, and we will converse about the darkness, and things that go bump in the night, and then . . ."

"And then?"

"I will let you see my precious books."

John did not respond, hating for anybody to have power over him, but . . .

"Is it a date?" Anastos asked.

He continued to wait, weighing his options, but the image of his wife bound to her hospital bed was enough to sway him.

"It's a date," John finally agreed.

And ended the call.

7

The princess bed was far too small, but it was the only place where Joyce Mckellan could grab any semblance of precious sleep.

Her husband, Bob, slept down the hall in their own room. He called it sleeping, but when she awakened, before slipping back down into the embrace of something more akin to unconsciousness brought on by exhaustion, she could hear him crying out.

Screaming their daughter's name.

In the morning, before the sun even began to think about rising in the sky, they would both get up—leaving their nighttime places—and silently walk to the stairs, where they would descend to the first floor and begin their wait for another day.

That was how it had been for the last nine days.

Since Rebecca had been taken.

They did not speak as they went about their business, one of them preparing the first pot of coffee for the day while the other checked their phones for messages just in case they might have missed a call. They barely even made eye contact. Grief was all that they could experience—were allowed to experience.

Over and over again Joyce recalled the day when Rebecca went missing. One moment she was there, watching television, and then she was gone.

Joyce's mind raced with the infinite possibilities of what could have happened. Had she left the house for some reason? Had someone, somehow, come into the house and taken her? Joyce found her mind drifting to the memory of a movie that she had seen on cable as a child, in which a little girl had been taken into another world—another dimension—filled with angry ghosts.

Right then she would have taken that insane answer to the question of what had happened to her daughter. At least it was more than what they had now.

Now all they knew was that their daughter had been there and then suddenly wasn't anymore.

Joyce sensed movement alongside her and watched as the steaming cup of coffee was placed beside her on the little table cluttered with other dirty mugs. Bob shuffled to his chair opposite the couch where she sat, and dropped into the chair, cell phone and portable landline lying in his lap.

That was where they would stay, drinking coffee.

And waiting.

Joyce looked to the clock on the cable box, calculating the number of hours before Agent Isabel would call. She called them every day with an update on the investigation. Joyce thought of the other parents with children who had recently gone missing. Agent Isabel believed that they were all somehow connected.

How many other kids had disappeared? She had to think for a moment to remember the number. Six. Six other children had disappeared from their homes without a trace.

Was it awful that she didn't care about the other children? That the only child she cared about was her Rebecca? That she would let all those other children stay missing if it meant her daughter could come home to her alive?

Yes, it was awful, but it was also the truth.

She picked up her mug, not in the least bit concerned that her hand was shaking and coffee was spilling over the rim to stain the cream-colored carpet. She sipped the scalding liquid, enjoying the sensation of feeling something other than grief for only an instant before thinking of Rebecca again. Her eyes again went to the cable box to check the time. It was ten minutes later than the last time she had looked, but she went through the process of calculating how long it would be before Agent Isabel called anyway.

Her husband began to sob and she looked at him sitting in his chair, staring off into space. She considered going to him, consoling him with some of her own strength but worried that if she did such a thing she might not have the power to deal with her own misery. She hoped that he would be okay as she continued to drink her coffee, waiting for the phone to ring.

Waiting.

Joyce found that she often slipped into a strange, fuguelike state, a weird place between being awake and asleep where time seemed to pass much more quickly. She actually enjoyed when that would happen, when she slipped away to where she could remember the happier times. She was almost in that state when a sound snapped her cruelly from it.

She immediately looked at her husband.

Bob had lifted the house phone to his ear, but the look of confusion on his face told Joyce that the phone had not rung. He looked at her when the sound came again.

Joyce stood up suddenly, her half-filled cup of coffee spilling onto the floor of the living room as the realization of what she and her husband were hearing became clear.

It was the doorbell.

The doorbell. At that hour? What did it mean? What *could* it mean?

"Oh God," she heard Bob say. He sounded as if he was going to be sick. He was standing as well, but not moving, as if frozen to that spot in front of his chair.

She was enraged. How dare he stand there, afraid to go to the door? What if it was something important? What if it was about Rebecca?

What if it was?

Joyce used her anger to force her legs to move, propelling her from the living room and into the hallway. She imagined pulling open the wooden door in front of her to see Agent Isabel standing there, a smiling Rebecca in her arms. But as she reached out to the doorknob, another scenario played out in the theatre of her mind. In this one, Agent Isabel stood there alone, an emotionless expression on her face as she blurted out, *"I'm so sorry."*

Sobbing, Joyce drew back the chain on the door. She turned the doorknob.

"Who is it?" Bob asked behind her, and she turned to see him peeking around the living room doorway like a frightened child, tears streaming down his cheeks.

Turning back to the door, she threw it open and stared out through the glass storm door at—

Nothing.

Joyce blinked wildly; hot tears burned her face.

There was nobody there. Had they been mistaken? Had they both somehow mistaken some other sound for the doorbell?

The early-morning sun illuminated the front porch in orange hues. She grabbed the latch on the storm door and pulled it down, pushing the door open.

"What?" she heard her husband cry. "What is it . . . who?"

She ignored him, stepping out onto the porch, her eyes darting from left to right just in case somebody had been there but left before she could reach the door.

The neighborhood was deathly quiet, and vacant of life.

"Who . . . ?" her husband called out again, this time closer. Brave enough now to come down the hallway.

"Nobody," she practically yelled back to him.

She stepped off the porch, still looking for something—anything. And then it caught her from the corner of her eye—a tongue of white protruding from the closed lip of the mailbox attached to the side of the house. Joyce stared at the envelope, trying to remember the last time she had retrieved the mail, pretty sure that it had been just the day before. They had received a stack of condolence cards, many of them from total strangers, and Agent Isabel had wanted to see them, envelopes and all.

Joyce opened the mailbox with a rusty-sounding whine and plucked the envelope from the slot where it had been fed. Something shifted inside—multiple things, sliding from one end of the envelope to the other.

"What is it?" her husband asked, fear in his tone.

She turned, shaking the envelope playfully. "Mail?" she said. "I don't know."

There were no markings on the envelope, no address, stamps, or postal dates. It was just a plain white envelope.

"Who is it from?" Bob asked as Joyce nearly pushed him out of her way on the way back into the house.

She felt her own fear rising as her imagination caught fire, and the words exploded suddenly within her brain.

Ransom note.

"Open it," he ordered, reaching to take it from her.

"Don't you dare," she spat, snatching the envelope away, hugging it protectively to her chest. Her husband recoiled with a look of hurt on his face, but she couldn't care about that.

Slowly she began to open the envelope. Her hands were shaking so violently that she briefly thought of her long-dead grandmother afflicted with Parkinson's. She slid her finger beneath the seal and began to run it beneath the lip, but her tremor caused the envelope to tear farther down than she expected. A jagged opening was torn through the paper, and the contents of the envelope spilled out onto the wooden floor, bouncing slightly at her feet.

"What . . . ?" she asked aloud, staring down at the pearly white kernels that littered the floor, unable to comprehend what she was seeing.

Her husband gasped, telling her that he knew what they were before she did. "Oh God," he said, the horror in his voice palpable.

And suddenly Joyce felt the strength leave her legs, as if the tendons and muscles had all been cut. She dropped to the hallway floor, jarred by the force of the impact, reaching down with trembling fingers to pluck the small white contents of the envelope up from the floor.

"Oh God," her husband wailed.

And this time she had to agree.

One by one she lovingly picked them up, collecting each and every piece in the palm of her hand, desperate to make sure that all the teeth had been retrieved. Then she closed her hand tightly about them and held them close to her heart. Joyce was crying now, too, remembering the last time she had seen them.

Displayed in the most beautiful of little girl smiles.

The knife cut through the perfectly prepared filet with little effort as John savored another bite of perhaps the best steak he had ever eaten. The sides were spectacular as well: grilled asparagus, creamed spinach, and a baked potato with all the fixings.

It was an amazing meal, but he found his enjoyment hampered by the memory of the secret library beneath the monastery, and more specifically the items that were missing.

"What about the episode with the teddy bear?" Anastos asked, making John look up from his food. The dark-skinned older man had fixed him in a steely gaze.

"The teddy bear?" John repeated, wiping his mouth with a cloth napkin. "I believe there were a few times that we dealt with toys."

Anastos drank from a bottle of Stella Artois, and set the bottle down. "The one where it looked as though it was dancing across the room. Don't you dare tell me that was real."

John chuckled. "Then I guess I won't say anything." He picked up his knife and fork and began to cut more of his meat.

"Seriously?" the multimillionaire laughed, slapping the hardwood tabletop with a large callused hand. "You're telling me that actually happened?"

"You told me not to," John said through a mouthful of steak as he reached for his glass of spectacular Merlot.

· "Get the fuck out of here!" Anastos exclaimed, wide-eyed. He snatched up his beer and took a long drink. "This is fascinating . . . absolutely fascinating."

"The world is a much weirder place than many suspect," John explained, feeling as though he were in the midst of a television interview.

"And it seems as though it's getting weirder," Anastos commented, going back to his own meal.

John said nothing, his thoughts flashing back to that night when everything had changed. Ever since then, things had been escalating, growing so much worse.

So much more evident.

"So, when will we see the next season?" Anastos asked, dark eyes twinkling mischievously. "You can tell me. I won't share with anyone."

John shook his head. "I really don't know," he said to his host. "I'm not sure if there will be one."

Anastos leaned back in his chair.

"Don't tell me that," he said. "Is it because of your wife? Has she recovered from the explosion?"

"She's still recovering," John said, absently playing with his potato. He allowed his host to believe an explosion was the cause of the catastrophe of their last broadcast, as did most of the world. After all, how does one explain that an old urn cracked and released demonic entities that now inhabited his wife's body?

"Is she all right?" Anastos asked. "Are they saying she'll recover?"

The image of his wife overtaken by the demons filled John's head. "Yeah," he said simply, setting down his fork, no longer hungry. "I'm sure she'll be fine."

"I certainly hope so," Anastos said, having more of his beer. "How was your steak?" he asked, changing the subject. "Cooked all right?"

"Perfectly, thank you," John replied.

"Can I get you anything else?"

"God, no," John said with a polite smile. "If I have anything else I'll burst."

Anastos looked to a corner of his dining room and gestured. A flock of white-coated waitstaff suddenly appeared and immediately began clearing the table.

"Thank you so much for your hospitality," John said, savoring his wine.

"It's my pleasure," Anastos said. "I am more than happy to play host to my favorite television personality."

"What? He or she couldn't make it?" John joked.

Anastos laughed. He then picked up his beer bottle and, seeing that it was empty, held it aloft, gesturing for one of his people to take the empty and bring him another. "You wouldn't believe the thought I put into getting you here," he said, a sly smile creeping across his tanned, handsome face.

"That was pretty slick," John said.

Anastos continued to grin. "You were actually the first person I thought of when I received the call about the Demonist library," he said.

John was taken aback by the man's familiarity with the ancient brotherhood.

"Ah, so you do know of the Demonists," John said. "I shouldn't be surprised, but their existence has all but been lost to the ages."

Anastos looked smug as one of his waitstaff brought him a new beer. "What, did you think my interest in the weird began with your show?"

John lifted his wine in a mock toast and took a sip.

"How lucky was it that I found a Demonist repository under a property that I owned? Pretty wild, eh?"

John studied him, and the smirk that was teasing the corners of his mouth. "Then it wasn't an accident?" he asked.

Anastos stood up from the table, holding the beer bottle by the neck. "There were hints in some old documents I uncovered about the possibility that the brotherhood had hidden their possessions beneath places of holy power," he explained.

"I'm guessing then that this isn't the first monastery you've purchased?"

"Bingo!" Anastos said, and began to laugh. "But let that be our little secret. I can just imagine what would happen if word got out that one of the world's richest men was obsessed with finding the hidden stashes of an ancient order of exorcists. Something tells me people just wouldn't understand." He brought his beer to his mouth and took a healthy pull on the bottle.

John drained his own glass and set it down on the table. Anastos immediately grabbed one of his waitresses as she passed, directing her toward the bottle on the table.

"No, thank you," John said, holding up his hand. The waitress smiled politely and took his empty glass away.

"You're going to make me drink alone?" the man asked. "Okay, then." He gestured for John to follow him.

John rose from his chair, following his host from the elaborate dining room. They walked down a long corridor, priceless paintings spaced sporadically on either side, and stopped before a set of double doors. Anastos set his bottle of beer down on a tall corner table that displayed a porcelain eighteenth-century Chinese vase from the Qianlong Dynasty. Anastos looked over his shoulder at John as he took hold of the doorknobs.

"Are you ready for this?" he asked, before throwing open the doors to a beautiful study.

John followed Anastos inside and at once saw the level of collector the man was. Some of the books he saw on the expertly crafted bookshelves were so rare that he'd only seen them before in museums, some in the forbidden archives of the Vatican Library.

"Impressive," John said.

Anastos sat on the corner of his desk and offered that smug grin again.

"Yeah, it's pretty good," he said, looking around the room and nodding. "But it's nothing compared to what was found in the secret library."

"I can imagine."

Anastos stared at him intensely. "I don't think you can."

"Show me."

"You don't think it's going to be that easy, do you?"

"We had steak together—thought we were bros now."

Anastos chuckled. "Oh no," he said.

"What do you need?" John finally asked.

"See, this is what I was hoping for," Anastos said. "Us talking . . . sharing."

John waited.

"I know there's so much more to you than a television star, a ghost chaser. I need your expertise . . . your accumulated knowledge . . . your experience."

"And if I give it to you?"

"The keys to the kingdom," Anastos said, and smiled wickedly.

An icy chill ran up and down John's spine. What was he getting himself into now?

It was like something out of a James Bond movie, John thought as he was led to an isolated section of Cyril Anastos' multimillion-dollar house, under armed guard and a sophisticated security system.

It appeared that Anastos had a thing for armed thugs, the black-suited security with their deadly submachine guns sneering at John as he followed their employer.

"This is pretty elaborate," John said as Anastos stopped before a chrome elevator door.

"And all completely necessary," the man said, pulling a small key from his pocket and inserting it in the lock. The metal doors parted, beckoning them to enter.

"After you, John," Anastos said with mocking familiarity.

John entered as Anastos followed.

"Does what you'd like my help with have anything to do with something found in the Demonists' library?" John asked, his curiosity getting the better of him.

"Something, yes," Anastos said as the doors slid silently closed and the elevator began its descent, the trip down taking far longer than John would have expected.

How deep had they gone? he wondered before they came to a stop.

Anastos looked over his shoulder and smirked, as if to say, *Prepare to have your mind blown,* or something to that effect.

And as the elevator doors slid open, John had to admit, the smirk was pretty damn correct.

Mind blown.

The Bond movie comparison continued.

The elevator had opened onto what looked to be a sprawling underground research complex, lab-coated technicians busily moving about. John tried to catch what they were doing, and saw with growing interest that they appeared to be examining items of great age.

Items likely removed from the Demonists' library cache and brought down here.

"So, what's all this?" he asked.

"A little of this and that," Anastos said, walking farther into the space. "Some cataloging, some translation, a lot of verification."

The shipping mogul stopped and looked around at the operation.

"It is said that many of these objects, liberated by the Demonists' brotherhood, were said to have a capacity for great power," Anastos said.

John glanced over to see a technician placing what appeared to be a golden crucifix beneath the lens of a powerful electron microscope.

"My business partners and I would like to know if this is true."

"Your business partners share your interest in the arcane?" John asked. "What are the odds of that?"

"Like minds and all that," Anastos said, crossing the room, as his employees greeted him respectfully. "They were very keen on you coming here, even before the Demonists' cache discovery."

"Before?" John asked. "And why was that?"

Anastos stopped before a room made entirely from glass, a transparent cube, filled with activity.

"This is why," Anastos said, not bothering to turn around.

John slowly sidled up alongside him, trying to see around the multiple technicians buzzing about inside. "What is . . . ?"

One of the techs moved aside to reveal a table, and the item that sat on it.

It took a moment for John to realize what it was.

"A Devil trap," he then said in reference to the cigar-box-sized container resting in the center of the table. The icy chill of foreboding was back, crazily running up and down his spine.

"Basically," Anastos said. "Though a tad more complex, we think. You wouldn't believe the number of supposed experts that we've had in to look at it."

John looked at him as Anastos continued to stare through the glass at his prized possession. "I want to get inside it."

"Are you saying that you want me to open the box?" John asked.

"That's exactly what I want you to do," Anastos said. "And in exchange I'll give you access to any and all findings from the Demonist library."

John stared at the box, taking in what details he could. In his vast research into the paranormal and ancient arcane, he had encountered similar Devil boxes. Sometimes they were just empty containers that were supposed to be receptacles for representations of people's guilt and trauma, while in other cases they were prisons for lesser and bothersome demonic entities, put there by competent practitioners of the magickal arts.

By the looks of this receptacle . . .

"May I take a closer look?"

"Of course," Anastos said excitedly, approaching the door to the cube and rapping a knuckle on the glass.

One of the men, a bespectacled gentleman with an enormous Afro of curly gray hair, looked up from a tablet, his eyes widening when he saw who was there. He swiftly darted to the door and pushed it open to allow his employer access.

"Good evening, Mr. Anastos," he said.

"Penderton," the millionaire acknowledged. "This is John Fogg. He's come to look at the box."

"Of course," Penderton said. "It's right over here."

The tech escorted him over to the table. The others who had been tending to the container quickly dispersed, leaving the glass room.

John stared down upon the box and immediately felt his heart begin to rapidly beat. This wasn't a container for trinkets, or troublesome spirits in need of taming. This was serious business. The first thing that he noticed on the lid of the wooden box was the engraving of the fifth pentacle of Mars—a scorpion surrounded by a circle of ancient symbols of binding.

"Terrible unto demons," John muttered beneath his breath as he continued to study the box.

"Excuse me?" Anastos asked. "What was that?"

"Terrible unto demons," John repeated. "It's what this is," he said, moving his hands above the box's lid. "It's from the lesser key of Solomon. A spell of entrapment."

"Impressive," Penderton said, nodding at his employer.

"I told you he knew his stuff."

John was annoyed by their interaction, but what lay on the table before him was far more a distraction. He leaned closer to the box and felt the air around it charged with some unknown energy, feeling the hair at the back of his neck stand on end.

He'd seen things sealed with similar spells from King Solomon's teachings, but there was something different here—something that would likely go unnoticed if . . .

John looked around the room.

"May I borrow this?" he asked no one in particular, snatching a magnifying glass from a workstation close by.

He brought the magnifier up to his eye and leaned toward the box's lid again.

"Interesting," he said.

"What?" Anastos asked.

"The binding spell has been altered," John explained.

"How so?"

"Whoever did this took the existing spell from Solomon's lesser key and changed it—made it something altogether different."

"Now I'm really impressed," Penderton said.

Anastos stood beside him smiling triumphantly.

"Good work," he said to John. "And that's exactly the reason why nobody else has even attempted to open it, and why I recommended you for the job."

"The alterations to the spell appear to be destructive in nature," John explained. "If not opened correctly—expertly—the box and its contents will be utterly destroyed." He leaned in toward the box again, taking another look. "As well as the person attempting to break the spell, I'd guess."

"Then you'd best be careful," Anastos said, patting his shoulder.

There was a growing tension in the small glass room that hadn't been there before. Something was most definitely not right, and John was beginning to sense that maybe he didn't want to be a part of it. "I'm sorry, Mr. Anastos—Cyril—but I'm afraid I can't do that."

Anastos cocked his head to one side as if confused.

"These seals are serious business," John started to explain. "Put there by a pretty powerful magick user—for a reason."

Anastos stared blankly, and then his face broke into a strange smile.

"Of course it was put there for a reason," he said. "As there was a reason to bring you here to my house." He paused and then pointed. "Open the box."

John slowly shook his head, his gaze going to the Devil trap, and then back to his wealthy host. "I'm not going to do that," he said. "And if that prevents me from gaining access to the items you took from the library, then I'll just have to live with that, I guess."

Anastos stared at him blankly and then looked to his man, Penderton.

"He has no idea who he is dealing with here," Anastos said with a sad shake of his head.

"I know exactly who I'm dealing with, Cyril, but I also know what this is." John looked to the trap. "Do you see these markings . . . these seals?" he asked. "These are warnings to stay away . . . to keep whatever is locked up inside this box inside this box. I have no intention of unleashing whatever it is in—"

Anastos moved swiftly, taking Penderton's tablet from his hands.

"I really hate to do this, John," Anastos said. "I was hoping that we could help each other here—you do something for me and I do something for you. It's how the world works, really."

John had no idea what the man was getting at, watching as the multimillionaire fiddled with something on the tablet screen. He then turned the screen toward John.

"Do you recognize this place, John?" he asked.

John stared, mouth agape. Of course he did. It was a shot from outside the Cho Institute.

"It's called a bargaining chip," Anastos said, turning the screen away from him and starting to pull up something else. "My partners thought I might need it, but stupid me, I defended you. I defended you, John. I told them that you were a highly intelligent man and that you and I could handle this transaction like adults."

He turned the tablet toward him again. "How about this?"

It was a shot of Theo sleeping in her bed.

"You son of a bitch," John muttered. "How did you get this?"

"Keep watching," Anastos ordered.

There was movement on the tablet screen, and John realized that he was watching a live moment. A man dressed as a security guard directed his phone toward his face and smiled.

"That's Kevin," Anastos said. "A recent hire at the Cho Institute.

He came highly recommended by one of my business associates. We had him put there just in case a situation like this arose. Personally I didn't think we'd have to use him, but . . ."

Kevin made it a point to hold up a syringe of some clear liquid and give it a shake.

John's blood turned to ice. "If you hurt her . . ."

"There's no reason to even think of such a thing," Anastos reassured him. "As long as you agree to do what I ask of you. It's quite simple really."

Kevin again pointed his phone toward John's sleeping wife.

"Do we have a deal?" Anastos asked.

John stared, the rage inside him growing, and growing. He tore his eyes from the screen to look at Anastos, and then turned his attention back to the Devil trap.

He had no choice.

"I'm going to need some things."

8

It was amazing how many violent deaths had occurred in some of the most quiet neighborhoods.

The deaths had happened over the years, tragic and terrifying, leaving a mark—a wound—upon reality, before eventually being forgotten.

Although the scar always remained.

That was how the Teacher traveled. That was how he gathered his students.

And on a picturesque street in a suburb of Chicago, Illinois, not long after the midnight hour, the Teacher went calling.

He arrived in the backyard of 37 Tremont Street, where young Abby Tisdale had landed after falling from a second-floor window in the summer of 1947. The wound in time and space had called to him, showing him the ghostly echoes of the teen's demise. In the corridor between locations, the Teacher had focused his thoughts upon the old injury, peeling back the healed-over skin of reality to pass through to his destination.

He stood silently in the cool of the night studying the home before him. His dark lord and master had placed this location in his mind while he slept, the place where his newest student would be found.

The Teacher approached the house, curtains of shadow trailing behind to shield his presence. Climbing the steps to the back entrance, he stopped at the heavy wooden door. He raised his right hand to the lock, moving his fingers, allowing shadow to flow into the keyhole like smoke, and solidified just enough to—

Click!

The door moved inward with a soft creak and the Teacher entered. The kitchen smelled of wonderful, home-cooked meals. Through the darkness, he stared at the square table across the room, imagining the family sitting there, eating and talking about their day.

Then he imagined how that would change once he acquired his newest student.

The thought of all the fear, misery, and sadness brought a smile to his face, and caused the mass on his chest to tingle sensually as it continued to grow. He stood for a moment in the center of the kitchen, concentrating on finding his student. He visualized the child—a young boy with a head of curly dirty blond hair—asleep in a room at the end of the upstairs hallway. He had the impression that this newest charge could be difficult and might need some extra attention.

So be it, he thought as he left the kitchen, walking through the dining room to the stairs. The Teacher had a way with problem children—the last to defy him had become much more manageable once he removed all her teeth.

He stood at the foot of the stairs, peering up into the semidarkness, before he began to ascend. He flowed down the hall to the last room on the right, eager for the latest lesson he would teach, and how much closer it would bring his lord to the world.

A sudden sound froze him in his tracks, and the Teacher turned to see a door open and a man step out into the hallway. He was a large man, and he held a gun in one hand.

"Don't you fuckin' move!" he shouted, raising the weapon and pointing it at the Teacher.

The Teacher stood still, his hand on the doorknob to the boy's room, calmly staring at the man in the hallway.

"What the fuck do you think you're doing?" the man raged, starting toward the Teacher, the weapon still aimed.

"I've come for your son," the Teacher answered truthfully. "He has much to learn before the arrival of Master Damakus."

He felt a tug on the doorknob and let go as the door to the child's room opened. As if summoned, the curly-headed boy appeared.

"What's goin' on?" he asked, rubbing the sleep from his eyes.

And that was when things became suddenly—active.

The child's father screamed for his son to go back into his room, but not before the Teacher had reached out and closed his hand around the boy's wrist.

"Hello there, I'm your new teacher," he announced.

And then there came a series of explosions, and the Teacher lost his grip on the boy's wrist as he was picked up and slammed backward against the wall. Dazed, the Teacher looked down at the smoldering, bloody holes that dappled the front of his dress shirt.

The pain was like a living thing, perched on his chest, chattering in his ear, encouraging him to give it all up—to let his life slip away. It was quite insistent, and the Teacher felt himself succumbing, sliding down the wall, to sit down hard upon the floor.

Through bleary eyes he watched his student race from his bedroom and jump into his father's waiting arms. An overwhelming sense of disappointment washed over him. He had failed. His lord Damakus had chosen him to prepare the world, to teach the young of his dark glory so that he might be reborn to the world.

But now it had been for naught.

He could feel the bullets embedded in his flesh, each one stealing away a portion of his life. It would not be long now, he knew, as his heart pumped frantically in a desperate attempt to keep him alive. But he could feel it tiring, slowing down as the blood left him, flowing out from the holes in his body.

The Teacher stared ahead, ready to die, watching as the father held his son in his arms, whispering to him that everything was going to be all right. That the bad man had been stopped . . . that the bad man was dead.

Not yet! the Teacher wanted to scream, but he was too weak, and by the time he could gather his strength, the father's statement would be true. He closed his eyes, and the curtain of darkness began to fall. The Teacher felt his life force leave him and was about to surrender to oblivion—

When something rushed in to replace it.

It was something similar to life, but different. Something that mimicked all the functions of a living being but was not of the earthly realm.

And that was when the Teacher knew he had been touched.

The blessed dark lord Damakus had deemed him worthy to continue the task for which he was chosen, and had given him the gift of continued existence.

"Go to my room and call 911," the Teacher heard his student's father order from what seemed like many miles away.

New strength surged through him then, and he opened his eyes to another chance at life.

To another chance at preparing this world for his master's return.

There was no pain anymore as he effortlessly climbed to his feet and strode down the short length of hallway toward the father, who had turned away from him.

Ignoring him in death.

The son saw him approaching his father and cried out, but it was too late. The father turned, weapon in hand, and looked at him, eyes wide with terror . . . terror that would be a lovely tithe for the coming lord.

With a strength that far surpassed what he'd had before, the

Teacher gripped the father's gun hand in his, snapping the wrist like a dry twig, causing the gun to drop to the floor.

"I guess I should thank you," the Teacher said, pulling the man closer. "Without your intervention, I would not have died and been reborn to fulfill my chosen appointment."

The father continued to struggle, and the Teacher could feel his fear, more attuned now than he had been before. Another gift from his most gracious and merciful master.

Not wanting to be cruel, the Teacher decided to end the tussle quickly. He wrapped his arms around the father and squeezed with all his might. Again he was surprised by the extent of his newfound strength, as the man's bones collapsed like the daintiest pieces of crystal.

The Teacher felt the father's fear abruptly end, and dropped the rag doll of flesh to the hallway floor. His student was gone, but the Teacher knew he couldn't have gotten far.

He stepped over the cooling corpse, walking to the next open doorway and peering inside. The boy was there, phone in hand, furiously punching buttons.

"There is no time for that, child," the Teacher said, flying across the room and slapping the phone from his student's hand.

"You're going to be late for school."

What did it all mean?

John pondered the bigger picture as he hovered over the Devil's trap, the question of why someone, or a group of someones, would want to release whatever it was that had been locked away inside the box a massive distraction to him.

And distraction could prove to be quite deadly.

"Do you have everything you need, John?" Anastos asked from the doorway behind him. He was standing there, along with Penderton and an armed guard. Just in case he decided to act up, John imagined.

"I believe it's all here," John answered, attempting to regain his focus. They'd brought him just about everything he could possibly need, even some texts that he hadn't been sure still existed. But here they were for his perusal.

He guessed that they had been found in the Demonists' library back at the monastery. Just a reminder of what could still be there made him practically vibrate, but he didn't need that distraction as well.

He had a Devil's trap to open.

In the four corners of the box he noticed tiny carvings, relatively elaborate interpretations of elemental spirits representing earth, wind, fire, and water. He had never encountered one himself, but had heard of Devil boxes so complex that they enslaved spirits of the elements to safeguard the most dangerous of contents.

"Are you absolutely sure you want to do this?" John asked. He still held out hope that somebody would come to their senses.

"Just open the trap, John," Anastos said. "I would hate for Kevin to get bored in your wife's room. He can be so unpleasant when he's bored."

The fact that Anastos was threatening his wife practically sent John into a rage, but he needed to stay focused; any wrong move could prove disastrous on so many levels.

Focusing on his work he attempted to recall what he'd read about these particular Devil traps. If he remembered correctly, each of the elemental spirits was a part of the locking mechanism, and they all needed to be rendered inert at exactly the same time, or they would be unleashed to wreak havoc on the unwary individual stupid enough to be trying to open the box.

He tried to recall the spell or rite he'd need to immobilize the spirits. As he glanced up from the ancient box, his eyes fell on the stack of texts that had been placed on a nearby workstation.

"Elementals," he called out.

"What about them?" Anastos asked.

"I'm guessing that somewhere in one of those texts is something that can be used to render an elemental spirit inactive. I need it or we're done before we can even begin," John quickly answered.

"You heard him, Penderton," Anastos commanded his lackey. "Get the man what he needs."

Penderton headed for the books and Anastos stepped into the room to stand beside John, admiring the box on the table. "I hope this isn't a way of stalling, to prevent me from getting what I want," he said.

John looked at him sternly. "If I attempted to open this box any other way, it wouldn't be good for me, you or anybody else in the vicinity. Whoever sealed this box was very serious about what's inside not getting out."

Anastos just smiled, and John felt a sickening weight continuing to grow in his stomach.

"Don't you worry about that, John. My partners are well aware of what's inside, and are quite eager to have it free."

"Found it!" Penderton suddenly announced, turning away from the workstation. He held a scroll, unrolled, in his hands and was reading it as he approached John and Anastos. "I believe this is what you're looking for," the man said. "It's in ancient Aramaic, but if you give me a few minutes, I can write down the translation for you. . . ."

"That won't be necessary," John said, quickly reaching for the scroll. "I can read Aramaic."

Penderton stared, surprised.

"Carry on," Anastos said, stepping back out of the way.

John read the Aramaic rite of quieting elemental spirits very carefully, searching for specific information on how it could be used to quell all four at a single time. He found what he was looking for in one of the last verses, but continued to stall, not wanting to complete the task.

What choice did he have? He thought of his poor wife, alone with that man at the hospital, and wanted to scream. He couldn't risk her safety, and if that was the case he had to do what was being asked of him.

But at what cost to the world at large?

He heard new voices chattering behind him and turned on his work stool to see a stretcher being wheeled into the glass room from a freight elevator at the opposite end. A thin, good-looking young man in a hospital johnny was lying on the stretcher and Anastos gave him the thumbs-up as he approached.

"What's going on now?" John asked, even more confused than before. "If you want me to get this right you're going to need to . . ."

"We do want you to get this right," Anastos answered. "And quickly."

"Who is this?" John asked, motioning with his head.

"He's not your concern," Anastos said.

More of his staff entered the room and hovered around the man, apparently checking vital signs.

"Why is he in here?" John demanded. "I can't be held responsible for any of this if I don't know exactly what's going on."

Anastos sighed, but answered.

"All right, John," he said. "When the trap is opened, another vessel . . . a compliant one . . . will be needed to house the box's contents."

Things were going from bad to worse.

"Don't do this, Cyril," John said. He sounded as though he were begging, and if that was the case, so be it, but the more he heard, the more he was certain that what they wanted him to do was a very dangerous thing.

"You don't need to worry about this, John," Anastos assured him. "Your primary concern should be that sick wife of yours back in the States. If you do what I am asking of you, everything will be all right. In fact, it will be better than all right . . . just think of all that wonderful knowledge you'll have access to, if you succeed."

John didn't believe a word that was coming out of his mouth. Everything about the situation—the Devil trap, the armed guards, the man in his wife's room—everything pointed to the fact that once he was no longer useful, he would be expendable.

And his wife would be as well.

"Are you listening, John?" Anastos interrupted his reverie.

John nodded slowly, having made up his mind.

"Do your job, and reap the benefits . . . that's all I'm asking. Do your job and be on your way. . . ." Anastos smiled that smile again. "Can't wait to see what you've got planned for season eight."

John turned his attention back to the task before him, but with a new purpose. He gave the scroll one more look before setting the ancient writing aside, and focusing on the lid of the box, he began the steps.

The words in Aramaic left his mouth in short, staccato bursts. The more he said, the more convinced he became that what he was about to do was right.

The next portion of the taming rite—the immobilizing rite—was something that could actually be seen. As he spoke the words the air around each of the elemental carvings began to swirl, miniature maelstroms of supernatural energy, each containing one elemental spirit.

"You're doing it, John," he heard Anastos say from nearby.

And from the corner of his eye, he could see Penderton with his phone, recording the ritual.

John spoke the final words of the rite, and the spheres of energy lifted up and away from the four corners, the Devil trap's main source of security deactivated.

John could feel all eyes on him, glancing over to the hospital bed, where the young man was sitting up, a disturbing look of euphoria on his simple face. He had to wonder if the poor guy had any idea of the torment he'd experience as the vessel for the entity contained within the box.

And it was an entity of extreme malevolence, John was certain of that. As soon as the elemental restraints were lifted, he could feel the wrongness of it all emanating from the box. It made his skin crawl as if covered with ants, his eyes burn and water as the smell of excrement filled his nose.

"Is there a problem, John?" Anastos asked, appearing at his side yet again.

"The elemental deterrents have been shut down," John explained, trying not to gag on the foulness leaking from the wooden box. "I'm guessing there are at least four more layers of security—maybe five— to get through before the trap can be opened."

Anastos glared.

"And you're not working on those now because of what?" the multimillionaire chided.

"Because what is inside this box wasn't meant to ever come out again," John said. "And whatever it is . . . it's going to stay in there."

Before Anastos could utter another word, to again threaten John with the safety of his wife or bodily harm, John did something that was incredibly stupid, but something that he knew would get results. He wasn't entirely sure what kinds of results, but he was certain they would be spectacular.

The Aramaic rite that he'd performed had created a kind of single circuit connecting all four of the elemental spirits.

The circuit was not supposed to be broken, but John did just that.

He stuck his hand between two of the corners, between wind and fire, temporarily interrupting the flow.

Breaking the circuit.

The reaction was explosive.

The wind elemental escaped its confinement with an ear-piercing wail and a gale-force breeze that exploded outward from the Devil trap. John was blown over backward in his chair and slid across the small lab in a shower of broken glass and scientific equipment. He witnessed others taken as well, the furious elemental spirit whipping up tornado-strength winds within the confined space.

And the fire spirit wasn't much happier.

John managed to find cover under a desk, peering around its corner to watch the elemental spirit exert its fury, appearing as a seething ball of flame, expanding outward like the sun to burn any who dared be present before it.

But wind and fire had never been able to get along, always at odds with each other. The wind elemental turned its anger to the fire, attempting to suck its equally enraged brethren into its swirling vortex. Fire responded in kind, meeting the attack with equal abandon, creating a spinning maelstrom of wind and flame as they fought.

Alarms were sounding, and people were panicking as the room and everybody inside it was caught up in the chaos that John had caused, even as he attempted to make his way toward the exit. He could see that wards had appeared upon the glass walls of the chamber, magickal symbols of containment etched there in case of emergency, to keep whatever might be accidentally unleashed from escaping.

The laboratory floor beneath John's feet started to vibrate, and crack, the heavy tiles pushed upward from the trembling ground. The earth elemental had awakened.

The wind and fire elementals continued their conflict as John struggled to stay on his feet as he ducked and weaved between the flying pieces of burning scientific equipment hurled about in the elementals' wake.

The sprinkler system triggered, and as the water rained down upon them, John could see the collected puddles begin to form a single, undulating mass on the floor, growing larger and larger as the sprinklers added to it. The water elemental was about to start some trouble as well.

An enormous bubble of clear fluid rolled across the lab, dousing the flaming pieces of debris that littered the floor. John watched in horror as the living water flowed over the faces of Anastos' lab technicians and scientists, forcing itself into their mouths and noses—into their lungs—drowning them where they cowered.

The glass room had become the personification of chaos, the floor cracking and opening up to swallow those who ran about in panic as fire, wind, and water wreaked havoc upon the tortured environment.

John saw an opportunity and made a dash for the exit. If he could get into the elevator and get up to the ground floor, he might be able to—

He recognized the sound of the single gunshot, before realizing that he'd been hit. The bullet entered his left shoulder, spinning him around as he fell through the cube's doorway to lie in shock on the floor outside the glass-enclosed lab.

He rolled painfully over and was greeted by the sight of a soaking Cyril Anastos standing over him, gun in hand, eyes twinkling.

"What did you do, John?" he yelled above the screams from within the glass room behind him. "What the fuck did you do?"

"I couldn't set it free," John said, shaking his head defiantly as he clutched his bleeding shoulder.

"You stupid, stupid bastard," Anastos growled. "You've ruined everything . . . and now your wife is going to suffer for it."

The mention of Theodora got John's attention, and he managed to push himself up from where he'd fallen despite the throbbing pain in his shoulder.

Anastos retrieved the tablet from a desk beside him, running his finger over the screen to bring it to life. "Before I kill you I want you to see what Kevin is going to do," the multimillionaire said with a feral snarl, turning the screen toward John.

And there was very little John could do but watch, watch as Cyril Anastos reached out to the man in Theodora's room and gave the order.

The command to kill his wife.

"Do it, Kevin," Anastos' voice commanded from the phone. "Kill the bitch, and make sure we can see it happen."

Kevin smiled. He hadn't been sure he would actually get to kill the woman, and he reveled in the pleasant surprise.

"Will do, Mr. Anastos, sir," he answered cheerily as he stepped toward the bed where Theodora was lying.

He'd been working for Mr. Anastos for the last ten years or so, and had never had a better boss. It was as if his employer had been able to see deep down into his soul, and could tell the kinds of jobs he would be perfect for.

Within the first few weeks of employment, Kevin had enjoyed participating in arson, witness intimidation, and good old-fashioned murder. He knew a good boss when he found one, and Mr. Anastos was a keeper.

"All right, sleepyhead," Kevin said as he pointed his phone at the woman before him. "Why don't we make this all the more permanent?"

He held the phone with one hand, and with the other slowly moved a hypodermic needle closer to Theodora's exposed neck. He was sure to move it extra slowly, wanting the woman's husband to get a good look at what was about to happen. That would teach him to piss off his employer. Served him right.

The tip of the needle was just about to prick the pale flesh of the sleeping woman's neck when—

"Excuse me," a man said as he opened the door and entered the room. "Have you seen Dr. Fine—"

"No," Kevin said, quickly putting the hand with the syringe behind his back, not sure how much the man had seen but secretly hoping for another opportunity to kill.

"Or Dr. Howard?"

"No, I really haven't any idea where—"

"Or the other Dr. Fine?"

"No, they're not here, and they haven't been here," Kevin said, annoyed by the interruption. "Maybe the receptionist upstairs . . ."

The man approached the side of the bed, looking down on the woman as if Kevin hadn't said a word. "She's really out, isn't she? Doesn't have a clue that you're not supposed to be in here."

Kevin reacted instantly. He launched himself at the man, fully prepared to waste some of the drug he was going to use on the woman.

But the man was fast, in one movement stepping to the side and taking hold of Kevin's arm as he lunged, bending it painfully back, forcing him to drop the needle.

"I found the security guard you knocked unconscious and put in the supply closet," the stranger said as Kevin struggled to free himself. "Looks like he got off easy. Mild concussion, maybe black eyes, but I think he'll be all right."

Kevin managed to free his arm, twisting himself around and bringing his knee up into the man's stomach.

The man avoided the worst of it, bringing his hands down to slow the thrust.

"But Ms. Knight here," the man said, driving an elbow into Kevin's face and knocking him back. "I don't think she was going to be as lucky."

Kevin managed to slip the folding knife from his back pocket and snap open the blade. He lunged at the stranger, and again the man proved faster. He sidestepped Kevin's dive, then moved in close to deliver a teeth-vibrating blow to the side of Kevin's face.

But Kevin was not to be outdone. He recovered quickly enough to slash the finely honed blade smoothly across the man's side. He heard a satisfying hiss of pain as the man stumbled back, looking down at the crimson stain already spreading across his green scrub top. Not wasting any more time, Kevin went at him again, determined that this man would fall.

Despite his injury, the man seemed to be ready again, but Kevin was relentless, slashing with the knife as the man struggled to disarm him. The man was soon covered with multiple gashes that wept freely. *It won't be long now*, Kevin guessed.

He had to admire this man; he was a good fighter. He couldn't think of the last time anybody had been able to put up this much of a struggle. It seemed kind of a shame to kill him. If they had met under different circumstances, they might have been friends.

But now wasn't the time for friendship.

Their skirmish had taken them across the room to the unconscious woman's bed. Kevin used his weight to push the man backward against the bed rails, where he lost his balance and fell atop the sleeping woman. Kevin bore down upon his foe, blade ready to part the pale flesh of the man's neck. Briefly he noted the scarring beneath the stranger's shirt as the man fiercely struggled. He managed to raise his hand just as Kevin slashed, cutting a bloody line across the taut flesh of the man's palm. Blood sprayed from the gash, covering the bed and the sleeping woman's pale face.

Kevin couldn't help staring at the woman. There was something eerily beautiful about the paleness of her flesh, adorned with the blood of his enemy.

He was taken aback when her eyes suddenly opened, and the corners of her mouth began to twitch. Kevin thought that she was starting to smile at him.

But then he saw the teeth.

There were far more inside her mouth than there should have been.

Griffin Royce had never again wanted to be in this hospital room with the likes of Theodora Knight. His one visit, when Elijah had sent him to confirm the reports of the woman's condition, had been more than enough.

But here he was, back in the hospital room he'd sworn never to return to, fighting for his life.

He would rather have been chauffeuring Elijah around Romania, but instead he'd been sent back to the States to ensure the safety of the woman whose husband had been caught up in a situation that he hadn't quite understood.

Griffin had known there was a chance things would get rough, but he had never imagined the extent.

The guy in the room with Fogg's wife was a killer, there was no doubt about it, and now Griffin had to keep not only the woman alive, but himself as well.

He had considered bringing a gun, but thought that his hand-to-hand skills would have been more than sufficient to handle the likes of anyone sent to harm Ms. Knight.

Note to self, always bring a gun.

The knife glided across the palm of his hand, opening his skin like a mouth, and he barely felt it. It was the blood spraying from the wound over the face of the woman he was supposed to be protecting that alerted him to the severity of the injury. Jamming the injured hand beneath his armpit to squelch the bleeding, Griffin threw himself backward, rolling over the woman and off the opposite side of the bed.

He quickly jumped to his feet, ready for whatever would come next, or at least he believed himself to be. He watched as his foe stood perfectly still, staring down at the woman he was sent to kill.

And that was when Griffin noticed that she was awake, her mouth widening in an enormous grin, but strangely enough it didn't stop there. The smile grew wider, and wider, and it appeared as if the woman's face had been somehow cut in two, and then he saw the teeth.

It was like looking into the grin of a great white shark.

Griffin and the hired killer both saw, and both understood, the severity of the moment, their eyes meeting briefly before—

The woman surged up from the bed, her movement so fast that it was a blur. Griffin jumped backward, stopping only when his back hit the wall. He froze, observing his foe's fate from what he prayed would be a safe distance.

The woman's mouth opened impossibly wide—wide enough to engulf the killer's head—then her jaws snapped shut on his neck, severing his head with a single bite.

Griffin could only stare, dumbfounded, at the sight of the headless corpse swaying from side to side as a geyser of blood shot up from the neck to paint the ceiling red, before it finally collapsed limply to the floor. The woman, her face hideously distorted and adorned in scarlet, chewed, powerful jaws grinding the skull to paste. The sight and sound of it made him want to gouge out his eyes and poke holes in his eardrums.

Then she turned to Griffin. Her face was suddenly relatively normal despite being covered in drying blood, and she smiled, a normal-sized smile.

"Thank you for trying to help me," she said as she gradually lay back down upon the bloody mattress and appeared to go quickly to sleep.

Griffin slid weakly down the wall, his legs no longer capable of supporting him. He had to steady himself a moment on the floor before reaching for the cell phone in his pocket. His hands shook as he touched the appropriate contact number.

"She's safe," he said into the phone, his eyes filled with the horrific imagery of what he'd just witnessed.

"But we have a bit of a situation."

9

Something didn't seem right.

Anastos turned the screen of the tablet toward himself while still pointing the gun at John.

"Kevin?" he asked. "Kevin, answer me. What's happening?"

His question was answered with the sounds of struggle.

"Kevin!" he demanded, his face twisted in anger.

Anastos locked eyes with John's. "Maybe you'll just have to go first," he said, lowering the tablet and raising the gun.

John tensed, preparing to be shot again.

Multiple shots rang out, and he couldn't help looking down at himself to be sure he hadn't been hit. He looked up at Anastos and followed the man's gaze toward the elevator, which had opened to disgorge several figures with guns.

Anastos shot at them, and they returned fire, causing the million-aire to duck below a hail of bullets as he ran back toward the glass enclosure where the Devil box still sat and the elemental spirits ran amok. Careful not to be shot himself, John pushed himself over into a corner and used the wall to push off against to help himself rise. He could see Anastos inside the glass laboratory, attempting to take possession of the Devil box.

Bullets raked across the front of the glass enclosure, causing the framework of the room to crumble, as well as obliterating the wards and sigils that had been etched into the transparent walls. With the glass shattered, the elemental spirits were now free, gaining in strength and ferocity as they escaped into the complex.

John watched as Anastos grabbed the box, tucking it beneath his arm as he headed for the exit. There was no way in hell that he was going to allow the man to escape with the accursed box, and he pushed off from the wall, keeping his head low beneath the gunfire as he went after him.

At the freight elevator at the back of the lab, John watched as Anastos retrieved a ring of keys from his pocket, found the one that he needed, and opened the metal sliding door.

John quickened his pace even though each footstep was excruciating, but he couldn't let him escape.

Anastos was sliding the door closed when John leapt. He managed some pretty good distance, blocking the elevator door with his good shoulder and then throwing himself inside, sending himself and Anastos both falling to the larger space of the freight elevator.

"What are you doing?" Anastos shrieked indignantly. He was still holding on to the box and swung it around, striking John on the side of his head with a corner. John fell backward into the wall, doing all that he could to stay conscious.

"I was actually going to let you live," Anastos said, climbing to his feet, gun in hand. He aimed the weapon and was about to fire. John lashed out, sweeping Anastos off his feet with one of his legs. The millionaire went down but still managed to keep his hold on the Devil trap, protecting it with his body. The gun fired, sounding like thunder in the confined space. John managed to avoid the shot, throwing himself toward the man and grabbing for the weapon. The barrel was hot and scorched his skin, but John held on, attempting to wrench the weapon away. Anastos fought crazily, kicking out, one of his feet connecting with John's injured shoulder and causing excruciating pain.

John lay there, gasping for air, hoping that the explosions of color in front of his eyes would pass. Through the fireworks of agony, he watched as Anastos got to his feet again, still protecting the box. The man reached down, retrieving the gun, and came to stand above John.

"I've had just about enough of you," Anastos said breathlessly, placing the cold end of the gun barrel against his head. "Maybe they'll do season eight with somebody else."

John's actions were sudden, and desperate. From what he remembered reading on the Demonist scroll, he began to recite one of the rituals. Specifically the ritual that had been used to trap the elemental spirits in preparation of binding them to the Devil trap.

He imagined it would be like waving a red flag in front of an angry bull as his voice grew louder, carrying outside the freight elevator, inciting the elementals to come to him. He hoped that they would get to him before Anastos had a chance to pull the trigger. He hoped that they wouldn't be too late.

The elevator shook as if held in the hand of some gigantic child playing with a rattle, signaling to John that the first of the elemental spirits had arrived. Anastos lurched to one side as he pulled the trigger, firing harmlessly into the elevator wall as the Earth elemental reacted to its summoning.

"What did you do?" Anastos asked, eyes wide with shock slowly turning to fear as he began to realize what John had started.

John continued to utter the words from the ancient rite, pushing himself away from the man who still clung tightly to the Devil trap. John knew that the spirits would be drawn to the Devil trap, the thing that had held them captive for so long.

They would be drawn to it, and they would be angry, seeking to destroy the object before they could be bound to it once more. The wind elemental was next, rushing into the enclosed space with a whoosh of air, picking the millionaire up in a shrieking maelstrom.

John pushed himself deeper into the far corner of the elevator. He could see the man staring helplessly through the wall of wind, his eyes begging for help. But John wasn't feeling the least bit merciful toward the man who was willing to hurt Theo to get what he wanted. The fire spirit rushed into the space next, merging with the cyclonic body of the air elemental. Again the two spirits were locked in conflict, battling as Cyril Anastos' body was burned and torn apart by the violent melding of the elements. The water elemental was late to the party, flowing into the elevator space and partially extinguishing the heat of the fire spirit while knocking Anastos' blackened remains from the grip of the swirling wind.

John watched in horror as the Devil trap fell toward the floor. He had no idea what the outcome would be if the box should break upon the floor.

Pushing off from the wall, John reached out as the trap continued to fall. Even though the floor of the elevator violently shook, he managed to get beneath the box, cradling it to his chest, all the while continuing to recite the ancient rite of binding, which returned the elemental spirits to the four corners of the container.

John lay there on the floor of the elevator, fighting to remain conscious, but it was a losing battle as the darkness around his eyes slowly began to close in.

And just as he was drifting off, he became aware that he was no longer alone, barely managing to open his eyes to glimpse who had joined him.

He recognized the older man from the hotel almost immediately, the horrific nature of his scars something he could never forget.

But what is he doing here? John wondered, feeling the Devil trap taken from his grasp as the darkness rushed in to take him down.

. . .

She had no idea how much longer she could hold out.

Theodora Knight pulled herself tighter into a ball within the darkness of her subconscious, listening to the taunts of the demonic entities that now shared her psyche.

"Why continue to fight, woman?" asked one.

"It's all for naught, it truly is," affirmed another.

"Give yourself over to us completely, and the pain and torment will end," said another.

Theodora ignored them, even though they were much closer to her now than ever before, the inner light that shone from her astral form growing dimmer the longer she remained trapped within herself. Soon it would be gone, and then . . .

"He can't save you," chided a voice more child's than adult's, but she knew better. "All his books and scrolls and words . . . they will never be enough."

"You belong to us now," growled a demon eagerly. "You just don't know it yet."

They were all laughing, trying to break her down, but she remained strong.

For now.

She could feel them reaching out, testing the light that emanated from her soul. They hissed and shrieked as the light burned them, but each time they touched . . . or poked . . . or pushed upon it, the glow diminished ever so slightly, as if a piece of the darkness that the demons represented was left behind to stain her aura.

Their attention to her was greater now that the light wasn't as strong, but she would not let the fire go out, feeding its heat and illumination with thoughts of love and words forged with the stuff of purity by good men and women whose purpose it was to fight back against the spread of evil and the demonic.

"Lovely words," cooed an entity so very close to her ear. "But they tarnish so very easily . . . smudges of black covering up their luster, and then . . ."

It was as if somebody had hit her with an axe.

The pain was intense—excruciating—and she cried out as the demons around her laughed and laughed.

Her guard was coming down, the pain that she felt chipping away at her resolve, and giving the entities the opportunity that they had been craving. They crowded all the closer, continuing with their words of encouragement.

"Won't be long now, sweetheart."

"That one must've hurt like the blazes," said one on the verge of laughter. "Let's do it again so she knows that her time is coming . . . that it won't be long until we're feasting upon her soul."

Theodora prepared to be struck again, fortifying herself the best she could, hoping and praying that it would be enough when—

The demons were screaming, crying out in pain the way that they used to when the aura of her soul was so much brighter. She wanted to know what was happening, but what if it was a trick? Something to make her drop her guard so they could attack?

The screaming went on, the sounds of their awful shrieks dwindling as they fled deeper into the shadow of her subconscious.

And then she heard the voice.

Stern. Powerful. Yet filled with kindness.

It was a voice that she'd heard before, but not in the realm of the living.

"Go on," the voice ordered. "Scurry back to the shadows where you belong. My granddaughter-in-law is not succumbing to you this day. Not if I have any say in the matter."

Theodora opened her eyes, confident now that it was all right, and saw her there, radiating with a light that forced the darkness away.

"Nana?" she called out, surprised that her voice sounded so weak—so frail. Perhaps things were even worse than she had believed.

The woman turned from watching the shadows, her beautiful old face stony at first, but then breaking into a smile.

"Hello, Theo," she said. "How's my girl?"

Nana Fogg was one of the most alive ghosts that Theo had ever encountered in all her years of being a medium. Even though she had passed from the physical world long before Theo and John had married, it truly didn't matter all that much because Nana's presence could always be felt.

Sometimes much stronger than others.

"I'm so tired, Nana," Theodora said, not wanting to break down, but barely keeping herself together.

"There's a good girl," Nana soothed, and she opened her arms to take her into her loving embrace. "You've got to hold on . . . you've got to remain strong for John."

"I know," Theo said as Nana's light seemed to infuse her with strength. "But it's been so hard—the demons are so strong."

"But it's a fight that you . . . ," Nana said, pushing her chin back so that they were looking into each other's eyes. "That the *world* cannot afford to lose."

In his dream John saw the jar.

Its bronze-colored surface glistened as if illuminated by some unknown source of light. John knew what it was, what it was going to do, for he had already lived it.

And then they appeared from the shadowy edges: Phil, Becky, Jackson . . . all alive again. They were moving closer to the jar, scrutinizing its coppery surface as the tiny, jagged cracks began to appear.

Get away from it, he tried to say, but the words wouldn't come—or maybe they had, but they just couldn't hear him. He tried again, this time louder, and still they leaned in closer, reaching out to touch the deadly container.

And then she was there, his beautiful wife. They reacted to her, backing up from the jar, and he found himself relaxing, breathing a sigh of relief as she moved to stand before the object. He told her that he loved her, and she looked at him, the hint of a smile tugging at the corners of her sexy mouth, before she turned her attention to the jar.

He screamed as she reached for it, her hands wrapping around the still-cracking surface. There was something that looked like smoke leaking out from the multiple fissures and swirling about her head. He was begging her to put it down, and to get away from it—for them all to get away from it—but she ignored him, holding the receptacle of evil in front of her, carefully studying it.

John tried to run toward her but found himself unable to move, as if he were bound by invisible chains that prevented him from reaching his love. He stretched his arms out to her, his fingers beckoning, but she ignored him, her entire focus riveted to the container.

And when it looked as though it was too late, that the contents of the jar were about to be released in a devastating explosion of supernatural ferocity, she—his wife—did the strangest of things.

Just as the container began to quake, the cracks spreading across the rounded surface like a wildfire unchecked, she opened her mouth incredibly wide, wider than any human should have been able, so wide that it would have required her jaws to become unhinged like a python's, or a boa constrictor's.

And she shoved the jar into her mouth, slamming her jaws closed and swallowing.

John watched the shape of it as it traveled ever so slowly down her throat, eventually disappearing into her stomach.

Theo then looked at him and smiled, extending her arms as her belly began to grow, the impression of clawed hands pushing outward upon the tight flesh.

"They're all inside me, John," she said, her words deafening inside his head.

And the others were all looking at her now, Jackson, Phil, and Becky, the fear in their expressions growing exponentially with the size of Theo's belly.

Until it burst, spewing evil like Pandora's box out into the world.

John's eyes opened to sunshine pouring in through an open window, and the sounds of birds chirping happily outside.

For a moment he considered that this was just another figment of his active imagination, and waited to see if it would suddenly turn to shit.

But it didn't.

He lay there, gradually waking up, trying to recall where he'd last been in an attempt to figure out where he was now. He tried to sit up and the pain was viciously sharp—startling—and he remembered that he'd been shot.

Anastos had shot him.

And then he remembered the entire, nasty affair, his thoughts freezing upon the fate of his wife.

He had no idea if she was all right.

Carefully pushing himself up in the bed, he saw that he was shirtless and his wound expertly bandaged. He gently probed the gauze where a quarter-sized bloodstain had seeped through.

He looked around the sparse room and saw a shirt and pants hung over the back of a nearby wooden chair. Cautiously he climbed from the bed on tenuous legs. The stone floor was cold beneath his feet as he crossed the room to retrieve the clothing. Images from the last moments he could recall flashed before his mind's eye. He remembered the box, and the evil that it contained, and the scarred old man who had appeared as his savior.

At least he hoped that was the case.

He needed to find a phone, some way to find out if Theo was . . .

Putting on his shoes and socks, which proved far more difficult than he would have expected, John walked to the door and stood.

Listening.

Wherever he was, it seemed to be incredibly quiet. Slowly he reached for the doorknob, turned it, and stepped out into a corridor. He looked from one end of the hall to the other, deciding which way he should venture. Not knowing one from the other, he took a chance, going left and passing other doors.

Based on the style of his surroundings, he gathered that he was in a rectory, priory, or convent. There was also an air about the place, a vibe that couldn't be missed. A sense of peace, of protection from the corrupted.

At the end of the corridor, he could go left or right and was considering his choices when the decision was made for him.

"Is that you, Mr. Fogg?"

John walked in the direction of the voice, finding an office with its door partially open. "Hello?" he called, placing his hand on the door and pushing it open some more.

The scarred old man was inside, standing at a coffee urn filling his cup.

"Good morning, how are we feeling?" he asked cheerfully, bringing his cup up to his mouth.

"I'm getting a strong sense of déjà vu," John said.

"Help yourself." The older man nodded toward the urn as he stepped behind a heavy wooden desk and sat down. "Oh yes, your wife is quite all right," he added. "Survived the incident unscathed."

"My wife . . . ," John began, feeling an overwhelming sense of relief. "She's all right, then? She's okay?"

The old man nodded as he drank. "My associate Mr. Royce confirmed her well later last night," he said, resting his cup in his hand.

"Did you have anything to do with—"

"Let's just say we kept a situation from escalating," the old man interrupted. "Please do have some coffee."

John hesitated for a moment but then decided, why not? He filled a cup and had his first sip.

"Good?" the old man asked.

"Excellent," John said. "Thank you."

"Please," the old man said from behind his desk, motioning to two chairs on the other side. "Take a seat. We have some things to discuss."

John walked to one of the chairs and sat, careful not to spill his coffee.

The old man reached across the desk and placed a tile coaster in front of him. "You can put your cup on that."

"I think some serious thanks might be in order," John said, feeling the need to start the ball rolling. "Not only did you save my life, but it looks like you saved my wife's as well."

The man lifted a hand, waving John's thanks away.

"Not necessary," he said. "We'd been waiting for an opportunity to raid Anastos' home for quite some time. You provided us with it."

"Who are you?" John asked before taking another sip of his coffee. "I'm guessing some sort of law enforcement organization? A division of Interpol perhaps?"

The old man stared, having some coffee, bringing a napkin up to the ragged side of his damaged face so as not to dribble.

"Okay," John said. "Could you at least tell me if I'm warm?"

"Did what you experienced last night look anything like something that Interpol would be involved with?"

John stared, ready for some answers.

"My name is Elijah," the man said finally. "And I am the leader of an organization—a coalition—that exists to attend to matters very much in the vein of what you experienced last night."

"So you deal with megalomaniacal multimillionaires who want to release ancient, supernatural evils out into world?"

"Far more often than I'd care to admit," Elijah confirmed with a chuckle.

"No connection to official law enforcement?" John questioned.

"Some are aware of our existence," Elijah said. "While others would prefer not to think of the things with which we find ourselves involved."

John finished his coffee and held up his cup. "May I?"

"But of course," Elijah said.

"Would you like some more?" John asked, reaching for the man's cup.

"Thank you," he answered. "That's very kind."

John took Elijah's cup, along with his own, and brought it to the urn.

"I'm not sure if you'll recall, but when we spoke in the hotel lobby, you talked to me about containers and the things that were inside them," John said as he pulled the spigot down and filled Elijah's cup. "I had a strange sense then that you weren't talking about coffee urns."

"And that sense was correct," Elijah said, taking the refilled cup from John. "Thank you again."

"You were talking about the jar"—John filled his own cup—"the container we found in the basement of the home we investigated for our Halloween show, weren't you?" He returned to his seat.

Elijah slowly nodded. "The jar was left there specifically for you and your wife to find," he said. "The Coalition has followed through with some research on that home's history, and found that much of the information that you received in order to consider the property for investigation had been tampered with, much of the research fabricated, the actual history far darker."

Elijah placed his cup down upon his own coaster.

"I don't believe that any of you were supposed to survive that

Halloween night. You and yours were to die horribly, and the great evils contained within the jar released out into the world."

"My wife," John started, imagining her lying in her hospital bed.

"Your wife saved you, and quite possibly many other innocent lives, by taking those demonic spirits into herself."

Elijah rose from his seat.

"The world has changed far more since that fateful All Hallows' Eve than you could possibly imagine, John," Elijah said, coming around the desk. "Walk with me, won't you?"

John set his cup down and did what was asked of him.

"It's as if the jar was some sort of trigger," Elijah explained as they walked down the long corridor to a set of stairs. "The first shot fired in a new war against the forces of light."

They descended the steps to a first-floor level filled with multiple desks, computers, and office equipment, clashing with the walls, which were painted with old, and quite gruesome, representations of the Stations of the Cross, depicting Jesus' torment and crucifixion.

"Interesting decorating choice," John said, eyeing the art.

"Left over from the previous tenants, the Blessed Sisters of Christ," Elijah explained. "The last sister of the order made me promise on her deathbed not to paint over it. As you can see, I keep my promises."

There were people working busily at their stations, not even noticing that they were there.

"This is where we do our research," Elijah explained. "Gathering information to determine whether or not we are to be involved. As you can see, we're quite busy."

A door at the far end opened and a thin man with a bald head entered the room, a travel bag slung over his shoulder.

"Ah," Elijah said in response. "Just the man I wanted you to meet."

The man approached. He had dark circles beneath his eyes and moved like somebody who was exhausted.

"John Fogg, Griffin Royce—the man who kept your wife from harm."

John gripped the man's hand firmly and gave it a shake. "Thank you so very much."

Griffin nodded, squeezing back. "She really didn't need my help," he said, and the expression on his face told John that something more had occurred, but before he could ask—

"I was just explaining to John about the Coalition," Elijah began.

Griffin studied him for a moment. "Think you'd fit right in," he said. "Scarred just like the rest of us."

"Scarred?" John asked, confused.

"Griffin is making reference to the fact that most of our members have been . . . damaged in some way by our encounters with the supernatural."

John could still feel the burning sensation of his wife's kiss upon his cheek.

"Don't tell me you're not sporting some scar tissue, John," Griffin said. "I've read quite a bit about you, and your past—and remember I've spent some quality time visiting your wife."

Suddenly John didn't care much for this Griffin. "And what about you, Mr. Royce?" he asked coldly. "What scars do you carry?"

"A dead wife and an eight-year-old daughter who misses her mother something terrible are the thickest right now," he said, his stare intense. "But as long as I'm with the Coalition, there will be more."

The sudden friction between him and Griffin was almost palpable, and Elijah, obviously sensing that things could take a turn for the worse, stepped in.

"Why don't you go and get some rest?" Elijah said, reaching out to take Griffin by the arm.

Griffin allowed himself to be moved along, but he kept his eyes on John.

"Yeah, I'm pretty exhausted," he said. "Want to see Cassie, too."

"Go on, then," Elijah said. "I think she was in the garden waiting for you to return."

"Nice meeting you, John Fogg," Griffin said. "Maybe we'll see each other again sometime."

John said nothing as the man slowly turned and strolled through the office toward the stairs, the staff acknowledging him with nods or smiles as he passed.

"He's rather—intense," John said.

"That would be an accurate description," Elijah said. "He lost his wife in a house fire when his daughter was just an infant."

"Very sad," John said. "You said that most members of the Coalition had been affected somehow by the supernatural. Was the paranormal involved with the fire?"

Elijah looked at him gravely. "His daughter, she caused the fire."

"But she was just a baby. How . . . ?"

"Pyrokinetic," Elijah said. "She was upset, as babies can sometimes be, when her unique ability manifested."

"She killed her mother," John said, horrified.

"She doesn't remember, and Griffin will never tell her," Elijah said. "But Griffin remembers . . . he remembers everything."

The room was silent then except for the clicking of computer keyboards as data were collected, as research was done.

"Why am I here, Elijah?"

"I would think it obvious," Elijah said. "I want you to join us . . . I want for you to be part of the Coalition."

John looked around the space, at the people as they scrutinized their computer screens searching for signs of something preternaturally amiss. He wondered about them, how the supernatural had touched each and every one of their lives.

"The world, and the many lives that live within, unbeknownst to most, is at constant war with the forces of the unnatural," Elijah explained. "Since man emerged from the shadows into the light, we have been there to fight this war. Call us what you will—Demonists, the Coalition—some form of our brotherhood has existed to battle the forces of evil."

"I'm sorry, Elijah. It's good that something like that exists, but . . ."

"Even more so now—since that fateful Halloween night," Elijah said. "The war has amped up, the attacks upon decency more pronounced. There appears to be a demonic incursion into the world since that night."

"So you're blaming me for the world quite literally going to Hell?"

"Of course not," Elijah scoffed. "You and your team were targets. Whoever was responsible wanted you out of the way. Removed from the world so that you could not intervene in what's to come."

Elijah paused, hoping that his words were sinking in, that John might be swayed.

"Elijah, I can't," John said with a sad shake of his head. "My focus needs to be on my wife, curing her of her affliction if I can."

The old man sighed, obviously disappointed. "Of course," Elijah said, "but I wouldn't get my hopes up."

"I can't give up before I try," John said. "I'm not going to give up on her."

"Of course you're not," Elijah said. He reached out and placed a hand on John's shoulder. "But evil of this magnitude is quite corruptive and your time is limited. I fear that you might already be too late."

"Which makes having access to the Demonists' library all the more important."

"Certainly," Elijah agreed. "Everything will be at your disposal."

"Thank you," John said.

They left the control center and returned upstairs in silence. At Elijah's office door they stopped.

"I'll have a driver take you back to your hotel to retrieve your belongings and then drive you to the airport," Elijah said.

"I appreciate it."

"The pertinent materials to be found in the Demonists' library will follow."

"Again, I can't thank you enough."

Elijah smiled, the twisted side of his face becoming even more grotesque with the attempt.

"I wish you the best of luck," he said, shaking John's hand. "But if you should fail in your endeavors . . ."

"I can't fail," John said. "I refuse to accept that as an option."

"Excellent," Elijah said, stepping into his office. He took something from his desk. "But if things turn grim, and you start to lose hope."

John took the business card with only a phone number printed on it.

"Call us," Elijah said. "Perhaps there is something that might still be done."

Elijah sat in his office reading through an extensive file on an ongoing FBI missing children investigation. There were some aspects of the report that made his facial injuries start to itch.

Always a bad sign.

A familiar knock landed upon the door.

"Come in, Griffin," he said.

The Coalition agent stepped into the office, and Elijah noticed that he'd changed his clothes, and smelled freshly showered.

"I thought you were going to sleep," Elijah said, closing the file and setting it down upon an ever-growing stack of files that would eventually need his attention.

"I'll grab a nap later," the man said, stepping forward to lean upon the front of the desk. "Well?"

"Well what?"

"What did he say? What was his answer?"

"It was what I expected at this time in John Fogg's life," Elijah said. "He needs to take care of his wife."

"I think it's too late for that," Griffin said grimly.

"But I'm not going to be the one to tell him," Elijah responded. "He'll have to determine that on his own."

"No loss, really," Griffin said, dropping down into one of the chairs. "Guy seemed like a jerk."

"Yes," Elijah said. "Not everybody can be as pleasant as yourself."

"What? I was good."

Elijah scowled, used to Griffin's somewhat abrasive style. "We'll just need to be patient, is all."

"Do we have time for patience?" Griffin asked. "Looking at the number of reports coming in . . . it's getting bad out there."

"What choice do we have? We will keep doing what we're doing, fighting this war, and hope that John Fogg contacts us."

"I still don't understand your fascination with the guy," Griffin said. "Sure, he's smart, well versed in the paranormal, but I'm sure there are plenty of guys out there with the same amount of experience. What makes Fogg so special?"

Elijah reclined in his chair, folding his hands across his stomach as he fixed Griffin in his stare.

"The fact that someone tried to murder him, killing his team, tells me that he is important," Elijah said. "And I believe that importance will be quite beneficial to us in the dark days ahead."

"You think it'll be bad?" Griffin asked.

"I don't think," Elijah said. "I know."

10

It was Brenna Isabel's first night home in . . .

How long was it? Two days? Or three?

It really didn't matter a helluva lot to her; this was as much home as the staff lounge, or her desk at the bureau.

Just a place to slow down for a bit and collect her thoughts, before starting all over again. She hadn't had a real place to call home since . . .

Her thoughts began to drift back to a time that seemed so very long ago, but in reality hadn't been that long at all.

She slammed the door as she entered the furnished rental, the noise loud enough to pull her from the painful recollections. It was so easy to get sucked into the past, to see over and over what had been lost—what had been taken from her.

Placing the plastic bag of Chinese takeout on the island counter-top, she moved around into the small living area and placed her satchel of files and laptop on the couch, where she would work until she eventually passed out, waking up at the crack of dawn to start the process all over again.

This was her life, she thought, going back to the kitchen to eat. This was what was left after . . .

There it was again, that painful reminder of what had been.

Her eyes drifted to the bookcase in the living room. She knew it was there—she knew exactly where it was.

She always did, both hating the idea that something so horribly painful was in her living space (it would never be a home) and overjoyed that a frozen piece of that wonderful past—no matter how painful it was—still survived.

Brenna felt herself pulled to it, but denied her desire. It wasn't time for that now; she needed to eat and then review her case files, and if she managed to get everything done, maybe . . .

Maybe.

She tried to forget it was there, distracting herself with General Gau's chicken, house fried rice, and a side order of fried wontons. Sitting on a stool at the island, she started off slowly, taking only a little bit from the various take-out containers, but quickly found that she was ravenous, finishing the chicken and eating nearly all the rice. She ate the wontons for dessert and then allowed herself two fortune cookies from the bottom of the bag.

Putting what was left of the rice in the refrigerator, she was reminded of how little was there, a bottle of spring water and a box of baking soda the only other things inside the fridge.

Maybe she should go shopping.

Maybe she shouldn't open the refrigerator. . . . The latter sounded the most appealing to her at the moment.

She left the kitchen, heading into the tiny bedroom, where she stripped off her work clothes and donned a pair of sweatpants and a Quantico T-shirt. Her every intention was to sit down on the couch and get to work, but her eyes wandered immediately to the bookcase as she stepped from the bedroom.

Not now, she scolded herself, grabbing the laptop from her bag and turning it on. She took the files from the bag and set them on the couch beside her. There was a part of her that knew that the likelihood of finding anything new in the files was a long shot. She'd nearly memorized every detail already, but no matter how minute the opportunity, she still felt compelled to try.

She opened the secure file on her computer, her eye drifting over the familiar words—the familiar faces. Eight children missing from different parts of the country, no one even recognizing that they were connected until the symbols were discovered: drawings of the same strange symbol found at all the scenes. On the inside wall of a closet in colored chalk, on a crumpled piece of construction paper on the floor of a room, on the sidewalk in front of a home: wherever the abductions took place, the symbol—whatever it was—was there.

And there wasn't a single clue as to who had left it or what it meant.

They'd brought it to anyone who might have had even a remote chance of knowing what it was: scientists, anthropologists, priests, and even experts in the supernatural.

She thought of the guy from that TV show, John Fogg, and how he'd never returned her call. He had said that he would be in touch once he got back from a business trip. Right. She made a mental note to call him again.

Her eyes eventually began to burn, signifying too much time on the laptop, so she switched to the hard-copy files. She flipped through the pages, spending a little bit of extra time on the pictures of the kids, silently promising them that she would do everything in her power to bring them home safely, and if that wasn't possible, to see whoever was responsible punished.

The last photo was of the only parent murdered—from the scene of the last abduction in Chicago.

Joseph Waugh, father of Christopher Waugh—now missing.

She stared at the photo, internalizing the violence depicted there. The ME had said that the father had been crushed by someone with incredible strength, that his bones were not only broken but pulverized. There had been blood at this scene—a lot of blood—believed to be from the perpetrator, but there hadn't been any match in their database.

Her mind started racing again. Was the one they were looking for badly hurt now? She had no idea. There hadn't been any further abductions, but there had been that delivery to the family of one of the little girls taken.

The teeth.

There were pictures of the teeth, and she stared at them again, feeling herself begin to sink into despair, into that dark place where she had been before and thought that she would never break free of.

But she'd surprised herself.

Brenna realized that she was no longer looking at work, but was back to gazing at the bookcase, her eyes finding the item that still had such a hold on her.

Maybe this was what she needed now, to remind herself of the beautiful things in the world, even though the beauty had been stolen from her. Maybe it would lift her up, or maybe it wouldn't. She never knew how it would affect her.

She hesitated, continuing to stare at the spot on the shelf. Maybe if she went to bed . . .

It wouldn't work; she was sure of it. Every time she had denied herself, it came back to bite her on the ass. Brenna tried to recall the last time she'd looked, and suddenly remembered how hard she had cried.

She hadn't thought she would ever be able to stop.

The time before that, though, she hadn't cried at all, feeling only an anger so intense that she was afraid she might hurt someone, or herself. She had locked her gun up that evening, just to be on the safe side.

And how about now? she wondered fretfully. What kind of night would this be? With what she had immersed herself in tonight, she feared the sadness but wasn't quite sure how she was feeling.

All she knew right then was that she had to look.

Brenna moved the hard files aside and slowly stood, all the while staring at the contents of the bookcase, eyes riveted to one particular area. She could just about make out the binding.

The book was calling to her.

Managing to tear her eyes from it momentarily, she went out to the kitchen again. In one of the nearly empty cabinets, she found what she was looking for in the form of a bottle of Irish whisky. Perhaps a few sips to take the edge off, she thought, pulling down the half-empty bottle—or was it half-full? Depended on the kind of night it was, she thought, finding an appropriate glass and rinsing it of dust in the sink. Unscrewing the top, she poured herself four fingers of the golden liquid, her keen sense of smell picking up on the strong aroma as soon as it started to flow into the glass.

She thought of whisky as the great equalizer, putting her brain in such a place as to make it easier to accept the emotions that the book would conjure. Bringing the glass up to her mouth, she took a good swallow, letting the burning fluid flow down her throat to her stomach, feeling the warmth already starting to spread.

Her husband had been right; she was such a lightweight.

Taking her glass, she left the kitchen again and went to the living room. There was no hesitation now. She went right to it—to the bookcase—eyes scanning the multiple titles. She had everything in there: how-to books, self-help, home improvement, biographies, embarrassing fiction, an encyclopedia of dogs from when they were considering getting a puppy before . . .

She took another long swig from her drink, letting the whisky do its thing.

Her hand went right to that particular book, the tips of her fingers running along the thin binding, as her eyes read the title as if it were something new, as if she'd never read it before.

Freddie Fox Plants a Garden.

She'd bought the book at a grocery store when she was only three months along.

It was to be the baby's first.

Brenna slowly—carefully—extracted the book from the shelf, afraid that if she was too rough it would somehow be irreparably damaged. The cover of the book always made her smile, the cute Freddie Fox in his blue overalls, tending his garden.

Clutching her prize to her chest, she returned to the couch and sat down, placing her half-full—or was it now half-empty?—glass down on the floor at her feet. Laying the book flat upon her lap, she continued to stare at the cheerful cover art, remembering the story inside with distinct clarity.

But it wasn't Freddie's story she was interested in. There was another story inside, a true story filled with so much love, and eventual sadness. A story that belonged to her.

She was amazed that no matter how many times she'd done this, her hands still trembled. It was almost as if she was afraid that somehow they wouldn't be there anymore when she opened the cover.

Brenna pulled back the cover and opened Freddie's adventure with gardening and found her own sad story in the shape of photographs.

There weren't all that many, just enough to paint a beautiful picture. The other pictures, the ones inside her head—and they were many—were for her, and her alone.

Opening the book, listening to the familiar cracking sound of the binding, she was careful not to let the pictures fall out. They were in a specific order, a special order.

The first picture always made her smile. She hadn't known it then, but it was the most perfect of times. She carefully lifted the photo by its corner, staring at the moment frozen in time. In the photo she saw a much younger, and prettier, version of herself, her husband, Craig, and their newborn son, Ronan. Her mind drifted back to the moment, remembering the sounds and the smells. It really was remarkable what the photograph could do; it was just like being back there again.

When things were good.

Perfect.

Before it all went wrong.

She didn't want to think of that yet, moving on to the next photo of her beautiful baby boy. He'd been less than a month when the picture was taken, so small and helpless, but so full of life. He was a loud one, that was for sure.

Brenna held back the sudden emotion, the urge to cry, as she heard the ghostly echoes of the past—her baby's cooing, and tiny cries of hunger—from inside her head.

She paused for a moment, reaching down to the floor for her glass. She needed more equalizer. The whisky went down without the burn now.

Feeling more in control, she went back to the pictures. The next was of Ronan's room. They were so proud of the job they'd done decorating it. The crib was front and center, and seeing it she could not help skipping ahead—

No. Not yet. There was still so much good to remember. So much happiness.

She could feel the love coming from the photos. It was always there, the love that they had had for each other as husband and wife, the love that they had had for their baby boy. She could see it on their faces in each and every picture. So much love.

One of the next pictures always triggered a reaction. The pumpkin. It was to be Ronan's first fall, his first Halloween, the first official holiday after his birth in August.

Happy Halloween, Ronan, the pictures said. Pumpkins and cartoon ghosts and witches. They'd decorated the house substantially. They'd said it was for the baby, but they knew better. The baby was just an excuse for Craig to embrace what he called his favorite holiday.

Brenna had some more of the whisky, not wanting to go to the next photos. There weren't all that many left and she knew that once she went beyond them, the other pictures, the ones inside her head . . . it would be their turn. She thought about stopping here, closing the book, and putting it back on the shelf until next time.

But she couldn't do it. If she'd come this far, she had no choice but to go forward. The whole story needed to be told, not just the good stuff. It was just how she was. She needed to go through to the end, from the past to the now. That was the story.

The next picture she loved, but hated. It filled her with happiness, and bone-crushing despair. She let the happiness come to her first as she looked at the image of her baby boy, propped up on the sofa, still too young to sit up on his own, dressed like a pumpkin. She remembered how Craig and she had laughed hysterically over the outfit, making up a story about how Ronan had been found in a pumpkin patch, retrieved from inside a broken gourd.

It had been a good story. Would have been a nice companion piece to Freddie planting his garden if somebody could have written it.

Her whisky was gone and she considered getting up and going for more, but she was almost done here.

The next pictures were of the inside of the house decorated for the holiday. Lots of orange lights and fake spiderwebs.

Brenna spent a little too much time on the photos of the house, not wanting to go to the last picture.

But she had to.

It was of Ronan's room, also done up for Halloween. It was a picture of him, still dressed in his orange pumpkin pajamas, sound asleep in his crib.

Staring at the picture, feeling the familiar sense of absolute dread return, she wondered again if there was something she could have done.

Something she should have noticed, and reacted to, to save her baby's life.

The picture that followed—the first of the ones that were inside her head—was very similar to the last one.

Trick-or-treating was over, the lights outside had all been turned off, and she'd gone into Ronan's room to check on him before going to bed herself.

Brenna had known something was wrong almost immediately upon entering the room. There had been a feeling in the air, a badness that hadn't been there before.

He looked as though he was sleeping, lying there in his pumpkin onesie. Something had told her to go to him, to make sure that he was all right. Brenna had done this countless times since he was born. If she had added up all the time that she had spent watching him sleep, making sure that he was breathing . . .

If she could only have that time back again—with him.

The tears welling up in her eyes were scalding hot as they tumbled down her face. She was careful to not let the tears land on the photos. She didn't want to ruin them.

She remembered how she had gone into the room, careful not to make a sound, and had stood over the crib looking down on her son, searching for signs that he was fine—deeply asleep and fine.

But this time she couldn't find any.

It felt as if hours had passed as she had stood over the crib, her eyes desperately looking for movement. She remembered how she'd berated herself for thinking such things. Of course he was all right. Of course he was just sleeping.

Brenna tensed with sensory memory.

Remembering how she'd reached down to take his tiny hand in hers.

It was so cold. Like plastic. Like a doll's hand.

Her first instinct was to rub his skin, to try and get the circulation back. It must have been too cold in his room, she'd guessed.

But then the realization began to dawn, and the panic like jagged bolts of electricity to sink in.

He wasn't waking up.

Ronan wasn't waking up.

Brenna braced herself against the torturous memories, setting the pictures back in the front cover of the storybook and closing it. She set it down on the couch beside her, letting the remembrances come.

She didn't really know how long she had tried to wake him up, snatching him from the crib, bouncing him in her arms. She remembered that she had begged him to wake up, to not scare Mommy that way.

It hadn't been long after that when she had begun to pray. She'd never been religious, but then, at that moment, she was as devout as any holy man on the planet.

She'd promised God anything and everything if He (*She?*) would help her son to wake up.

The screaming and crying started not long after she realized that God wasn't listening, the only one to hear her cries being her husband. And he was as useless as God.

The memories that followed were a blur: EMTs, hospitals, doctors explaining about SIDS, the autopsy—

They had cut her baby open to find out what had killed him, and the answer had been less than satisfactory. There was something wrong with his breathing, something completely unnoticeable, something that had become a problem that Halloween night.

Something that had decided to act up and end his life.

Picking his tiny coffin was the next, strongest memory. Imagining her baby being placed inside that box and being put into the ground. The day Ronan was buried, a large part of her was buried with him.

The part that cared about going on, about continuing with her life.

The breakdown nearly took her, and at the time she wouldn't have cared. She had been hospitalized for nearly six months, and during that time as they struggled to heal her, her world continued to die.

Craig left three months into her hospital stay. He said that he couldn't do it anymore, and that he was sorry. She didn't have the strength to argue, and they sold their dream house, and he went away. There were divorce papers that she barely remembered signing, and that was the last time she'd heard anything about him.

She still wondered where he had gone, and whether or not he had found some semblance of peace.

Brenna placed the flat of her hand on the book cover, sealing the memories away once again. She got up from the couch and returned the book to the shelf, sliding it back into the open slot.

Until next time.

Her mind was a jumble of images and emotion, and she considered her options at the moment; she could most certainly do some more work, or she could try and get some sleep.

Doubting very much that sleep would be attainable, she crossed the room and snatched up her empty glass from the floor. She would have a little bit more whisky while perusing her files and then . . .

It took her a moment to recognize the sound of her cell phone ringing. Having to remember where she had left it, she went to her bag and rummaged through the multiple pockets frantically, wanting to catch the call.

"Isabel," she said, holding the cell to her face.

There was silence, which made her start to believe that she was too late when somebody spoke.

"Yeah, it's Grinnal," the reedy, high-pitched voice of one of the odder members of her forensics team said.

"What's up?"

"Sorry to bother you," he said. "I debated on whether or not to call, but decided that maybe—"

"What's up?" she asked again, letting a little petulance slip into her tone.

"It's the teeth," he said.

"The teeth?" For a moment she had forgotten one of their more gruesome pieces of evidence. "What about them?"

There was another long pause.

"Grinnal?"

"Yeah," he said. "You might want to come in so I can show you."

He went silent, and for a moment she believed that he might have hung up.

"I think there's something written on them."

Franklin Cho had owed John and Theodora a tremendous debt.

He'd never believed in the supernatural, in ghosts or anything of that nature, until he'd been confronted with something that he couldn't explain.

Cho was thinking of those things as he walked the corridor of the supposedly secure wing of his psychiatric hospital, on the way to check in on a patient who was also the closest of friends.

Theodora had put him immediately at ease. All the fear that he had been experiencing at the time of the inexplicable events had seemed to melt away after spending less than ten minutes with the woman.

He stood at the door staring through the small window at the sleeping Theodora Knight, saddened by the events that had brought her here. He still didn't know precisely what it was that had happened but understood that it had something to do with her and her husband's unique area of expertise.

Dr. Cho had been experiencing what could best be described as high-level poltergeist activity when he first met the parapsychologists who would become his friends. When it first began, he had believed that he was imagining things, that the strange events that had started to interfere with his normal day-to-day activities were just unusual happenings—flukes—that could be easily explained away. Strange banging noises, items from his home disappearing, only to be found in other locations outside the residence, furniture and appliances moving inexplicably on their own: these were just a few of the bizarre experiences plaguing him.

And then they got worse.

Mechanical devices breaking down, lightbulbs exploding, an overwhelming sense of being watched when nobody else was present.

Cho had been at the end of his rope when the answer to his problems presented itself at a fund-raiser for cancer research, in the form of two guest speakers: celebrity stars of a very popular television program about ghosts and whatnot.

A show that he'd never seen, nor had cared to see. He'd always been more of a PBS guy when he actually had the time to watch television.

He hadn't even wanted to be at the event, having not had a decent night's rest in weeks thanks to a mysterious voice that cried whenever he closed his eyes, but a dear friend—unaware of his situation—had asked him to attend, and he hadn't wanted to disappoint her. He'd planned on going, being seen, making a donation, and then leaving as quickly as he could. The TV stars had been wrapping up their talk when he arrived, allowing him to stealthily enter, make his pledge, wave to a few of his colleagues, and start on his way when he was stopped by the woman speaker as she left the stage.

Theodora Knight.

She'd said that she wanted to talk to him . . . she wanted to help him with his—*problem.*

Cho rapped gently on the door and stepped in to find a nurse administering medication through an IV. They were giving Theodora lorazepam, a calming agent for the overly anxious. It had been used quite successfully with dementia patients suffering from severe anxiety, and it seemed to be having equally good results with Theodora.

"How's she doing, Stacy?" he asked, picking up and looking at her chart.

"She seems fine," Stacy said, finishing with the IV. "Resting comfortably."

He heard a cough from the corner of the room and turned to see a security guard sitting and reading a magazine. There had been some kind of incident in the room the other night involving unauthorized personnel that he had still been unable to quite figure out, and thought it might be best to assign somebody to keep watch over her.

Cho finished reviewing the chart and stepped closer to the bed, looking down at his friend. She looked thin, her skin an unhealthy pallor. Whatever it was that was affecting her was certainly taking its toll. He remembered how she had looked the first time they met, the vibrancy that seemed to come off her in waves.

When she'd mentioned his problem he remembered feigning ignorance, pretending to not understand. He recalled the look she had given him then as clearly as if she were staring at him now, as well as what she had said.

"He'll never leave you alone until you acknowledge he was here," she'd said. He'd been even more confused then, asking her who she was talking about, who would never leave him alone.

"Your brother," she'd said.

His suspicion that she was nothing more than a charlatan was verified at that moment. He'd never had a brother. In fact, he was an only child. And he'd told her so, believing that he'd seen through her performance, catching her off guard.

But Theodora had been completely unfazed. She'd stuck to her story and even gone on to explain that he had indeed had a brother, but they had never known each other outside the womb.

"I'd like some time alone with my patient," he said softly. Stacy understood, and quickly left. It took a moment for the security guard to get the picture. "Take a break," Cho told him. "I'll keep an eye on things for a while."

The security guard stood and left them alone, and Dr. Cho pulled a chair up alongside Theodora's bed. To see her like this, as if her very life force was being drained away, was truly something terrible.

He reached beneath her blanket and took her hand in his, hoping to will some of his own inner strength into her. There was no natural reason for her to be in this condition, which left only the most disturbing of alternatives.

Again, he went back to that night when he'd first met her. He had gone home shaken by her strange words. The unusual events that had been plaguing him began to intensify, so much so that the constant, unexplained disruptions were even beginning to affect his work. He'd been unable to stop thinking of what Theodora had said about a brother, unable to rest, and finally he worked up the courage to ask his elderly mother about it. He'd been certain that she would scoff at the idea, but to his surprise she hesitated.

Cho squeezed Theodora's hand. "Can you hear me, Theo?" he asked. "It's Franklin."

She continued to sleep, showing no signs that she could hear him, but that didn't stop him.

"I'm sorry," he said. "I'm sorry for not being able to help you, like you helped me."

Cho's mother had finally explained that when she had first found out that she was pregnant, the doctors had believed that she was having twins, but a follow-up visit several weeks later showed evidence of only one child. The doctors had said that the second child was a victim of a phenomenon called vanishing twin syndrome, where one of the two children in utero is miscarried and then absorbed by the other, healthier child. She had always believed the doctors had just been wrong.

He remembered thinking over and over again, *She was right. Theodora Knight was right.*

"I was at the end of my rope, and you helped me," he said to the unconscious woman. "You gave me my life back . . . and helped my brother to finally rest."

Cho had contacted Theodora Knight almost immediately after learning about his twin, practically begging for her help. He had been beyond desperate by then, and she couldn't have been more gracious.

Together they explored his life before the strange activity had begun. Cho had shared that he had a benign cyst on his lower back that had been discovered just before the poltergeist activity began. He had been planning to have it removed, but those plans had taken a backseat to the chaos his life had become.

Theodora had felt that it was all connected, and had encouraged Cho to proceed with the surgery. Cho hadn't understood, but by then he had learned not to question Theodora's advice. He'd had the cyst removed and was stunned by the pathology results. The sac had contained embryonic residue of his twin.

Theodora had explained that those remains needed to be acknowledged for what they were, and interred with some level of respect. Cho had done as she directed, and the unusual phenomena affecting him had stopped as suddenly as they had begun.

Theodora had basically saved his life by showing him the existence of another reality, and now she needed him, his expertise, and he would do anything that he could to save her.

He continued to hold her hand, carefully studying her face for any signs of improvement. And his vigilance was rewarded, as she suddenly began to stir.

"Theo?" he called, standing and leaning over her. "Theo, it's Franklin. Can you hear me?"

Her eyes opened and she looked at him vaguely.

"Hey there," he said, gently smoothing the hair away from her face. "How are you feeling?"

Her eyes closed slowly, and then opened again, wide, as the expression on her face grew rigid.

"Is there anything I can do?" he asked her. "Anything to make you more comfortable?"

Her mouth started to move, and he leaned closer to her, placing his ear near to her mouth. "What is it, Theo?" he asked her. "What can I do for you?"

And then he heard the words, soft yet clear and forceful.

"Kill me," she said simply.

Cho pulled back, shocked by her words, then even more surprised as he watched her expression change from one of desperation to absolute savagery.

As she sprang up from the bed with an animalistic growl and attacked him.

The ride from the airport to the institute seemed to take forever.

John had called ahead, telling Franklin that he was on the way and that he needed to speak with him about his wife's condition and her treatment.

Cho had mentioned that some items had been delivered to the institute for him, and he questioned if those might have something to do with the conversation they were going to have.

John had noticed a strange coldness in his friend's tone as they spoke, and wondered if the strain of caring for Theo was becoming too much for him.

The cab finally pulled up in front of the building and John was out of the car before it had come to a complete stop. Quickly paying the fare, he retrieved his luggage from the trunk and made his way up the stairs to the main building.

John strode into the lobby, telling the receptionist that Dr. Cho was expecting him, and was allowed to continue down to his office. He'd intended to bring Franklin a nice bottle of wine, a lovely old bottle of Chardonnay perhaps, but with all that had happened he never got the chance. With an apology on his lips, he rapped a knuckle upon the wooden door, before stepping into the office.

"I had every intention of bringing you a lovely bottle of something, but . . ."

It was dark in the office, the blinds pulled down, the curtains closed. Franklin sat in a pocket of shadow, his back turned away.

"Franklin?" John questioned, already sensing that something was off. "Why are you sitting in the dark like that?"

John looked for the switch on the wall.

"Don't turn on the lights," Franklin warned, turning slightly in his desk chair. "Not yet."

John didn't understand. He set his bags down and moved closer to the desk.

"I need to . . . I need to explain some things to you first."

"Franklin, what's going on? Is Theo—"

"Your wife," he began, freezing John in place. "I paid her a visit last night . . . to check on her."

"Franklin, what happened?" John asked, sensing a near-electrical tension growing in the atmosphere of the office. He reached out for the Tiffany lamp on the corner of the desk and pulled the short chain below the green shade.

The light came on, illuminating the surface of the desk, as well as the person sitting behind it. Dr. Cho recoiled.

And as much as he didn't want to, John gasped at what he saw.

"It's not as bad as it looks," Cho said with a pained chuckle. "I'd hoped that most of the swelling would have gone down by now, but . . ."

Dr. Cho looked as though he'd gone ten rounds with a heavyweight boxer, his face battered and bruised, eyes swollen nearly shut. The way he moved, John could tell that it wasn't only his face that had been hurt.

"Theodora," John said, feeling his anger begin to surge. "She . . . she did this to you?"

Cho leaned back, slumping in the chair.

"I don't think she did, John," he said through swollen lips. "Just before . . . just before the attack, she . . ."

One eye was open more than the other, the bloodshot orb focusing upon him.

"She begged me to kill her, John," Dr. Cho said.

John couldn't stand it anymore, a rush of anger propelling him out the door and down the hall toward the secure ward where his wife was supposedly recovering.

"John, please," he heard Cho call out from behind him.

"Stay in your office, Franklin," John said over his shoulder. "This is between my wife and me."

He tried to get control of his emotions as he walked, but it was like holding on to fire, and the more he was burned, the angrier he became. Slamming through the door to the secure unit, he marched directly toward his wife's room. He stopped before the door to her room, peering through the tiny window as he finally reined in the rage.

Theodora was sitting up in bed, as if waiting for his arrival.

"Hello, dear," she said, and smiled sweetly as John entered the room. "What is it? You seem upset."

John stood at the foot of the bed, fixing her in his furious gaze.

There was part of him that wanted to go to her, to take her lovingly into his arms, but he knew that what he was seeing was a lie, that something else was wearing the face of his love.

Something that had to be stopped, before it hurt anybody else.

"What is it, John?" it asked him, doing the best imitation of his wife's lovely voice. "You're scaring me."

It was starting to crawl down to the end of the bed toward him, the restraints mysteriously undone.

"Please, John . . . what's happened?"

He needed to be fast, to immobilize the body before it could attack.

"In the name and power of the Lord Jesus Christ, I command all supernatural action from any entity in this room to cease. The Lord Jesus Christ commands you."

It was as if his wife had been struck, her body flipping violently backward to the head of the bed.

He continued without pause.

"We bind you by the power of the Blood of Jesus Christ, only begotten of God."

The thing wearing his wife's body thrashed upon the bed, as if held down by some enormous, invisible hand.

"What are you doing, John!" it screamed. "You're hurting me . . . please, John!"

He could feel its power working on him, attempting to instill doubt in him, trying to quell his words long enough for the entity—*entities*—inhabiting his wife's body to attempt to gain the upper hand.

"I bind you to this form, foul creatures," John roared, refusing to listen. "I hold you in this place so you might be extracted—excised from this form of flesh so that it might eventually be cleansed of your foulness!"

His wife . . . *no, the things inside her* . . . began to scream and thrash.

"You're hurting me, John! What are you doing?"

He had no idea how long these words would last. They were old words, strong words, but he did not think that they would be enough. Something far older would likely be necessary.

"You bastard!" the entities shrieked, finally exposing themselves. He could hear the multiple voices, all vying to be heard. "You miserable son of a bitch!"

He needed something new, yet ancient. Words that had not been uttered for a very long time.

"Help me!" the demons screamed, using the voice of his wife again. "Somebody help me, please!"

She was thrashing violently on the bed, crying out in pain, although physical hands had not been laid upon her.

"You will stay as you are told, foul things," John commanded. "You will stay until you are removed, one by one, plucked from this poor prison of flesh and blood, her soul eventually cleansed of your—"

The door to the room came open, a security team, their guns drawn, rushing into the room.

"Sir, step away from the bed," one of the men ordered, his eyes darting nervously from John to Theodora writhing upon the bed.

"Thank God," one of the demons screamed in its most pathetic of voices. "Thank God you're here . . . please, help me!"

"Please, you don't understand," John began, moving toward the men. They pointed their weapons at him. He needed to make them understand before . . . "This is my wife and I—"

"He's hurting me!" she screamed. "I don't know what's wrong with him. Oh God, you have to help me."

"It's all right, miss," the man said. One of the other security officers moved toward the bed.

"Don't go near her!" John shouted, but it was too late.

Just as the officer reached the side of the bed and placed a comforting hand on her arm, the demons struck.

They just couldn't resist.

She moved in a flash, shucking off the binding ritual to strike. The poor bastard didn't know what hit him as his arm was wrenched savagely to one side, the sound of the bones breaking nearly deafening in the room, followed by his pathetic wails of pain.

And the demons began to laugh.

John began to move toward the injured man but stopped when he realized that the other guards were aiming their weapons directly at him, looking as though they would have no problem firing.

"Get him away from her," John said, pointing to the man who had dropped to his knees and was leaning against the mattress, moaning.

The guard started to move, but he was too slow. Theo lunged across the mattress, grabbing the crying, moaning man by the head. He began to scream all the louder.

"Release him!" John cried out authoritatively, and the demons wearing the woman's body froze.

"And why should we listen to you, John?" they asked. "Why shouldn't we rip this poor soul's head from his body and toss it against the wall?"

"Because I compel you," he said. "Because the power of the Lord God compels you!"

The demons screamed out, their voices so loud in the tiny room that the remaining security staff covered their ears.

"No!" The demons shook his wife's head. "Not this time . . . this time we are ready."

"Then attack me," John commanded. "Come at me." He spread his arms. "Where is your strength now, hellions? Where is your power?"

The woman scowled, releasing her moaning captive, tossing him away with such force that he struck the wall across from her and remained still.

"You're pressing your luck, John," one particular demon said, its voice a throaty growl. "It seems as though you want to hurt her. . . . Is that true, John? Do you really want to hurt your lovely wife?"

"I love my wife with all my heart and soul," he said, stepping toward the bed.

The demons wearing her body began to crawl backward, away from him.

"Which is what gives me the faith and power to bind you here," he said, remembering the words he'd already spoken, letting them replay within his mind as he locked eyes with the possessed woman.

The demons bent to his will, dropping down to the rumpled sheets and torn mattress.

"We're going to hurt her, John," the demon said. "We're going to hurt her so fucking bad."

He looked over to see the security team huddled around their fallen member, staring at the scene unfolding on the bed.

"Get out of here," he commanded them.

They didn't seem to know how to react, staring at each other.

The sound of the door opening distracted them all.

John looked to see Franklin Cho. His condition appeared even worse in the light of the hospital room, and John felt his anger toward the things that hurt him ignite even further.

"Go," Cho said to his team. "Go on, get out."

The security guards didn't have to be told again, helping their man with the broken arm to stand.

"Have Dr. Kurothers look at him," he said as they passed, practically dragging the man behind them.

Cho watched as they disappeared down the corridor. He then turned to look at John through his swollen lids, stepping away from the door and letting it slam behind him.

"Was that necessary, Franklin?" John asked, annoyed. "They could have been killed . . . or worse."

"I thought," Cho began, his gaze going to Theodora on the bed. "I thought you might hurt her."

The demons laughed uproariously. "All alone again, John?" the demon voices said in unison. "Just us, against you?"

He was ready to do what was needed, to face the monsters alone if he had to.

But perhaps that wouldn't be the case.

"Franklin, that delivery you mentioned earlier. Would you get it for me?"

Without a word, Cho left the room, only to return moments later with a silver transport case, grunting with the weight of it as he set it down on the floor at John's feet.

The demon struggled to raise itself from the bed, to look, to see what had been brought into the room.

"Is what's inside this case going to help cure Theodora?" Cho asked.

"I hope so," John said.

"I want to help," Cho said, looking toward the bed and the woman who now crouched there, growling like something wild.

Something inhuman.

John squatted down, undoing the latches on the case. "Let's get started."

The rite went on for hours.

Page after page of ancient text that had not been utilized for more than a millennium.

It was all new to him, but John Fogg needed to be strong, needed to read those powerful words aloud with utter conviction, spurred on by absolute faith.

And still the evil fought him.

The demons were deeply entrenched in his wife, clinging to her soul with all their might even though the ancient ritual hurt them, like hungry ticks to the flesh of an animal, feeding not on her blood but on the goodness of her soul. It made him sick to see what they were doing to her.

And the horrors that were still likely to come.

John was exhausted, but he did not let on, for he knew that they were watching through her eyes. He showed them his strength, moving from one part of the ancient rite to the next without hesitation. He remembered an old priest who had taught him many years ago, how he had used boxing as a metaphor for the rite of exorcism.

"Get 'em on the ropes," the old man had said, reminding John more of an old-time trainer than a man of God. *"Never let 'em recover."*

And that was what John was doing, moving from one difficult level to the next even harder. The Demonists were brutal in their war on the demonic, their rites of exorcism like an intricately woven rug, each powerful thread connecting to the next to form the entities' eventual demise.

But so far the demons had proven themselves to be far stronger than John would ever have imagined.

Blood streamed from his wife's nose as she lay on the rumpled, torn, and stained bedcovers. She wanted him to look at her—*they* wanted him to look at her, but John remained strong, pausing only an instant to drop one scroll and unroll the next.

"Can I check on her?" Dr. Cho asked, coming up alongside him.

"You just did," John said rather cruelly, unfurling the document, letting his eyes familiarize themselves with the language before beginning anew.

"John, that was over two hours ago," the doctor cautioned.

John looked at the man, and saw the concern in his swollen, bloodshot eyes. It was good that Cho was there; a man of medicine was often needed at the most critical of junctures. Sometimes the human body could only be taken so far before . . .

"Go ahead," John said, letting his eyes touch briefly on Theo before returning to the scroll. "But be careful."

Cho turned toward the bed, but John grabbed his arm, stopping him. Quickly he checked the wards of protection he'd scrawled on the back of the doctor's hands and on his forehead earlier. Seeing that they were still intact, he allowed the man to continue on to Theo.

John kept one eye on the scroll he was about to read and the other on the man administering to the subject.

The subject.

He hated being so cold, looking at her then not as his wife whom he loved with all his heart and soul, but only as a vessel containing vast amounts of evil, a jar that had to be emptied and cleansed before it could again be filled with good.

"I'm ready to start again," John said to the man.

"John, please," Cho said. "Her vitals are slipping."

"She's strong," John said flatly, trampling down on his emotion. "Stronger than the vermin infesting her."

"I . . . I'm not sure how much longer her body can stand it," the doctor tried to explain. "Her blood pressure is through the roof. She could have a stroke. . . . I think we should stop for now and—"

"Get away from her, Doctor," he commanded.

"But—"

"Doctor—please."

John saw it on his friend's face, the realization that he would get nowhere with him. Sadly Cho stepped away from the woman's bed and back to the corner of the room where he'd been sitting throughout the ritual, waiting to be needed.

John began again, the powerful words flowing from his mouth, directed at the vessel lying prone on the bed before him.

The vessel. Not his wife. The vessel.

He had to think of her that way, not letting any sign of emotion show. To the demonic, emotion was like blood to sharks.

The words of the ancient rite spilled from his mouth, as if the ancient power found in the writings of the Demonists had accepted him, recognizing in him one of its own.

His wife . . . the vessel, began to scream again, but these sounds were different from the others. He could hear actual pain in them, real fear from the monstrous entities hiding in their stronghold of flesh, blood, and bone.

The cries made him stronger, feeding him—feeding the power in the words that poured from him.

The vessel began to thrash, her body to bend and contort in such a way that was physically impossible, but there it was, happening before his eyes.

"John," Cho warned. "John, I'm concerned that—"

"Hold your concern, Doctor," John commanded in a booming voice filled with the righteousness of the power he was now wielding. He continued to bombard the vessel, to get her on the ropes as his teacher had instructed.

The subject's body had begun to swell, the exposed flesh turning a fiery red as it expanded. She arched her back and continued to shriek and wail. Her stomach grew, and grew, the hospital johnny so taut across her expanding gut that he was certain that it would tear.

Evil was attempting to thwart its demise. Evil was attempting to escape out into the world.

John continued to pummel the demons with the ancient words, sensing their weakness, feeling that victory might be close.

The sight of her then was nothing that he would ever have wanted to see, the bare skin of her arms and legs splitting, bleeding.

Emotion threatened to overcome John, but he forced it back, refusing to reveal his own weakness. He needed to be strong . . . as strong as the words he read in a tongue that was ancient before the birth of Christ.

The rite was reaching its crescendo, the words now flowing from him sounding like a song.

A song of evil's demise.

The swollen thing on the bed continued to tremble and shake, expand and bleed, and he had not the slightest idea where this would go. All he knew was that the demonic entities entrenched within the subject . . .

His wife.

The vessel.

Theodora.

. . . were on the cusp of their destruction. Soon they would be gone. Soon they would be no more.

John moved closer to the bed, holding up the scroll as he read the last lines of the ancient ritual, stressing each and every word so that the entities within the woman would hear, and know that their time in the world of man was at an end.

Her body shook convulsively, blood vibrating from the gashes that now covered her entire body, spattering the bed, the walls, and even the floor, but he continued to read, unwavering in his determination to see these spiritual monstrosities gone from the body of the woman he loved.

The woman he loved. His beloved wife. Theodora.

John wasn't sure if it was this brief moment of weakness that was responsible, but the woman's body suddenly—violently—arched upon the bed, the sound of her creaking spine loud and disturbing as its limitations were tested. It was followed by horrible, guttural screams as her head bent back, and her mouth opened wider, and wider still as if something were about to emerge.

He felt Dr. Cho grab his arm, but he didn't waver, finishing the last lines of the rolled parchment.

"John—what's happening?" Cho asked, fear dripping from his words.

"We're winning," John said, and for the briefest of moments, he actually believed that to be true.

The subject's body had swollen to more than four times her natural size and had continued to vibrate to the point where the sight of her had become a blur. And then, suddenly, it all came to a stop. The screaming, bleeding, and shaking ceased, filling the hospital room with a deafening silence.

Theo lay on the bed, perfectly still, eyes so wide that it appeared the milky orbs were about to explode from their swollen sockets.

John had reached the end of the last scroll, quickly darting over to the box to make sure that was really the case. It was, the box was empty. He waited, eyes riveted to the body on the bed.

The gurgling came first, a bubbling, roiling sound from within the woman's still-expanded body.

Cho's grip on his arm was back, growing tighter in anticipation, as John continued to watch, and wait, and pray, for a sign that the ritual had succeeded.

That the power of goodness had won.

The subject's mouth snapped violently open, the sounds of bubbling internal happenings filling the room, followed by a rush of burning bile shooting up from her open mouth in a stinking column that struck the ceiling and cascaded down upon the room.

The vomit was like lava, burning everything that it touched. Within seconds, sections of the room had started to burn. Once again fire alarms blared and the sprinklers triggered, dousing the room in another round of artificial rain.

"It's still burning," Cho said, panicked.

John's eyes were still locked on the subject, who was now convulsing.

"Get an extinguisher," John said, pushing the doctor toward the closed door. "I'll be fine for the moment."

Cho dashed for the door, going out into the hall.

John approached the bed, avoiding smoldering piles of bile eating away at the floor. He had grabbed the first of the scrolls he had read, ready to begin the rite all over again if that was what it would take.

Looking at the subject, he was preparing to affirm his authority and power over the evil when she turned her head and looked at him.

"John," she said, and he knew at once that it was her. His wife.

Theodora.

"John, you have to listen to me," she said. Her voice was a harsh whisper. "I don't have much time. . . ."

He moved to sit upon the bed, taking her hand in his to lend her strength.

"We're going to help you," he said. "We've almost succeeded, we just need to—"

"Shut up and listen," she said in near panic.

John fell silent.

"If this continues, I'm going to die," she said.

"You can't," he interjected. "You're strong, you'll—"

"Please, shut up," she said again, with a sad shake of her head. "I'm going to die, and then . . . and then they'll be free. It's what they want."

Her words slowly began to sink in, filling him with a weighty dread.

"This is their plan, to fight you, to let you think you've won . . . but I'll be dead, their prison no longer able to hold them . . . *I'll* no longer be able to hold them."

She squeezed his hand.

"You have to do something . . . something now," she said to him, bloodshot eyes begging.

"What?" he asked.

Cho came storming into the room with the fire extinguisher. He paused, watching.

"Take care of the room," John ordered, and he immediately went to work putting out the burning piles and stains on the ceiling, walls, and floor, as the artificial rain fell down upon them.

"What?" John repeated to his wife, bringing her hand to his mouth and kissing the swollen, blistered skin.

"They need to be kept in my body," she said, nodding. "But I can't do this any longer. . . . I'm not strong enough to go on."

"I . . . I don't understand," John said.

"Kill what's me," she said. "But leave my body alive."

And then he realized what it was that she was asking of him. She wanted him to destroy her mind, her brain, but allow her body to remain alive.

A living, breathing prison for the demons festering inside her.

"No," he said.

"Yes," she affirmed. "I can't hold them for much longer, and if they were to escape . . ." She closed her eyes, and the tears began to fall. "I'm . . . I'm not strong enough."

John released her hand. He stumbled back, banging into Dr. Cho, who was still extinguishing what was left of the smoldering bile.

"What?" the doctor asked. "Is she all right . . . did we . . . did we win?"

John could not answer as he continued to back away, moving toward the door.

"Please, John," Theo called weakly to him, her trembling hand beckoning. "You have to . . . *need* to do this."

John knew then that he wasn't strong enough. He'd been convinced that the Demonist writings would work, that he would expel the demonic entities inhabiting his wife, and all would be well again.

But he had been so wrong, things had progressed so much further than he'd been willing to see.

"John," she cried as he reached the door.

He couldn't bear to look at her anymore, to see his failure before him. Yes, he had beaten back the demons, perhaps even hurt them in some way, but they were still inside the subject.

Still inside Theodora, ready to be strong again. Ready to be free, or to take control if they could. Either would most certainly be fine for them.

Out in the hallway he nearly collapsed with exhaustion, but he pushed himself toward the stairs. He had to get out of there; he needed to breathe air not stinking with the smell of evil and despair.

He heard it as he stepped out onto the first floor, the rumble of thunder. He was drawn to it, toward the exit, pushing his way through the glass doors out into a real rainstorm and not an artificial one.

The rain pelted him, soaking through his clothes to his skin, and what felt much deeper than that.

John Fogg knew then and there that he was at a crossroads. Deep down he knew that Theo was right, that the twisted things inside her could not be allowed to escape, but he couldn't bear the thought of what she was asking him to do.

It would kill him, that he knew.

But there was another option, one that he hadn't wanted to consider, but now, looking at the choices he might be forced to make, it seemed to be the lesser of two evils.

He reached for his wallet as lightning cut the sky in a jagged jack-o'-lantern smile, and removed the business card that he'd been given in Romania.

Dialing the number on his cell, he placed the phone to his ear and waited.

"Yes," a voice answered.

"Elijah," John said.

"Hello, John," the leader of the Coalition said. "I thought I might be hearing from you."

"I need your help," he said to the man.

There was a long pause that seemed to last for centuries.

"And you are willing to help us in return?" Elijah asked.

"Yes," John agreed, at this stage willing to make a deal with the Devil himself to save the woman he loved.

"Very good, John. We'll be in touch," the old man said, ending their call.

As thunder crashed and the heavens cried.

11

Elijah hadn't been back to the States in over fifteen years.

The leader of the Coalition sat in the back of the black Land Rover with his handpicked team, on their way to the home of John Fogg and a confrontation with the forces of darkness.

It was quiet in the vehicle, the seven others lost in thought, most likely about what they would soon encounter, what they were about to attempt. They were the best at what they'd been trained for, but that did not mean that this particular evil might not be better.

To be overconfident could easily bring about a horrible defeat. Elijah knew that better than anyone, being forced to wear the scars of his complacency for such a moment.

Gazing out the window, he fought to keep his eyes open. It had been a long flight, and the previous two sleepless nights as they had prepared for their journey had left him physically and mentally exhausted. He closed his good eye, convincing himself that a moment's rest—a brief catnap— might be exactly what he would need to revitalize his energy stores.

But as soon as the eye was closed, the memories came. Memories of his times in the United States, and how the Vatican had entrusted him with the most important of missions.

He had been a priest of the Roman Catholic faith, recruited by the Vatican to become one of their chief exorcists. Not something that was openly talked about, the Vatican exorcists were an important weapon in the ever-growing battle against the forces of evil. They were like the marines of the faith, sent in to vanquish supernatural evil before it could gain a foothold in the material world.

Elijah remembered how unprepared he had been for the truth of the matter, that powerful supernatural forces were indeed loose in the world, and a perpetual threat to the safety of humanity.

But he had learned his job well, and soon became one of the Vatican's rising stars. The evil he had seen, and vanquished. It was a never-ending battle, but one they—*he*—were ready to fight.

So many encounters . . . so many victories. There were times when it had been close, when it looked as though the minions of the pit would be victorious, but he never gave up, fighting to the bitter end.

Fighting until evil could fight no more and had no choice but to succumb.

His skills became legendary to the others of the profession, instilling in them a sense of superiority that served them all well.

Until it didn't.

Until his fall.

Elijah stirred in his sleep, fighting to awaken, but the memory had him as it often did, wanting to show him the error of arrogance once again.

A case of demonic possession had been reported, and verified, in the city of Fall River, Massachusetts, a working-class city on New England's south coast. He had been assigned to the case, as he was already in the Boston area dealing with a case of Devil worship at an Ivy League school. Elijah went directly to Fall River, wanting to be done with his work as quickly as possible, so that he might return to Vatican City for some welcome time off.

Elijah twitched, and moaned softly as he remembered the neighborhood tenements, the images inside his mind distorted by a fitful sleep. He recalled how he'd actually been amused when he reached the address given to him by his Vatican superiors. It wasn't a home or an apartment building, as he'd expected to find.

It was a convent.

If his memory had served him right, the Sisters of the Blessed Virgin had been a part of this working-class community since the early 1920s, establishing schools and building rest homes for the old and the infirm. They were an older order, and one that would likely be gone in a few years because very few young women were joining the convent anymore. It was a sad fact, but a reality nonetheless

As if impatient with his recollections, the dream—or was it a nightmare?—skipped ahead to his meeting with the order's mother superior, Sister Margaret Joseph. She had been so relieved to see him, for the sisters were at their wits' end over what to do. They were congregated outside the subject's cell, their mouths moving in silent prayer as they manipulated the rosary beads in their ancient hands. They watched him as he approached with the mother superior, knowing who he was, and why he had come.

The subject's name was Sister Bernadette Michael, and she lay on her bed in the sparsely furnished room, wearing only a white cotton nightgown. She stared upward toward the ceiling as if transfixed by something that she saw there.

There was a stink of something foul in the air, something that Elijah had encountered many times before in his work for the Vatican. It was the smell of the profane, of the unholy.

Of evil.

He turned toward the doorway to see the sisters still praying with their rosaries. He had a speech that he would often give to the loved ones, to the concerned of those afflicted, but he just didn't have the strength that day, and instead he'd asked the sisters for some privacy. But before closing the door on them, he'd warned that they might hear some things out of the ordinary from within the room, and asked that they remain strong, lending him some of their strength through prayer. They of course agreed, clutching their beads all the tighter, and he'd shut the door and prepared to go to work.

He'd brought his bag of tricks with him. That was what he jokingly called the black leather satchel that carried all the necessary items for expelling demons.

The old nun had been bound to the bed by what appeared to be clothesline, and lay atop sheets stained with bodily waste.

The Vatican file sent over to him had provided him with some basic information on the subject. He found it odd that the file never bothered to mention that she was a nun, but he imagined it wasn't important to his superiors. Evil was evil no matter where it festered. His job was to excise the threat whether it be in the body of a child, or a woman of the faith, or an old man.

The rite had gone exactly as expected, the beginning steps in the ancient ritual causing the demonic entity to act out: shrieking obscenities, spitting, ranting and raving in some unintelligible demon tongue, and vomiting.

Lots and lots of vomiting.

In a matter of hours, the old woman appeared clear, showing no sign of the demonic entity that had possessed her. Elijah had believed that the evil entity had been vanquished by the holy words of the exorcism ritual, what remained of the monstrous spirit dispersing in the ether never to bother another living soul.

And that was where his arrogance—his assumptions had gotten the better of him.

The old woman had been moaning from the aftereffects of the exorcism, and before allowing her fellow sisters to come into the room to administer to her, Elijah had gone to the bed to untie her and assure her that everything was now fine and that the evil that had taken control of her was gone.

As he had comforted the woman, she suddenly became hysterical, correcting him, explaining through the tears that the entity that had been inside her was still there with them.

Was still in the room.

Instead of instantly reacting, he had paused to explain to the nun that she was mistaken.

And with that arrogant pause he had set himself up for attack, and eventual failure.

The demon excised from the body of Sister Bernadette Michael had not been destroyed, dissipated to the ether by the rite of exorcism, but had in fact remained alive, awaiting an opportunity to infest a new and unsuspecting host.

Elijah came awake with a start, his forehead slamming against the window as the vehicle passed over a rut in the road. His team were staring at him, their eyes all showing concern.

"Are you all right, sir?" one of them asked. "Is everything okay?"

"I'm fine," he said, the memories unleashed by his exhaustion still prevalent in his mind. He couldn't stop them now if he'd wanted to, turning back to the window seemingly to watch the scenery go by, but instead reliving the terror of that night.

With Elijah's guard down, the demon had taken him, worming into his body—his soul.

Elijah still remembered the feeling, a lingering sensory nightmare that he would have done anything to forget. It was the experience of all the sadness and anger of the world shoved down into his soul, and just when he thought he could never survive, he did. And it just continued to go from bad to worse for what seemed like an eternity.

He had wanted to die more than anything.

But the evil had said *no*.

The evil hadn't finished with him.

The old nun was the first to be murdered, her fragile throat collapsing as the Vatican exorcist's priestly hands wrapped around her thin neck and squeezed with all his supernaturally enhanced strength.

Elijah still saw the woman's dark brown eyes as they bulged wider and wider still. Eyes that watched the holy man who was supposed to save her taking her life instead.

The other sisters were next. The demon had allowed him to leave Sister Bernadette's bedroom to find the others. They were gathered in the convent's kitchen, huddled around a coffee urn, and they all looked to him, their eyes filled with hope, as he entered. The demon inside him had to hold back a chuckle as it informed them that there was nothing that could be done, and that their sister in Christ had succumbed to the evil that had taken her, and that her soul was now experiencing the eternal torments of Hell.

Elijah remembered how the sisters had cried and prayed—the demonic entity feeding off their pain and misery. Growing stronger from their sorrow, as well as his own helplessness.

The demon let them cry for quite some time before putting the blame of their sister's possession squarely on them, telling them that they were all sinners and would be damned like Sister Bernadette Michael.

It was the mother superior who finally confronted him, scolding him in her fury and demanding that he leave at once.

The demon inside him did not care to be spoken to in that way, and Elijah was forced to watch from a prison of his own flesh as his hand grabbed a knife from a strainer by the kitchen sink and cut the old woman's throat from ear to ear. And before the others could react, he attacked them as well, the demonic entity taking even more pleasure from strangling the nuns with their rosary beads and bludgeoning them with a heavy wooden crucifix that had been hanging on the wall.

Oh how the demon had laughed as he killed them, and while the foul spirit was wrapped up in its monstrous glee, Elijah had made his move, regaining partial control over his body. He began to pray, believing that his Lord and savior would give him the strength to fight the evil that had invaded his body.

He truly had believed that, until the monster inside him painfully proved him wrong.

The demon took back control with ease and turned the wooden crucifix that he still clutched in his hand against him. The demon wanted to show him how little this symbol of good meant to one such as it, taking great joy at the amount of damage the crucifix could do to his face.

The demon allowed him to feel the pain, each stab and gouge and strike as the crucifix was repeatedly slammed against the side of his face. Over and over the corners of the cross struck, ripping the skin, breaking the bone, damaging one of his eyes beyond repair.

And once the demonic entity was finished with its bloody and brutal task, it took his torture even further by allowing him to live.

The demon left him there amongst the murdered sisters, the side of his face reduced to pulverized bone and ragged meat.

Left him there to suffer for his failure—for his arrogance.

The left side of Elijah's face began to painfully throb with the recollection of what the demon had forced him to do to himself, and to the nuns he had been sent to save.

It was something impossible to forget, something that set him on a totally new path.

The Vatican had protected one of its own, removing him from the bloody scene and painting him as one of the victims of the crime that had claimed the lives of the Fall River Order. He was flown back to the Vatican, where he physically recovered under the care of their doctors. Plastic surgery was offered to repair his damaged appearance, but Elijah refused, wanting to wear the scars as a reminder of evil's rising power in the world, as well as a show of what his arrogance was responsible for.

The Land Rover came to a stop, and Elijah realized that they had at last reached their destination. The sounds of seat belts being unsnapped filled the inside of the vehicle as the team that he'd brought for the special job prepared to exit.

He felt as though he knew each and every one of them, specifically selecting them based on their talents. Similar to what the Vatican had done with him when he was released from the hospital. He could no longer be a priest, the taint of the evil he'd carried having poisoned his soul, but he could most definitely help in the battle against the encroaching darkness. They had offered him the position as director of an organization that worked outside the constraints of the church to combat threats of a supernatural nature.

There was no other choice but for him to accept, as it was for the team that he'd selected for this operation.

Elijah was the first to exit the vehicle and stand in front of the entrance to the mansion. He noticed the lights, inside and out, had started to flicker. The others, now getting out of the vehicle, took notice as well.

"What's up with the lights?" Griffin Royce asked as he climbed from the driver's seat.

The front door opened and John Fogg stepped out to greet them.

"Thank you for coming," he said, hand outstretched as he descended the steps.

Elijah accepted the man's handshake, which was firm, but clammy, evidence of Fogg's nervousness about what would be attempted this evening.

"You're most welcome, John," Elijah said. "But let's save our thanks until after we know if our endeavors were successful."

The team had come around to the front of the Land Rover, standing there.

"Obviously this is your team," John said.

"I won't bother to introduce you," Elijah said, starting up the stairs. "They know why they are here, and that quite possibly they will not survive the night. Any connection made between you and them would be a waste."

Elijah was halfway up the steps to the house when the lights started to flicker again. He looked to John. "Your wife?"

"She's awake," he said. "It's as if she knew that you'd arrived."

"I'm sure she does," Elijah answered, continuing up to the door, where he let himself in.

There was a thin, blond-haired man standing in the lobby, arms crossed defensively.

"This is my personal assistant," John said, coming in behind him with the others. "Stephan Vasjak."

"Mr. Vasjak," Elijah said with a slight nod as the lights continued to go on and off.

"You're going to help her?" Vasjak asked, stepping closer to them. "You're all here to help her?"

"We are here to attempt something that may indeed prove beneficial to Ms. Knight, yes," Elijah answered.

"Do anything and everything that you can to help her," Vasjak said with grim seriousness. "But if you hurt her in any way . . ."

The threat hung thickly in the air of the lobby.

Elijah moved in close to the wispy man, fixing him in his good eye. "I'm sorry to say, there is nothing that we could do that would be worse than what she is already experiencing."

That silenced the young man long enough for Elijah to turn toward his host.

"If you would please take us to your wife," he said to John. "There are some things we need to prepare before we begin the ritual."

John followed Elijah and his team up the stairs to the level that housed his wife.

Dr. Franklin Cho was waiting just outside her door.

"This is Dr. Cho." John introduced Elijah as they reached the landing. The men shook hands.

"How is she physically, Doctor?" Elijah asked.

"She's weak," the doctor responded. "The constant battle to not allow these . . ." He was having a hard time finding the right words.

"It must be difficult for you, Doctor," Elijah said. "A man of science having to confront the existence of dark forces that have been here since creation . . . and perhaps before."

"It's been—interesting," Cho acknowledged. "But John and Theodora have helped to open my eyes."

"I'm sure they have," Elijah said, what could have been an attempt at a smile tugging at the scarred corner of his mouth.

The lights pulsed on and off.

"She's becoming impatient," the Coalition leader said, turning to address his team. "We'll need to be quick and precise if we're going to have even the slightest chance of success."

The seven-member team nodded in unison, ready to do what needed to be done.

John stepped forward. "Is there anything that I can do to help?" he asked.

"Ah yes," Elijah said. "There is. You'll be going in with us."

Cho watched them, wondering.

"Dr. Cho, I believe you can sit this one out."

"Are you sure?" Cho asked.

"We're good," Elijah said, then turned back to his people. "Are we ready?"

Elijah moved toward the door.

"What should I be doing?" John asked him.

"You are to wait until I tell you what to do," Elijah said, turning the doorknob and pushing the door open into the room.

Theodora was bound to the bed using soft restraints, her head and neck bent in such a way that looked nearly impossible, and quite painful.

"Theodora Knight," Elijah's voice boomed as he entered the room, his people flowing in around him to encircle the bed. "My name is Elijah, and I and my people have come to offer you assistance."

"John . . . ," Theo cried, pulling on her bonds. "John, who are these people?"

John started to answer, but Elijah gave him a glare with his good eye that kept him silent.

"Begin," the old man instructed.

One of the team, a heavyset man with a shock of curly red hair and a large Viking beard, stepped toward the bed as he reached into the leather satchel that he carried. In one swift movement he'd removed a silver vial and dipped his finger inside it. As the finger came out, John could see that it was covered in something gray and powdery—ash, he believed. The bearded man proceeded to draw a strange symbol on Theodora's forehead.

She immediately began to scream, the intensity of her wails actually pushing the man backward, where he bumped violently against the room's wall and slid down to the floor.

"Next," Elijah said, unfazed, as a woman on the other side stepped forward.

"Don't you dare come near me, bitch!" Theo—or the things inside her—began to threaten.

Ignoring the outburst, the woman began to recite something that might have been Sumerian, but John couldn't be sure.

"Shut up!" Theo screamed, her neck stretching abnormally long.

The woman had just finished the verse when she began to choke, and insects—cockroaches, it appeared—began to spill from her mouth. She, too, stepped back, then dropped to her knees, and John heard her begin to pray aloud.

Elijah watched unflinchingly, nodding to the next of them.

Another woman darted toward the bed, laying a gloved hand upon John's wife's stomach and reciting the next verse of this Sumerian rite. As she spoke, she removed the glove to reveal a hand covered in a strange, swirling-patterned tattoo that seemed to move as if alive as it hovered above Theo's stomach.

Theo's body went completely rigid, as if her limbs were being pulled taut by invisible ropes. Her shrieks intensified as she fought against the forces that were being worked upon her.

The woman's tattooed hand suddenly burst into flame, and she stifled a scream as one of her other teammates ran forward to suffocate the orange fire with a towel.

Elijah then nodded to another of them, a thin-faced man with twitchy, nervous mannerisms who quickly stepped to the bed and extended both hands above the subject, reciting even more of their rite.

Theodora began to roar.

It was as if there was an entire zoo inside her, the shrieks, wails, screams, and howls coming from her vibrating the very air of the room.

The animal sounds eventually began to dim, followed only by the pathetic sobs of a woman in obvious pain.

"Theo?" John asked, looking first to Elijah before moving.

The old man nodded to him, and John sat down on the bed next to his wife.

"Something's happened," Theo said, her eyes drooping from exhaustion. "The demons . . . they're . . . they're trapped . . . locked away."

"Is this true?" John asked, stroking his wife's sweaty hair and enflamed cheeks.

"It is," Elijah said. One of his people came over to him with a black leather medical bag, and he took it.

"How long?" John asked, knowing that this was only temporary.

"Long enough to do what is next required," Elijah said as he removed a long protective case from within the bag.

"Which is?" John asked.

"Which is your job," the old man said as he opened the case to reveal a syringe filled with a golden liquid.

"What's that?" he asked cautiously.

"When you are told, this is what you will inject into your wife," he said.

"Okay. And what will I be injecting into my wife?"

Elijah approached, offering him the syringe.

"It's a fast-acting poison that basically shuts down the entire nervous system," the old man explained.

"You can't be serious."

"I've never been more serious, Mr. Fogg," Elijah said. "With your wife being technically dead, we can then turn our full attentions to the demonic entities inside her, without concern."

"You . . . you're going to kill her?"

"Only temporarily," he said. "As soon as we're done with the demons, we'll administer the antidote and then—"

"I can't do this," John said. "I'm not going to kill my wife."

"Then your wife will die anyway," Elijah said. "You heard your friend Dr. Cho. She is growing weak. The entities are becoming stronger with every passing day. Theodora only has so much time left before the demons totally dominate her, and at that stage your wife will no longer exist."

Elijah shoved the syringe at him.

"Take it," the old man said. "Do your part, and then we will do ours."

He couldn't believe he was doing it, but John took the syringe in his hand. Theodora was delirious, her temporary relief from battling the demonic forces inside her having taken its toll.

"Time is of the essence, John Fogg," Elijah informed him.

"Don't you dare rush me," John yelled. "What you're asking me to do . . . I . . ."

"I am asking you to trust us," Elijah said. "Without this . . ." The old man went silent, and John knew that this was likely his wife's only chance at surviving her affliction.

Without any further words, or thought, John removed the plastic cover from the tip of the needle and prepared to do what was asked of him.

"Damn you to Hell if this doesn't work," John said through gritted teeth, bringing the needle to his wife's throat.

"There's a very good chance we'll all be damned if we're not successful," Elijah responded.

The tip of the needle punctured the pale flesh of her neck, a crimson bead welling up at the point of entry. John then applied pressure to the plunger, slowly injecting the poison into his wife's already depleted system.

Her eyes at once grew wide, and he bent down nearly overcome with emotion to kiss her lovingly upon the lips.

"I'm so sorry," he said to her. "But it's for your own good."

Her mouth moved as she tried to speak, but the poison was as fast as Elijah had explained.

All John could do was stare, watching as his wife's life drained away.

"Oh my God," he said, watching her die.

Elijah then took him by the arm, escorting him toward the door as his team began the next phase of their operations.

"What's going to happen?" John asked, turning around to see what they were doing. They had undone her bindings and were removing her pajamas.

"What . . . ?" he asked.

"John, please," Elijah said. "Let us try to help her."

Elijah pulled open the door, pushing him out into the hall. John took one last look just as the old man closed the door. The Coalition agents were all standing over his wife, having taken items from their bags that he had seen before while visiting some of the more primitive cultures in his research. They were items made of bone and used for puncturing and injecting ink beneath the skin.

Tools used for making tattoos.

John sat outside the locked bedroom door for what felt like days. It had been, in fact, a little more than twenty-four hours, but the reality of the actual amount of time that had passed did little to comfort him.

There had been screams, and there had been moans from the other side of the door; some had been from his wife, and others . . . The number of times he had risen, and almost pounded upon the door, demanding entry, was too great to consider at this point.

The disturbing and curious sounds had diminished over the last few hours, and John found himself back on the landing floor, leaning wearily against the balustrade.

What was happening on the other side of the door, he obsessed, and would it result in his wife being returned to him? Elijah had offered no guarantees, but as long as the slimmest hope remained, he needed to hold out.

"Anything?" a voice asked, coming up the stairs from the first floor.

John turned his head as Stephan passed.

"Nothing," John said.

Stephan reached the top, holding a tray of steaming mugs. Dr. Cho followed with another tray, this one holding three plates with a sandwich on each.

"I told you I wasn't hungry," John said as he stood, taking a mug of hot coffee from Stephan's tray.

"You haven't had anything substantial in close to fifteen hours. I've decided that yes, you are hungry," Stephan said. "Have a sandwich."

Franklin came to stand beside Stephan with the tray.

"I don't want anything," John said, before taking a sip from his mug.

"Believe me," Dr. Cho said. "Take a sandwich."

"See, someone listens," Stephan commented.

John shook his head, exasperated by the badgering, but knowing better than to argue with his assistant. He did as he was told, taking a sandwich from one of the plates.

"There you go," Stephan said, helping himself to one as well. "You won't believe how much better you'll feel once you have something in your stomach."

John grunted a response, lowering himself to the floor, careful not to spill his coffee. Franklin took the spot beside him, and Stephan plopped down beside him. They all began to eat, staring at the closed doors.

"I wonder how much longer they'll be?" Stephan asked, taking a large bite from his sandwich, chewing slowly.

"It's making me a bit crazy that I can't check on her," Franklin said. "Her vitals were so iffy that . . ."

"She might be dead," John stated, eyes fixed upon the barrier before him. The statement of fact was true, no matter how abrupt and potentially painful, and he felt as though they should all get used to the possibility.

"I don't think that they'd still be in there with the door closed if she was dead," Stephan said. He set the plate with the half-eaten sandwich down on the floor beside him. "I don't even know why I'm eating that. I'm not even hungry."

"Is that how you're choosing to deal with this now?" Franklin Cho asked him. "To assume the worst, and take it from there?"

"I injected her with a neurotoxin," John said.

"Which was part of a procedure," Franklin then added. "One that I believe is extremely dangerous, but a part of their procedure nonetheless."

"I just feel we should all entertain the possibility that Elijah and his people might not be successful," John said. He took another bite of his sandwich, chewing slowly.

"But again," Stephan said, "they might be. You've always been that half-empty guy, John. You really do need to start thinking more positively."

"We're going to do this now?" John asked him. "Have you seen anything positive around here these last few days? Maybe I've missed it."

Stephan looked away and began to silently sip on his coffee.

"We don't even know what they're doing to her in there," John said, the primitive tattooing tools prevalent in his thoughts.

"Yes, we do," Franklin chimed in. "They're trying to help her."

"Are they?" John asked. He looked to his friend. "They made me agree to help them with their war against the forces of evil, or whatever, in exchange for whatever the hell they're doing." He motioned toward the door, his voice growing louder. "God knows what they're trying . . . they could just be going through the motions so I keep my part of the deal."

He thought about his wife, as she lay in her hospital bed at the Cho Institute when he'd attempted to save her. When she had begged for him to make her a vegetable, permanently trapping the demons in her still-living body, but freeing her of the torment.

He was beginning to think that maybe there had been something to her request, and it was killing him inside.

"Let's hope that's not the case," Stephan said, getting up from the floor with a loud grunt. He had started to retrieve the plates and empty mugs—

When the bedroom door came open.

Elijah stood in the doorway, looking much the worse for wear. His clothes were wrinkled and stained, the sleeves of his dress shirt rolled up to the elbow. He looked as though he could use a shave and a shower.

John sprang to his feet, going to the door. Elijah blocked his way.

"Not yet," the old man said. "Give it some time first. Let her rest and recover."

"Then she's all right?" He was looking into the room, and saw some things that he wished he hadn't. There was blood on the walls, and on the floor. One of Elijah's crew was zipping up someone in a black plastic body bag.

Immediately John felt his heart skip a beat with the sight, looking at once to the bed, making sure that he saw his wife lying there. And she was, curled in a tight ball, covered with a sheet, trembling as if cold.

He wanted to go to her, to hold her—to warm her with his body.

One of her bare arms shot out from beneath the sheet, and he saw the markings.

Just by looking at them, he could tell that the symbols were ancient, and filled with power.

One of Elijah's people went to the bed, gently taking her exposed arm and sliding it back beneath the covers.

"What have you done?" John asked Elijah, still feeling images of the black, tattooed symbols that he had just seen on her flesh writhing in his brain. "What did you do to her?"

Elijah looked back into the room before grabbing the doorknob and closing the door once more behind him.

"Hopefully we've helped her," he said. "Given her a chance to live with the evil that infests her. Hopefully we've given her control."

12

My name is Christopher Waugh, the boy repeated in the echoing cavern of his mind, *and I lived in Chicago.*

Live *in Chicago,* he corrected. *I live in Chicago.*

The image of his father lying dead in the upstairs hallway almost made him cry, but it was so hard for the tears to come these days.

Is it possible to actually cry out all your tears? he wondered.

Looking around him, he thought it might be.

He'd had his head down on his desktop, resting, and raised it to look about the room. There were several others in the classroom with him; most of them were sleeping

They rarely moved, rarely cried out, never pulled at the chains that bound them to the wooden floor beneath their desks.

None of them were doing all that much these days—

Except learning about Damakus.

That was what they were there for . . . what they were living for.

Damakus was the eye in the center of creation, and through his teachings he would come again and he would . . .

Chris silenced his fevered mind. He didn't want to think about that, or the one who had brought them all there.

The Teacher.

With just the thought of the man, Chris felt his body start to shake, to break out in a cold, tingling sweat that made it feel as though he had millions of tiny spiders crawling up and down his back. He shifted in his chair, his chains rattling on the floor and filling the silence of the classroom with noise.

Some of the other students stirred.

That was all he knew them as, *students*.

The Teacher did not want them to be anything more than that. They had no names anymore. They were the students, and he was the Teacher. That was all there was to know.

And they were there to learn about Damakus so that he could live again.

The girl across from him—a little bit of a thing who couldn't have been any older than six—looked at him with eyes that showed nothing. He wondered how long she'd been in the classroom. She'd been there when he arrived. There was dried blood all over her mouth, which probably had something to do with the fact that she didn't seem to have many teeth. There was another boy in the first row whose hand was bandaged.

He wanted to talk to them, and was about to speak to the toothless girl when she seemed to sense his intention and immediately put her head down upon the desk as if hiding from him. The other students were stirring as well, but they refused to look at him, or one another.

The Teacher had warned them about this.

He didn't know why he bothered, but he slid down from his seat to the floor to examine where the chain attached around his ankle. He moved aside the stinking metal bucket where he went to the bathroom, and again studied where the chain connected to a plate in the floor. Using all his strength, he tugged upon it, but only succeeded in causing a painful throb inside his head. Nothing was any different, the thick chain remaining attached to the plate bolted into the wooden floor. He even picked at the wood around the plate, but that had gotten him nowhere.

Christopher emerged from under his desk and slipped back onto his seat. The others had been watching him, but they quickly looked away when he looked in their direction.

They'd put their heads back down upon their desks, hiding from him, hiding from what he was doing.

At least I'm doing something, he thought, disgusted by the fact that they all seemed so accepting of their situation.

He wondered how long it would be until he was that way and felt a surge of anger course through him, the memory of what that man, what the Teacher, had done to his father accompanying the rush of rage. And before he could stop himself, he started to scream, tossing his head back and reaching down deep to cry out as loudly as he could. He knew he had done it before to little effect, but maybe this time . . . maybe this time somebody would hear.

The others had all lifted their heads and were staring at him intensely, their eyes telling him to stop, that it would all be for nothing. But Christopher couldn't help himself. He had to try before . . .

Before he became like them.

He screamed until his voice gave out, ragged and raw, and sat there panting, listening for a sign that somebody had heard.

"Maybe," he said to them, his voice little more than a dry croak.

One by one, they just looked away, putting their heads back down upon their desktops.

And then he heard the sound . . . they all heard the sound.

It was loud and powerful in the silence, a clattering sound as if something . . . *someone* . . . was coming in through the door from the outside.

Someone must have heard, he thought, and he began to scream again, though the sound emerged from his throat as little more than a sickly squawk. Just to be sure, he began to thrash his legs, letting the chain around one of his ankles whip about, banging off the floor and the legs of his desk.

He thought for sure that the others would join him in being heard, but they all sat dumbly silent, their eyes fixed upon the doorway.

Waiting for their savior.

The front of the shopping cart came through the doorway first, and Christopher let out a happy squeak, jumping to his feet on legs that trembled from lack of use.

He was ready to be rescued . . . ready to be free, but found his anticipation shattered like brittle bone as the pusher of the shopping carriage entered the room.

"And who's making all that noise?" the Teacher asked, his dark beady eyes moving about the classroom until they fixed upon Christopher.

"Ah, there you are," the man said, shoving the cart farther into the room and down one of the rows between the desks. "My, aren't we rambunctious today?" the Teacher said, maneuvering the cart to stop before Christopher.

"What do you have to say for yourself, student?" the Teacher asked.

He had no idea why he said it, but the words just seemed to spill from his mouth.

"I'm Christopher Waugh," he said, desperate to hold on to who he was. "I'm Christopher Waugh and I want to go home."

The Teacher's dark eyes grew immense as he stared.

"You still have so much to learn, student," the Teacher said, his gaze like twin laser beams burning into the flesh of his face.

Christopher was ready for anything, ready to be punished for his behavior, but the Teacher continued on, pushing the shopping cart filled with stuff to the back of the room.

They all turned in their chairs, watching their teacher. Christopher took note of the cart's contents, curious as to what the horrid man was planning on doing with an empty fish tank.

The Teacher left his cart and dragged two empty desks closer to the shopping cart, placing them side by side.

It was hot and steamy inside the classroom, and Christopher wondered how the man wasn't suffocating in all the layers of clothing he was wearing, not to mention the long coat.

The Teacher hefted the empty fish tank from out of the shopping carriage and set it down atop the two desks. He hovered over the empty tank, peering down into the nothingness before returning to the cart. There were multiple plastic jugs of some nasty-looking liquid that the Teacher then began to open and pour into the tank.

One of Christopher's fellow students, the little girl with no teeth, whimpered as if she knew something that he didn't.

The tank was about half-full now, the water—or whatever it was—a nasty, yellowish color filled with dark floating bits.

"Should we perhaps add some of your tears?" the Teacher asked, chuckling to himself as he emptied the last of the containers into the tank. "There isn't enough time," he answered the question himself, reaching down into the brackish fluid as if to check the temperature.

Christopher's mind raced as he tried to grasp what could possibly be happening now. *What is the tank for?* he wondered.

"Is this what you want?" the Teacher said to the liquid contents. "Is this what you need?" He appeared to react to his own question, rearing back as he clutched at his chest, doubling over as if in pain. "Yeeearr-rrrrgh," the man screamed as he bent nearly in half.

He panted with exertion, slowly righting himself.

"Today you will see what your learning has wrought," the Teacher said to them. "What your belief in Him has created."

Christopher still didn't understand, but he wanted to cry as much as the toothless girl beside him had. There was a feeling in the room, a sensation even worse than it had been.

Something was going to happen, he was sure of it. Something really, really bad.

"You," the Teacher said, pointing at him. "The one that was making all the noise."

He twitched in his seat from the attention brought to him.

"Come here, student," the Teacher instructed, motioning him closer.

Christopher did not want to leave the protection of his desk, and shook his head.

"You will do as your Teacher tells you!" the man screamed. He was bending over again, gripping his stomach and chest through the heavy trench coat he wore. "Come here!"

It was as if Christopher were caught in some powerful invisible current, his body pulled away from his desk toward the makeshift table where the tank of filthy water sat.

The Teacher came around to stand in front of him, before the eyes of the other students.

"Why did you cry out?" the Teacher asked. "Was it so that someone might hear . . . so that they might come to rescue you?" He looked up over the classroom. "You haven't a clue as to what is going on here . . . the history you are about to witness . . ."

He started to unbutton his heavy woolen coat, to reveal a red-checked shirt beneath. He shucked off the coat.

That was when Christopher noticed his shape, the way in which the Teacher's shirt clung to his body.

It looked *wrong*.

"What you are about to become a part of." The Teacher started to unbutton his shirt, and all the boy could do was stare in rapt attention. The Teacher pulled open his shirt to reveal the swollen mass of pulsating flesh. For a moment, Christopher thought of his friend Tommy Stanley's mother, who was going to have a baby. But this growth was higher, and more strangely shaped than Mrs. Stanley's stomach, and it throbbed and writhed as something moved eagerly just beneath the skin.

"Behold what my teachings have planted," the Teacher commanded. "And what your beliefs and fears have grown."

Christopher backed away, repulsed by the sight of the man's awful stomach.

"No, no," the Teacher said. "You, my noisy cherub, have a job to do . . . an assignment to perform."

The Teacher went to the shopping wagon and carefully bent forward to retrieve something from the bottom of the cart.

"Your tool," he said, holding up what he had found and extending the rusty blade.

Christopher recognized it as an old box cutter.

"Take it," the Teacher ordered.

Christopher recoiled from the offer.

"Take it!" the Teacher exclaimed, his swollen belly moving and expanding all the faster in his excitement.

Reaching out with a trembling hand, Christopher took the box cutter. He was shocked at how cold it was to his touch. Staring at the cutter, he was suddenly aware that it had the potential to be so much more.

Can this be how it all happens? Christopher thought. How he was able to kill his captor and escape from the filthy classroom? Staring at the pointy tip of the blade, he wondered if he could do it . . . would it be possible for him to use this object to harm?

"I can practically hear your thoughts," the Teacher said. "The question of whether or not I have just handed you your freedom."

The Teacher smiled, and Christopher's skin crawled.

"I offer you so much more than freedom," the Teacher growled, rubbing one hand across the taut, veined flesh of his growth.

The Teacher stepped menacingly toward him.

"Cut me," he demanded, offering his stomach to the youth.

Christopher stepped back, gripping the box cutter all the tighter.

"Go on," the Teacher said, thrusting his protruding belly at him. "You know that this is your desire. Run the blade across my flesh . . . do it and learn the reason that you are here."

Christopher continued to back away, untrusting of the situation.

"Do it and learn the reason why your father had to die."

His father.

Christopher saw the man he loved inside his mind, the image then shifting to how the Teacher had left him, broken in the hallway of his Chicago home.

"Do what I tell you and learn why it was all worth it."

Something let go within the boy, something that reminded him that even if he were to get away, his life would never be the same again, that his father was gone, and now he was alone.

"Do it!" the Teacher screamed, providing him with the most perfect of targets.

Christopher lunged with his arm raised, and brought it down in a quick slash across the bulbous flesh. "Gahhh!" was all that he could manage, the ability for human speech impossible at that moment. It was all about anger, and rage, and violence.

The Teacher cried out, both hands going to his protruding stomach, the gash the boy had cut in the skin bleeding heavily.

"Oh, you wonderfully wicked child," the Teacher cried. "Your father would be so proud!"

The mention of his father was all the fuel he needed, and Christopher again rushed toward the Teacher, cutting at the exposed flesh.

"Oh yes!" the Teacher wailed, his hands now covered in gore. The wooden floor of the classroom was spattered with blood as he stepped back away from the boy, hauling his swollen and bleeding midsection over to where the fish tank sat.

Christopher stood ready, his body tensed to fight some more—to inflict more harm—but it appeared that this wasn't going to happen.

That it was no longer necessary.

The Teacher stood before the tank, his fingers moving across his lacerated stomach. It was suddenly apparent that he wasn't trying to stem the flow of blood, but instead was pulling the cuts in his skin apart, opening the flesh to get his fingers—his hands—inside the gaping wounds

What is he doing? Christopher wondered, his brain completely numb as he bore witness to the nightmarish sight unfolding before him.

"What had been forgotten is remembered again," the Teacher said, his hands disappearing into the wounds in his body. "Given life through the belief of the innocent."

The Teacher withdrew his hands and they were not empty. Something had been extracted from inside his person, something that squirmed and splashed in the blood of birth.

Something alive.

Something that had not existed until he . . . *they* had been taught of it.

The newborn nightmare squealed and writhed as it was brought to the edge of the fish tank and released over the side to splash down into the filthy water.

And as Christopher watched the newly birthed life swim within the fluids of the tank, he understood what it was they had been responsible for. An old god had been reborn this day, and it was the students who had given it life.

He let the blood-covered box cutter drop from his hand with a clatter as he stared at the tank and its new inhabitant.

"Praise Him, He has returned," the Teacher said, swaying from side to side inside a circle of his own blood.

"Damakus," Christopher said, understanding then why he and the others had been brought to this place.

And with that understanding, the god within the tank started to grow.

"Damakus," the students said in unison.

"*Damakus.*"

John Fogg stood in the doorway of their bedroom watching his wife.

Theo had been out of it for three days and had barely moved since the last time he checked in on her. Squinting in the darkness, he looked for signs that she was indeed breathing.

Franklin had given her a quick checkup once Elijah and his people left. He said that she was actually good, better than good really. There was a calmness to her now that hadn't been present since . . .

John grabbed hold of the doorknob and was about to pull the door closed when he heard his name softly spoken.

"John?"

Damn it, he thought. He hadn't wanted to wake her.

"Yeah," he answered, leaning into the darkness of the room. "Just checking to see if you were all right. Go back to sleep."

"Well?"

The door was halfway closed again, and he pushed it back. "Well what?"

"Am I?" she asked sleepily.

"I think you're good."

"I feel . . . different," she said.

"It's to be expected," he said. "You need to rest. Then you'll feel better." He started to close the door again. "Now go back to sleep."

"Hey, John," Theo called out.

"Yes," he answered.

"I wanted to tell you . . . I wanted to say that I love you. I think it's been a long time since I've told you that."

He found himself genuinely smiling for the first time in months. It was taking everything he had not to go to her, to take her in his arms and . . .

"I love you, too, babe," he said. "Now get some rest."

The door finally closed, and he allowed himself to feel something that he had not experienced since the events involving his wife began.

Hope.

Elijah and the Coalition had seemingly given it back to him. It was time that he began repayment on his debt to them.

Brenna had been staring at the pictures for hours, similar in nature to the single symbols found at all the kidnapping scenes.

Strange, jagged shapes in succession, primitive writing long forgotten even by scientists who proclaimed themselves to be experts of such things.

Written on the extracted teeth of a six-year-old.

They had noticed the gouges when the teeth were collected from the parents, scratches in the yellowish enamel. At first they had believed them to be some natural defect.

But then Grinnal had looked closer.

The markings were intentional, put there for a reason.

But why?

To send the child's parents even farther down the rabbit hole to insanity? That was at least one sure bet, but there was something else to it as well. Something that the agent couldn't quite put her finger on—yet.

Brenna remembered her coffee and picked it up for a sip. Ice cold. She made a face, disgusted, and set it back down on her desktop. She guessed that more time had passed than she would have expected.

She was considering heading out to get another cup when there came a knock at her door. A secretary—she believed her name was Nadine—stuck her head quickly inside the office.

"Agent Isabel?" the woman asked. "There's somebody here to see you about your missing children case. He said that he's expected."

Brenna wasn't expecting anybody. "Did he give a name?"

The woman shook her head. "No."

Brenna got up from her chair, going to the door and peering out. "Where—" she had started to say just as Nadine pointed him out.

John Fogg stood in front of Nadine's desk, hands clasped in front of him, head bowed. He looked as though he might be praying.

"Should I tell him you're busy, or . . ."

"No, I'll see him," Brenna said. "Just give me a second."

She went back to her desk, placed the pictures of the teeth back in their folder, and put them away inside her drawer. Returning to the door, she leaned out, motioning for John to come down.

He smiled pleasantly when he saw her and headed down the aisle between workstations to her office.

"Mr. Fogg," she said, holding out her hand. "Nice to see you again."

He took her hand and squeezed lightly.

"Agent Isabel," he said. "I'm sorry that it's taken me this long to get back to you."

"Come in," she said, ushering him into her office. Brenna closed the door, then walked behind her desk, gesturing for him to take the chair opposite her as she sat. "Please," she said.

"Thanks," he replied, sitting down.

She was trying to be polite, but it was hard for her not to show her annoyance. She'd been trying to communicate with this guy for nearly two months and hadn't heard a peep.

"So," she said, leaning back in her chair. "To what do I owe this visit?"

Fogg leaned forward. "I doubt that I'm your favorite person right now," he said with what appeared to be genuine sincerity. "But you did ask me for my help, and I'm here to offer it to you."

"Really?" she asked, unable to contain her annoyance with the television celebrity any longer. She seriously doubted that he had anything

200 · *Thomas E. Sniegoski*

to offer and was about to blow him off. "How nice of you to offer, but right now we've got a pretty good handle on the case and—"

"That's not what I was led to understand," he said, his delivery quite serious.

"Oh, really?" she said, leaning forward in her chair. "And should I perhaps be asking the source of your information?"

"Let's just say there are people paying attention to certain . . . things going on in the world at large," he said. "Things that I believe pertain to the case that you're working on."

She wanted to rake him over the coals, to dig for specifics, but the way he was staring at her, the intensity in his demeanor, she came to the conclusion that maybe she'd be better off if she didn't know.

"Please, let me help," he then said, and she knew that she couldn't send him away, that maybe—maybe there was a chance he really could assist in some way.

She pulled open the desk drawer and removed the file that she'd been looking at. Laying it down upon the desk, she opened the folder to reveal the photos within and slid them toward him. "What do you make of this?"

John Fogg delicately picked up the tiny incisor with a hand encased in rubber.

He held it beneath the high-intensity magnifying glass and looked at the markings that had been etched there. Studying the strange configurations, his eyes tracing each and every shape, he felt an icy chill run up and down his spine.

This was something very bad.

"Well?" Isabel asked from the corner of the room. "Can you read it? Does it look like anything you've seen before?"

"No," he said, setting the tooth down with the others. He wanted to pick them all up, each and every one, and examine them, but was sure that the outcome would be the same. "It's definitely a language, but nothing I've ever encountered. I can tell you that it's very old."

John moved on to the other items left at the homes of the missing children in the last few weeks. He felt the familiar chill again with the sight of the tiny figurine. It had been carved from the finger bone of one of the children. It was a simple carving, the major details being on the figurine's face—its eyes and mouth open wide as if in surprise.

"And all of these objects"—he ran his hand over the tabletop with even more evidence laid out, printed numbers beneath each—"were found after the children's disappearances?"

"Yes," Isabel said, moving closer to the table. "Every home has received some strange piece of paraphernalia in connection to their missing child." She leaned her hip against the table's edge, her eyes moving over each of the familiar items. He wondered how many times she had already done that very same thing. "Almost as if the son of a bitch responsible was rubbing it in, reminding these poor people that their children were gone."

"And that he has them," John said.

She looked at him hard.

"There haven't been any bodies found, or remains," he explained. "I'd guess that whoever is responsible still has them. Whether or not they're still alive . . ." He shrugged, turning his attention back to the table of gruesome oddities.

"Would it be possible for me to have copies of the case files?" he asked. He could see that she was about to object, but he was persistent. "I have an extensive library at home, as well as contacts that run the gamut of just about every strange topic imaginable. There might be answers readily available. We'll just need to sift through tons of bullshit to find them."

She appeared to be considering his question, arms crossed defensively across her chest. "Let me check with my director," she said, striding toward the door. "Give me a moment."

Agent Isabel stepped out and he made his move.

John reached down, taking one of the teeth and slipping it into the pocket of his navy blue blazer. Pictures were all well and good, but to have one of the actual teeth, with the markings made by the kidnapper. He wanted to touch it—to feel it beneath his fingers without the gloves. He wanted to possess it.

It could make all the difference in the world.

Certainly he could go through all the proper channels, the Coalition capable of pulling some strings, but he believed time was of the essence. If the children taken were still alive, they would need to move as quickly as possible.

Agent Isabel stepped back into the room and he turned toward her.

"Yes," she said. "I can have copies made up of all the pertinent information for you to continue your review."

"Excellent," John said, removing his rubber gloves. "As soon as I receive the files, I'll go through them with a fine-tooth comb and hopefully find something that will help us to crack this case."

There was a small barrel in the corner of the room and he tossed the used gloves inside.

"Thanks so much for agreeing to speak with me," he said as he stood beside the agent in the doorway to her office.

"And thank you for finally responding to my requests," she said sarcastically.

"I deserved that." He extended his hand. She took his hand in hers. The grip was firm, powerful. This was a woman to be reckoned with, but he wasn't sure if even she had the strength to handle the darkness that might be approaching.

"These people you mentioned earlier," she said as she squeezed his hand, looking him hard in the eye. "Will they be offering you assistance with this?"

"I'm sure they will," John said.

She stared at him harder as she loosened her grip.

"So they're aware," Agent Isabel began.

"Aware?"

"Aware of how things are now," she said.

He knew exactly what she was talking about.

"Very much so," he said.

"That's good."

He started through the doorway, his business there done. "I'll be in touch, Agent Isabel."

And she nodded at him as he left, the last look that he saw in her eyes changing his opinion.

Maybe she was indeed strong enough.

13

The demons believed that they would soon be free, their frail prison of flesh, blood, and bone brought to death.

They imagined their escape out into the earthly realm. So much life, so much frailty, so much goodness to corrupt; it would be a most glorious thing to be free.

They were all ready, waiting, deep down in the darkness. They could feel their host dying by inches, her life functions gradually shutting down one at a time, and as this occurred they rose.

Closer to the surface.

Ready to leave the fleshy trap that had ensnared them when they were freed from the jar.

The jar. Thoughts of their original imprisonment brought a wave of confusion and anger. They had no memories of how they had come to be within the jar, awaiting their prey.

But that was a mystery for another time . . . for when they were truly free.

And they were ready. The life of the woman that held them inside her was coming to a close.

An end for her.

A beginning for a multitude of evil.

The demons swarmed closer, digging their claws and talons into her fading soul as they ascended.

The demons were of a common mind, a hive mind so to speak, each of them sharing with one another their twisted and awful desires for themselves, as well as for the world of man.

But suddenly something was wrong.

The flesh had died, but something kept them there . . . something of a magical nature.

The demons were enraged, throwing themselves against the confines of their fleshy prison . . . which appeared to be exactly what someone had intended.

They had been corralled, trapped, damned up within an area of the human woman's body, the magicks being used ancient and so very powerful.

So powerful that their human host would not have survived if they were used upon her.

Most of the demons ranted and raged, but some admired the trickery used.

The magick had trapped them, bound them, and now the body that they had possessed had been returned to life, and even more powerful magick was being used upon her—

Upon them.

Even though their numbers were legion, they could not escape. They were bound to their host, grafted into the fabric of her being.

Where they had expected to be free when the cage of flesh expired, now they were as one. If she were to die, they would die as well.

The demon swarm roiled in a last-ditch attempt to take control of their host, but something prevented them.

Something held them back.

Marks, symbols, black tattoos inscribed upon her soft and supple flesh.

The demons saw these marks and knew terror and despair, for they were powerful sigils designed by their most reviled enemies.

Designs that gave those adorned with them power over the forces of shadow.

That gave those adorned with these figures power . . .

Over.

Them.

Theodora stood naked before the mirror in awe of what had been put upon her skin.

At first she had been horrified, shaken to the core that these strange sigils had been inked upon her body. The marks flowed up her arms, around her neck, and down her back to circle her waist like a belt. From there they continued, seeming to slither down her hips, to explode outward on either side of her vagina, before winding around her thighs and legs and onto the tops of her feet.

Look at me, she thought, turning in the mirror, admiring her shoulders, lower back, and buttocks.

All covered with the ancient marks.

But the shock had been short-lived, for she could feel the strength that they gave her, the power over the forces that had infected her.

She could still feel them there, inside her—waiting.

There was no doubt that the demons were still strong, powerful beyond words, and she was certain that if it wasn't for the strangers who had come into her home to work their magick, and put these marks upon her, she would have fallen by now. Would have died, allowing the malignant forces out into the universe to infect many other poor souls and eventually bring about their demise and the doom of any who loved them.

They had saved her. Somehow they had done what her husband, with all his arcane knowledge, could not.

For a moment she remembered a needle in the hands of her husband, and how he had injected her with its contents, and how she was pretty sure that she had died.

But only temporarily.

She remembered a sense of peace—an inner calm as her spirit was released from its corrupted flesh to flow upward from the earthly realm to a place of warmth and light.

She thought she would have been content to stay there, to join with the stuff of creation, but Nana Fogg had told her that it was not yet her time, that she still had much to accomplish.

She and the love of her life.

It was that love that had brought her back, that had given her soul the weight and strength to return to a body still infected with a multitude of evils.

But the vessel—her body—had been fortified, made stronger by the magickally infused sigils that had been inscribed upon her flesh, their power flowing under the skin to the muscle, sinew, blood, and bone beneath.

Yes, the evil—the demons—was still there.

Theodora held out her hand, feeling the influence of one of the demonic entities as it attempted to assert itself. She could feel it slithering beneath the flesh, entwining around her fingers. She watched as the flesh grew leathery and spotted, the nails at the tips of her fingers growing longer, hooking as they grew thicker, becoming more like a bird's talons now.

She knew what the demon wanted. It wanted her to reach up with those nasty claws to her delicate throat and rip the flesh away. The hand rose, and the long, spindly fingers trembled in anticipation of the violent act it was going to commit.

And she said, *No.*

208 · *Thomas E. Sniegoski*

With that simple command, the flesh softened, the talons receding, changing, until they were nothing more than fingernails again. Theodora flexed the hand, opening and closing her fingers, and she smiled

Yes, the evil—the demons—was still inside.

But it was now she who possessed them.

John Fogg held the tooth in his fingers, trying with all his might not to think of where it had come from.

"There are repeated patterns," he said as he brought the tooth under the focus of the magnifier lens that he had attached to his glasses. "Which convinces me that these scratches are most definitely part of an alphabet, but not one I've encountered before."

Elijah grunted in response.

John looked away from the tooth, to the image of the Coalition leader on his computer screen. In his office in Romania, the scarred old man hovered over the multiple photographs taken of the teeth from the files Agent Isabel had given them.

"We've run the patterns through our database with no luck," he said. "Perhaps what we're looking at here is older than the data we've collected. So old it has been lost to time."

John removed his glasses, rubbing at his tired, burning eyes. "Or our perpetrator is more ambitious than we thought and has created his own alphabet and written language."

"There is a man in Sicily who has helped us on occasion," Elijah said as John watched him slowly lower himself down into a chair. "Ever since an accident on a construction site that caused a steel bolt to be lodged in his skull, he has been capable of deciphering Enochian script. Perhaps he might be able to do something with—"

"Hello," said a voice.

John nearly jumped out of his skin, spinning around in his desk chair to see his wife standing there.

"You scared the shit out of me," he said, and watched an apologetic smile creep across her pale features.

"Sorry," she said with a shrug. She hugged herself nervously. "I heard voices and thought that maybe . . ."

Theo focused on his computer screen, seeing Elijah there.

"I thought so," she said, recognizing the old man and moving toward her husband's desk and the small video camera built into his screen. "Hello."

"Theodora," Elijah said. "I must say, you're looking well. How are you feeling?"

"Good, Elijah," she said, leaning against the desk. "More myself every day."

John watched her communicating with the Coalition leader, paying attention to her every word. She appeared to be telling the truth, seeming to be getting better each day, but he was still cautious, watching for signs that the sigils they had placed on her body weren't performing as intended.

So far, so good, but he didn't want to let his guard down.

"And the itching?" Elijah asked. "Has that diminished?"

"Lots of body lotion," she answered, running her hands up and down her arms, across the exotic markings on her flesh that kept the demons trapped inside her at bay.

John could see them move, changing their configuration in order to counter whatever new threat the evil inside his wife might be attempting.

"That will pass with time," Elijah said.

"I'm sure," Theo agreed. "I want to thank you again—you and your people—for what you did for me."

"You are so welcome, my dear," the old man said. "Now you must get well again so that you and your husband can assist the Coalition in our future endeavors."

John cringed at this reminder but remained silent. He no longer wanted his wife involved in any form of investigation, especially the cases that the Coalition would bring, but that was a discussion for another time.

There was a pause in the Skype conversation and John decided that it was time to wrap things up for the evening.

"So you're going to take the pictures of the teeth to your man in Sicily?" he asked.

"Yes, that might be the best approach right now," the old man said.

"Pictures of teeth?" Theo questioned.

John nodded. "I'm consulting with the FBI on a case and there is some evidence—a child's teeth that appear to have been inscribed with—"

"May I see?" she asked.

"I actually have one of the teeth," he admitted ashamedly. He had put it away in an envelope on his desktop. He poured it into his hand to show her.

"May I?" she asked, tentatively reaching down to take it from his palm.

"We were saying that neither of us has ever seen symbols or writings such as this before," Elijah said through the computer speakers. "And that maybe the language is something far older than—"

"It is," Theo gasped, closing her eyes as she wrapped her fingers around the tooth and began to swoon.

John reacted, jumping from his seat, ready to catch her if necessary.

Theodora swayed where she stood, her entire body trembling.

"Theo, what is it?" John asked.

"I . . . ," she began haltingly. "I . . . *he* . . . he knows what this is," she finished, her fist still wrapped around the tooth.

"Theo? Are you all right?" Elijah asked. "John, what's going on?"

"It appears that she's having some sort of reaction—to the tooth."

She had brought her closed fist to her chest and was holding it tightly as she seemed to struggle. John saw that the exposed tattoos on her arms and neck were moving, slithering across her skin as they attempted to reconfigure.

"Who knows about the writing on the tooth, Theo?" John asked.

"One of them," she answered. "One of them inside . . ."

She dropped to her knees, in the midst of some great inner struggle. "He knows what it is . . . what the writing is. . . . He can read it. . . ."

John squatted down beside her as she started to laugh—but it wasn't her laughing; it was something inhuman . . . monstrous . . . demonic. "Theo! Theo, are you all right? Are you there?"

He saw that her eyes had changed. They looked reptilian now—crocodile-like—to be more specific.

"If you only knew," the voice of the demon said, Theo holding out the tooth to him.

"Elijah, what should I do?" John asked, unsure if there was something he should be doing, something he should know.

"She should be able to fight them off," the Coalition leader said. "Give her a moment before—"

The demon screamed, Theo's neck swelling up like a bullfrog's. She began to thrash, bending forward until her head touched the floor.

"Theo?" John asked. He reached out cautiously, wanting to touch her but . . .

"I'm all right," she said breathlessly. "I'm all right now. . . . He said that . . . he said that he wasn't going to tell us what is written on the tooth."

John squeezed her shoulder. "That's perfectly fine," he said. "Let me help you up and—"

"But I told him that's not how it works anymore," she then said, a touch of maliciousness in her tone.

"And?" John questioned.

She smiled, and the hair on the back of his neck stood on end.

"You might want to grab a pen and a piece of paper."

She had gone back inside again.

Sitting on the floor of her husband's office, she'd closed her eyes and dove into the darkness, where the monsters lived inside her.

They were all there, waiting in the shadows. She couldn't quite believe the number that had found their twisted way into her body, affixing themselves to the stuff of her soul.

The demons sensed her at once, coming at her in a tidal wave of jabbering obscenity, and for a moment she was afraid.

But then she remembered who held the true power now.

"Stop," she commanded them, and as much as they did not want to, and as much as they struggled and fought against the words, her magick was strong.

Theo noticed her flesh, the markings that had been put upon her naked body. In the material world these sigils were as black as a murderer's soul, but here, they glowed as if white hot.

They glowed like the stars in the sky.

They screamed at her, this demonic army, threatened her with bodily harm and worse, but they did not move.

They could not move.

She looked out over the sea of them, at all their twisted and horrible faces, searching. She was looking for one of them in particular.

One of them who had information that she wanted.

"Where are you?" she asked them as they continued to screech and wail, still held in place by the markings on her body. "Where is the one that knows about the tooth, and the writings scratched upon it?"

The demons writhed as one, an undulating ocean of wickedness.

"Give him to me," she commanded, her words making them shriek and wail as if they were being hacked to bits.

They did not want to obey her, but the sigils burned all the brighter, their magickal radiance touching their horrible flesh, making the demons act on her command. They singled out one of their own, grabbing him up and lifting him above their heads, moving him across the ocean of their evil toward her.

The demon protested, cursing his brethren's existence as he was handed over, one demon to the next.

He was a foul, awful thing, piglike in appearance, with a tail that was a hissing serpent, and tiny, baby's hands instead of hooves. As he drew closer, he attempted to escape, to crawl across the surface of his awful kind, but they propelled him forward.

Toward the woman who commanded them.

Theo watched as the demon was ejected toward her, his corpulent pink form landing upon a solidified platform of darkness with a wet-sounding slap. The demon lay there, head bowed, trembling before her. Slowly it lifted its porcine face to glare.

"The things I will do to you when the opportunity arises," the monstrous thing spat, the inside of his mouth filled with writhing, plump maggots.

She moved closer to the demon, the light emanating from the markings on her naked flesh making him squeal as it touched him. The demon tried to get away, to turn tail and run back into the mass of inhumanity, but his fellow demons blocked his way.

"When the opportunity arises," Theodora repeated, squatting down in front of the piggish demon. "*If* the opportunity arises. Guess we'll have to cross that bridge when we come to it." She reached out, grabbing the hideous thing and pulling it into her arms in a hug. "But until then, you're nothing but my bitch."

Theo seemed to have gone into a kind of fugue state, sitting on the floor of John's office.

He watched her as she sat there, both fascinated and terrified by how quickly the symbols on her flesh were moving—writhing, expanding, and contracting.

"What's happening, John?" Elijah asked over the Skype connection.

"I'm not really sure," he answered. "She appears to be in some deep, meditative state. The sigils, though . . ."

"She is communicating with them," Elijah said. "The demon spawn that possess her are likely attempting to regain control, but the sigils give her the power now. The power over them."

"I just wish that she'd come out of it," John said. He couldn't help himself, gingerly reaching out to stroke the softness of her ruby-flushed cheek.

Theo opened her eyes and gasped.

For a moment he saw the eyes not as his wife's, but as someone else's—*something* else's—but they quickly changed, and once again, he was looking into his wife's loving gaze.

"Hey," he said to her. "You all right?"

"Yeah," she said, nodding. "You ready to talk to him?"

He looked at her. "Him?"

"The demon," she explained. "I'd tell you his name, but it sounds more like a cat hawking up a hair ball than a proper handle."

"Is she all right?" Elijah asked from Romania.

"She appears fine," John said.

"I'm good," Theodora answered for herself. "Are we ready for this?"

"Elijah, she says that she's going to allow us to communicate with the demon that knows about the writing on the tooth."

"Fantastic."

"Can she do this?"

"Of course I can do this," she answered, a touch of petulance to her tone.

"That is what the sigils are for," Elijah explained. "They give her the power to have control of the demons inside her instead of the other way around."

John could see that the sigils on her body were still moving across her flesh like a swarm of army ants.

"All right," John said. "How do we do this?"

"Are you ready to ask the questions?" she asked. "I'm not too sure how long I'll be able to keep this up, or how compliant the demon will be."

"I'm ready," John said, grabbing the pen and notepad that he'd brought out earlier.

He watched her take a deep breath, and her eyes slowly closed.

"Be careful," he suddenly said.

Her eyes opened and she looked at him.

"Careful as mice," she said, and smiled in such a way that his heart began to swell with the love he had for her.

She went back to it, closing her eyes.

"Get over here," she said in a powerful voice, and for a moment, John considered moving closer to his wife until he realized it wasn't him that she was talking to.

Theo's face suddenly changed, the bone structure altering, the flesh growing thicker—grayer—and her eyes opened, but they weren't her eyes that now looked at him.

The demon gazed around the room and smiled, a thick stream of foul-smelling bile trailing from the corner of its twisted mouth.

"I could get used to this," it said, and then chuckled with a horrible gurgling sound. "Just imagine how much nicer it could look covered in a healthy arterial spray."

It laughed again, and John had to suppress the urge to attempt to drive this filth from his wife's body.

But as Theo had said, that wasn't how this worked.

"We're not here to talk about my office," John said to the thing.

Its eyes . . . its dark horrible eyes . . . focused on him.

"Hello, John," it said. "That is your name, right? John."

"And yours?" John asked.

The demon shook his wife's head from side to side. "Not gonna get that from me," it said. "Names are power . . . but you already know that, John."

"I'm getting tired of you," John said. "I have some questions that you're going to answer."

"Ya think?" the demon responded.

Suddenly the demon's body was racked with what could best be described as a horrible spasm. It looked quite painful.

"You'll answer the questions or I'll hurt you." Theo's voice suddenly came through, replacing that of the demon's.

"Fucking bitch," it snarled.

"I wouldn't test her," John said. "She means what she says."

The demon seemed to consider this.

"Ask him the questions, John," Elijah said through the monitor speakers.

The demon looked up from the floor to the computer. "I love this fucking show," it murmured. "I thought it was canceled."

"Are you ready?" John asked it, bringing its attention back to him.

"Sure," the demon said. "What have I got to lose?"

John found the tooth and held it out to his wife.

"This," John said.

"The tooth fairy is gonna give you at least five bucks for that beauty," the demon said, and then chuckled again.

"You know what it is."

"A small fortune," the demon said, just before his—*her*—face twisted up in pain, and the monster let out a pathetic squeak.

"Tell us," his wife's voice commanded. John was amazed at what she was doing, controlling this twisted abomination from within her own body, but he worried about her endurance. How long could she keep this one monstrosity under control, while keeping watch—and control—over so many others?

"The marks on the tooth," John said, holding it up to the demon so that he could see. "It's writing, isn't it?"

"It's writing, all right," the demon agreed.

"What does it say?"

The demon held its tongue.

"Do you want her to hurt you some more?" John asked. "I could most definitely ask her to do that for me. We have a bit of an agreement."

"Fuckers," it snarled.

"Occasionally," John agreed with a nod. "Actually, quite a bit." It was John's turn to smile. "What does it say?" he then asked, the smile quickly disappearing.

The demon simmered, its horrible eyes attempting to inflict some sort of terrible damage with the intensity of its stare.

"Theo," John said. "Hurt him really bad this time."

The demon's eyes went suddenly wide, and it began to talk.

"It's a declaration . . . ," the demon cried out.

"A declaration," Elijah repeated. "What kind of declaration?"

"A declaration of return," the demon said, his breathing becoming rapid. "He wants everybody to know that he's coming back."

"Who?" John asked. "Who's coming back?"

The demon didn't want to say, but Theo convinced him that he should. The demon fell sideways to the floor, writhing as if he'd been doused in acid. John hated to see his wife's body used in such a way, but he needed to be strong as she was being.

They needed to get their answers.

"Damakus," the demon said pitifully. She had done a job on him this last time.

"I'm not familiar," John said. "Demon?"

"A lord," the demon said. "A king."

"Mustn't have been anything too special," John said. "Never heard of him."

The demon chuckled. "Which was all part of their plan."

John waited. The demon knew that it had to explain everything that it said or Theo would—

"The other lords at the time feared him . . . feared his growing might," the demon explained, not wanting to be hurt anymore. "So they tried to erase him . . . anything and everything that knew his name was excised—wiped from the world."

"And that would hurt him?"

The demon looked disgusted by John's stupidity.

"It's how he fed . . . how he grew strong," the demon told him. "To know of Damakus was to fear him . . . that fear gave him form . . . strength . . . power."

"So to eliminate any mention of Damakus was to take away his might."

"He ceased to be," the demon said. "Or at least the lords and kings thought."

"This message," John said, presenting the tooth again. "And the message written on the other teeth . . ."

"There's more?" the demon asked, springing up from the floor. "Can I see them? How about if I said please?" The demon smiled horribly, a thick stream of something foul smelling running over Theo's bottom lip to the floor.

"Even though we can't read it," John said, "this message calls him back?"

"It's the language of Damakus, fool," the demon said. "Just to see it is to remember him . . . to call him back from the brink of the void."

"Someone is trying to call him back?" John said, realizing what this all meant.

"Oh yes," the demon responded excitedly. "And once he's back . . . once they know of him, and see his glory . . ."

The demon paused, making sure that his words were sinking in. "No one will ever forget him again, and his power will grow and grow and he will live as lord over this festering pile-of-shit world forever."

John stared at the demon wearing the guise of his wife and felt his anger surge. He'd had just about enough of this.

"We're done," he said, hoping that his wife could hear.

"Don't you want to know more?" the demon asked. "I'm sure there's all kinds of shit that you don't know . . . about how bad it's going to get around here. Damakus is only the first of your concerns."

What the demon said was tempting, but one problem at a time, John thought. They would hopefully be able to deal with Damakus, and then . . .

The demon began to squeal like a pig being dragged to the slaughterhouse, and John watched helplessly as his wife's body writhed upon the floor of his office before going suddenly still.

The sigils were flowing wildly but then began to slow, and he waited to see if she was all right.

Theo's eyes flickered open, and she let out a low, tormented moan. He could only imagine how it must have felt to have something like that within her body, never mind a thousand.

"I need to brush my teeth," she said, her face twisted up in disgust.

"That would probably be a good idea," John said. He reached down and pulled her up from the floor, taking her into his arms.

"You might not want to . . . ," she began, struggling for a moment, but succumbing to his comforting advance.

"Don't tell me what I want or don't want," he said, glad to have her back with him.

"Did that help?" she asked, face pressed to his chest.

"Yeah, I think it did," he answered.

"Damakus," Elijah said from the computer.

"Somebody is trying to bring him back," John said in review. "To know of him is to make him stronger. . . . Fear feeds him. And that same person took the children."

Theo pulled away slightly to look up at him.

"If he feeds on fear, then the missing kids . . . ," she said, obviously having the same realization that he was.

"There's a chance they might still be alive."

14

Too much whisky had left her on the sofa, startled awake to a morning of throbbing pain.

Driving down the early-morning streets of Arlington, she did her best to ignore the pounding inside her skull, as well as her aching back and joints. What she wouldn't give for a cup of coffee and a couple of Advil, but they would have to wait.

The call had come from the Boston police, a wellness check on the Fitzgerald family. The Fitzgeralds had been the first to lose their son to the kidnapper she was tracking, the police having been left strict instructions from her office to let her know of anything that might be going on with the family since their child's disappearance.

Recently they'd received a gift from the man who'd stolen their child, a crude drawing of a city on fire—the drawing having been done on a five-inch-by-six-inch piece of skin.

Brenna found a parking spot on the opposite side of the residential street, and carefully hauled herself from her car. Every joint screamed in protest, and her head joined in just to make sure that it was not forgotten. She felt suddenly nauseated and guessed that she was probably dehydrated.

Crossing the street to where multiple cruisers were parked, she was met by a patrolman who looked as pale as she felt.

"Agent Isabel?" he asked. She already had her identification out, and he quickly checked it before continuing.

"Mrs. Fitzgerald's sister had called us early this morning to do a wellness check. The sister hadn't heard from either Mr. or Mrs. Fitzgerald in the last few days. I guess they normally speak daily."

Brenna continued on to the front porch where other patrolmen waited. They all had that same pale look as she climbed the steps. They watched her, their eyes warning her—*you don't want to go in there . . . you don't want to see what we saw.*

"Go on," Brenna said, stepping through the open door into the hallway. "I'm guessing they didn't answer the door?"

"No," the patrolman said.

"So you let yourselves in," Brenna continued as she entered the kitchen, her eyes taking everything in. There was no sign of anything out of the ordinary. She saw the sink and went to it. The police officer watched her cautiously.

"Excuse me," Brenna said, grabbing a plastic cup from the strainer and turning on the water to fill it. "If I don't have a drink of water I'm going to pass out."

The officer nodded as she leaned back against the sink to swallow the cold water in multiple gulps. From where she was standing she could see into the small living room.

"In there?" she questioned, pointing out the location with the cup.

The patrolman looked briefly in the direction and then quickly looked away. He didn't want to see what was inside the living room again.

She finished her water, preparing herself for the inevitable. Rinsing the cup, she put it back in the strainer and headed through the doorway into the living room.

The Fitzgeralds had seemed like a lovely couple, but now . . .

She remembered first meeting them, how devastated they'd been. It was as if their very souls had been taken.

Brenna had understood that feeling completely, secretly studying them, wondering if they would have the strength to make it back. Wondering if they would survive this horror, or would they—*not*?

Or would they eventually become something like her?

That question was answered. She stood before them as they sat so very still on the sofa.

They would not.

The Fitzgeralds were dead, but how they had left this life was something that wasn't readily apparent. "This is exactly how you found them?" Brenna asked as she moved closer, checking for clues as to how they'd died. The couple was still dressed in their robes and pajamas. They were holding hands, but their bodies appeared mummified, as if they had died a long time ago.

"Yeah," the patrolman confirmed from the doorway, clearly not wanting to come any closer. "We came in through the back door and this was what we saw."

She took a pen from her coat pocket and moved the collar of Mr. Fitzgerald's pajamas to examine the area around the neck. There weren't any wounds to be found around the dried, wrinkled flesh on him or his wife.

It looked as though the very stuff of life had been sucked from their bodies, leaving behind these dried, withered husks.

"What could have done something like that?" the cop asked.

She didn't even have the beginning of an answer, so she remained completely quiet, staring at the corpses and remembering them as they'd been. She'd promised them that she would find their son, and now she silently reiterated that pledge.

There were more sounds from the front door, and she guessed that Forensics had arrived.

"Hello?" someone called out, and she turned to see that Grinnal had come with a few of the others from his department.

"Jesus Christ," she heard one of them mutter as they came into the living room.

Brenna stepped back, allowing them access. Grinnal looked at her, and then moved his head awkwardly in one direction. She guessed that he wanted a word in private, and gestured for him to follow her to a corner of the kitchen.

"What's up?" she asked, tempted to have some more water, but holding back for now.

"Both our asses are going to be handed to us if we don't find it pretty goddamn quick," he said, suppressing his anger.

She'd never seen Grinnal angry, or had ever even heard him raise his voice, so she was a little confused.

"What are you talking about?" she asked, keeping her voice down.

"A tooth," he said, eyeing her as if he suspected she knew all about it.

"A tooth," she repeated. "Is that supposed to mean something to me and—"

"From evidence," he hissed. "There were twenty, and now there are only nineteen. One of the teeth is missing. I checked all over, just to be sure, and realized that I last saw the full set . . ."

She remembered the last time she had handled all the teeth.

"Got it," she said. "Let me look into this." She was mulling over the fact, feeling her anger rising.

"You'd better," Grinnal stressed angrily. "If anybody comes looking and finds that—"

"I told you I'll handle it," she snapped, the intensity of her gaze shutting the squirrelly forensics specialist down.

Brenna left him standing in the Fitzgeralds' kitchen and headed for the door.

She had a visit to make, and a piece of evidence to reclaim.

. . .

John placed a red pushpin in the center of Chicago on the map he'd hung haphazardly on the wall, stepped back, and stared.

How is this possible? he wondered, looking at the locations where all the children had been taken from. Looking at the dates and times, John found it nearly impossible for the children's abductor to make it from these locations across the country even if he or she owned a private jet. Maybe something with warp speed, but seeing as that—as far as he knew—hadn't been invented yet . . .

Theo came to stand beside him, staring at the map intensely.

"Perhaps there's more than one follower of Damakus," he mused aloud. "All of them collecting their victims and then bringing them back to—"

"No," Theo answered, eyes still affixed to the map. "He chooses a single herald to spread his name, a disciple, but only one who is truly worthy of the task."

John looked at her. "And you know this . . . ?"

"Having bonded with the demon . . . I know things now," she said, still looking at the map. "Things that I didn't know before."

"So this is the work of one person," John said. "But how?"

He glanced over to see that Theo's face was scrunched up, which gave him the impression that she was either in pain, thinking incredibly hard, or . . .

"John," someone called out, and he temporarily looked away from his wife to see Stephan peeking into the office. He looked quite concerned.

"What is it, Stephan?" he asked, moving away from his wife.

"Ah, I tried to hold her off, but—"

The door was pushed wider as Agent Isabel stormed in around the personal assistant.

"Thanks so much," she said to Stephan.

John gave him a look that said that they would be having a long discussion about this later.

"She has a gun," Stephan explained in a panicked hiss. "And something tells me she's not afraid to use it."

"Thanks, Steph," John said. "I'll take it from here."

His assistant quickly backed out, closing the door behind him.

"Agent Isabel," John said. "Coffee?" he offered, moving across the room to where a coffeemaker sat gurgling. "I just made a fresh pot."

"No, thank you," she said curtly. "I'm here about the—"

"I was just about ready to call you," he said, taking his mug from his desk and bringing it over to the coffeepot. He filled his cup.

"How convenient," she said. "Guess I saved you the call."

"My wife and I . . ."

Theodora turned from the map to look at the woman, noticing for the first time that somebody else was there.

"Your wife?" Agent Isabel questioned. "I thought she was . . ."

"She's feeling a good deal better," John said. "Isn't that right, Theo?"

Theo stared at the woman for a little too long, and John was about to intervene when—

"Agent Isabel," Theodora said, coming forward to shake her hand. "It's a pleasure."

The FBI special agent and John's wife shook hands. "Nice to see that you're feeling better," Agent Isabel said.

"Yes," Theo responded with a brief smile, turning away and going back to the map.

"We believe that we may have found a motive for the kidnappings based on the evidence you've shared," John said, holding his steaming mug of coffee before him.

"Ah yes, evidence," Agent Isabel said as she moved closer.

John guessed what she was getting at, and why she looked so angry, but hoped to deter her wrath with facts that would move the case forward. "We believe that the kidnapper is a worshipper of an ancient demonic entity called—"

"I could arrest you now," Agent Isabel interrupted him. "Slap the cuffs on you and haul your ass to federal prison."

"I'm sure that you're more than capable of all sorts of unpleasant-ries," John said. "But if you care to listen—"

"I trusted you, but I shouldn't have," Isabel continued, not want-ing to let it go.

"I know what this is about, and I shouldn't have done it, but in this line of investigation—"

"You couldn't have asked?"

"You would have said no," John said flatly.

She thought for a moment, shrugged, and went on. "Perhaps, but if you'd stated your case—"

"You would have said no," John said again even more forcefully.

"By stealing that evidence you've jeopardized this case, and your standing with the FBI, never mind my own reputation with—"

"Are we done with this?" It was John's turn to interrupt, tired of the nonsense. There wasn't time for it. "If we are, we can move on to what we've learned, and what we believe our kidnapper is up to."

Agent Isabel glared, flesh-singeing laser beams shooting from her eyes. "This is not over," she said with an angry snarl. "But I would be remiss in my duty and my responsibilities to all the parents whose children are missing if I didn't listen."

She crossed her arms, waiting for him to continue.

"As I was attempting to explain before," John said, "we believe the kidnapper is a servant of an ancient, demonic god called Damakus, a god whose existence had been believed wiped from history . . . until now."

Isabel's brow furrowed. "A demonic god," she said, adjusting to the concept. "If this demon god was wiped from existence, how did our kidnapper know . . . ?"

"We're not a hundred percent sure, but we think that Damakus has somehow reached out to our perpetrator and—"

"Damakus reached out?" she asked.

"He wasn't quite as dead as the other demon lords and kings thought," Theo answered.

Agent Isabel looked at them as if they were both totally insane.

"Hear us out before you have us both committed," John said. She went quiet, doing as he asked, but he saw that his time was limited.

"We believe that the demon lord reached out to this individual and gave him a purpose, that purpose being to collect children, to teach them about Damakus. And in learning about him, learning to fear him."

She was glaring at him.

"That fear and belief would then aid in bringing him back into reality."

Agent Isabel laughed out loud. "I can't believe I'm standing here listening to this bullshit."

"Call it what you want, but that's what we think is happening," John explained. "We read the tooth. It's part of a proclamation—an announcement that Damakus is coming back from the brink of the nonexistence that he'd been banished to."

"You read the tooth?"

"It's one of the reasons that I needed the actual item," he explained. "Our methods here are a bit unusual sometimes and . . ."

Isabel stepped back, turning away from them. He wasn't sure if she was getting ready to leave, or . . .

She turned back, seeming to be struggling with a concept, an idea.

"The families," Agent Isabel began.

"What about them?"

"A connection has always been maintained between the kidnapper and the parents of the children," she stated.

"Yes," John agreed. "The objects delivered to the parents were, I believe, part of this ritual of returning Damakus from—"

"I think they're being targeted now," she interrupted, her demeanor changing. "I've just come from the home of the first kidnapping victim. The parents are dead."

"Dead?" John asked. "Care to elaborate?"

She thought for a moment. "I've spent time with this couple. They were probably in their mid to late thirties, but the bodies that were found . . ."

Agent Isabel stopped to consider her next words, and John Fogg tensed.

"The bodies looked hundreds of years old—mummified."

John looked over to his wife. "That isn't good," he said.

"Not good at all," Theo agreed. "The disciple is harvesting. . . . There won't be much time now before—"

"Harvesting," Agent Isabel interrupted. "What does that mean?"

"It means that Damakus is close," Theo said. "The fear and belief of the families chosen are being collected—harvested—in order to return him to life."

"Damakus . . . a demon is coming back to life?" Isabel asked, as if saying it out loud would help her wrap her brain around the insane concept.

"As crazy as it sounds," John said, "that's what we think is happening."

He knew that there was something different about Agent Brenna Isabel, that she suspected that the world was changing, that darkness was becoming that much stronger.

She walked closer to them, turning her attention to the map.

"So the kidnapper . . . this disciple of Damakus," she said. "He's harvesting."

"Yeah, I think he is," John said.

"Then there's a chance," she said, still eyeing the map. "There's a chance that the kids . . ." Her voice trailed off.

"That the children are still alive," John finished for her. "Yes, I do believe that's a possibility."

"We need to find them," Agent Isabel said, a sound of desperation in her tone. "We have to find where he's taken them before . . ."

She didn't want to believe what they had told her. John could see this in the way she hesitated, but there wasn't any other way around it. A demon lord was attempting to return to life.

"Before Damakus can be reborn," John finished, so she didn't have to.

Agent Brenna Isabel hung up her cell phone after communicating with the last of the police departments connected to families of the missing children. She'd informed them to be on full alert for anything out of the ordinary, that the kidnapper might be returning to the scenes of the crimes.

She'd gone no further than that, not quite sure how she would have explained the resurrection of an ancient demon lord.

"Can I get you anything?"

Brenna turned to see Stephan.

"No, thank you," she said, sliding the phone into the pocket of her dark blazer.

"A sandwich maybe? Or a bottle of water?" he suggested. "It's no problem really."

She smiled at his kindness as she stood outside Fogg's office door. She could hear Fogg and his wife talking heatedly inside.

"So, how long have you worked for them?" she asked, pointing toward the door.

"John and Theo?" he asked, thinking a moment. "I think it's been close to six years now."

She nodded slowly.

"You want to know what it's like, don't you?" he asked.

"Yes, I do."

"It's different—unlike any other job I've had before." He smiled, nodding.

She looked to the door again, and then back to him.

"Are they nuts?" she asked. It came across as joking, but there was a vein of truth to it. She needed to know—she needed to be sure. There was a part of her that hoped that they were. It would have made things so much easier, but deep down she knew.

"They're probably a little bit crazy, yeah," Stephan answered. "But at the same time I've never seen two people more dedicated to the field of paranormal research. Even after the Halloween event—"

Brenna went rigid with the mention of the holiday, immediately thinking of her own situation. The image of her baby son lying perfectly still in his crib exploded inside her head, and she couldn't get it to leave no matter how hard she tried.

"Are you all right?" Stephan asked. "Do you want to sit down?" He took her arm as she found herself starting to swoon.

"No, I'm good," she said, getting a hold of herself. "But maybe I will take that water if it's not too much bother."

He excused himself as she pulled herself together. She'd known that there was some sort of accident that Fogg and his television crew had been in, but never made the connection with the fact that it had happened that last Halloween night.

The same night that her son . . .

The voices inside the office had grown a bit louder, and she moved toward the door, knocking before she entered.

"Is everything all right in here?" she asked.

Theodora was standing at her husband's desk, holding something in her hand. It took her a second, but Brenna realized what it was.

The missing piece of evidence. The tooth.

"Hey, that's—" she began.

"You need to put that down, Theo," John said, moving toward his wife.

"I have to do this," she said, backing away. "The longer we wait, the less chance we'll have of finding them alive."

"She's talking about the kids, right?" Brenna asked. "What is she getting at, John?"

"My wife wants to do something that I feel might be dangerous to her health," John explained. "Theo, please . . ." He held out his hand to her, moving his fingers for her to hand the tooth over.

"I need to do this, John. I'm sorry," she said, backing into the corner of the room and popping the tooth into her mouth as if eating a breath mint.

"What is she doing?" Brenna asked, now moving in her direction as well.

She began to chew, the crunching sounds emanating from inside her mouth sounding incredibly painful.

"She's eating our evidence," Brenna said, not believing what she was seeing.

Stephan came into the room with her bottle of water and immediately froze.

"What's going on?" he asked.

No one answered as Theodora's eyes rolled back into her head, and she went limp, falling to the floor.

Brenna reacted, moving toward the unconscious woman. John's hand shot out, grabbing her by the arm, stopping her from reaching his wife.

"What are you doing?" she asked. "Something's wrong—she's probably choking. We need to—"

"She's not choking," he said with a sad shake of his head.

"Well, whatever's happening, we have to help her," Brenna said, yanking her arm back.

"I wouldn't get too close," John warned.

She was about to ignore him and help the woman but noticed something strange. The tattoos that covered quite a bit of the woman's flesh appeared to be moving. The woman's body had begun to vibrate, every inch of her thrumming so powerfully that Brenna could feel it through the soles of her shoes on the hardwood floors.

"All right, spill it, John," she said, backing up ever so slightly. "What the hell is happening?"

"My wife is afflicted with an unusual condition," John started.

They were both watching her now, the dark markings flowing on her skin like ink injected into water. And then her limbs began to snap—to bend in impossible positions—to change.

"John, that's . . . that's not normal," Brenna said, watching in awe as the woman's body reconfigured, becoming something . . .

"No, it's not," John said. "The night of the incident—"

Halloween. It happened on Halloween. For a moment she saw her son, lying in his crib. Did she remember him dead or alive?

"She became inhabited . . . possessed by a number of demonic entities."

The woman's changing body flipped, landing on her stomach, where her newly elongated limbs lifted her onto all fours. She resembled some sort of giant reptile now, a purplish forked tongue shooting out snakelike to taste the air.

It was taking everything Brenna had not to pull out her gun and shoot the horrible thing dead.

"Recently, with the help of some—associates—we were able to gain some control over the problem."

The woman's body had continued to shift and alter, spiny protrusions pushing out from her already bruised flesh, giving her a strange, armored appearance.

"This is control?" Brenna asked, not liking the sound of panic she heard creeping into her tone.

John's wife sprang up to her feet, the sound of her spine snapping, popping, and reconfiguring incredibly grotesque.

"Hello, fuckers," the woman said through a mouthful of incredibly sharp teeth, a thick stream of bloody drool oozing from the corners of her mouth to puddle at her clawed feet.

Brenna went purely on instinct, pulling her gun from its holster and aiming.

"There's the gun," Stephan said from the far corner of the room where he cowered. Brenna hadn't remembered that he was there.

"I hope that won't be necessary," John said, moving over to her.

The monstrous woman laughed to herself, admiring her new form by holding out her long, spindly arms and flexing her spiderlike hands.

Brenna continued to aim; a head shot would probably be best.

"Put that fucking thing away," the demonic woman roared, stretching her neck incredibly long to glare at her.

John moved toward his wife.

"Theo," he said. "Theo, are you there?"

The demonic entity glared at him with yellow, red-rimmed eyes.

"She wants to be," the demon said in a low, ominous tone. "But I've decided to—"

The demonically afflicted woman went suddenly rigid, her terrible eyes going wide. She shook her head wildly from side to side, sending tendrils of thick, bloody mucus through the air as she did.

Brenna aimed down the sight of the weapon, just in case, but the monstrous woman suddenly grew calm, turning her attention back to them.

"You can lower the weapon, Agent Isabel," Theodora Knight said, though her voice did sound somewhat strange—raw and ragged. "I'm in control now."

Theo held out her hands, moving the long, clawed fingers, examining what her body had become.

"This is awful," she said in a sad, sad whisper.

"What the hell's happened to you?" Brenna asked, lowering her weapon, but not by much. Still, just in case.

"Let's just say I've gotten in touch with my inner demon," Theo said. "Or at least one of them."

Brenna's phone started to ring, and she was tempted not to answer, but . . .

"Yeah," she said, lowering her gun even more and turning her back to them for privacy. The voice on the other end was from the main office, rattling off information that made her brain hurt.

They wanted her to come in, to return to the office to regroup, but she knew that wouldn't help.

She hung up even as the person on the other end continued to talk. She would have to make up some story about her phone, how it had for some reason cut out, refusing to work.

"The disciple or whatever the hell you want to call him has tried again," she announced to the room, John and his wife looking at her. "Multiple attempts over the last hour or so in multiple states."

"And was he successful?" Theo asked.

Brenna shook her head. "No, local law enforcement was ready and waiting," she said, thinking again about what she had been told over the phone. "Shots were reportedly fired in each of the attempts, and the perpetrator was hit."

"Let me guess," John said. "No body was found at any of the scenes."

"How is that even possible?" Brenna asked, feeling her grip of reality loosening that much more. "All over the country in a matter of an hour, hit by multiple gunshots?"

She waited for something—*anything*—to be said to return the world to some semblance of normalcy, but doubted that it was coming anytime soon.

"I'd say Damakus is very eager to return," John said. "Which leads me to believe that our timetable has likely been sped up."

"Which is why I did this," Theo stressed, holding out her arms and showing the state of her form. "One of the things inside me. This thing." She looked at what she had become again with total disgust. "It is a tracker . . . a bloodhound of the demonic. With a single drop of blood . . . a strand of hair, a fingernail . . ."

"Or a tooth," Brenna added.

Theo slowly nodded. "It could track the little one from whom it was taken to the ends of the Earth."

She then dropped to the floor and extended her neck and head. There came an awful, regurgitating type of sound, followed by the smacking of lips.

"Do I even want to know what you just did?" Brenna asked.

"No," Stephan called from the back of the room. "I would rather we didn't."

Theo's head began to move from left to right, her enlarged nostrils flaring as she attempted to capture the desired scent.

Still on all fours, the woman scampered from the office incredibly fast, stopping outside on the landing to test the air again. She jumped over the railing, falling to the foyer below.

"Follow her," John said, and he and Brenna took a more conventional path down the stairs.

Theo had already found her way outside the house and was squatting on the lawn, head tossed back, her eyes closed.

"Well?" Brenna asked, coming up behind her.

"He's gone," Theo said. "I've lost him."

"I thought you said that you could track him anywhere on Earth?" Brenna asked angrily.

"Anywhere on Earth," Theo said, turning her elongated neck to look at her. "He's not on Earth anymore."

15

Christopher Waugh was dying. They all were.

The boy sat in his seat, in the stifling heat and stink of the classroom, trying to keep his eyes from closing, fearing what would follow if he should fall asleep.

He looked around the room at the others and felt his hope begin to slip away. They were dying. He was dying.

There was a part of him that wanted to quit, to give in and escape this living nightmare.

The sound of something splashing in the tank behind him made him sit rigidly upright in his chair. The thing that had been inside the Teacher's stomach was becoming more active. Christopher knew that it could very easily escape the fish tank, throwing its horrible form over the side of the tank and slithering across the floor to get them.

The thought was terrifying, and the more he imagined it, the more active the thing in the tank at the back of the room seemed to become. It was as if the thing could sense his fear.

Christopher attempted to calm himself, to remember a time when he wasn't in this terrible place.

The thing in the tank continued to splash, slapping its many arms against the glass. It was hungry. Christopher could practically hear its thoughts inside his head. Damakus was hungry and soon they would all be food to sustain his awesome glory.

For a moment that seemed perfectly fine to him. Perfectly reasonable. They were all here for Damakus. . . .

The thing in the tank was inside his head and he found himself sickened by its psychic touch. Christopher screamed briefly, nothing more than a pathetic yelp really, bringing his forehead down as hard as he could upon his desktop to drive away the squirming sensations inside his head.

He knew that this was the beginning of his end, that the thing in the tank—Damakus—would slither itself into their brains and prepare them for their deaths. They were going to be its sacrifice, one of the final steps of returning the creature—this god—to its former glory.

As it had been inside his head, Christopher had gotten a glimpse of what was inside the creature's.

Did it even have a head? He didn't think so.

The question was enough of a distraction for him to begin to panic. He didn't want to die, and he knew that if he didn't do something very quickly, that would most certainly be his fate.

He could feel it trying to slither even farther into the crevices of his brain, to assure him that everything was just fine, but Christopher didn't want to hear it.

The boy decided that he had to do something. He had to get away from this room—from this building—from the thing inside the tank.

Damakus.

He reached beneath his desk, grabbing hold of the filthy chain and pulling with all his might. It was foolish for him to try—he already knew that, having done the same thing over and over again—and still the chain was too strong.

But he knew that the answer to his problem was somehow connected. The chain was what kept him here, in this room.

The chain.

Christopher slid out of his chair again to the floor beneath his desk. He'd done this all before, but he could not help himself as he inspected each and every link of the chain, stopping at the metal ring that encircled his boney ankle.

He grabbed at the circle, turning it around on the chafed skin above his foot. Christopher became entranced, staring at the metal cuff, wondering if the thoughts that were taking shape inside his mind could be translated into some form of reality.

He knew that he had lost weight since being brought here, since the ring had been placed around his ankle. The ring was sized for how he had been.

Not how he was now.

He sat on the floor and pulled his foot closer to him. Grabbing the ring, he attempted to pull it down over his heel, but there was still too much foot.

But not as much as there had been before.

The fact of too much foot did not deter him, and he continued to pull down upon the ring, twisting and turning with all his might. The process was painful, and he temporarily considered any alternative, but there wasn't anything else at the moment.

Christopher continued to work, trying to ignore the pain and think of how things would be when he was able to escape. The thoughts of his murdered father just fueled his efforts all the more, giving him that little bit of extra strength to try and force the ring down over the top of his foot and heel.

Time was his enemy. He had no idea when the teacher might return. The pain was making him dizzy, but something told him that if he was to stop he would never begin again and he would die here with all the other students.

The thing in the tank at the back of the room became more active, splashing about in its filthy habitat.

Christopher's heart raced, and he was panting from the exertion.

Wouldn't it be better if you slowed down for a bit? asked a voice from somewhere inside his skull. *Wait a few minutes for the pain to recede and then—*No.

His actions became all the more furious. He wondered if the others noticed what he was doing, roused from their stupor to see that he was going to try and live, that he was not content to sit here and eventually die, sacrificed to whatever that nasty thing in the tank—

It responded violently, throwing its muscular form against the aquarium glass. *Is it trying to get out?* Christopher wondered. *Is it trying to break free to stop me from—*

He chanced a fleeting glimpse at his foot, and nearly died then and there from the shock of what he saw.

An empty metal ring.

It took a moment for that to sink in, to permeate through the cloud of agony.

The ring was no longer around his ankle. Christopher wasn't sure if he was seeing that properly, maneuvering himself on the filthy wooden floor for a closer look, just to be certain.

Yes. Yes, the ring was empty.

He was free. He'd done it. He was free.

He scrambled to his feet, expecting the others to be watching him with curiosity, but they remained silent and still, heads down on their desktops.

Waiting for their end.

The thing in the tank called to him, a horrible tickling sensation, an itch that he was unable to scratch.

Holding on to the side of his desk, he cautiously looked toward the back of the classroom where the tank waited. The thing in the filthy water watched him, multiple sets of yellow eyes pressed to the glass.

It compelled him to come closer, but Christopher chose instead to look toward the front of the room, and the open doorway beyond it.

"I'm leaving," Christopher announced to anyone who was listening, moving out into the center of the classroom aisle and almost falling.

The pain in his foot was nearly crippling, but he couldn't let that stop him. He had his eye on the prize, and that prize was the open doorway and an eventual path to freedom.

He was limping crazily, but he was making progress.

He was getting closer to the doorway.

With that realization the thing in the tank surged up out of the filthy water, thick black tentacles covered in razor-sharp spines glistening in the faint light of the room as they hung over the lip of the aquarium.

It beckoned to him, the thing that would eventually become a god extending its muscular limbs and calling him back. Again he felt it inside his head, telling him to return to his seat, that all would be fine if he only came back.

Christopher actually caught himself turning back, but then he saw her. The little girl with no teeth had raised her head, and was looking at him with dark, hollow eyes.

Go, she mouthed.

And he did as she told him, practically throwing himself toward the open doorway and the darkness behind it. He would do it for her. He would get out into the world and bring people to help her and the others, before it was too late.

Christopher experienced a surge of strength, adrenaline coursing through his veins as he made it out into the hallway of the schoolhouse. He had no idea of the size of the place and was surprised to see how small it was. It was practically a one-room structure, like something that would have been used in the olden days, he thought as he searched the darkened hall for an exit.

There was a door up ahead of him, the exit sign above it dark. He limped to the door, slamming all his body weight against the metal bar and pushing it open to freedom.

Freedom.

Christopher wobbled upon the top concrete step that led down into . . .

Nothing.

There was some grass that circled around the front and to the back of the building, but beyond that there was . . .

Nothing.

It looked like fog, but it was more than that.

Or less.

He carefully stepped down to the grass, limping to where it suddenly stopped, peering into the white of . . .

Nothing.

Balancing on one leg, Christopher shoved his hand into the wall of white. It was incredibly cold within and he quickly pulled back.

His thoughts were a jumble as he studied the area, the schoolhouse sitting on top of a small piece of land, an island in a sea of . . .

Nothing.

At first Christopher wasn't sure what was happening; it had been so long since he'd last experienced the warmth of the fluids spilling from his eyes.

Tears. He was crying. He hadn't used them all up after all.

It was no consolation as he stood there before the wall of shifting white, trying to understand where he was. Christopher was so deep in thought that he didn't hear the sound of the Teacher's arrival.

"And what do we have here?" the Teacher asked, stepping from the cold embrace of nothing onto the grassy island.

The boy jumped back, losing his balance and falling to the grass.

The Teacher's filthy clothing was covered in blood and pocked with holes. He strode across the ground to loom over Christopher, two bubblelike spheres undulating in the air around the man's head. They reminded Christopher of jellyfish that he'd seen on a school field trip the previous year.

"You," the Teacher said with a snarl, obviously remembering the trouble that Christopher had caused before. "I'm surprised, really," he said, reaching down to grab him by the front of his pajama top and haul him up to his feet.

Christopher's eyes were drawn to the bullet hole in the middle of the Teacher's forehead, but he forced himself to instead watch the strange spheres that floated around the Teacher's head. They were like bubbles of very thin skin, and he could see that something moved around frantically inside the weightless globules, as if trying to escape.

"You almost make me doubt my skills as an educator," the Teacher said, tossing Christopher over his shoulder and heading back for the schoolhouse.

"But that just means I'll need to work a little harder."

"What the hell does that mean?" Agent Isabel asked frantically.

Theodora listened to the woman's question. She'd fallen forward to the ground outside the house, trying to return her body to its human shape. To push the demon back where it belonged.

"He's not here anymore," she said in between pained grunts and the popping of joints. "He's not here . . . or at least the child isn't."

The FBI special agent looked around, not quite sure what she should be doing now.

John came to kneel beside her.

"Are you all right?" he asked, concern in his tone.

Theo started to stand, her spine cracking noisily as it returned to its natural—*human*—shape.

"If he's not here . . . on Earth, where?" Agent Isabel asked, confused by the whole affair. "Mars? Is he on fucking Mars?"

Theo shook her head. "I don't know," she said. "The child isn't on this plane of reality," she attempted to explain.

"What the fuck is that supposed to mean?" the agent asked again, not understanding this in the least.

"It means exactly what she said," John said, coming to his wife's defense. "Somehow the child has been taken away from this reality to another. That probably explains how he's been able to travel unnoticed all over the country in such short periods of time to collect his victims."

Agent Isabel listened, tried to digest, but obviously had little luck.

"You've completely lost me," she said. "Are you saying that our perpetrator could be on some other planet or something? That he could actually be on Mars?"

"Not another planet," Theo interjected. "Another plane of reality . . . another dimension. A world that exists alongside this one . . . another side."

Theo watched the woman. She seemed to get smaller, crushed beneath the weight of this latest revelation.

"So there's no way to get to him . . . to track the children," she said.

"I'm sure there's a way," John said. "But it would probably take days of research to find exactly what we're searching for, and by then it will likely be too late."

Theo could see the frustration working on her husband as well.

And then she heard the laughing somewhere deep inside her skull. The demons were amused by their human antics, their human perception of things. She silenced them with a thought, but there was one voice that remained. One that said that it just might have answers to their questions.

She moved away from the others.

"Theo?" her husband called to her.

"So, what now?" Agent Isabel demanded to know. "Do we just sit around and wait for some resurrected demon god to show up and—"

"You don't want that," Theo heard her husband say. "That would be very bad."

Theodora ignored the sounds of her husband's concerns, standing alone in a patch of darkness to reach out.

To communicate.

"Theo," she heard John call to her again.

"John, please—just a moment," she said angrily, holding out a hand to stop his progress.

She let her thoughts go, traveling inside her mind to the deep darkness where they waited.

Where answers might still be found.

The demons had gone deep, driven to hide in the nooks and crannies of her subconscious.

"I'm here," she announced, the sigils on her flesh creating a shimmering corona of yellowish orange around her.

She knew they were there, watching her silently, and she extended a hand to disperse the light from her body so that she might see them.

They were there as she sensed, a sea of evil and inhumanity, the ones closer to where she stood shielding their horrible eyes from the discomfort caused by her inner light.

A thousand demons. This was the number that inhabited her body, a fact that suddenly filled her head.

One of them was being cute, reaching out, providing her with answers to questions she had pondered.

"Well?" she said, looking at them all, showing them that she was unafraid.

And the demons stared back, but not as afraid as she imagined they should be.

"Which one of you is it?" she asked. "Which one of you wants to talk?"

They looked at one another, these horrible manifestations of evil, and eventually all turned their attentions back to her.

"All right, then," she said, her patience waning. "I could force you—hurt each and every one of you—but I just don't have the time."

She had begun to withdraw, to return to the physical world, when she noticed across the sea of the demonic that a fissure was starting to form. That something was moving down the center of them, the monstrosities parting to let it pass.

Theo paused her return to the physical and waited.

The demons in front moved to either side, and a child emerged.

Theodora gasped, feeling a violent knife stab of emotion in her heart.

"You wicked, wicked things," she muttered beneath her breath, wishing then and there that she was capable of killing them all in the most horrid and painful ways possible.

There was snickering amongst the demons as the child presented himself.

"I would have thought you would be comforted by this form," the demon wearing the shape of Billy Sharp said.

Theodora glared, her anger simmering.

Billy Sharp had lived next door to the Knights when she was a young girl, a lovely little boy with a contagious smile and a mischievous way about him, who died two weeks before his sixth birthday from drowning.

Only a few years older herself at the time, Theodora remembered the nearly overpowering sadness at the loss of the younger child whom she treated like her baby brother.

It had always bothered her that neither she nor her mother had been able to communicate with the dead child's spirit. That he seemed to have moved on to the afterlife without a trace.

"I found the image of the child just *floating* around your psyche and believed that it would put you at ease," the demon wearing Billy's form said. "It appears that I was mistaken."

"You found him just floating around, did you?" she asked, reacting to the cruelty of the demon's specific words, but what would one expect from a demon?

"Perhaps we should do this another time," the demon said, starting to make his way back into the monstrous crowd.

"Wait," she called to it. She hated to think of it as a child—as Billy.

The demon stopped, turning toward her again. She noticed that he was wearing the striped shirt, short pants, and running shoes that Billy had been wearing on the day he died.

"You hinted that there might be answers to a particular quandary we are experiencing," she continued.

The little boy slowly nodded. "There very well might be," he said.

"And do you know what that problem is?" she asked.

"We know all your problems," the demon said, smiling with the beatific face of a child.

"Don't fuck with me," Theo warned, her anger simmering just below the surface.

"Wouldn't dream of it," the demon child said.

The others roared, laughed, shrieked, and tittered their amusement, and the child turned his attention toward them.

"Silence," he commanded, and they did as they were told.

Who was this mysterious demonic presence to warrant such a level of respect? Or was it something more akin to fear? Theodora wondered.

The child looked back at her, the expression he now wore vacant of any sign of innocence.

"You and your people are searching for the disciple of Damakus," Billy said in a matter-of-fact tone. "But he's not to be found on the earthly plane. Oh where, oh where could he be?"

"That is most certainly the question," Theo said. "Lives are at stake," she added. "The lives of children."

"Yum," Billy said, and for a brief instant his baby teeth were razor sharp and plentiful.

"Don't," she began.

"I know, I know," Billy said. "Don't fuck with you."

"Well?" she demanded, growing tired of the dance. "Do you have answers for me or not?"

"It all depends," Billy said.

"On?"

"On what you can do for me."

Theo laughed at the monster's audacity. "Seriously?" she asked. She extended her bare arms, presenting her sigils, the light that they threw bathing the child and the front row of demons behind him.

"You sound as though you've forgotten who's in charge now," she said.

The demons recoiled from the searing light, but the child stayed, averting his gaze ever so slightly.

"I've done no such thing," Billy said. "Please," he asked her, motioning for her to turn the illumination away. "If you wouldn't mind, it makes it difficult to speak."

Theo lowered her arms.

"I want that information," she stated.

"And I will give it to you willingly," Billy said. His face had blistered where her light had touched him. "If you will do something for me—for us."

She shook her head. "No."

The force of the child's gaze was like being punched.

"I'd be lying if I said I wasn't disappointed," Billy said. "But it is your choice."

He turned and started to leave, the demons parting to let him pass.

"Where do you think you're going?" she asked. "I didn't say you could leave."

He stopped but didn't turn. "If you must know, I'm returning to my little pocket of shadow nestled nicely inside what remains of your soul."

"You're going nowhere without telling me what I need to know," Theo said.

Billy turned.

"I could tell you everything, but it would do you little good," he said.

She didn't quite understand but said nothing, not wanting to show any weakness.

"You need me to comply—us to comply," he said, motioning with tiny hands to the demonic gathering about him. "We could give you the knowledge . . . the talent to traverse the veil," Billy explained. "To open a door normally closed to one such as you."

She glowered at the demon wearing the form of her dead friend.

"I could force you," she said, her hands clenched into trembling fists. The sigils glowed all the hotter in her frustration.

"You could try," Billy said. "But I'd be willing to bet that you would have nothing for your troubles when it was all said and done."

"I could try," Theo stressed.

"And for that you would be commended," Billy said. "Even though it would be useless."

They stood like that for a while, neither wanting to budge, but then she thought about the children who could very well still be among the living, and the fate that awaited them if the disciple was to finish his chores.

"What is it you want?" she asked.

Billy almost smiled but seemed to know better.

"We ask for only one thing," he said.

"What?"

"Permission."

"Permission for what?"

And Billy's smile grew wider, and wider still, and she listened to what the demon wanted, and what only she could grant them.

And the answer she gave was—

Yes.

. . .

John knelt beside his wife.

He watched her carefully for signs, paying extra-close attention to the markings on her flesh. They had been flowing—realigning—quite heavily for a moment, but now appeared to be calming.

"What's wrong with her now?" Agent Isabel wanted to know.

"Hey," John called, leaning in to the woman he loved, placing a comforting hand upon her back.

Her eyes were closed, and she appeared as though she might be asleep.

"Maybe we should get her inside," Isabel suggested, coming to assist him.

"Give it a sec," John said, watching his wife.

"Those kids don't have a second, John," Isabel answered sharply.

His wife's eyes opened.

"No, they don't," she said, rising to her feet.

"What's up?" John asked her.

"Are you two ready?" his wife asked them, moving to a more open area alongside the house.

John looked at Agent Isabel.

"Ready for what?" she asked.

"I've got our answer," she said, and John noticed the pained expression on her normally beautiful features. "The solution to the problem."

"What did you do, Theo?" he asked, concerned.

"Doesn't matter," she said, shaking her head. "Are you ready?"

"Yeah," Isabel said. "Yeah, we're ready."

John wasn't sure what he was supposed to be ready for, but he guessed that now was probably as good a time as any, especially with the lives of children at risk.

Theo wasn't waiting any longer, standing there, her posture sort of crouched. It looked as though she were getting ready to jump—to leap from the tallest cliff into oblivion.

And in a strange kind of way, she was.

He knew where she had been moments ago, the darkness inside her so tempting with its twisted power. She had gone back to the well for further answers, and appeared to have found what they were looking for.

But at what cost?

"Come closer," Theo summoned them, her eyes focused on an area of open air directly in front of her.

He could see that her body was trembling, and yes, the sigils were on the move, flowing and swirling in an attempt to keep up with the dark power that was attempting to manifest.

She let out a horrible, pained moan, and he wanted nothing more than to take her in his arms, to comfort her, and lend her some of his own strength to endure whatever the task was that she was attempting.

"All right, you twisted fucks," Theo snarled.

Agent Isabel looked at John, but he knew that his wife wasn't talking to them; instead she was addressing those that infested her soul, those that had somehow provided an answer to the problems now confronting them. And again he considered the high cost of such knowledge.

"Give me what you promised," Theo demanded, and then emitted a low, thrumming growl, as what—*who*—she was speaking to finally responded.

Her arms shot out before her as if beckoning for some invisible offering. John winced, and held back his need to go to her when the sounds of cracking bone and morphing flesh again filled the air.

Theo's arms grew incredibly long, and John was reminded of the front limbs of a praying mantis. Her hands expanded, doubling in size as each finger grew longer, her fingernails turning to claws, the tips becoming crystalline and razor sharp.

"Jesus Christ, John," he heard Agent Isabel say beside him as she watched the latest transformation before them.

He didn't respond, unable to find the words. Tears streamed down from his wife's eyes, and he was compelled to stop whatever it was that she was doing, but he couldn't. She had done this for them . . . for the missing children . . . and he couldn't allow what she had sacrificed to be for naught.

Long black spines had erupted from her back, sparks of electricity arcing from their ends to dance in the air above her head. It was this power that she seemed to require, reaching up behind her with obscenely long arms to pull the threads of crackling energy from the air. And in her monstrously altered hands, begin to manipulate this strange power.

To begin to create something.

The crystalline claws at the ends of each elongated finger teased the bluish energy, stretching and kneading the humming substance, and then adding to it from the source leaking from the spines on her back.

John was reminded of a spider as it wove its silken strands, making a web—or imprisoning its prey. He watched in a combination of horror and wonder at what his wife was creating. At first he couldn't quite understand what it was, but as the shape grew, he saw that the crackling strands of unearthly energy were being knitted together to form a kind of hole.

A passage from this reality to another.

The doorway hung within the air, humming and crackling like an impending summer storm.

"I don't understand," Agent Isabel said as she stared at the pulsating circle of darkness as it floated there weightlessly.

"There's very little to understand," Theo said, her words garbled because her mouth was now filled with far too many teeth. "We need to get to where the disciple is performing the final ritual . . . where he has taken the children. This will bring us there."

As Theo spoke she continued to weave, her long, spindly arms moving in the air as if she were conducting some silent orchestra.

The opening in time and space grew steadily larger, and soon was emitting a mournful moaning sound. Theo moved back from the passage, a corona of cracking energy surrounding an iris of absolute black.

"It's done," she said, admiring her demonic craftsmanship with a tilt of her head.

"Yeah," Agent Isabel said warily. "Now what are we supposed to do?"

John walked close, feeling the pull of the hole in reality. "We go through," he said.

"I don't know if I can do that," the FBI special agent said, stepping back.

"Do you want to stop this guy . . . save those kids if possible?" John asked her.

She remained silent, but her eyes said everything.

Theo darted in front of him, pushing him out of the way as she plunged her mantislike arms into the blackness of the passage.

"I'll go first," she said, drawing her body toward the center, and finally she was gone, passing into the eye to the other side.

"Are you coming?" John asked, about to follow his wife. "I hope that you are, because I don't have a gun or any weapons."

Agent Isabel hesitated, coming forward but stopping. She was scared, and he didn't blame her. Feeling the pull of the passage before him, John held out his hand to her.

"C'mon," he said.

He still wasn't sure how she was going to react, but she quickly came forward and took hold of his hand in a bone-breaking grip. And without further hesitation, they dove into the center of the opening, which would supposedly take them to another plane of reality.

Together.

16

"Hello, class," the Teacher said as he walked across the front of the room, the student on his shoulder thrashing, but only weakly.

The Teacher could feel their stares on him, those whom he had been teaching the ways of the dark lord these past weeks. He could feel their respect, but he could also feel their fear.

And fear was what it was all about, for fear would restore the great Damakus to his full glory.

The two fleshy bubbles continued to hover around him like balloons dragged along by a toy vendor at a holiday parade.

There should have been more, he thought.

This was yet another gift bestowed upon him by his dark master. The ability to remove the life force of a living thing had been a lost art form for countless millennia, a gift presented to only the most holy and worthy of disciples.

But there should have been more. He had failed in the harvest. Somehow the authorities had anticipated his coming after the first two parents were claimed, denying him—*denying Damakus*—his harvest.

He dropped the squirming child on the floor in front of his desk.

From his pants pocket the Teacher found the key and opened the manacle ring to accept the student's ankle once again.

"Your foot," the Teacher said, motioning with his fingers for the child to obey.

The student glared at him defiantly, pushing himself back across the floor.

"Don't test me, boy," the Teacher growled, and reached out, grabbing hold of the student's foot, yanking him closer.

But before he could get the manacle around the boy's ankle, the Teacher sensed that something was amiss. He released the student and stood, looking around the classroom. The two bubbles of life force had drifted away from him and were now hovering above the heads of the students still chained to their seats.

The female student who had given up her teeth stared at the pulsating globules, reaching a tiny filthy finger up to one as it undulated above her head.

"Don't you dare touch that!" the Teacher bellowed.

The child looked at him then, fear in her eyes, but quickly turned her attention back to the hovering sphere.

"Pretty," she squeaked, her index finger going up toward the weightless bubble.

The Teacher threw himself toward the child, but he wasn't quite quick enough, as the child's index finger made contact with one of the sphere's fleshy surfaces, pressing upon it until—

There was a flash of energy, an explosion of warm light that temporarily chased away the darkness of the classroom.

The light repelled him, burning the Teacher's pale, bullet-riddled flesh as he stumbled backward. He blinked repeatedly, attempting to wash away the writhing blots of brilliant color that now obscured his vision.

"You insolent brat!" he raged.

The little girl looked at him with different eyes now, eyes that had been filled with fear and misery now overflowing with something else entirely.

Hope.

The other children watched yearningly, the soul spheres now drifting toward them.

The Teacher had to stop this. He grabbed the girl and pulled her in close. He opened his mouth wide and inhaled, drawing first the filthy scent of the female student into his lungs, followed by the energies she had stolen. She tried to hold on to her prize, but his strength was too great, and he took the soul stuff into his own body.

The fear in the room was once more palpable, the awful emotion driving the spheres of life energies away as if carried by a strong gust of wind. The Teacher called them back to him, and they had no choice but to obey and resume orbiting around his head.

"There must be order here," the Teacher proclaimed. He then regurgitated from inside him that which had been stolen, blowing the precious life energies like smoke, back into the fleshy spheres of containment.

But his satisfaction was short-lived as he remembered there was still another unruly student to deal with. He looked around to find that the boy had crawled down the aisle to the incubation tank, where his master grew.

"And where do you think you're going?" the Teacher asked, striding down the aisle.

The student looked at him defiantly, and the Teacher could see that he meant the master harm as he grabbed hold of the tank's edge, attempting to pull it over.

"You test me, boy," the Teacher said, reaching for the student as he struggled to tip the tank but was not strong enough.

The infant Damakus acted, two barbed tentacles shooting out from the tank to wrap hungrily around the fleshy globes that still hovered near the Teacher's head. The muscular limbs squeezed until the bubbles popped, the crackling white energy within eagerly absorbed by the boneless appendages.

"O dark lord," the Teacher said in a powerful voice. "Let this meager offering satisfy your needs. The life forces of two who loved, and nurtured, filled with the horror and fear of terrible loss. Energies—souls—tainted with the sweet, sweet tang of angst. Sustenance to spur the growth of your return."

The Teacher smiled. He hoped that the offering, and the sadness of the children that now permeated the room, would be enough to satisfy his master.

But his hope was short-lived, for he sensed a sudden intrusion to his safe haven, his place of teaching, and the land that it inhabited. This was his world given to him by his master so he could carry out Damakus' bidding unhindered.

"How can this be?" he muttered beneath his breath. He grabbed the student by the back of his pajama top, hauling him down the aisle to his seat, where he was properly shackled, then stormed from the classroom.

Drawn toward the source of the disturbance.

John Fogg dragged Agent Brenna Isabel from the shifting clouds of white, the two of them collapsing to a patch of lawn.

They were both trembling, their teeth chattering in reaction to the extreme cold that they experienced while traveling from their world to—

Here.

"Well, that's something I wouldn't care to do again," John said, rubbing his hands furiously up and down his arms in an attempt to get some of the warmth back.

Agent Isabel lay curled into a tight ball, her body shaking on the ground.

"C'mon," John said, attempting to haul her up. "That's it. You've got to move around—get the blood circulating again."

"Oh. My. God," Agent Isabel said, each word forced from her mouth. She was still trembling uncontrollably, and John had no choice but to help her get warm.

"You've got to move," he told her again, rubbing his hands up and down her arms, and back. "Come on now."

He didn't mind the action, for it helped him with his own circulation, and he actually started to feel somewhat normal again.

"What . . . what did we just do?" she asked. Her lips were a purplish blue, and there were even some touches of frost at the tips of her auburn hair. John hugged her closer, rubbing her arms vigorously.

"We've gone to another place," John said, still rubbing but now looking around. The cold mist was thick and blowing about, but he was now able to see the structure that seemed to appear before him.

"Son of a bitch," he said. The building was small, run-down, and painted a god-awful shade of red. It was like something he'd seen a million times in books on early Americana. The little red schoolhouse in all its quaint glory.

"Of course there's a schoolhouse," John muttered beneath his breath. "Where else could he teach them about Damakus?"

Agent Isabel's shaking had calmed down, and she suddenly pulled away from him, uncomfortable with his familiarity toward her.

"Thanks," she said, stiffly moving away. "Where is your wife?"

"I don't know," he said, looking around. He was tempted to call out her name, but something told him that maybe that wouldn't be wise.

Agent Isabel turned to the wall of fog behind her, sticking her hand inside. She gasped, pulling it back, a look of shock on her face.

"It's so cold," she said, shoving her fingers beneath her armpit to warm them.

"The cold of nothing," John said, looking to the curtain of shifting white. "It appears our disciple has been given a special place to perform his duties."

At first John wasn't sure that he'd actually heard it, glancing quickly over to Agent Isabel to see if she'd noticed. She had stopped and was listening as well, looking toward the schoolhouse.

"You heard it, too?" he asked.

"Yeah," she said, reaching down to unsnap her holster and remove her gun.

They both stood perfectly still, the thick gray mist blowing around them on a silent wind.

"There," Agent Isabel said, now moving toward the building.

He'd heard it as well, and there was no mistaking what it was. John followed closely behind her, the two of them drawn toward the almost ghostly sound of multiple children.

All of them crying.

Theo did not wait for the others.

The entities inside her were wild, compelling her to run from the passage toward the mist-enshrouded building.

She could feel them inside her, pumping her heart, flowing through her blood, engorging her muscles, attempting to change her in such a way as to deal with what she would find in this tiny pocket of reality.

"No," she grunted aloud, forcing herself to stop—to take control.

They fought her, but to no avail; she was stronger than them, the magic inscribed upon her flesh making her superior.

The demons protested, but she was capable of suppressing them for now, giving her a chance to check out where she was. Theo was at a back entrance to the building, a rusted chain and lock woven through the door handles to prevent anyone from coming, or going. She approached the door, touching the chain with the tips of her fingers, knowing that she needed to be inside.

Any volunteers want to help me get in? She put the question out there to the demons, feeling a multitude of stirrings. Grabbing the chain in both hands, she waited to see if any would volunteer, opening up the dam of her control just a little to allow one of the demonic beasts to come through long enough to assist her. There was a sudden, painful surge of power down her arms, and she felt her skin stretching to accommodate the powerful musculature that had begun to manifest. Her fingers grew thicker, the skin like rock, as she took the chain in both hands and pulled in opposite directions.

The center links came apart with ease, falling to the ground in front of the door, allowing her to remove the chain. The demon that had lent her its strength wanted to stay a bit longer, desperate to tear the doors from its hinges, and rampage through the structure mangling anything that dared get in their way, but Theo promptly informed the entity that it was done, pushing it back down where the others of its ilk congregated.

In control again, she grabbed hold of one of the door handles and pulled it open to reveal a figure in filthy, tattered clothing standing there to greet her.

"One needs the proper authorization to enter this building," the man said, winding back and punching her square in the face.

Theo flew backward, landing hard upon her butt, rolling backward to the ground, stunned by the strength of the blow.

"Do you have the proper authorization?" she heard the man ask as he left the building walking over to where she lay. "I don't believe that you do."

Theo tried to react, to recover enough to get up from the ground before more harm could be done, but she couldn't escape the darkness as it closed in all around her, putting her back with the demons inside her.

"He's likely going to kill me," she informed the gathering of demons that encircled her.

Billy Sharp, or the demon wearing the benign shape of the little boy, pushed through the crowd to speak to her.

"Do you recall what was promised us?" he asked in his high-pitched child's voice.

"He'll kill me, and you will all die. You're bound to me in such a way now that if I die, you die with me," she told them all. "So it would benefit you to—"

"Do you recall?" Billy insisted.

She didn't want to remember what she had done to acquire the information that they'd needed, what she had agreed to.

"Yes," she said. "I remember."

"And you will give us this?" he asked her.

She didn't answer, feeling a terrible constriction about her throat. She could only imagine what the man was doing to her.

"Yes," she finally agreed. "You'll get what you want . . . what I told you I would do."

The demon child studied her with dark, cautious eyes.

"Yes," she finally screamed at him. "I swear."

The boy smiled, happy with her response. "Okay, then," he said. "Would you like a little help?"

Theo opened her eyes, looking into the face of the man who was attempting to kill her. This close, he looked like a walking corpse, and he held her by the throat, before his horrible face, studying her.

"Who are you?" he asked, realizing that she was awake. "And how on earth did you get here?"

She couldn't breathe, the pressure on her neck excruciating. It was only a matter of seconds before the fragile workings within her throat would collapse and she would be as good as dead.

The demons waited just long enough, almost as if wanting to show her how needed they now were.

How valuable they could be.

Theo experienced the physical changes almost immediately, the muscles, cartilage, and bone around her neck and throat thickening in such a way as to prevent any damage.

She could breathe again, taking in the foul stench of her enemy.

The man smelled of rot, as if the flesh on his body had begun to decay. The stink of him was obscene, and she wanted nothing more than to be free of his clutches.

The disciple was squeezing with all his might, waiting for the inevitable collapse of her trachea beneath his powerful grip, but the new makeup of her throat wasn't about to let that occur.

She looked into his dull, film-covered eyes and saw a moment of realization there, the recognition that something had happened to steal away the murder he was about to perpetrate.

That maybe he should have been more careful.

Her body had morphed as well, the muscles in her legs having grown thicker, and more powerful, the feet inside her shoes growing so large—the nails on her toes so sharp—that they shredded through the sneakers on her feet. Theo pulled her legs up, the remains of her footwear dropping like discarded skin as she dug her new talonlike toes into the front of the man, raking down the front of him, tearing away clothing as well as the foul skin beneath.

The man cried out, releasing his grip on her neck as he stumbled back.

Theo crouched upon the ground, watching the man as he looked down upon the damage she had wrought. The gray flesh of his stomach was lacerated and weeping a milky substitute for blood.

"That wasn't very nice," the disciple of Damakus said as she watched his belly push outward, the skin letting go with a disgusting, tearing sound, his insides uncoiling and spilling out to the ground.

The demons inside her went wild with the disgusting sight, enjoying the obscenity of it all with such intensity that she actually found herself smiling with them at their victory.

Which might have been a bit premature.

The man was on his knees, his internal workings displayed before him. She could hear him muttering to himself as he reached down to the rubbery innards, picking them up in his hands and shoving them back inside the open stomach cavity.

The demons were suddenly impressed, showing their approval with screams and laughter.

The organs stayed where the man had shoved them, his sickly flesh rapidly healing around the open wounds.

"Now, then," the man then said as he rose. "Where were we?"

17

Brenna moved down the schoolhouse corridor, gun ready to fire if required.

"Stay close," she said as she walked, eyes darting to patches of shadow just in case.

The crying was louder the closer they got to the open doorway at the end of the short hall. Her heart was being torn apart by the hopelessness of the sound, but she curbed the urge to run blindly into the room.

In a situation such as this, she needed to be careful.

She thought of her son as she cautiously moved toward the doorway, thinking of how she wished that he had cried out, had given her some kind of chance to save him. But whatever had taken him—SIDS, crib death—whatever name was given to the crippling phenomenon, it had struck with terrible efficiency.

From somewhere in the building they heard a loud, banging sound as if heavy emergency doors had been thrown open. They stopped, listening for what might follow.

This just spurred them on to move all the faster, Brenna making eye contact with her partner at the open doorway.

"Ready?" she asked, and he quickly nodded as she came around the corner into the room, her gun aimed for business. Her eyes scanned the location, taking in the rows of old-fashioned desks and the five children sitting there.

"We've come to get you out of here," she told them, attempting to stifle the flow of powerful emotion that she could hear in her own voice.

John had already moved to the first desk, a boy she recognized as Christopher Waugh watching cautiously as he squatted down beside him.

"They're chained," John announced, already looking around for a possible solution. "We need a key, or something to break the chain with."

She holstered her weapon, going to the heavy wooden desk at the front of the room.

"Look at the lock," she instructed. "What does it look like?"

"Simple manacle," John answered. "Nothing fancy."

She moved around to the front of the desk, pulling open side drawers, top and bottom, which were empty. She then tried the center drawer, which was pretty much the same except for dirt, an old pencil, and . . .

Bingo!

There were two paper clips inside amongst the filth and she snatched them up as if they were the most precious of rare jewels.

"Check on the condition of the others," she said, coming down the aisle toward where Christopher sat, bending the paper clips into the appropriate shape for what she was going to try.

"It's been years since I've done this," she said to anyone who was listening.

"What—" the little boy started, his voice a terrible dry croak.

"I'm going to try and pick this lock," she said, getting down on the floor. She went to work on the boy's chains but not before she noticed the dried blood covering his foot.

"This one," she heard John say. Brenna looked over to see what he was doing. In the next row, John was squatting down next to a little girl, who appeared to be sleeping.

"Is she . . . ?" Brenna asked, afraid of the answer.

"She's alive," John said, laying a gentle hand upon her back. "But she's in rough shape. All these kids need medical attention as soon as possible."

"He's going to kill us," the boy, Christopher, croaked. "He's going to feed us to . . ." The boy turned his head, and Brenna followed his gaze to a tank at the back of the room, something swimming around in the filthy water.

She could see that the boy was on the verge of complete emotional collapse, his lips quivering and his face twisting up with sorrow.

"Let's get you kids out of here," she said, looking away before she, too, began breaking down.

She slipped the thin ends of the paper clips into the lock of the manacle around Christopher's ankle, trying desperately to remember her college days and how she'd taught herself to pick locks out of necessity because she was always locking herself out of her dorm room.

The lock was clogged with dirt, but she was still able to get in, manipulating the simple mechanism to release the clasp and set the boy free.

"There you go," she said, looking at him. He'd gotten control of himself, but she could still see that vacant look of shock in his eyes. "You just sit there while we help the others," she told him.

He agreed with a slow nod.

She then turned to the little girl across from him. "You're Rebecca, aren't you?"

The child attempted a smile, and Brenna felt her rage inflame. The monster who had abducted her had taken her teeth. In a way, she had been the one to lead them here, the horrible act committed against her actually contributing to them getting here. Brenna reached out, laying a gentle hand upon the little girl's hair, and spoke softly to her.

"We're going to get you home." She then proceeded to pick the lock on the child's manacles, freeing her in less time than it had taken with Christopher's restraints. It was all coming back to her.

Brenna turned to Christopher. "Can you keep an eye on Rebecca while we free the others?"

He said that that he would, and she reached out, giving his shoulder a gentle squeeze, and was horrified by the touch. She remembered the photo of the husky boy, in his Pop Warner football uniform; now he was nearly skin and bones.

"This is Cindy," John said as Brenna joined him, leaning down beside another little girl who could barely keep her eyes open.

"Hello, Cindy," Brenna said, squatting down beneath the desk. "Let's get those chains off you."

She did that two more times, each child grateful, but not having the strength to do much of anything else other than sit there and . . .

"What's he up to?" John asked.

Brenna looked to where he was looking and saw that the boy, Christopher, had hobbled to the back of the room and now stood before a filthy fish tank, looking at it with hateful eyes.

"Chris, what's up?" Brenna asked, standing up from where she'd been squatting, working on the last of the locks.

"It's being quiet," the boy said, swaying because of his injured foot. "It doesn't want you to know it's here."

There was sudden movement within the tank, the filthy water splashing.

John moved down the aisle. "Christopher, I think you might want to—"

"It's because of *him*," the boy said, reaching out to grab hold of the edge of the tank.

"Who, Christopher?" John asked, almost to the boy.

"Damakus," the boy said, almost as if spitting something poisonous from his mouth. And as the name was said, he pulled upon the tank's edge, using all his strength to tip it from where it rested on the two desks.

The tank fell from the desks, shattering upon impact, spilling its foul-smelling water, and something else, onto the classroom floor.

John ran toward where the boy was standing, staring with rapt attention at the hideous monstrosity that now flopped and writhed upon the wet, glass-covered floor. He grabbed the boy, yanking him back away from the thing as it immediately lashed out at where the child had been standing, one if its tentacle-like appendages snapping the air like a whip.

"What the hell is that?" Brenna asked.

"That, I believe, is the demon lord Damakus," John said, watching the thing as it thrashed about.

"Good to know," Brenna said, walking a few steps closer, aiming her gun, and firing multiple shots into its fleshy, undulating mass.

She let the demons' attributes flow, allowing her body to shift and change, to manifest their various traits.

This would be needed if she were to survive.

The disciple of Damakus was fast, evading her claws with ease while pounding her with fists like rock.

Theo lay on the ground, shaking the fog from her mind. She attempted to evade him, to spring away from his reach, but he again proved too fast. One of the disciple's hands grabbed a handful of her thick black hair, yanking her back to him.

"What are you exactly?" the man asked inquisitively. "I've never seen the likes of something like you before."

She struggled in his grasp, and then felt her hair let go.

Theo was suddenly free, scrabbling away from her foe, who was left holding only a large handful of her hair.

She ran a clawed hand over a newly smooth scalp. One of the demons had caused her hair to fall away, leaving her now bald, and quite angry about the change. Theo loved her hair, and hoped—for the sake of whatever demon had been responsible—that they would somehow return it to its fullness and luster as soon as this matter was settled.

But until then she would use the anger over its loss to her advantage, springing off from the ground in a terrific leap, landing upon her foe's chest and driving him back to the ground.

"You want to know what I am?" she asked, perched on the disciple's chest. She could feel the inner workings of her mouth changing, her teeth re-forming in her gums, growing sharper—longer. "I'm the thing put out there in the world to make something like you afraid."

The man fought to throw her off, but she held fast, the claws of her toes and hands sinking into the putrefying flesh to hold on as she drove her head and mouth forward, to sink her teeth into the skin of his throat.

Theo should have been revolted by the act, but she wasn't—the demon that was giving her the strength and rage to fight her foe dismissed the disgust and replaced it with something akin to hunger.

The man tried to scream, but his damaged throat was filled with blood, or whatever foul juices coursed through his disgusting body. Theo bit down harder and yanked back, tearing away a large chunk of neck. Part of her wanted to consume the prize, but her humanity won out, and she spat the piece away. Caught unawares, the disciple bucked wildly, and she was thrown from her perch on him.

One hand pressed to his damaged throat, he climbed to his feet. Theo waited, in a tensed crouch, growling like something fresh from the jungle.

The disciple pulled his hand away from the nasty bite, and she watched in horror as it healed before her eyes.

"That was nasty," the man said, his voice at first a strained whisper, but suddenly stronger. "But I can be nasty, too."

He charged at her, grabbing her around the waist and tackling her to the ground.

The demons inside Theo all cried out, each and every one of the thousand trying to come forward. It was more than she could handle as her psyche was deluged with the demonic, giving her adversary the upper hand.

The disciple was wild with rage, his fists raining down upon her, ripping flesh and shattering bone. Theo attempted to fight back to the best of her ability, but she was easily swatted aside, one of her limbs grabbed, twisted, and broken with such savagery that she found her mind going completely numb to the onslaught.

Allow me, the demonic entity that sounded like little Billy Sharp echoed inside her head.

And she did just that, raising an arm broken in at least two places, as a razor-sharp spine, like something from the shell of some prehistoric insect, sprouted from the palm of her hand, stabbing into the side of her attacker.

The disciple cried out, grabbing at her offending arm and ripping it from her shoulder. Theo cried out in agony, managing to throw the man from her body. She climbed to her feet, gripping the bleeding stump of her arm, silently commanding the entities within her to stem the flow of blood.

The disciple stood up, examining where he had been pierced. He picked at the side wound, plunging his index finger and thumb into the wound and slowly extracting the barbed spine from inside.

He studied the dripping appendage with fascination.

"I think I'll make you eat this," he said, his horrible eyes darting from the demonic weapon to her.

She was ready, but seriously doubting that she would have the strength to continue to fight, when something inexplicable happened.

The disciple went suddenly rigid, the spine-covered appendage falling from his hands as he turned toward the school.

"Damakus," the disciple said beneath his breath, darting toward the open door and disappearing inside.

Fearing for her husband's and Agent Isabel's safety, Theo moved to follow, but her damaged body had other plans as she pitched forward, unconscious before she even hit the ground.

18

John watched as the abomination writhed upon the classroom floor, cries like those of injured infants emitting from the multiple bullet holes that had been shot in its loathsome body.

He still held on to the boy, Christopher, moving him along the back of the room, toward where Brenna Isabel was standing with the other children.

"We should probably think about getting them all out of here," he said, just as what felt like an ice pick plunged into the center of his skull and into his brain.

John let out a scream, his shoulders bunching up tightly against his neck. Something had found its way inside his skull—inside his brain—and from the looks of Agent Isabel and the children, they were experiencing it as well.

He managed to look to the back of the classroom, to where the infant form of the demon lord Damakus lay amidst the filthy water and broken glass. Multiple sets of horrible eyes were fixed upon him—*upon them all*—eyes that held them in contempt, promising nothing but pain and misery.

Damakus spread its tendrils within the folds of his brain, showing
him the truth of the world and the terror of a future yet to come.

John snapped awake, his fingers still poised upon the keyboard.

"Shit," he said, squeezing his eyes tightly shut and opening them.
He gave his head a little shake to clear away the fog, and looked at the
last line of the paragraph he'd been typing and laughed.

Kahisdhgpoashidgpaosidhgasdp89yuwe9p8y9hsa, it said.

Good one, he thought. *Another* New York Times *bestseller for sure.* He
deleted the gibberish, saving the document in multiple places before
shutting the computer down for the night. When he was falling asleep
at the keyboard, there wasn't much sense in pushing it any further, even
if he did have an insane deadline breathing down his neck. He'd get
back to it in the morning when his brain was fresher.

He glanced at the cuckoo clock in the shape of a haunted house
on the wall of his office and saw that it was much later than he thought
it should be. *How long have I been asleep at the keyboard?* he wondered,
rolling his chair back from his desk.

John had been killing himself on this latest book, a recounting of
the whole Damakus affair, give or take some details that might cause
the general populace to totally freak out. It was bad enough having to
deal with the threat of the world under attack by dark, supernatural
forces. It would be near impossible to deal with if the average citizen
was truly aware.

Standing up from his chair, he turned away from his desk toward
the front of his office, and was surprised that she was standing there.

"Hey," he said to his wife. "You scared the shit out of me. I didn't
hear you come in."

She stood there staring and smiling at him.

"I was falling asleep at the computer, guessed that it might be time
to get some sleep."

She'd gone up to bed hours ago and he was surprised to see her awake.

"Are you all right?" he asked.

She nodded quickly. "I went to your room, but when I saw that your bed was empty I figured you were still in here."

They hadn't slept in the same room, or bed, since her change.

These days Theo often had nightmares, most likely spurred on by the demonic entities that continued to reside within her body. The sigils that the Coalition had tattooed upon her body gave her control of them in her conscious state, but when she was unconscious, things had the potential to become more dangerous.

They both thought it would be wise if he slept in one of the mansion's guest rooms until she had a better control of the situation.

She stepped closer to him. "Thought you might need to be reminded to go to bed."

"Yeah," he said, and laughed. "It's getting to be that way these days."

He was suddenly very aware of her proximity to him, feeling the heat from her body. She was wearing a Ramones concert T-shirt and nothing else, and he couldn't remember her being any more beautiful.

Or desirable.

Their relationship since the whole demonic possession thing had been strained. She was still dealing with so much in regard to her mental state, never mind the physical manifestations, and it had driven them apart. John was well aware that she needed time to adjust, and was more than willing to oblige.

But he loved her so much, and to be kept from her, to not be able to be with her, to touch her—it was killing him inside.

Theo moved even closer and looked him square in the eye.

"It's time to go to bed, John," she said. She was standing so close that he could feel the warmth of her breath on his face.

"Thanks for the reminder," he said, fighting desperately not to take her by the shoulders and pull her to him.

They'd talked about this before, about waiting until they knew it was safe.

She put her hand on his chest, and he jumped, as if shocked by electricity.

Theo laughed, a sexy sound that he hadn't heard often enough these past months.

"What are you doing?" he finally had the courage to ask her.

She ran her fingers down his chest while looking at him. "Getting you ready for bed."

"That's not getting me ready for bed," he said, and laughed nervously.

Her fingertips left his chest, moving down to his stomach. "It's not?"

He shook his head.

Though it pained him to do so, he grabbed her wrist.

"This probably isn't—" he began.

"No, it is," she corrected him, twisting her hand free from his grasp and continuing her progress, only this time much lower.

"Theo, we talked—"

"And talked, and talked," she said, moving herself closer as her hand found what it had been searching for.

The pleasure of her touch was something that he knew he'd missed, but until then he hadn't been aware of how much.

"I'm tired of waiting," she said, bringing her lips to his in a kiss that made his heart race, and his blood pump. "I'm done with it . . . we need to get used to the new normal."

He was considering protesting, to ask her if she was absolutely sure, but it all became sort of fuzzy as her hands undid the buckle of his pants, and he found his own hands suddenly on her, frantically pulling her close as their lips locked hungrily together.

John believed that her intention had been to go back to what had been their bedroom, to finish what had been started, but things proceeded far quicker than they'd both likely anticipated.

At the moment, he'd found it incredibly unfair that he was wearing so much clothing, the effort of peeling away the layers taking away from the intense pleasure of their acts upon the floor of his office. He didn't mind the hardness of the wooden floor, or the abrasiveness of the area rug around his desk; it all became part of the sensations of the moment.

Sensations that were absolutely incredible, and so very missed.

After, they lay there on his office floor, naked and drenched in the sweat of their strenuous activity, listening to the sounds of the office—of the old house around them.

"Still awake?" he asked, pulling her closer and kissing her on the side of the head.

"Why?" she asked. "Want to go again?"

He laughed out loud, seriously considering the offer. It had been too long.

She rolled out from beneath his arm, sliding her naked body on top of his, and looked down into his face.

"That was good," she said.

"Nice to know that we haven't lost it," he said.

She smiled at him. "Not at all," she said, pushing herself up to sit astride him. "In fact, I think it worked on the very first try."

He wasn't sure what she meant.

"What did?" he asked as he ran his hands down the sides of her smooth, muscular legs.

She ran her hands across her stomach. "Your seed," she said, her intoxicating smile beaming down to bathe him in its radiance. "It's taken root."

"I don't—" John began as she leaned down to him, her long black hair tickling his face and upper body as her lips hungrily locked to his.

She broke the kiss with a throaty laugh, rising again to gaze down on him.

"It's already growing," she told him, her hands now rubbing across a stomach that suddenly appeared larger to him, and more pronounced.

He instantly knew that something was wrong, noticing signs that perhaps his wife was no longer in control. He tried to throw her off, but her weight suddenly had increased threefold, pinning him to the floor. Thinking fast, he dredged up some powerful words of immobilization, words that would perhaps buy him some time to get away from the demons who had most likely hijacked his wife's body so that he might do something to help her regain control and—

It was as if the demons sensed what he was going to do, a stinking stream of viscous fluid splashing down from her open mouth to cover his own, filling his mouth and sealing his lips closed so that he could not speak.

Could not utter the words.

She tossed her head back and laughed, her naked stomach growing increasingly larger, swelling from within.

He tried to fight her, to force her from atop his body, but he wasn't strong enough, his efforts swatted away with little concern.

"Look at what you've done," she said in a voice that did not belong to her. "Look at what you've helped us do."

Her belly was huge, the skin stretching before his eyes. He tried to speak, to wipe the viscous substance from his face, but it had become like some sort of rubbery solid, bonding with the skin of his face. He could no longer tell where the substance started and his own skin began.

"With your love," she said, her fingers probing at the tight skin just below her protruding belly button, "you've given us substance . . ."

The nails at the tips of her fingers had become long and yellow and sharp and they dug into the taut skin of her belly, ripping at the flesh.

"Shape . . ."

Her fingers had disappeared beneath the flow of blood, digging deeper as she tore at the skin, pulling the jagged rend that she'd made apart with both hands.

"Body . . ."

The skin of her belly came apart with a horrible ripping sound, and the contents of her insides spilled down upon his naked form.

"You've given us life!"

Finger-length larvae, awash in a stinking mixture of pus and blood, poured down on him. Even though he knew that he couldn't, John tried to scream as he bucked wildly beneath her incredible weight.

He could see the things that covered his body, the thickness of their milky white undulating bodies, their all-too-human faces—mouths open in high-pitched wails of hunger.

He saw his wife, stomach wound gaping wide, looking down upon him, and their newly born spawn lovingly, urging them to eat.

And eat they did, as John Fogg silently screamed.

The terror from the one called Fogg was delicious, and the Lord God Damakus could feel his divine personage, cut by glass and punctured by gunfire, begin to heal.

And his mass begin to grow.

It hoped that the female's horror would be just as delectable and sweet.

It was a gorgeous fall day, and Brenna had brought flowers and a balloon to the grave.

There was a part of her that thought the business of leaving things at the grave of a loved one kind of foolish—the person was dead, what would he care if she left something there or not?

But then there was the part of her that asked, what if somehow he actually liked the gifts?

So she brought flowers, and an Elmo balloon, just to be on the safe side.

Brenna stood over the plaque in the grass, reading her baby son's name, and the date that he died, feeling that awful disconnect that she often did, that something very special was missing from the universe these days.

There were other people scattered about the cemetery, visiting with their lost loved ones, so she refrained from talking. She knelt down at the grave, tying the string of the balloon to the flowers, and set her offering down alongside the bronze-colored plaque.

Her psychiatrist said that it would be good for her to visit here, to sit and reflect on the past, and what had been lost. He said that it would better prepare her for the future.

Her child was gone, her husband was gone; all she had left was her job.

A chill ran down her spine, and she realized that she had been staring at her son's name on the grave marker so intensely that her eyes now hurt, and her vision was blurry. Brenna looked away, blinking and rubbing at her eyes, and she noticed that it had become suddenly overcast, a surprisingly cool breeze now whipping over the graves.

She also noticed that the cemetery now appeared empty, and wondered how long exactly she had been staring at the plaque. She made a mental note to bring up the odd passage of time to her psychiatrist, just in case it might be something he should be made aware of.

Brenna had reached the point of her visit a little bit quicker than she usually did, when she'd reflected enough on the painful past, and the equally painful future ahead of her, and was preparing to leave when she heard it.

Soft and muffled.

A baby's cry.

Brenna listened to the sound, processing the auditory information, ready to pass it off as the wind blowing through the trees, or the afternoon cries of some sort of animal, but there was nothing more distinct at that moment.

A baby was crying—her baby was crying. Beneath the cemetery dirt, within the tiny white casket, her baby son was crying.

Brenna had no idea how it was possible, but there was no mistaking the sound. She knew his cry, distinct and special, a part of her that could never be forgotten. A cry that she hadn't heard since that fateful Halloween night when . . .

She saw him inside her head, in his crib, silent and still, the image as she continued to gaze at the grave marker morphing into a vision of him wailing within the coffin nestled in the embrace of the cold, dark ground.

And she knew right then that there wasn't a question—she had to get him out. Her mind raced with the things that she could do, that she probably *should* do, like finding someone who worked for the cemetery, or calling the local police, but what if there was some sort of time limit, what if this miracle—because that was what this was, a miracle—what if this special happening had an expiration time? What if she only had this moment . . . this now, to act? What if she waited, and did the rational things, and her son died again?

Again.

The fear of this was incredible, a palpable living and breathing thing, perched on her shoulders and screaming, *Go, go, go, go!* And the thoughts of the rational things that she should have done were cast aside like a heavy sweater on an August afternoon as she plunged her fingers down into the dirt and began to rip the layers of turf away, tossing them aside with abandon, furiously digging a hole to get to her son.

She was afraid she wouldn't get to him in time, afraid that she would be too late.

Afraid that the miracle would be over.

Afraid as she madly dug, hearing the muffled cries of her baby—her son—from within his white casket, under the dirt.

Somewhere under the dirt.

Brenna dug, what fingernails she had breaking and painfully splitting at each new handful of soil, of rock, that she tossed aside to get to her son. Her eyes were fixed to the hole in the ground, watching for a sign . . .

A sign of white—the lid on her baby's casket.

To her his cries sounded louder, which meant she was getting closer, that it wouldn't be long now, that she wouldn't miss it—that the miracle wouldn't be wasted.

This time she heard him; this time she wouldn't be too late.

But what if? She considered, throwing handfuls of dirt over her shoulder, making the hole that much deeper, eyes desperate for a sign of white.

What if the crying was to—stop?

What if she was late—again?

Her fear intensified, growing like the hole beneath her.

Growing as she wildly dug, focused upon the cries of her child. Waiting for the next handful of dirt to reveal what she'd been digging for, fearful that her child's cries would suddenly stop before she got to him.

Late again.

Fearful.

Digging as fast and as deep as she possibly could.

Afraid of silence, and what it would mean.

Late.

Again.

Damakus had grown at least three times larger, the fear present in the classroom so very rich and nourishing. If this were but a sample of what the human world was like, of the kind of sustenance he would find out there, he would be unstoppable.

Nothing could stop his return.

Theodora Knight knew that she was close to death, and wondered if perhaps this was a good thing, that if it was to happen, she and all those that she loved—as well as the world—might be better off.

She was lost inside that place again, where the demons waited. They huddled around her, hanging on her silence, waiting for what was next to come.

They wanted something from her—something that she'd promised.

Something that was very important to them.

"Well?" Billy Sharp asked impatiently. "Why are you still here? Go after the disciple. . . . We've healed you, given you our strength—go."

She could feel them trying to force her out, but she clung to the darkness of her psyche, unsure if it was safe to go back.

"He's growing stronger, you know," Billy said, pacing in front of where she huddled, surrounded by the infernal.

"Who?" she asked.

Billy laughed with little humor before answering, "Damakus."

She remained silent.

"Not far from where your body lies . . . within the wooden struc-ture, the demon lord feeds on the most nourishing of fears."

"The children," she said, suddenly remembering the driving force behind coming to this strange pocket of reality floating amidst the nothing.

"The children were but a snack," Billy warned. "An appetizer before the main course."

She immediately knew whom the demon was referring to.

"So much fear from one who appears so strong," Billy cooed.

John.

"And the woman . . . it's a wonder she can leave the house."

Agent Isabel.

Theo had been curled in a tight ball, shadows wrapped around her like a blanket, and had been seriously considering dying.

But now.

She unfurled, climbing to stand amongst the demonic once more. They stepped back away from her, the light from the sigils on her body growing stronger, brighter.

"Going someplace?" Billy asked.

"I'm going to need to heal more if I'm going to stop Damakus," she said.

"We can help you with that," Billy said.

"Do it."

"Certainly," the demon child agreed. "And when it is time, you will allow us our moment like we agreed?"

"I wish I was stronger," Theo then said.

"Stronger how?" the demon asked with an odd tilt of his little boy head.

"Strong enough not to care about dying, and to take you miserable sons of bitches with me."

The demon smiled at her, reaching out to take her hand in his tiny hand.

"Sometimes there is greater strength in knowing that one is not strong enough," Billy said.

19

The Teacher entered the room gripped by panic.

His eyes first went to where the tank, the artificial womb where his lord and master gestated, had been. The sight of it gone from the desks and shattered on the floor of the classroom nearly stole away his life.

But then he saw his master.

The Master. In all his glory.

The Teacher wanted to cry. The sight of Damakus was magnificent. He had grown nearly five times the size he'd been, his many limbs—in which he would embrace the world and take it into his maw—spread out, extending across the classroom floor.

Looking about the classroom, the Teacher came to understand the situation: the foes of the great Lord Damakus had entered the classroom attempting to steal away the loving angels who would give his lord of lords their fear, their love, and their lives to return him from the brink.

But they had been stopped. Frozen in their tracks by the holy omnipotence of his dark lord and master.

Relieved beyond words, he glared at the intruders and his students, held in the grip of his master's power. They would all be punished for their insolence in thinking that they could ever escape the wonder that was Damakus.

And then he felt it, a painful tickling at the center of his brain as if . . .

Damakus was touching him, reaching out to feed upon his own fear.

But he feared nothing now that his master was here, healthy and growing, and he tried to show his master this. The Teacher allowed Damakus to probe, to stimulate, but he knew that there was nothing in existence that could ever make him afraid again.

"Where did you go?" someone called out, and the Teacher was startled by the sound of the question, turning around toward the front of the classroom, surprised to see a familiar form.

A familiar form that brought to him the sensation that he believed up until a few glorious seconds ago had been excised from this genetic makeup.

"I didn't think we were quite finished yet," she said, walking down the aisle to where he stood.

Fear, he recognized with absolute revulsion. The woman brought him fear.

Theo was in absolute agony.

The demons were helping her heal, but they weren't doing her any favors in the pain department. In fact, they loved that she was hurting, taking an immense amount of pleasure from the pain that healing her many gashes and breaks, never mind growing her a new arm, was causing her.

She wanted to hit something—to kill something—and entering the creepy classroom where she'd found her husband, as well as Agent Isabel and the missing kids, Theo thought it looked as though her wish was about to be granted.

The demons inside her roared at the sight of the disciple, as well as the monstrosity spread out on the floor in front of him.

A part of her was revolted by the sight of the shapeless thing, her brain attempting to define it in some way, but coming away with only one designation.

Nightmare. The thing was what nightmares were made of, and that was saying a lot coming from a woman possessed by a thousand demonic entities.

"Where did you go?" she called out to the disciple.

She watched as he turned, enjoying the look of fear that appeared on his loathsome face.

"I didn't think we were quite finished," she said to him, preparing herself for what was likely to be another nasty bout.

But she was ready—

As were the nightmares that lived inside her.

His children were eating him.

For that was what they were . . . spawn of his seed, vomited from the womb of his wife.

His children.

John lay there on the floor of his office, totally immobilized, as his children fed upon his flesh. He guessed that there was some sort of natural narcotic in their saliva, something that killed the pain of their consumption of him, something that made it strangely—

Pleasurable.

His wife had retreated to a far corner of the room, curling up into a tight little ball to heal, he believed. It took quite a bit out of one to give birth by ripping open one's stomach. She needed her rest, and he'd be damned if he begrudged her that.

John lay there, eyes closed, listening to the sounds of his children chewing.

Resigned to his fate.

He was going to die, everything that he was going into the bellies of his demonic spawn. The idea was terrifying to him, and he felt the intensity of his emotion race through his numbed body, almost returning some semblance of his pain response.

But he did not feel the pain, only the terror of what was to come after he had passed. What he was responsible for, and how it would affect the world.

The chewing was louder, accompanied by a low droning sound that signified to him that his children were content.

He imagined that he should have taken some pleasure from the fact that his children—his spawn—were happy.

The voice inside his head was sudden, sharp, and cutting.

Look at you.

He knew the voice, and he opened his eyes to see his nana standing above him, looking down with disapproval.

"And you wonder why I haven't gone on into the light," she said in disgust. "Where would you be—where would the world be really—if I wasn't around to pull your ass from the fire? You're going to need to be better at this if you and yours are to succeed," she said with a disappointed shake of her gray head.

He couldn't help smiling up at her.

Nana put her hands on her hips, looking him over.

"That's disgusting," she said. "And I've seen just about enough of it."

Nana pulled her pack of Camels—unfiltered—from inside the pocket of the apron she always wore, and placed one in the corner of her mouth. She then returned the pack of smokes to the same pocket and produced her lighter. John loved that lighter, and always wanted to play with it as a child, but she always told him that he'd burn the house down.

"Are you ready?" she asked him, the cigarette in the corner of her mouth bobbing up and down. "Or do you want to wait until they get to your liver?"

He really wasn't sure what he should be getting ready for, but he told her that he was just so she wouldn't be angry with him.

"That's good," she said, bringing the flame from the lighter to the tip of her Camel. "'Cause I was going to do this whether you were ready or not."

And before he could question, she pulled upon the end of her cigarette, the red tip burning angrily as she sucked fumes deeply into her lungs, and then exhaled a cloud of noxious chemicals down onto him.

He felt it at once, the tingling, burning sensation as the fog drifted over his body, as well as the reaction of his children. They had started to panic, to cry out, their mouths still filled with the vestiges of their fleshy meal as they screamed.

The smoke was hurting them—killing them—and he found himself nauseated by the idea that he was feeling pangs of emotion as the voracious larvae dropped from his body, writhing and dying upon the floor.

The smoke had grown thicker as the demon children had died, his office around him practically disappearing as he lay, now seeming to be floating in nothingness.

Still puffing upon her cigarette, Nana looked around her and seemed satisfied by her act. She then returned her attention to him.

"Now get up," she commanded.

And John did as he was told, realizing that he was whole again, his body and flesh restored.

"We've still got work to do," Nana finished, dropping the remains of her unfiltered cigarette into the hungry void she had created.

Theo lifted her head back and sniffed the air.

"Is that fear I smell?" she asked, a nasty smile that wasn't her own teasing the corner of her mouth.

The disciple glared.

"I left you for dead," he said. "I'm guessing there's more to you than meets the eye."

"You have no idea," she said, releasing the psychic leashes that she held on the entities that possessed her.

She felt the changes at once, dramatic and quite painful, and began to scream as she charged toward her foe. The disciple of Damakus reacted in kind.

The two collided, arms swinging like clubs as they each attempted to take the other down. One of his stonelike fists connected with her chin, and she felt something snap as she was knocked aside, crashing into the last row of desks. The disciple did not hesitate, plowing across the room to inflict even more savagery upon her.

Theo was shocked by the sensation in her jaw, and was horrified as it came away in her hand, replaced by something far more nasty.

The disciple tossed aside the classroom furniture that was blocking his access, bearing down as she turned her transformed gaze to him.

The disciple hesitated, startled by her new appearance, but that was all that she needed. Theo sprang, the newly formed muscles in her legs like coiled metal springs. Stumbling back from her attack, the disciple put his hand out, attempting to halt her advance. Theo saw this as an opportunity, unhinging her newly formed jaws and opening her mouth incredibly wide.

It was quite impressive, she had to admit.

Her jaws snapped closed just above his wrist with a muffled snap and crunch as she dropped down to the floor.

She didn't think he understood what had just happened, slowly raising his arm to look in awe at where his hand had once been. The disciple then turned his stunned gaze to her.

Just as she began to chew.

"I'm coming, baby," Brenna Isabel cried, her mouth filled with dirt.

She had dug down far deeper than she would have imagined possible, the walls of the hole all around her crumbling and rolling back down to where she continued to dig.

And still her son cried.

And still she dug, handful after handful, searching for that hint of a white coffin lid.

It was getting more difficult to clear the opening as she threw the handfuls of dirt and rock as high as she was able, much of it falling back down for her to pick up and attempt to remove from the hole again.

Brenna could feel herself getting tired, the muscles in her arms burning and trembling as she scooped and hurled.

Scooped and hurled.

She would stop from moment to moment, and listen—desperate to hear the sounds of her son's cry. Terrified that she wouldn't . . . Terrified that she would be too late again.

Yes, yes, he was still there . . . still alive. All she had to do was get to him and get him out of the little white coffin.

It'll be a miracle, she told herself, scooping up another handful of the rich black earth and trying to throw it up and out of the hole she had dug.

A miracle.

"Agent Isabel," called a voice down into the hole. "Brenna?"

She didn't want to stop digging but she figured that maybe whoever it was could help her.

"Yes?" she called up, her hands full of dirt.

A face appeared in the circle above, peering down at her. "Brenna, it's me, John Fogg."

She knew the name, but she didn't have the time to dwell upon it. She needed to get to her son before . . .

"Get out of the way," she called up, throwing the handful of dirt. The head momentarily disappeared, only to return again.

"Brenna, you have to stop," he told her.

Is he insane? she thought. Didn't he know how important this was?

"Go away!" she screamed at the dirt, continuing to dig at the soil. "I don't have time for this!"

"You have to come out of there," John Fogg called down to her. "The children . . . they need us."

She had no idea what he was talking about. There was only one child who needed her, and . . .

And suddenly she realized that his cries had stopped.

"No," she screamed, listening with all her might for the muffled, screechy sound. "No, please . . ."

"Brenna, please," the man's voice said. And with terror-filled eyes she looked up to see that he was somehow much closer to her, his hand reaching down for her to take.

"I . . . I can't," she said through the tears, starting to dig again. "I can't leave him like this. What if . . . what if he needs me . . . what if . . ."

"The children need you," John Fogg stressed to her. "Christopher, Rebecca, Cindy . . ."

"The children?" she questioned. Why didn't she know what he was talking about? Why didn't . . .

And she suddenly remembered the missing children, and how they had found them in the strangest of places.

"The children," she said, momentarily forgetting why she was inside the hole.

"Take my hand," John said.

For a moment, just as their hands were about to touch, she heard the faintest of sounds.

Like a baby's cry from somewhere deep down beneath the dirt.

But that can't be, she thought as she took his hand and was pulled from the confines of the grave.

Clutching his oozing wrist, the Teacher turned toward his dark lord, praying for his assistance.

"Lord Damakus!" he proclaimed. "Your most humble servant, the purveyor of your magnificent glory, begs your assistance!"

Damakus pulsated and writhed upon the floor, growing even larger before his eyes.

And from inside his skull, he heard his god's answer to his pleas.

And the answer was *No*.

The Teacher could not believe what had been said. Had he not been the most faithful and dedicated of servants? Had he not been the one responsible for bringing the dark lord back from the brink of nothing?

He stumbled toward his master, begging to be heard . . . begging for his petition to be reconsidered.

And the high dark lord Damakus denied him yet again.

No.

The answer was like a blade, plunged deeply into his putrefying heart. And he understood then that the gods, even the ones that had promised him a world to teach, were selfish, desperate to keep all the power for themselves.

With a sadness so strong that it was like a thing alive, the Teacher turned back to face his foe. She crouched there, picking the flesh of his hand from between elongated teeth that would have made a Tyrannosaurus tremble with envy.

"This is where it ends," he said to her, no longer having the urge to fight in the name of his master.

She slowly stood, her body making the strangest of noises as bones elongated and thickened and limbs sprouted spines that glistened sharply before his eyes.

"You're right," she said, darting toward him in a flash.

Moving so quick that he didn't even feel the razor-sharp claws of her hand as they passed through the flesh and bone of his neck.

Severing his head from his body.

. . .

John Fogg opened his eyes to a reality as fucked up as the one he'd left behind.

The demon lord Damakus had continued to grow, its disgusting mass having expanded across the schoolroom floor. Its flesh split and was sloughed off to reveal its next, newer, and larger form, only to begin all over again.

He turned to Brenna Isabel, who still appeared to be in a kind of trance, and gripped her arm, giving it a violent shake. Her eyes snapped open, and she raised her gun, pointing it at him.

"Whoa!" John said, throwing up his hands. He saw the realization come into her eyes, followed by absolute terror at the sight of the continuously evolving demon god before them.

Agent Isabel turned to see the children cowering behind her, and stepped forward with her weapon. "Get them out of here while I—"

"You'll do no such thing," Theo called out from across the room.

John looked over to see something that he knew was once his wife. Her body was misshapen, covered in spikes and spines, her limbs twisted and malformed.

There was a headless corpse at her feet.

"Is that . . . ," Brenna started to ask.

"Yeah," John answered, feeling as though he might be sick.

"Get out of here," his wife ordered. Her mouth was like that of a shark, enormously wide and filled with rows and rows of razor teeth. "Take the kids with you and go," she again commanded, waving them away with appendages that looked more like a bird of prey's talons than hands.

The children were still in the grip of Damakus, their bodies twitching and moaning as it continued to feed upon their nourishing fears. Brenna knelt down to the children, attempting to rouse them.

"Theo," John said, beginning to approach.

She held out a claw. "No," she said. "Just go."

"John," Brenna called to him, and he turned from his wife to assist the FBI special agent with the children.

The children started to gradually awaken, and Damakus reacted, its multiple limbs flexing and lifting its growing mass up off the floor. The demon lord threw its body toward them in an attempt to halt their leaving, but a child's desk was thrown across the room, striking its amorphous head and knocking it back.

"Get the hell out of here—now!" Theo screamed as the demon lord turned its attention to her.

John did as he was told, helping Brenna drag the children to the front of the classroom and toward the doorway. The kids were crying, actually frightened to leave the environment where they'd been imprisoned and tortured for so long. It had become what they knew, and they were afraid to leave it.

They were almost through the door when John stopped, turning for one last look before going.

Damakus towered over his wife, the demon's monstrous form rising as its many-tentacled limbs waved threateningly. John watched as she crouched down, preparing to attack her prey, when Damakus struck. One of its muscular limbs darted forward, a spearlike appendage at its tip impaling the woman, pinning her to the floor of the classroom.

"No!" John screamed, moving to go to her, but Brenna grabbed hold of his arm, preventing him from going any farther.

"The children," she said to him. "The children need us . . . *you* if we're to get out of here alive."

He heard Brenna's words and knew them to be true, but how could he leave Theo there like that?

It was almost as if his wife could hear his thoughts, and she turned her now monstrous gaze to him, her eyes telling him that it was all fine.

Brenna continued to tug upon his arm, and he finally allowed himself to be taken, ripping his gaze away from the horrors of the room.

And the love he was leaving behind.

Theo gazed down at the pulsating appendage sticking out from her chest. She could feel the demon lord's mind attempting to find its way inside her skull, to feast upon the fear of her impending demise, but she would not let it in.

Not yet.

She glanced over to see the old woman standing nearby.

"Nana?" she asked.

The old woman approached, kneeling down beside her.

"It's time now," Nana said as Theo looked at her. "Give them what they want."

Theo could feel them huddling at the border of her psyche, waiting for what had been promised to them.

"I never wanted this," she said, and felt the heat of her tears as they streamed down from her eyes.

"I know, dear," Nana said. "But a bargain is a bargain."

"I don't know . . . I don't know if I'll be strong enough to come back." Nana smiled, laying a cool, ghostly hand upon Theo's fevered cheek.

"The smartest thing my grandson ever did, marrying you," the old woman said as she bent down to lay a gentle kiss upon Theo's brow. "Now send that miserable piece of shit back to the nothingness where it belongs."

Nana was gone, her words a gentle echo inside her skull, gradually replaced by the yowls of the demonic.

It was time to give them what they'd asked for, Theo admitted as she peered into her psyche to see them all standing there, the little boy, Billy Sharp, out in front.

"Well?" the demon child asked.

"Make it quick," Theo said, temporarily lifting the magick that kept the demons in check. "And make sure that you return it to me in one piece."

The demon child laughed, a happy sound escorting her down into oblivion.

As the demons took control.

20

The floor beneath their feet heaved upward, wood snapping, walls cracking, windows shattering as the schoolhouse shook in its death throes.

The children screamed as chunks of the plaster ceiling rained down upon them. John charged ahead, herding them all toward the doors and hopefully to some semblance of safety.

The noises coming from back in the classroom were unlike anything he had heard before, the nearly deafening howls of something not of this Earth crying out in pain—

Or was it pleasure?

He found himself frozen in the foyer of the school, staring down the hallway from where they'd come, contemplating the fate of his wife. He was tempted to go back, to do anything that he could to help her—to save her if he could.

To die with her if he had to.

The building shook as if in the hands of some enormous child playing with a dollhouse, a large portion of the ceiling breaking away and falling down toward him.

298 · *Thomas E. Sniegoski*

He was struck from the side, tackled to the floor as the plaster chunk crashed down to where he'd been standing.

"What the hell's wrong with you?" Brenna Isabel asked, lying atop him.

He really didn't have a satisfactory answer, figuring that dying with his wife wouldn't have been all that popular a response.

She hauled him up, dragging him across the uneven floor to where the children huddled.

They all looked at him, their eyes wide and wet and filled with fear—but there was something else. There was hope in their gazes, hope that they were going to be rescued. Hope that he and Agent Isabel were going to take them away from this nightmarish place.

John chanced a final look down the corridor and watched in horror as it shook so violently that the walls and ceiling caved inward in a choking cloud of asbestos dust and dirt.

He'd seen enough, running toward the front doors and hitting them with full force. The doors didn't open, and he bounced backward, nearly falling on his ass.

"Are they locked?" Brenna asked, panic setting into her tone. "Don't tell me that they're fucking locked." She ran at them then, and they still didn't budge.

He looked at the doors carefully and saw that the frame had been bent in such a way that the doors were being held shut.

"No," he said, running at the doors again. "The doorframe is bent— help me," he said.

They went at the door, grabbing it in such a way, pushing and lifting in an attempt to free it from where it was caught.

The cries of the demonic in the background grew even louder, and he hoped and prayed to any deity that might be listening that they wouldn't be too late to save the children.

He was guessing that someone, or something, might have been

listening—or maybe it was just good luck—as the door popped free of the twisted frame, swinging outward with a tortured shriek.

They all spilled out onto the grass, the air still thick with fog.

He turned and gazed at the school building, watching as it shook, the brick façade cracking and starting to crumble in many places.

"C'mon," he said, moving the children along from where they had come out. "Get as far away as you can."

They could hear the building crumbling over the sounds of something inhuman crying out.

"Is it coming for us?" one of the children asked, a little boy with snot streaming from his nose. "Is Damakus going to get us?"

John told the child no, but then felt guilty. He had no idea what was going to happen.

They went as far as they could, then stopped, watching the building as it trembled, shook, and fell apart.

And they waited.

For what they did not know.

"Do you know who we are?" the demon spokesman asked through the mouth of his physical host as the tentacles of the lord Damakus attempted to crush the life from her ever-changing body.

"I do not care," the dark lord's voice boomed within her mind. "I am the end times—the beginning of a new age—an age of fear that will be built upon the putrefying corpses of humanity."

"All well and good," the spokesman, who'd worn the form of Billy Sharp to put his host body at ease, said. "But there are questions that must be asked."

The demon lord continued to grow and evolve. Damakus pushed upon the walls and ceiling of the dilapidated structure, threatening to bring it all down upon them.

The woman's form was far smaller than her foe—and quicker—avoiding the thick, oozing tendrils that wanted to smash and crush, to reduce her to little more than a stain on the schoolhouse floor.

But Damakus' wants were far from the demons' concern. They needed to know things, and they believed that the newly resuscitated demon lord could provide them with some of the answers that they sought.

The woman threw herself upon Damakus' undulating mass, sinking thick black claws into the demon lord's abhorrent flesh, climbing his body to look him in the multiple sets of eyes.

"The detonation of an infernal artifact brought you back from the brink of nothing," the demon spokesman said, clinging to the writhing head of Damakus. "A jar that contained one thousand of the underworld's most powerful demons. Who was responsible?"

The demon lord screamed and roared, thrashing its boneless form in order to dislodge his relentless attacker, but the woman clung tick-like to his body.

"How dare you question the likes of me?" Damakus' voice boomed inside the woman's skull. "You are insignificant in the grand scheme of things!"

"Who?" the spokesman questioned, allowing more of his demonic brethren to come forward, transforming the woman's body into something that barely held the semblance of humanity.

"Who put us in that jar?"

Damakus' form reacted to the question violently, managing to dislodge the woman, sending her hurtling across the room and into a wall, bringing the rubble down atop her.

"We all have our parts to play," High Lord Damakus' voice pulsated through the ether. "You and yours were nothing more than refuse, castaways after your function was performed."

The high lord's giant mass sinuously moved across to where the wall had fallen.

"Refuse?" the demon spokesman, whose female host form now appeared lacking in any form of femininity, or humanity, questioned as she rose from the rubble to gaze upon her foe with malicious eyes.

Damakus reared away, taken aback by the startling transformation.

"Castaways?" the spokesman continued, unable to contain his own writhing furor, as well as the furor of the others that resided within their host body.

Lord Damakus attacked, his monstrous form colliding with that of the demon spokesman's newly transmogrified host form. Walls collapsed and ceilings fell as the two were locked in combat.

"As high lord, I will be obeyed," Damakus proclaimed, his commanding voice echoing inside the host body's skull. The spokesman could feel the human attempting to come back—to regain control over her form.

But they were not yet ready.

"Tell me," demanded the spokesman, as claws tore away oozing chunks of Damakus' flesh, "would mere refuse have the need to obey the commands of authority?"

Damakus fought wildly, powerfully, but the spokesman and his demonic brethren were a force to be reckoned with.

"Would castaways bow before the might of those deemed superior?"

The spokesman drove Damakus down to the shattered schoolhouse floor, his psychic screams deafening as his body was torn asunder.

"I think not," the spokesman said, pulling away large chunks of writhing flesh from the body of the high lord and hungrily shoving them inside her mouth.

"There is knowledge to be found in the flesh of one's enemies," the spokesman declared, and the other demons agreed.

As they all partook of the high lord's body and all that it would tell them.

Feasting upon the flesh of a demon god.

. . . .

The schoolhouse gave one last mournful moan before collapsing in upon itself, thick clouds of dust and dirt mingling with the chilling fog.

John made a move toward the wreckage but realized the futility of the action and came to a stop at the structure's outskirts.

All he could think of was her, and how maybe this wouldn't have happened if he had stayed with her inside and . . .

"John?" Brenna called.

He turned to see Agent Isabel approaching before turning back. The dust from the collapsed building filled the air, clinging to his face and clothes.

"I'm so sorry," she said, standing beside him.

He kept his emotions in check, attempting to reassure himself that Theo had died for a good cause, and that hopefully the demon lord Damakus had been returned to the oblivion from where it had been pulled.

"Do you think . . . ?" Brenna began. He knew she was talking about Theo.

"Do you?" he questioned. "The place is in ruins. I doubt anything could have survived."

John flinched as he felt her hand on his shoulder, and turned to look at her.

"We should probably see to the kids," she said, quickly removing her hand. He agreed, turning from the rubble. The children were all sitting on the grass, the wall of mist at their backs. Looking at them, he was reminded of photographs from World War Two, and the liberation of the concentration camps. The look in the eyes of the survivors, it was very much the same.

Haunted, but alive. Survivors.

"We have to get them out of here," he said beneath his breath. He scanned the fog behind them, trying to remember from where he and Brenna had first arrived in Theo's wake.

"Do you think it's still there?" Brenna asked. "The opening?"

"I have no idea," he said, walking over to where a section of mist seemed particularly thick. "I'm thinking that maybe the passage was like a tear—a rip in reality and that—"

One of the children started to scream.

They spun around, running to where the kids sat. Rebecca was now standing and screaming like a banshee as she pointed to where the school once stood.

"What is it, honey?" Brenna asked, trying to calm her down.

John looked to where the child was pointing. At first he saw nothing more than the shifting mist, and the outline of the schoolhouse rubble beyond it, but then—

"What?" Brenna asked, seeing his reaction as he started to move closer. "What is it?"

A shape had emerged from beyond the rubble, appearing not at all human, and his blood ran cold. What new nightmare would they be forced to deal with now? he pondered as the thick mists blew across the moving figure, temporarily obscuring their view. Brenna had pulled her gun once again, standing beside him at the ready, as they both squinted into the fog.

The figure reappeared even closer and Brenna raised her weapon.

"No," John said, pulling down her arm as he realized who it was coming toward them through the mist.

Theo was completely naked, and covered in blood that did not appear to be her own. John ran to her across the short expanse of grass, reaching her just in time as she collapsed in his arms. He noticed how heavy she seemed, as well as the swollen nature of her stomach.

As if she'd eaten a really large meal.

Brenna took off her suit jacket, wrapping it around the woman's naked shoulders as they walked toward where the frightened children waited.

"Damakus," Brenna said to her.

Theo's head slowly turned to look at her.

"Is he gone?" the FBI agent asked. "Did you . . ."

She didn't finish the question.

"He's gone," Theo said in a voice so very small. And John noticed that as she answered about the dark lord's whereabouts, she rubbed her swollen belly.

"Then we won," Brenna said. And John could see that she was forcing a smile. "We won," she stressed again, waiting for her enthusiasm to be reciprocated.

John was about to agree in some way, maybe with a smile and nod—or maybe even a hearty high five.

But then Theo began to laugh, a horrible mocking sound, as she took them toward the mist, and hopefully the passage that would take them home.

"We won a battle," she said, pulling Brenna's coat tighter around her, against the cold, the words that followed chilling him to the core.

"But the war has just begun."

EPILOGUE

It was their ten-year anniversary and they'd decided to celebrate.

They had heard about the Blue Ox in Lynn from a few of their food critic friends and had decided to give it a try.

John sipped from his tumbler of whiskey, carefully watching his wife across the table from him for any signs that things might be turning sour. Between their own productions and the activities of the Coalition, they'd had very little personal time lately, and he wanted to make sure that it wasn't too much for her.

"What?" she asked over her glass of red wine, as she caught him staring.

"Doing okay?" he asked.

"Doing fine," she said. "The natives have been put to sleep," she added, making reference to the demons that remained a part of her. "How about you?"

He set his glass down. "I'm good," he said, attempting a smile, attempting to make it seem as though everything really was just fine.

Things had been relatively quiet since the Damakus affair, and he was seriously beginning to wonder. There had been some minor investigations: a haunted distillery in Boston, a possible bogart infestation in northern Maine, which had turned out to be raccoons.

Odds and ends with a paranormal bent, but nothing that pointed to the level of danger that had been foreshadowed. He found it all a bit unnerving, waiting for the other shoe to drop.

"Even after ten years you haven't gotten any better at it," she said.

"At what?"

"Lying."

"And who's lying?" he asked incredulously.

"There's that face again," she said with a laugh that made his heart beat triple time.

She had been doing better with her situation, experts from the Coalition flying in from time to time to offer her pointers on how to continue maintaining total control. She said that they helped her quite a bit, but then there would be the nights when she desperately needed to be alone, and would go down to a special room they'd set up for her in the mansion's basement. A room that either John or Stephan would lock from the outside when the demons needed to stretch their talons.

"Seriously, I'm fine," he said, and they smiled at each other, each pretending that things were fine. That they had returned to how things used to be.

Their appetizers arrived: a heaping plate of lemon hummus, grilled pita, pickled vegetables, marinated olives, and olive oil. It was delicious, and they made short work of the plate.

Theo brought up anniversaries past, and they laughed with the memories. It was as if they were talking about old friends who had moved away—or died. Although there were laughs, there was a certain sadness to every recollection.

They shared a bottle of wine as they ate their meals. He had the special, which was an amazing rib eye, medium rare, with grilled asparagus and a lobster risotto, and she had the roasted Faroe Island

salmon, Sardinian couscous, garlic, sautéed spinach, smoked toma-
toes and basil, with lemon.

It was all incredibly delicious, and they both cleaned their plates.

They contemplated dessert, but instead decided to sample an after-
dinner wine, which was beyond sweet, and pleasant, and was accompanied by a story of how the grapes were the last of the season, picked
at the beginning of winter, with the harvesters wearing special linen
gloves to protect the delicateness of the grapes.

The wine was outstanding, as was the story that came with it.

The manager that night, whose name was Charlie, stopped by the
table to see how their evening had been, and they offered nothing but
praise.

Then stepping out into the cool evening, they walked arm in arm
to their car, neither of them speaking as they headed home to Marblehead.

The house was dark as they approached, Stephan having gone
home hours before. They found a vase of flowers waiting for them in
the kitchen as they came in, a note attached from Stephan and his
husband.

"They're beautiful," Theo said, leaning in to sniff one of the flowers.

He watched her as she moved, in awe of her, amazed that something so incredibly beautiful could belong to him.

But did she?

She caught him watching her again, but he didn't look away. Theo
smiled at him, and he thought he might've caught just the slightest
hint of sadness there. He understood, especially on a night like this.

They closed up the downstairs for the night, shutting off lights
and setting the alarms, and he followed her up the winding staircase
to their rooms.

Their rooms.

Since her possession, they hadn't shared a room, or bed, the Coalition specialists believing it best that she gain a level of control over her situation before . . .

Theo stopped at her door.

"Happy anniversary," she said to him.

"Happy anniversary," he responded, leaning in to kiss her.

Their lips touched, inflaming memories of other kisses, other anniversaries, of the way things used to be.

John started to pull away, but her arms came up, wrapping themselves around his neck and making the kiss last all the longer. He responded in kind, hungry for something other than an incredible meal.

But he knew that it couldn't be that way.

He pulled his lips from hers, looking into her icy eyes. There was that sadness again. He wondered if she saw the same in his.

"I've missed you," she said so very softly, as if not wanting to be too loud and wake something up.

He kissed her again, not really knowing what to say. He missed her, too, the wife and lover who was the center of his world, the other half of his soul.

But she was gone now—changed.

As if in response to his thoughts, she spoke.

"I'm still here, John," she said, her eyes wet with emotion. "I'm still here fighting to keep myself above it all, fighting to be who I was—but also who I will be."

He held her tighter, understanding what she endured every single moment of her existence, willing his strength into her.

"I can't do it alone, John," she said. "I can't win the battle without you."

And he understood at that moment, more than he'd ever understood anything ever before.

He kissed her then, as he'd kissed her before, all the love and admiration he had for her flowing through his lips and into her.

Giving her his strength to fight the darkness that was inside her, lending his light to hers.

And she took his hand, leading him into the darkness of the bedroom.

Their bedroom.

"Let's go to bed," she said to him, and he followed.

There was a battle to fight.

A war to win.

Brenna Isabel couldn't remember the last time she'd felt this—*right*.

Sitting at her desk, reviewing the file on her latest investigation: a potential case of human sacrifice where it appeared that the bodies had been partially eaten by some sort of animal.

It was the some-sort-of-animal part that had gotten her interest, and she had experts at the Smithsonian examining plaster casts of the bite wounds found on the victims' remains. So far, everyone claimed to have never seen anything like them before.

She had an energy now that she hadn't had in years. She guessed that it had something to do with the fact that she was eating better, exercising more, and drinking less.

And getting a decent night's sleep.

She smiled at the thought of sleeping, believing the act had far more to do with her positive mental state than she cared to believe. That and the dreams that accompanied it.

It shocked her how powerful dreams could be.

They'd started right after the Damakus abductions case was closed. They were always the same, which was perfectly fine with her. She was in the cemetery where Ronan was buried, visiting his grave. The cemetery was always beautiful in the dream, colorful flowers blooming, filling the air with the most fragrant of smells.

And while she was admiring the beauty all around her, she could hear it, a baby's gurgling coo. In the dream she was almost afraid to turn around, expecting there to be nobody there, but she was wrong. There was . . .

An older woman standing by an ancient oak, holding a baby in her arms.

Brenna knew at once that the baby was her son . . . her lovely Ronan. And the older woman smiled at her, bouncing the happy baby in her arms.

Brenna went to them, carefully walking between the graves, afraid that they would disappear as if they'd never been there—this was a dream, after all.

But they remained, and the old woman spoke to her.

"We just wanted you to know that he's fine," she said, looking at the baby adoringly. "Nana won't let anything happen to him."

Brenna stood there, adoring the sight of him in Nana's arms.

Nana. The older woman called herself Nana.

Brenna closed her eyes as she sat at her desk, remembering her dream.

"May I hold him?" she'd asked the woman.

Then he was with her again, so warm and filled with life in her arms. Brenna held him tight, never wanting to let him go, but knowing that she must.

For this was only a dream.

Nana had smiled at her then, taking baby Ronan back from her. The old woman told her that they would visit again, that all Brenna need do was to go to sleep and think of him.

And dream.

The knock on her door startled her.

"Yes?" she called out.

Her boss stuck his head in the doorway. "You got a minute?" he asked.

She got up and followed the man down the hallway between the rows of workstations.

He was talking as he walked, telling her that her special department was about to be teamed up with an international bureau investigating the things that she did, but on a worldwide scale.

She didn't get a chance to comment before he led her to another office door, telling her that her liaison was inside and that he wanted to meet her.

Agent Brenna Isabel watched as her boss gently knocked upon the door and pushed it open.

"Good luck," he said, motioning her in, then turning quickly away.

She watched him disappear around the corner, then approached the open door.

"Hello?" she called out, pushing the door wider as she stepped in. The office was as sparse as hers. A figure stood behind the desk, looking out the window.

"Come in, Agent Isabel," the older gentleman said, slowly turning around to address her.

She was immediately taken aback by the horrible scarring on the left side of his face, wondering what on earth could have done such damage.

He came around the desk, extending his hand.

"My name is Elijah," he said, taking her hand in a powerful grip.

"And it appears we're going to be working with each other."

Read on for an excerpt from

A KISS BEFORE THE APOCALYPSE,

a Remy Chandler Novel by Thomas E. Sniegoski.
Available in print and e-book from Roc.

It was an unusually warm mid-September day in Boston. The kind of day that made one forget that the oft-harsh New England winter was on its way, just waiting around the corner, licking its lips and ready to pounce.

Remy Chandler sat in his car at the far end of the Sunbeam Motor Lodge parking lot, sipping his fourth cup of coffee and wishing he had a fifth. He could never have enough coffee. He loved the taste, the smell, the hot feeling as it slid down his throat first thing in the morning; coffee was way up there on his top-ten list of favorite things. A beautiful September day made the list as well. Days like today more than proved he had made the right choice in becoming human.

He reached down and turned up the volume on WBZ News Radio. Escalating violence in the Middle East was once again the headline, the latest attempts for peace shattered. *Big surprise*, Remy thought with a sigh, taking a sip from his coffee cup. *When hasn't there been violence in that region of the world?* he reflected. For as long as he could remember, the bloodthirsty specter of death and intolerance had hovered over those lands. He had tried to talk with them once, but they used his appearance as yet another excuse to pick up knives and swords and hack one another to bits in the name of God. The private investigator shook his head. That was a long time ago, but it always made him sad to see how little things had changed.

To escape the news, he hit one of the preset buttons on the car's radio. It was an oldies station; he found it faintly amusing that an "oldie" was a song recorded in the 1950s. Fats Domino was singing about finding his thrill on Blueberry Hill, as Remy took the last swig of coffee and gazed over at the motel.

He'd been working this case for two months, a simple surveillance gig—keep an eye on Peter Mountgomery, copy editor for the Bronson Liturgical Book Company, and husband suspected of infidelity. It wasn't the most stimulating job, but it did help to pay the bills. Remy spent much of his day drinking coffee, keeping up with *Dilbert,* and maintaining a log of the man's daily activities and contacts. *Ah, the thrilling life of the private gumshoe,* he thought, eyeing the maroon car parked in a space across the lot. So far, Mountgomery was guilty of nothing more than having lunch with his secretary, but the detective had a sinking feeling that that was about to change.

A little after one that afternoon, Remy had followed Peter along the Jamaica Way and into the lot of the Sunbeam Motor Lodge. The man had parked his Ford Taurus in front of one of the rooms, and simply sat with the motor running. Remy had pulled past him and idled on the other side of the parking area, against a fence that separated the motor lodge from an overgrown vacant lot littered with the rusting remains of cars and household appliances. Someone had tossed a bag of garbage over the fence, where it had burst like an overripe piece of fruit, spilling its contents.

The cries of birds pulled Remy's attention away from Mountgomery to the trash-strewn lot. He watched as the hungry scavengers swooped down onto the discarded refuse, picking through the rotting scraps, and then climbing back into the air, navigating the sky with graceful ease.

For a sad instant, he remembered what it was like: the sound and the feel of mighty wings pounding the air. Flying was one of the only things he truly missed about his old life.

He turned his attention back to Mountgomery, just in time to see another car pull up alongside the editor's. *Time to earn my two-fifty plus expenses,* he thought, watching as Peter's secretary emerged from the vehicle. Then he picked up his camera from the passenger's seat and began snapping pictures.

The woman stood stiffly beside the driver's side of her boss's car, looking nervously about as she waited to be acknowledged, finally reaching out to rap with a knuckle upon the window. The man got out of the car, but the couple said nothing to each other. Mountgomery was dressed in his usual work attire—dark suit, white shirt, and striped tie. He was forty-six years of age but looked older. In a light raincoat over a pretty floral-print dress, the woman appeared to be at least ten years his junior.

The editor carried a blue gym bag that he switched from right hand to left as he locked his car. The two stared at each other briefly, something seeming to pass silently between them, then together walked to room number 35. The secretary searched through her purse as they stood before the door, eventually producing a key attached to a dark green plastic triangle. Remy guessed that she had rented the room earlier, and took four more pictures, an odd feeling settling in the pit of his stomach. The strange sensation grew stronger as the couple entered the room and shut the door behind them.

This was the part of the job Remy disliked most. He would have been perfectly satisfied, as would his client, he was sure, to learn that the husband was completely faithful. Everyone would have been happy; Remy could pay his rent, and Janice Mountgomery could sleep better knowing that her husband was still true to the sacred vows of marriage. Nine out of ten times, though, that wasn't the case.

Suspecting he'd be a while, the detective turned off his car and shifted in his seat. He reached for a copy of the *Boston Globe* on the passenger's seat beside him, and had just plucked a pen from his inside coat pocket to begin the crossword puzzle, when he heard the first gunshot.

He was out of the car and halfway across the lot before he even thought about what he was doing. His hearing was good—unnaturally so—and he knew exactly where the sound had come from. He reached the door to room 35, pounding on it with his fist, shouting for Montgomery to open up. Remy prayed that he was mistaken, that maybe the sound was a car backfire from the busy Jamaica Way, or that some kids in the neighborhood were playing with fireworks left over from the Fourth of July. But deep down he knew otherwise.

A second shot rang out as he brought his heel up and kicked open the door, splintering the frame with the force of the blow. The door swung wide and he entered, keeping his head low, and for the umpteenth time since choosing his profession, questioned his decision not to carry a weapon.

The room was dark and cool, the shades drawn. An air conditioner rattled noisily in the far corner beneath the window; smoke and the smell of spent ammunition hung thick in the air. Mountgomery stood naked beside the double bed, illuminated by the daylight flooding in through the open door. Shielding his eyes from the sudden brightness, the man turned, shaken by the intrusion.

The body of the woman, also nude, lay on the bed atop a dark, checkered bedspread, what appeared to be a Bible clutched in one of her hands. She had been shot once in the forehead and again in the chest. Mountgomery wavered on his bare feet, the gun shaking in his hand at his side. He stared at Remy in the doorway and slowly raised the weapon.

"Don't do anything stupid," Remy cautioned, his hands held out in front of him. "I'm unarmed."

He felt a surge of adrenaline flood through his body as he watched the man squint down the barrel of the pistol. *This is what it's like to be truly alive,* he thought. In the old days, before his renouncement, Remy had never known the thrill of fear; there was no reason to. But now, moments such as this made what he had given up seem almost insignificant.

The man jabbed the gun at Remy and screamed, "Shut the door!" Slowly, Remy did as he was told, never taking his eyes from the gunman.

"It's not what you think," Mountgomery began. "Not what you think at all." He brought the weapon up and scratched at his temple offhandedly with the muzzle. "Who . . . who are you?" the editor stammered, his features twisting in confusion as he thrust the gun toward Remy again. "What are you doing here?" His voice was frantic, teetering on the edge of hysteria.

Hands still raised, Remy cautiously stepped farther into the room. As a general rule, he didn't like to lie when he had a gun pointed at him. "I'm a private investigator, Mr. Mountgomery," he said in a soft, calm voice. "Your wife hired me. I'm not going to try anything, okay? Just put the gun down and we'll talk. Maybe we can figure a way out of this mess. What do you think?"

Mountgomery blinked as if trying to focus. He stumbled slightly to the left, the gun still aimed at Remy. "A way out of this mess," he repeated, with a giggle. "Nobody's getting out of this one."

He glanced at his companion on the bed and began to sob, his voice trembling with emotion. "Did you hear that, Carol? The bitch hired a detective to follow me."

Mountgomery reached out to the dead woman. But when she didn't respond, he let his arm flop dejectedly to his side. He looked back at Remy. "Carol was the only one who understood. She listened. She believed me." Tears of genuine emotion ran down his face. "I wish we'd had more time together," he said wistfully.

"The bitch at home thought I was crazy. Well, we'll see how crazy I am when it all turns to shit." The sadness was turning to anger again.

"This is so much harder than I imagined," he said, his face twisted in pain.

He lowered the gun slightly, and Remy started to move. Instantly, Mountgomery reacted, the weapon suddenly inches from the detective's face. Obviously, madness had done little to slow his reflexes.

"It started when they opened up my head," Mountgomery began. "The dreams. At first I thought they were just that, bad dreams, but then I realized they were much more."

The editor pressed the gun against Remy's cheek. "I was dreaming about the end of the world, you see. Every night it became clearer—the dreams—more horrible. I don't want to die like that," he said, shaking his head, eyes glassy. "And I don't want the people I love to die like that, either." The man leaned closer to Remy. He smelled of aftershave and a sickly sour sweat. "Are you a religious man?"

If he had not been so caught up in the seriousness of the situation, Remy Chandler would have laughed. "I have certain—beliefs. Yes. What do *you* believe in, Peter?"

Mountgomery swallowed hard. "I believe we're all going to die horribly. Carol, that was her name." He jerked his head toward the dead woman on the bed. "Carol Weir. She wanted to be brave, to face the end with me. But she was too good to die that way."

He smiled forlornly and tightened his grip on the gun. "I would have divorced my wife and married her, but it seemed kind of pointless when we looked at the big picture. This was the nicest thing I could do for her. She thanked me before I . . ."

Mountgomery's face went wild with the realization of what he had done, and he jammed the barrel of the gun into Remy's forehead. The muzzle felt warm.

"Would you prefer to die now, or wait until it all goes to Hell?" the editor asked him.

"I'm not ready to make that decision."

Remy suddenly jerked his head to one side, grabbing the man's wrist, pushing the gun away from his face. Mountgomery pulled the trigger. A bullet roared from the weapon to bury itself in the worn shag carpet under them.

The two men struggled for the weapon, Mountgomery screaming like a wild animal. But he was stronger than Remy had imagined, and quickly regained control of the pistol, forcing the detective back.

Again, the editor raised his arm and aimed the weapon.

"Don't you point that thing at me," Remy snarled, glaring at the madman. "If you want to die, then die. If you want to take the coward's way out, do it. But don't you dare try to take me with you."

Mountgomery seemed taken aback by the detective's fierce words. He squinted, tilting his head from left to right, as if seeing the man before him for the first time. "Look at you," he said suddenly, with an odd smile and a small chuckle. "I didn't even notice until now." He dropped the weapon to his side.

It was Remy's turn to be confused. He glanced briefly behind him to be sure no one else had entered the room.

"Are you here for her—for Carol?" Mountgomery continued. "She deserves to be in Heaven. She is—*was* a good person—a very good person."

"What are you talking about, Peter?" Remy asked. "Why would I be here for Carol? Your wife hired me to—"

Mountgomery guffawed, the strange barking sound cutting Remy off midsentence. "There's no need to pretend with me," he said smiling. "I can see what you are."

A finger of ice ran down Remy's spine.

With a look of resigned calm, Mountgomery raised the gun and pressed the muzzle beneath the flesh of his chin. "I never imagined I'd be this close to one," he said, finger tensing on the trigger. "Angels are even more beautiful than they say."

Remy lunged, but Mountgomery proved faster again. The editor pulled the trigger and the bullet punched through the flesh and bone of his chin and up into his brain, exiting through the top of his head in a spray of crimson. He fell back stiffly onto the bed—atop his true love, twitching wildly as the life drained out of him, and then rolling off the bed to land on the floor. His eyes, wide in death, gazed with frozen fascination at the wing-shaped pattern created by his blood and brains on the ceiling above.

Remy studied the gruesome example of man's fragile mortality before him, Mountgomery's final words reverberating through his mind.

I never imagined I'd be this close to one.

He caught his reflection in a mirror over the room's single dresser and stared hard at himself, searching for cracks in the façade. *Is it possible?* he wondered. Had Peter Mountgomery somehow seen through Remy's mask of humanity?

Angels are even more beautiful than they say.

Remy looked away from his own image and back to the victims of violence. *How could a case so simple turn into something so ugly?* he asked himself, moving toward the broken door, followed by the words of a man who could see angels and had dreamt of the end of the world.

He stepped quickly into the afternoon sun and almost collided with the Hispanic cleaning woman and her cart of linens. She looked at him and then craned her neck to see around him and into the room. Remy caught the first signs of panic growing in her eyes and reached back for the knob, pulling the door closed. In flawless Spanish he told her not to go into the room, that death had visited those within, and it was not for her to see. The woman nodded slowly, her eyes never leaving his as she pushed her cart quickly away.

ABOUT THE AUTHOR

Thomas E. Sniegoski is a full-time writer of young adult novels, urban fantasy, and comics. His works include the *New York Times* bestselling Fallen series, the Remy Chandler novels, the graphic novel *The Raven's Child*, as well as contributions to famous comics such as *Batman*, *Buffy the Vampire Slayer*, and *B.P.R.D.*

CONNECT ONLINE

sniegoski.com
facebook.com/thomas.sniegoski
twitter.com/tomsniegoski